"Act... ...
And what you're doing is ignoring me and Rose."

"I'm not ignoring the baby, I'm ignoring *you*."

"Why?" Lilah demanded, tossing both hands high.

Could she really not see what it cost him to avoid her company? Was she clueless about the attraction sizzling between them? Well, if so, Reed thought, it was time to let her know exactly what was going on here.

Her scent reached for him, surrounded him and he threw caution out the damn window. "Because of this."

He grabbed her, pulled her in close and kissed her as he'd wanted to for days.

* * *

The Baby Inheritance is part of
Mills & Boon's no.1 bestselling series,

Billionaires and Babies:
Powerful men… wrapped around
their babies' little fingers.

THE BABY INHERITANCE

BY
MAUREEN CHILD

First Published in Great Britain 2016
By Mills & Boon, an imprint of HarperCollins*Publishers*
1 London Bridge Street, London, SE1 9GF

© 2016 Maureen Child

ISBN: 978-0-263-91867-0

51-0716

Maureen Child writes for the Mills & Boon Desire line and can't imagine a better job.

A seven-time finalist for a prestigious Romance Writers of America RITA® Award, Maureen is an author of more than one hundred romance novels. Her books regularly appear on bestseller lists and have won several awards, including a Prism Award, a National Readers' Choice Award, a Colorado Romance Writers Award of Excellence and a Golden Quill Award. She is a native Californian but has recently moved to the mountains of Utah.

To Patti Canterbury Hambleton—Best friend since first grade and still the absolute *Best*.

For all the laughs and tears and crazy adventures.

I love you.

One

"Divorce is reality," Reed Hudson told his client. "It's marriage that's the anomaly."

Carson Duke, America's favorite action-movie star, just stared at his attorney for a long minute, before saying, "That's cold."

Reed shook his head slowly. The man was here to end a marriage that most of the country looked on as a fairy tale come to life, and still he didn't want to accept the simple truth. Reed had seen this over and over again. Oh, most of the people who came to him were *eager* to end a marriage that had become inconvenient or boring or both. But there were a few people who came to him wishing they were anywhere but in his office, ending a relationship that they'd hoped was forever.

Forever. Even the thought nearly brought a smile. In his experience, both business and personal, there was no such thing as *forever*.

"Like I said," Reed told Carson with a shake of his head, "not cold. Reality."

"Harsh." Then Carson snorted a short laugh and crossed his legs, his ankle on top of his knee. Frowning a little, he asked quietly, "You ever been married?"

Now Reed laughed. "Oh, hell, no."

Just the idea of him ever getting married was ridiculous. His reputation alone, as what the tabloids called the "divorce attorney to the stars," was enough to make sure no woman he was involved with developed long-term plans. And representing most of Hollywood and New York in high-profile divorce cases had all started with a single client five years before. Reed had represented television's most likable comedian in a nasty split from a wife who made the "bunny boiler" look like a good time.

Word had spread in Hollywood and across celebrity lines, and soon Reed's practice was littered with the rich and famous. He enjoyed his work, relished protecting his clients from bad relationships and shattering the occasional prenup. And, if there was one thing he'd learned through the years, it was that even the best marriage could dissolve into misery.

But, he hadn't exactly needed his clients to teach him that lesson. His own family was a sterling example of just how badly marriages could go. His father was now on wife number five and living in London, while Reed's mother and husband number four were currently enjoying the heat and tropical atmosphere of Bali. And from what Reed had been hearing, his mother was already looking for husband number five. Thanks to his serially monogamous parents, Reed had ten siblings, full and half, ranging in age from three to thirty-two with another baby sister due any minute thanks to his father's ridiculously young, and apparently fertile, wife.

For most of his life, Reed, as the oldest child in the wildly eclectic and extended immediate family, had been the one who stepped in and kept things moving. When his siblings had a problem, they came to him. When his parents needed a fast divorce in order to marry their next "true love," they came to him. When the apocalypse finally arrived, he had no doubt that they would all turn to him, expecting Reed to save all of their asses. He was used to it and had long ago accepted his role in the Hudson clan. The fact that his experience as a mediator had served him so well as an attorney was simply a bonus.

Looking at his latest client, Reed thought back over the past year and remembered the innumerable articles and pictures flashed across the tabloids. Carson Duke and his wife, Tia Brennan, had graced the covers of magazines and the pages of newspapers, and the two had been favorites on the celebrity websites. They'd had a whirlwind romance that had ended in a fairy-tale wedding on a Hawaiian cliff overlooking the Pacific.

Stories proclaiming the nearly magical connection between the two, holding them up as examples of what "real" love looked like, had been printed, pored over and discussed all across the world. Yet here Carson sat, a little more than a year later, hiring Reed to represent him in a divorce that promised to be as high-profile as the marriage had been.

"Let's get down to business then," Reed said and looked at the man across from him. Just like in his movies, Carson Duke looked tough, determined and had the cool, hard gaze of a seasoned warrior. Not surprising, since the star had been a US Marine before turning to Hollywood. "First tell me what your wife thinks about all of this."

Carson sighed, shoved one hand through his hair and then blurted out, "It was her idea. Things have been rough between us for a while now." It looked as though every word he spoke tasted bitter. "She—*we*—decided that it would be better, for both of us, if we just end the marriage and walk away now, before things get ugly."

"Uh-huh." Duke sounded reasonable, but so many of Reed's clients did when they were first entering the muddy swamp of litigation. Couples determined to remain "friendly" eventually succumbed to name-calling and vicious diatribes. Reed wasn't looking forward to watching Carson and his wife go down that path. "I need to know—are you seeing someone else? Is another woman at the bottom of all this? I will find out sooner or later, so it would be better for all of us if you tell me now so there are no surprises."

Carson stiffened, but Reed held up a hand to silence what would no doubt be a tirade of insult and outrage. All of his clients tended to paint themselves as the injured party, and if Reed wasn't careful, he could be blindsided by a scorned lover testifying for the opposition. Better to have as much information as possible from the jump. "These are questions I have to ask. If you're smart, you'll answer."

Carson stewed in his chair for a second or two, looked as though he'd like to punch something, then surged to his feet in one smooth motion.

"No," he snapped, and paced across the room to stop at one of the wide windows overlooking the sweep of ocean stretching out into the distance. He stared through the glass for several long seconds, as if trying to calm down, then turned his head to look directly at Reed. "No. I didn't cheat. Neither did Tia."

Reed's eyebrows arched. First time he'd heard a client *defend* a spouse. "You're sure about her?"

"Absolutely." Carson shook his head and looked back through the glass at the sunlight dancing on the ocean's surface. "This isn't about cheating or lying or any other damn thing."

Intriguing. The old *irreconcilable differences* plea was usually just an excuse to keep secrets private. There were always reasons for a divorce, and in Reed's experience, cheating was right at the top of the list.

"Then why are you here?" Reed asked, leaning back in his black leather desk chair.

"Because we're not happy anymore." Carson laid one hand on the glass. "It started out great," he continued as if to himself. "Tia and I met and it was like…magic. You know?"

"No," Reed said, smiling. "But I'll take your word for it."

Carson shook his head. "We couldn't keep our hands off each other. From that first moment, there was something powerful between us." He smiled, and shot Reed another quick glance. "It was more than sex, though. We used to talk all night, laughing, planning, talking about moving out of Hollywood, having kids. But the last few months, between work and other demands on both of us…hell. We hardly see each other anymore. So why be married?"

Pitiful excuse to sentence yourself to divorce court, but then, Reed silently acknowledged, he'd heard worse. He'd once represented a man who claimed he needed a divorce because his wife kept hiding cookies from him. Reed had almost advised him to buy his own damn cookies, but had figured it was none of his business. Because the cookies weren't the real reason. They were simply the excuse. The man wanted a divorce; Reed would get it for him. That was his job. He wasn't a marriage counselor, after all.

"All right then," Reed said briskly. "I'll get the paperwork started. Tia won't be contesting the divorce?"

"No." Carson shoved both hands into his pockets. "Like I said. Her idea."

"That'll make it easier," Reed told him.

Wryly, Carson whispered, "I suppose that's a good thing."

"It is." Reed watched his client and felt a stir of sympathy. He wasn't a cold man. He knew that people came to him when their worlds were dissolving. In order to maintain a professional distance, he sometimes came off as harsh when all he was trying to do was to be a rock for his clients. To be the one stable point in a suddenly rocking world. And as he studied Carson Duke, he knew the man didn't need pity, he needed someone to guide him through unfamiliar waters. "Trust me," Reed said. "You don't want a long, drawn-out battle described daily in the tabloids."

Carson shuddered at the idea. "I can't even take the trash out at my house without some photographer leaning out of a tree for a picture. You know, on the drive down here from Malibu, I was telling myself that it'd be a hell of a lot easier on most of us if your office was in LA—but getting away from most of the paparazzi is worth the drive."

Over the years, Reed had told himself the same

thing about relocating to Los Angeles many times, but damned if he could convince himself to move. A quick glance around his office only reinforced that feeling. The building itself was old—built in 1890—though thankfully it had been spared the Victorian ginger-bread so popular at the time. He'd bought the building, had it completely remodeled and now, it was just as he wanted it. Character on the outside, sleek and elegant on the inside, plus the office was only a fifteen-minute drive from his home.

Besides, Reed preferred Orange County. Liked the fact that Newport Beach sprawled out in front of his two-story building crouched on the Pacific Coast Highway and he had the majestic sweep of ocean behind him. Sure, in the summer the streets were crowded with tourists—but he'd have the same problem in LA without the beautiful setting. Newport Beach was more laid-back than LA, but upscale enough to convince clients they were with the right attorney. Besides, if he had to drive the 405 freeway every night to get from his office to his home at the Saint Regis hotel in Laguna Beach, he'd be spending more than two hours a night just sitting in traffic. If clients wanted the best, then they'd better be ready to do the drive.

"I'll have the papers drawn up and messengered to you in a few days."

"No need," the other man said. "I'm taking a few days. Staying at the Saint Regis Monarch. I've got a suite there."

Since Reed lived in a massive suite at the exclusive, five-star resort, he knew the hotel would give Carson the distance he wanted from Hollywood and the scoop-hungry photographers who would be hunting him once news of an impending divorce hit the media. And it would hit, no matter how they tried to keep it quiet. If Carson or Tia's people didn't release the news, then someone along the chain of information would. There were always leaks no matter how hard you tried to keep things confidential. It wouldn't come from Reed's staff, that he knew. They were paid extremely well—not just for their expertise, but for their discretion—and knew their jobs depended on their ability to keep their clients' business to themselves.

But there were others out there Reed had no control over. Everyone from valets at the Monarch to desk clerks and hotel maids. Once the media found out where Carson was staying, they'd continue to dig until they found out why the action star was holed up sixty miles from his house.

"You live at the Monarch, don't you?" Carson asked.

"Yeah, I do. So once the paperwork is completed, I'll have it all sent to your room for signing."

"Convenient, huh?" Carson said wryly. "Anyway, I'm registered under the name Wyatt Earp."

Reed laughed. The wildly famous usually signed into hotels under false names to keep those *not* in their immediate circle from knowing where they were. "Got it," he said. "I'll be in touch."

"Right." Carson nodded. "Thanks, I guess."

Reed watched the man go and once the office door was closed again, he walked to the windows behind his desk and stared out at the view of the ocean as his client had done only moments ago. He'd been through this so many times now, with so many people, he knew what Carson Duke was feeling, thinking. The big decision had been made. The divorce was in play. Now he was feeling a mixture of relief and sorrow and wondering if he was doing the right thing.

Oh, sure, there were plenty of people who divorced with joy in their hearts and a spring in their steps. But they weren't the rule. Generally, people felt the pain of losing something they'd once pinned their hopes and dreams on. Hell, Reed had seen it in his own family time and again. Each of his parents invariably entered a marriage thinking that *this* time would be the last. The *one*. True love and they would finally live happily ever after.

"And they're never right," he murmured, shaking his head.

Once again, he was reminded that he'd made the right life choice in *never* letting himself fall into the trap of convincing himself that good, healthy lust was some kind of romantic love destined to transform his life.

At that thought, he snorted in amusement, then walked back to his desk to begin drafting Carson Duke's divorce papers.

Lilah Strong took her time driving along Pacific Coast Highway. The scenery was wildly different from what she was used to and she intended to enjoy it in spite of the hot ball of anger nestled deep in her belly. She didn't like being angry. It always felt to her like a waste of emotion. The person she was furious with didn't care how she felt. Her anger affected no one but *her*... by making her a little nauseous.

But knowing that did nothing to ease the underlying tension that burned inside her. So rather than try to ease that uncomfortable feeling, she briefly distracted herself by glancing out at the ocean.

It was lovely—surfers gliding toward shore on the

tops of waves. Sunlight glinting off the deep blue surface of the sea. Boats with jewel-toned sails and children building castles in the sand armed with nothing more than tiny buckets and shovels.

Lilah was a mountain girl, through and through. Her preferred view was of a tree-laden slope, wide-open meadows covered in bright splashes of wildflowers or the snowy mountainsides that backed up to her house. But looking out at the Pacific was a nice change. Of course, she had time to look at the sea while driving only because she wasn't actually "driving." It was more...parking.

Pacific Coast Highway was completely backed up with locals, tourists and, it seemed to her, every surfer in Southern California. It was the middle of June and Lilah could imagine that the crowds would only be getting thicker as the summer went on. But thankfully, that wouldn't be her problem.

In a day or two, she'd be back in the mountains, leaving her companion here in Orange County. That thought gave her heart a hard squeeze, but there was nothing she could do about it. It wasn't as if she'd had a choice in any of this. If she'd been someone else, maybe she would have considered ignoring facts. But she couldn't live a lie. She had to do the right thing—even if it felt wrong.

Glancing into the rearview mirror, she looked at her companion and said, "You're awfully quiet. Too much to think about to leave room for talking, hmm? I know how you feel."

Her own mind was spinning. Lilah had been dreading this trip to California for two weeks and now that it was here, she was still trying to think of a way out of the situation she found herself in. But no matter how she looked at it, Lilah was stuck. As was her friend in the backseat.

If she were doing this on her turf, so to speak, she might feel a little more in control. Back in her small mountain town in Utah, she had friends. People she could count on to stand with her. Here, all she had were her own two feet and that sinking sensation in the pit of her stomach.

Orange County, California, was only an hour-and-a-half flight from Lilah's home, but it might as well have been on the other side of the world. She was walking into the unknown with no way out but *through*.

By the time she parked, helped her friend out of the car and walked into the law office, Lilah's stomach was swirling with nerves. The building was Victorian on the outside and a sweep of glass and chrome on the inside. It was unsettling, as if designed to keep clients off guard, and maybe that was the idea. The floors were a polished, high-gleam hardwood, but the walls were decorated with modern paintings consisting of splashes of bright color. The reception desk where a stern-faced, middle-aged woman sat sentry was a slab of glass atop shining steel legs. Even the banister gliding along the wood staircase was made up of steel spindles faced with a wall of glass. It was cold, sterile and just a little intimidating. Oh, she was now sincerely prepared to dislike the man she was there to see. Lilah stiffened her spine and approached the reception desk. "I'm Lilah Strong. I'm here to see Reed Hudson."

The woman looked from Lilah to her friend and back again. "Do you have an appointment?"

"No. I'm here on behalf of his sister, Spring Hudson

Bates," Lilah said and watched a flicker of interest glitter in the woman's eyes. "It's important that I see him now."

"One moment." The woman watched Lilah as she picked up a phone and pressed a single button. "Mr. Hudson, there's a woman here to see you. She claims to have been sent by your sister Spring."

Claims? Lilah swallowed the spurt of impatience that jumped into her throat. It took another moment or two before the receptionist hung up and waved one hand at the staircase. "Mr. Hudson will see you. Up the stairs, first door on the left."

"Thank you." Lilah and her companion walked away, but as she went, she felt the other woman's curious gaze follow her.

At the landing, Lilah paused to settle herself outside the heavy double doors. She took a breath, then turned the knob and walked inside.

The outer office was small, but bright, with sunlight pouring through windows that overlooked the ocean. Lilah stepped inside and took a breath, pausing long enough to appreciate the elegant furnishings. The wood floors shone. In one corner, there was a healthy ficus tree in a silver pot. A pair of gray chairs separated by a black table sat against one wall.

A young woman with short black hair and brown eyes sat at a sleek black desk and gave Lilah a friendly smile as she entered. "Hello. I'm Karen, Mr. Hudson's executive assistant. You must be Ms. Strong. Mr. Hudson's waiting for you."

She stood and walked to a pair of double doors. Opening them, she stepped back and Lilah steeled herself before she walked into the lion's den.

The man's office was enormous—no doubt designed

to impress and intimidate. *Mission accomplished*, she thought. A wall of glass behind his desk afforded a spectacular view of the ocean, and on her left, the glass wall continued, displaying a bird's-eye view of Pacific Coast Highway and the crowds that cluttered the street and sidewalks.

The wood floor shone here, too, with the slices of sunlight lying on it sparkling like diamonds. There were several expensive-looking rugs dotting the floor, and the furniture here was less chrome and more dark leather. Still didn't seem to fit in a Victorian building, but it was less startling to the senses than the first-floor decor. But, Lilah told herself, she wasn't here to critique the results of what some designer had done to the stately old building. Instead, she was here to face down the man now standing up behind his desk.

"Who are you?" he demanded. "And what do you know about my sister Spring?"

His voice was deep, rumbling around the room like thunder. He was tall—easily six feet three or four—with thick black hair expensively trimmed to look casual. He wore a black, pin-striped suit and a white dress shirt accented with a red power tie. His shoulders were broad, his jaw square, his eyes green, and as they focused on her, they didn't look friendly.

Well, she thought, that was fine, since she wasn't feeling very friendly, either. He was as intimidating as the plush office, and far more attractive—which had nothing to do with anything, she reminded herself.

Still, she was glad she'd taken care with her appearance before this meeting. At home, she went days without even bothering with makeup. Today, she wore her own version of a power suit. Black slacks, red shirt and short red jacket. Her black boots had a two-inch heel, adding to her five-foot-six-inch height. She was as prepared for this meeting as it was possible to be. Which wasn't saying much.

"I'm Lilah Strong."

"I was told who you are," he said. "What I don't know is why you're here."

"Right." She took a deep breath, then blew it out again. Deliberately striding across the floor in a quick march, she heard her heels click on the wood then soften on the rugs as she approached him. When she was so close she caught a whiff of his aftershave—a subtle scent that reminded her of the forests at home—she stopped. With his wide, black matte desk between them, she looked into his deep green eyes and said, "Spring was my friend. That's why I'm here. She asked me to do something for her and I couldn't say no. That's the *only* reason I'm here."

"All right."

That deep voice seemed to reverberate inside her, leaving her more shaken than she wanted to admit. Why was he so gorgeous? Why did the wary look in his eyes seem sexy rather than irritating? And *why* was she letting an unwanted attraction scatter her thoughts?

"I'm curious." His gaze flicked briefly to Lilah's friend before shifting back to her. "Do you usually bring your baby with you to meetings?"

She lifted her chin and glanced down at the baby girl on her left hip. Here was the reason for leaving home, for facing down a man with ice in his eyes. If it had been up to her, Lilah never would have come. She wouldn't be standing here in Reed Hudson's office with a ball of cold lead in the pit of her stomach. But this wasn't her choice and no matter how hard it was, she would do as Spring had asked.

Rosie slapped both hands together and squealed. Lilah's answering smile faded as she turned her gaze back to the man watching her.

"Rose isn't my baby," she said, with more than a twinge of regret as she met his gaze coolly. "She's *yours*."

Two

Instantly, Reed went on red alert.

The cold, dispassionate demeanor that had made him a legend in court dropped over him like a familiar jacket. The woman looking at him as if he were a worm, just slithering out from under a rock, was beautiful but clearly delusional.

Over the years, there had been a few predatory women who'd tried to convince him they were pregnant with his child. But, since he was always careful, he'd been able to get rid of them easily enough. And this woman, he'd never been with. That he was sure of, since a man didn't forget a woman like this one.

"I don't have a baby." The very idea was ludicrous. Given his background, his family, his career, if there was one lesson he'd learned it was don't build a family of his own. Since he was sixteen, he'd never been without a condom. "If that's all," he continued briskly, "you can show yourself out."

"Nice," she commented with a slow shake of her head.

The tone of her voice caught his attention. It was just as coolly dismissive as his own. His gaze caught hers and he couldn't mistake the anger and disdain shining in those clear blue eyes. "Problem?"

"No more than I expected from a man like you," she countered and bounced a little, as if to entertain the baby babbling on her hip.

"A man like me," he repeated, curious now. "And you know me, *how*?"

"I know that you were Spring's brother and that you weren't there to help her when she needed it." Her words rushed out as if flowing on a tide of fury. "I know that when you see a child who looks just like your sister you don't even ask a question."

His eyes narrowed. "My sister."

She huffed out a breath. "That's what I said." Briefly, she looked at the baby and her mouth curved slightly. "Her name is Rose and she's Spring's daughter." At the mention of her name, the tiny girl bounced in place and slapped her hands against the woman's shoulder. "That's right, Rosie. You're your mommy's girl, aren't you?"

As if in answer, the baby clapped tiny hands and chortled in some weird baby version of a giggle. And while the two of them smiled at each other, Reed shifted his gaze from the lovely woman to the baby in her arms. *Spring's daughter.* Now that he knew, now that he wasn't on automatic defense, he could see his sister's features, miniaturized on her child. Fine, black hair curling about

a rounded face. Eyes so green they shone like emeralds—
the same shade as Spring's.

As his own, come to that.

Instantly, without even being told, he *knew* his sister
was gone. Spring had looked all her life for real love.
There wasn't a chance in hell she ever would have left
her daughter if she'd had a choice.

And the baby was clearly a Hudson. Then there was
the fact that even in so small a child, he saw the stubborn chin his sister had boasted. Spring had a daughter
he'd known nothing about. He understood the woman's
anger now. Her accusation of not being there for Spring
when she needed him most. But he would have been,
he assured himself silently. If she'd come to him, he'd
have—how was it possible that she *hadn't* come to him?
Everyone in his family came to him for help. Why hadn't
Spring?

Then he remembered the last time he saw his younger
sister. More than two years ago, Spring had come to
him, wanting him to arrange for an advance on her trust.
She'd been in love. Again.

Frowning, he remembered his reaction, too. Spring
was one of those people who went through life wearing rose-colored glasses. She saw only the best in people—even those who had no best at all. Spring refused
to recognize that *some* people simply weren't worth her
loyalty or her affection.

It had been the third time she'd been in love—and
that last time was just like the others before had been.
Without fail, Spring seemed to migrate toward men with
few morals, little ambition and less money. He'd always
thought it was because Spring thought she could "save"
them. And that never worked.

Always on the lookout for love, she would invariably end up in Reed's office asking for money to pay off the latest loser so she could move on with her life. But that last time, Reed had been forewarned by yet another sister. Savannah had met Spring's lover and she'd been worried enough that she'd called Reed. He'd run a background check on Spring's love of the moment and found a criminal background—fraud, identity theft and forgery. But Spring hadn't wanted to hear the warnings. She had insisted that Coleman Bates had changed. That he deserved a second chance.

Reed recalled clearly telling her that the man had *had* a second chance—even a third—and hadn't changed. But Spring was in love and wouldn't listen. Standing there now, though, in front of the child she'd left behind, Reed frowned, remembering he'd told Spring to grow the hell up and stop expecting him to sweep in and take care of whatever mess she created. Hurt, angry, Spring had walked out of his office. So later, when she'd really needed him, his sister hadn't called on Reed. And now it was too late for him to make it up to her.

A swift stab of guilt pierced the edges of Reed's heart but he fought it back. Regret was indulgence. It wouldn't help Spring, couldn't ease the pain of her loss. He'd done what he thought was best for his sister at the time. For the family. And if she had come to him for help in extricating herself from the relationship, he assured himself, he would have done all he could for her. Now all he could do was find answers.

"What happened to Spring?"

"She died two months ago."

He gritted his teeth as the harsh truth shook him to his bones. He'd known it, *felt* it, but somehow hearing it made it harder. A quick, sharp slash of pain tore at him and was immediately buried beneath a fresh wave of regret, sorrow. Reed scrubbed one hand across his face then focused on the baby again before shifting to meet Lilah Strong's clear blue eyes. "That's hard to hear."

Spring was his half sister on his father's side and five years younger than Reed. She'd always been so bright, so happy, so damn trusting. And now she was gone.

"I'm sorry. I shouldn't have said it so abruptly."

Shaking his head, he stared into those eyes of hers. So blue, they were nearly violet. They shone with sympathy he didn't want and didn't need. His pain was private. Not something he would share with anyone, let alone a stranger.

To cover the turmoil raging within, he said simply, "There is no way to soften news like that."

"You're right. Of course, you're right." Those eyes shifted, changed with her emotions, and now he read grief of her own mingling with a simmering anger in their depths.

He was no more interested in that than he was in her sympathy.

"What happened to my sister?"

"There was a car accident," she said simply. "Someone ran a red light…"

His eyes narrowed. "Drunk driver?"

"No," she said, shaking her head and patting the baby's back all at once. "An elderly man had a heart attack. He was killed in the accident, as well."

So there was no one to hold responsible. No one to be furious with. To blame. Reed was left with an impotent feeling that he didn't care for.

"You said this happened two months ago," he said

quietly, thoughtfully. "Why are you only coming to me now?"

"Because I didn't know about you," she said, then looked around the office. "Look, the baby needs a change. Do you mind if we take this conversation over to the couch?"

"What?"

She was already headed for his black leather sofa. Before he could say anything, she'd set the infant down and reached into what had to be a diaper bag slung over her shoulder for supplies.

Struck dumb by the action, he only watched as she expertly changed the baby's diaper, then handed the folded-up used one to him. "What am I supposed to do with this?"

Reluctantly, it seemed, her mouth curved and damned if he didn't like the look of it.

"Um," she said wryly, "I'd go for throwing it away."

Stupid. Of course. He glanced at his small office trash can, then shook his head, crossed to the door and opened it. Signaling to his assistant, he held out the diaper and ordered, "Dispose of this."

"Yes, sir." Karen accepted the diaper as she would have an explosive device, then turned away.

Once the door was closed again, Reed looked at the baby, now standing alongside the glossy black coffee table, smacking both hands on the surface and laughing to herself. Shaking his head, he thought of Spring and felt another quick twinge of pain. Still watching the baby, he asked Lilah, "What did you mean you didn't know about me until now?"

She tossed that thick mass of wavy red-gold hair behind her shoulder and looked up at him as she repacked the baby's supplies. "I mean, that until last week, I didn't know Spring had a family. She never talked about you. About any relatives at all. I thought she was alone."

That stung more than he would have thought possible. His sister had wiped him from her life? So much so that her best friend didn't even know of his existence? He scrubbed one hand across his face and regretted that last conversation with his sister. Maybe he could have been kinder. More understanding. But he'd assumed, as he supposed everyone did, that there would be more time. That he would, once again, be called on to dig Spring out of trouble, and so he'd been impatient and now she was gone and the chance to make things right had vanished with her.

"She left two letters," Lilah said and held out an envelope toward him. "I read mine. This one is yours."

Reed took it, checked that it was still sealed, then noted Spring's familiar scrawl across the front. He glanced at the baby, still entertaining herself, then he opened the envelope and pulled out the single sheet of paper.

Reed. If you're reading this, I'm dead. God, that's a weird thought. But if Lilah brought you this letter, she's also brought you my daughter. I'm asking you to take care of her. Love her. Raise her. Yes, I know I could ask Mom or one of my sisters, but honestly, you're the only one in our family I can really count on.

Well, that hit him hard, considering that in their last conversation he hadn't given her the help she'd wanted. Gritting his teeth, he went back to the letter.

Rosie needs you, Reed. I'm trusting you to do the right thing because you always do. Lilah Strong has been my friend and my family for almost two years, so play nice. She's also been Rosie's "other mother," so she can answer any questions you have and she can be a big help to you.

As usual, you were right about Coleman. He left as soon as I got pregnant. But before he left, I got him to sign away his rights to Rosie. She doesn't need him in her life.

I love you, Reed, and I know Rosie will, too. So thanks in advance—or from the grave. Whichever. Spring.

He didn't know whether to smile or howl. The letter was so like Spring—making light of a situation that most people wouldn't think about. In seconds, vignettes of Spring's life raced through Reed's mind. He saw her as a baby, a child who followed him around whenever they were together, a teenager who loved nothing more than shocking her parents and finally, a woman who never found the kind of love she'd always searched for.

He folded the paper slowly, then tucked it away again before he let himself look at Spring's child. The baby was clearly well cared for, loved…happy.

Now it was up to him to see that she stayed that way. At that thought everything in Reed went cold and still. He knew what his duty was. Knew what Spring would expect of him. But damned if he knew a thing about babies.

"I see panic in your eyes."

Instantly, Reed's normal demeanor dropped over him. He sent Lilah a cool stare. "I don't panic."

"Really?" she said, clearly not believing him. "Because your expression tells me you're wishing Rosie and I were anywhere but here."

He didn't appreciate being read so easily. Reed had been told by colleagues and judges alike that his poker face was the best in the business. Knowing one small baby and one very beautiful woman had shattered his record was a little humbling. But no need to let her know that.

"You're wrong. What I'm wondering is what I'm going to do next." And that didn't come easy to him, either. Reed always had a plan. And a backup plan. And a plan to use if the backup failed. But at the moment, he was at a loss.

"What you're going to do?" The woman stood up, smiled down at the baby then turned a stony stare on him. "You're going to take care of Rosie."

"Obviously," he countered. The question was, *how*? Irritated, he pushed one hand through his hair and muttered, "I'm not exactly prepared for a baby."

"No one ever is," Lilah told him. "Not even people who like to plan their lives down to the last minute. Babies throw every plan out the nearest window."

"Wonderful."

Rosie squealed until the sound hit a pitch Reed was afraid might make his ears bleed. "That can't be normal."

Lilah laughed. "She's a happy baby."

Tipping her head to one side, Lilah watched him. "After I found out about Spring's family, I did some research. I know you have a lot of siblings, so you must be used to babies."

Another irritation, that he'd been looked into, though

he knew potential clients did it all the time. "Yeah, a lot of siblings that I usually saw once or twice a year."

"Not a close family," she mused.

"You could say that," Reed agreed. Hard to be close, though, when there were so damn many of them. You practically needed a spreadsheet just to keep track of his relatives.

"My family's not at issue right now," he said, shifting his gaze away from blue eyes trying to see too much to the baby looking up at him with Spring's eyes. "Right now, I've got a problem to solve."

Lilah sighed. "She's not a problem, she's a *baby*."

Reed flicked Lilah a glance. "She's also my problem. Now."

He would take care of her, raise her, just as his sister had wanted. But first, he had to get things lined up. He'd made his fortune, survived his wildly eclectic family, by having a plan and sticking to it. The plan now entailed arranging for help in taking care of Spring's daughter.

He worked long hours and would need someone on site to handle the child's day-to-day needs. It would take a little time to arrange for the best possible nanny. So the problem became what to do with the baby until he could find the right person.

His gaze settled on Lilah Strong. And he considered the situation. She already knew and cared about the baby. Yes, she still looked as though she'd like to slap him, but that didn't really matter, did it? What was important was getting the baby settled in. He had a feeling he could convince this woman to help him with that. If he offered her enough money to compensate her for her time.

He knew better than most just how loudly money

could talk to those who didn't have any. "I have a proposition for you."

Surprise, then suspicion, flashed in her blue eyes just before they narrowed on him. "What sort of proposition?"

"The sort that involves a lot of money," he said shortly, then turned and walked to his desk. Reaching into the bottom drawer, he pulled out a leather-bound checkbook and laid it, open and ready, on top of his desk. "I want to hire you to stay for a while. Take care of the baby—"

"Her *name* is Rosie…"

"Right. Take care of Rosie then, until I can arrange for a full-time nanny." He picked up a pen, clicked it into life then gave her a long, cool look. "I'll pay whatever you want."

Her mouth dropped open and she laughed shortly, shaking her head as if she couldn't believe what was happening. Fine. If she was unable to come up with a demand, he'd make an offer and they could negotiate from there. "Fifty thousand dollars," he said easily.

"Fifty?" Her eyes were wide. Astonished.

"Not enough? All right, a hundred thousand." Normally, he might have bid lower, but this was an emergency and he couldn't afford to have her say no.

"Are you crazy?"

"Not at all," he said with a shrug to emphasize that the money meant nothing to him. "I pay for what I need when I need it. And, as I believe it will take me at least a week or two to find and hire an appropriate nanny, I'm willing to buy interim help."

"I'm not for sale."

He smiled now. How many times had he heard that

statement just before settling on the right amount? Everyone had a price—the only challenge came in finding the magic number. "I'm not trying to buy you," Reed assured her, "just rent you for a week or two."

"You have enough arrogance for two or three people," she said.

He straightened up, shot her a level look. "It's not arrogance. It's doing what needs to be done. I can do that with your help—which allows you to continue to be a part of the child's—"

"Rosie's—"

"—life," he finished with a nod at her correction. "You can stay, make sure the person I hire is right for the job. Or, you can leave and go home now."

Of course, he didn't believe for a moment that she would leave the baby until she was absolutely sure of the child's well-being. That was written all over her face. Her body language practically *screamed* defensive mode. And he would use her desire to protect the baby for his own purposes. Reed Hudson always got what he wanted. Right now, that included Lilah Strong.

He could see her thinking and it wasn't difficult to discern her thoughts from the expressions flitting across her features. She was still furious with him for whatever reasons, but she wasn't ready to walk away from the baby yet. She would need to see for herself that Rosie was settled into her new home.

So, whether she realized it or not, Lilah Strong would do exactly what Reed wanted.

"I'll stay," she said finally, still watching the baby stagger around the coffee table like a happy drunk. "Until you've found the right nanny."

Then she turned and looked at Reed. "But I won't be paid. I won't be *rented*. I'll do it for Rosie. Not you."

He hid a smile. "Good. Now, I've a few more appointments this afternoon, so why don't you and the—" he caught himself and said instead "—*Rosie* head over to my place. I'll be there at about six."

"Fine," she said. "Where do you live?"

"My assistant, Karen, will give you all of the particulars." He checked the platinum watch on his wrist. "For now…"

"Fine. You're busy. I get it." She slung the diaper bag over her shoulder, then reached down to scoop up the baby. Once Rosie was settled on her hip, she looked up at him. "I'll see you later then. We can talk about all of this."

"All right." He kept the satisfaction he felt out of his voice. She walked past him and her scent seemed to reach out for him. Lemons, he thought. Lemons and sage. It was every bit as tantalizing as the woman herself.

He watched her go, his gaze sliding from the lush fall of that golden red hair down to the curve of a first-class behind. His body stirred as her scent seemed to sink deep inside him, making him want things that would only complicate an already messy situation.

Knowing that, though, didn't ease the hunger.

"You *live* in a hotel?" Lilah demanded the moment Reed walked through the door later that afternoon.

For hours, she'd wandered the expansive suite, astonished at the luxury, the oddity, of anyone actually living in a hotel. Okay, her own mother and stepfather lived on board a cruise ship, traveling constantly from country to country. They enjoyed being somewhere different every day, though it would have driven Lilah crazy.

But living in a hotel? When there were a zillion houses to choose from? Who did that? Well, all right, she'd heard of movie stars doing it, but Reed Hudson was a lawyer, for heaven's sake. Granted, a very successful, obviously very *rich* lawyer, but still. Didn't the man want a home? A hotel was so…impersonal.

Though she'd noticed a lot of framed photos of what had to be members of his family scattered throughout the two-bedroom, two-bath suite. So, she told herself, he wasn't as separate from the Hudson clan as he pretended. That made her feel both better and worse.

Better because Rosie would have more family than just this one seemingly cold and distant man. But worse because if he did care about his family, why hadn't he been there for Spring when she'd needed him?

He shut the door behind him, then simply stood there, staring at her. Those green eyes of his seemed to spear right through her and Lilah could only imagine how good he must be in court. Any opposing witness would quail beneath that steady, cool stare.

"You have a problem with the hotel suite?" He tucked both hands into the pockets of his slacks.

"It's lovely and you know it." And, unlike his office, the space was decorated in more than black, chrome and gray.

The living room was wide and dotted with twin lemon-yellow chairs opposite a sky blue sofa, all of them overstuffed and just begging someone to drop in and relax for a while. The tables were a honey-colored wood and the rugs on the tile floor were splashes of jewel tones. There was an oak dining set at the edge of a small, stocked wet bar, and a grouping of cream-colored lounge chairs on the terrace ran the length of the suite. Each of the two bedrooms was done in shades of cream and green and the bathrooms were luxurious, spa-like spaces with stand-alone tubs big enough to hold a party in and showers studded with full-body sprays.

From the terrace, there was a spectacular view of the ocean in the distance, with the meticulously cared-for golf course and a sea of red-tiled roofs in the surrounding neighborhood closer up. The hotel itself looked like a castle plunked down in the middle of a beach city and felt light-years away from her own home, a cabin in the mountains.

Though it was much smaller than this hotel suite, her cabin afforded beautiful views, too, of a lake and the mountains and a meadow that in spring was dotted with wildflowers and the deer that came to graze through it. She was out of her element here and that made her feel slightly off balance. Which, Lilah told herself, was not a good thing when dealing with a man like Reed Hudson.

"Where's the baby?" he asked, his gaze shifting around the room before settling on her again.

"Rosie—" she emphasized the baby girl's name "—is asleep in the crib the hotel provided." Honestly, how was he going to be a parent to the little girl if he couldn't even seem to say her name?

"Good." He slipped out of his jacket, tossed it across the back of a chair and walked toward the wet bar near the gas fireplace. As he reached for a bottle of scotch, he loosened the precise knot of his tie and opened the collar of his shirt. Why that minor action should strike Lilah as completely sexy, she couldn't have said.

"I called ahead," Reed was saying. "Told Andre you

were coming and to see that you had everything you needed."

"Andre." Lilah thought back to the moment she'd entered the hotel to be greeted by an actual *butler*. If it hadn't been for the man's friendly smile and eagerness to help, she might have been completely intimidated by the snooty accent and his quiet efficiency. "He was wonderful. Couldn't do enough to help us and Rosie loved him. But I can't believe this suite comes with a butler."

One corner of his mouth quirked as he poured himself a scotch. "Andre's more than a butler. Sometimes I think he's a miracle worker."

"I'm convinced," she admitted. "He arranged for the crib and had a wide selection of baby food stocked in your pantry. He even provided a bright blue teddy bear that Rosie already loves."

Reed smiled and even from across the room Lilah felt the punch of it. If anything, her sense of balance dissolved just a bit more.

"You want a drink?"

She thought about refusing, simply because she wasn't ready to relax around him yet. But after the day she'd had… "Wine, if you have it. White."

He nodded, got the wine from the refrigerator and poured her a glass. Carrying both drinks to the sofa, he sat down and handed the wine to her when she joined him, taking a seat on the opposite corner.

Lilah took a sip, let the wine settle her a bit. Being this close to Reed Hudson was a little unnerving. The anger she'd been living with for the past few weeks still simmered deep inside her, but looking at him now, she had to admit it wasn't only anger she was feeling. She had another slow sip of wine and reminded herself just why she was there.

"Why are you so willing to raise Rosie?" she asked, her voice shattering the silence.

He studied the golden scotch in the heavy glass tumbler for a long moment before taking a swallow. "Because Spring asked me to."

"Just like that."

He looked at her, his green eyes as clear and sharp as emeralds under a spotlight. "Just like that. The baby—*Rosie*—" he corrected before she could "—is a Hudson. She's family and I look out for my family."

"Enough to change your whole life?"

A wry smile curved his mouth briefly. "Life's always changing," he mused. "With a family like mine, nothing ever stays the same."

"Okay, but…" Waving one hand to encompass the elegant surroundings, Lilah said, "You're not exactly living in a baby-friendly environment."

"I know." His gaze slipped around the open room, then he nodded at her. "That's one of the reasons you're here. You've got more experience with babies than I do. So you'll know how to baby-proof this place temporarily."

"Temporarily?" she asked.

"Obviously, I'll need a house," he said, taking another drink of his scotch. "Until now, the hotel's worked well for me. Butler service, daily maids and twenty-four-hour room service."

"It does sound good," she admitted, but didn't think she'd be able to live in such a cutoff, sterile environment for long.

"But a baby changes things," he added, with a slight frown into his glass.

"Yeah, they really do."

Abruptly, he pushed to his feet and reached out for her hand.

"What?" she asked.

One eyebrow winged up. "Don't be so suspicious. Just come with me for a minute."

She placed her hand in his and completely ignored the buzz of something electric that zapped through her. If he felt it, too, he was much better at not showing it than she was. Not a flicker of response shone in his eyes as he pulled her to her feet.

He tugged her behind him as he walked around the sofa, across the room and out onto the terrace, stepping into the encroaching shadows. Then he let her go and walked up to the stone railing, looking out over the view as lights began to wink into existence in the homes below, and a handful of stars began to glitter in the sky.

Lilah followed his gaze briefly, then half turned to watch him instead. His sharp green eyes were narrowed against the cold wind that ruffled his thick, wavy black hair. Somehow he seemed more…approachable. Which should probably worry her.

"I can't stay here," he said, his voice soft enough that she leaned in closer so she wouldn't miss a word. "Rosie will need a yard. And a terrace that doesn't include a couple-hundred-foot drop to the street."

Lilah shivered and looked over the edge of the railing. She'd had the same hideous thought herself. A tiny Rosie crawling out to the terrace and somehow climbing up on furniture and pitching right over. Deliberately, she pushed that mental image away and told herself it was good that Reed had come to the decision to move on his own—without her having to mention it.

"So just like that, you'll buy a house."

"Just like that," he assured her, turning to lean one hip against the stone balustrade. "I'll find something this weekend."

She laughed. How could she not? Lilah's friends worked and saved for months, sometimes years to sock away enough money to maybe look for a house. Reed Hudson would simply pull out his magic checkbook. "Is everything so easy then?"

"Not easy," he assured her, his green eyes meeting and holding hers. "But if there's one thing I know—it's that if you want something, you go get it."

Three

Oddly enough, Lilah could understand that statement. Okay, the spur-of-the-moment buying of a house was way out of her league, but the *attitude* was something she believed in. Going after what you wanted and not giving up until you had it.

Isn't that how she'd run her own life?

How strange that she found herself agreeing with a man she'd expected to loathe on general principle. But as much as she was still furious on her friend's behalf, she had to admit that Spring had left her daughter to Reed's care. That said something, too, didn't it?

Spring had loved her daughter more than anything. So Lilah had to assume that there was more to Reed Hudson than she'd seen so far. Rose would not have been entrusted to him if Spring hadn't believed he could and would love that little girl.

Maybe, Lilah thought, instead of just holding her own anger close and nurturing it, she should give him a chance to show her she was wrong about him.

"How does Rosie fit into your plans?" she asked.

He looked at her for a long minute and Lilah just managed to keep from fidgeting beneath that steady stare. Her hormones were stirring to life, and that was so unexpected. She'd come here reluctantly, to turn over a baby she loved to a man she didn't know or trust. Now her own body was lighting up in a way she'd never known before, and she didn't like it. Being attracted to this man wasn't something she wanted—but her body didn't seem to care.

Under the gaze from hot green eyes, she shifted uncomfortably and silently told herself to get a grip.

"Rosie's mine now." Cool words uttered simply and they drove a knife through her heart.

Instantly, she told herself that she should be glad of it. That's why she was here, after all. But she'd loved Rose from the moment of her birth. Lilah was Spring's coach all through labor and delivery and she'd held Rosie herself when the little girl was moments old. She had been a part of the baby's life from that day on, helping to care for her, worrying about her, *loving* her. And since Spring's death more than a month ago, Lilah and Rosie had been a team. A unit. Now she had to give up the child she loved so much and it tore at her.

"I'll take care of her," he was saying. "Just as Spring wanted me to."

"Good," she muttered, and paused for a sip of wine. "That's good."

"Yes," he said wryly. "I can hear just how pleased you are about it."

Caught, she shrugged. "No point in pretending, is there?"

"None." He nodded. "Truth is much easier and far less trouble."

"Are you sure you're a lawyer?"

One eyebrow winged up. "Don't much like lawyers?"

"Does anyone?"

His mouth twitched briefly. "Good point. Though I can say my clients end up very fond of me."

"I'll bet," Lilah muttered. In all of her research, she'd learned just what a shark Reed Hudson was in a courtroom. He was right, his clients did love him, but, oh, his opponents had plenty to say—most of it sour grapes, but still.

Frowning, he gave her a hard, long look and asked, "So is it lawyers you loathe or just *me* in particular?"

"I don't know you well enough to loathe you," she admitted, which wasn't really answering the question. She gave a sigh, met his gaze and said, "I came here already not liking you much."

"Yes, that was clear when we met."

Lilah winced a little. She was never deliberately rude, but her emotions had nearly been choking her. It wasn't really an excuse, but it was the only one she had. "You're right. But losing Spring, then having to hand Rosie over to someone I'd never met…"

She watched him think, consider, before he finally nodded. "I can see that," he acknowledged with another long look into her eyes. "I appreciate loyalty."

"So do I," she said and thought they'd finally found some common ground.

"I spoke to our parents," he said abruptly. "Well," he amended, "our father, Spring's mother."

So strange, Lilah thought, different parents, same family, tangled and twisted threads of connections. Lilah had had no idea that Spring was a member of such a well-known family. Until her death revealed her secrets, Spring had gone by her ex-husband's last name, Bates. So Lilah hadn't been at all prepared to face down the powerful Hudson family.

Worry tightened into a coil in the pit of her stomach. What if Spring's parents wanted Rosie? Would he give the baby over, in spite of Spring's request that he raise her? And if he wanted to, how could Lilah fight him on it? From what she'd learned about the Hudsons, she had to think their parents were less than interested in their own children. They wouldn't give Rosie the time or care she needed. Even while a part of her started plotting just what she might do if she had to take on Spring's parents, Lilah asked, "What did they say?"

He sighed and for the first time he looked more tired than irritated. Or maybe, she thought, *resigned* was the right word.

"Just what I expected them to say," he told her with a wry twist to his lips. "My father reminded me that he already has a three-year-old in the house and his wife is about to give birth to another baby."

She blinked. It sounded strange to hear about siblings born more than thirty years apart.

"And Spring's mother, Donna, said she's got no interest in being a grandmother—or in having anyone find out she's old enough to *be* a grandmother."

"Not very maternal, is she?"

"The words *alley cat* spring to mind," he admitted. "My father has interesting taste in women. Anyway, I told them both that Spring left her child to me. I was only calling them to give them a heads-up."

A quiet sigh of relief slid from Lilah's lungs. He didn't sound as though he had any interest in handing Rosie over to those people, so one worry down. "So basically," she said through the quiet sigh of relief, "they're leaving Rosie with you."

He looked at her. "I wouldn't have given Rose to them even if they'd wanted her—which I was certain they wouldn't."

Now surprise flickered to life inside her. Lilah would have expected him to *want* someone to relieve him of the baby. Hearing him say just the opposite made her wonder about him. "Why?"

Frowning, he took a drink, then said, "First and most importantly, Spring asked me to take care of her daughter."

Lilah nodded. She understood and appreciated that he would take his sister's request to heart. In everything she'd read about him, he was a cold, merciless attorney. What she hadn't known about was the loyalty she saw now, etched into his expression.

And even though her heart ached at the thought of going home and leaving Rosie behind… Lilah felt a bit better about going knowing that at least Reed would do what his own sense of duty demanded. It wasn't enough for a child to grow on. A child needed love before anything else. But it was a start.

Still, she asked, "What else? What aren't you saying?"

His mouth firmed into a tight line as he shifted his gaze from hers to the ocean, where the dying sun layered brilliant streaks of red and gold across the water. "Your parents," he asked, "still together?"

A bittersweet pang of old pain shot through her chest. "They were," she said quietly, watching his profile as he studied the sea as if looking for answers. "Until my father died in an avalanche five years ago."

He looked at her then, briefly. "I'm sorry."

"So were we," she said, remembering that loss and how keenly it had been felt. "A couple of years ago, though, my mother met someone. He's a very nice man and he makes her happy. They were married a year ago, and now they spend all of their time traveling."

Stan was retired, having sold his business for millions more than ten years ago. When he met Lilah's mother on a ski run in Utah, it really had been love at first sight, for both of them. And though it had been hard to accept that her mother could love someone other than Lilah's father, she couldn't deny how happy Stan made her mom.

Curiosity sparked in his eyes. "Going where?"

"Everywhere, really," she said, with a half laugh. "Mom and Stan live on a cruise ship, going from port to port and, according to my mother's emails, having a wonderful time."

Now he turned, a small smile curving his mouth, and looked down at her. "You were surprised that I live in a hotel, but your own mother lives on a cruise ship."

She shrugged. "But a hotel's on land. Near houses. A cruise ship is something else again."

"Odd logic."

Smiling, she said, "It works for me."

"Yeah." He turned his face into the wind again and said, "So, my family's different. They like having children, they just don't like having them around. Nannies, governesses and boarding schools are the favorite child-rearing tools for the Hudsons."

Before she could say anything about that, he went on, "Spring hated it. It was a kind of torture for her to be locked away in a school she couldn't leave." He swiveled his head and stared at her. "How could I give Rose over to people who would only do the same thing to her that they did to her mother? No."

Warmth opened up in the center of her chest and Lilah was caught off guard. The cold, hard lawyer seemed to have disappeared and she didn't know quite what to make of the man he was now.

"You've agreed to stay," he was saying, and Lilah came up out of her thoughts to listen.

"For a while, yes." For Rosie. For Lilah's own sake, she would stay until she was sure the baby girl would be safe. Happy. She'd closed her artisanal soap shop temporarily and could run the online business from her laptop, so there was no rush to get home.

Reed had wanted to *pay* her to stay. What he didn't realize was he would have had to pay her to *leave*.

"Then you can help me choose the house." He finished off his scotch. "And furnish it. I won't have time for a decorator."

Stunned, she just looked at him. "You want me to—"

"Don't all women like shopping?"

She laughed shortly. "That's completely sexist."

"Sue me. Am I wrong?"

"No, but that's not the point," she said.

"It's exactly the point. You'll have free rein," he tempted her. "You can pick out the furnishings that'll make the house baby friendly."

Help choose the kind of house Rosie would grow up in? How could she refuse? Shopping to outfit an entire house on someone else's dime? What woman wouldn't accept that offer? Besides, if left to his own devices, Lilah was sure he'd furnish the whole place in black and white, and that thought was just too hideous to contemplate.

"Free rein?" she repeated, wanting his assurances.

"That's what I said."

"So you're okay with lots of color."

His eyes narrowed. "How much color?"

He was worried and that made her smile. "Free rein," she reminded him.

Buying a house wasn't that difficult when you were willing to pay any price to get what you wanted when you wanted it. The Realtor quickly decided that Lilah was the person she needed to convince, and so Reed was able to hang back and watch the show. He had to admit, Lilah was picky, but she knew what would work and what wouldn't. She wasn't easily swayed by the Realtor's practiced patter about square footage, views and school districts. He admired that.

But then, he was finding the whole package of Lilah Strong intriguing. She wasn't sure of him still, so there was a simmer of anger about her he couldn't miss. Most women he knew were cautious enough to only let him see carefully constructed smiles. They laughed at his jokes, sighed at his kiss and in general tried to make themselves into exactly what he might want.

Strange, then, that the woman who didn't care what he thought of her was the one he found the most intriguing. Hell, watching her move through an empty house, the Realtor hot on her heels, was entertaining. And damned if the view wasn't a good one.

She wore a long-sleeved white button-down shirt with

a sleek black vest over it. Her blue jeans hugged a great behind and an excellent pair of legs, and black boots with a two-inch heel completed the look. Casual elegance. Her reddish-gold hair hung loose to the middle of her back in a cascade of waves that made him want to bury his hands in the thick mass.

But then, he remembered she'd looked damn good the night before, too, wearing only a sky blue nightgown that stopped midthigh.

He woke up at the sound of the baby crying and realized that this was his new reality. Rose was his now and he took care of what was his.

Moving through the darkened suite, he walked to the room Rose and Lilah were sharing, gave a brief knock and opened the door. Lilah was standing in a slice of moonlight, the baby held close to her chest. She was swaying in place and whispering things Reed couldn't make out.

"Is she all right?" he asked, keeping his own voice hushed.

"Just a little scared," Lilah told him, giving the baby soothing pats as she rocked her gently. "New place."

"Right." Wearing only a pair of cotton sleep pants, he walked barefoot across the room and scooped Rose right out of Lilah's arms, cradling the baby to his chest.

For a moment, it looked as though Rose would complain. Loudly. But the baby stared at him for a long minute, then sighed and laid her little head down on his shoulder.

That one action melted something inside him and felt...powerful. He held that tiny life close, felt her every breath, every shuddering sigh, and knew in that one shining moment he would do anything to keep her safe.

Then he looked into Lilah's eyes and found her mea-
suring him. Her hair was a tangle of curls around her
face, her eyes were wary and she crossed her arms over
her chest, lifting her breasts high enough that he got
a glimpse of cleavage at the V-neck of her nightgown.

"Sorry she woke you," Lilah said, voice soft as a
feather.

"I'm not," he said, surprised to find it was nothing but
the truth. "We have to get used to each other, don't we?"

"Yes, I guess you do." She reached out one hand to
smooth her palm over Rosie's dark curls. "She's usu-
ally a good sleeper, but her routine's a little messed up
right now."

"She'll get a new routine soon."

At that, Lilah let her hand drop to her side and stared
up at him. "Are you ready for that?"

He looked down at the baby asleep on his shoulder.
"I will be."

And in the quiet of the night, with a sleeping baby
between them, he and Lilah watched each other in the
silence.

Reed had wondered then, as he did now, if she had
felt the heat that snapped and sizzled between them.

Today, her blue eyes were sharp and clear as she in-
spected the kitchen of the fifth house they'd seen that
morning. She stepped out onto a brick patio, with the
Realtor hot on her heels. Reed walked out after them,
listening to their conversation.

"I like that there's a fence around the pool," Lilah
said, looking at it as if she could judge its strength with
the power of her gaze.

"Electronic locks with a parental control," the Realtor said, giving a wide, plastic smile as she smoothed

black hair so stiff that it probably wouldn't have moved even if she were in the middle of a tornado. "There's a top-of-the-line security system in the house as well, and both remotes are accessible in the garage as well as the house."

"Security," Lilah mused thoughtfully. "So this isn't a good neighborhood?"

The Realtor paled while Reed smothered a smile.

"This is one of the finest neighborhoods in Laguna," the Realtor protested. "A security system is simply for peace of mind."

Reed saw the humor in Lilah's eye and knew she was just giving the other woman a hard time.

"I do like this yard," she said, turning in a slow circle to admire the picture.

Reed did as well, and he had to admit that of the houses they'd seen so far that morning, he preferred this one. The house itself was a larger version of a California bungalow. It had charm, character but plenty of room, and it wasn't sitting on top of its neighbors. He liked that. Reed also liked the yard. The pool took up a third of the lot, but alongside it ran a wide green swath of lawn that would give a kid plenty of room to run. There were trees and flower beds, and since they were situated high on a hill, there were spectacular views of the ocean. The brick terrace boasted an outdoor living space, complete with a backyard kitchen, and the interior of the house was just as perfect. Five bedrooms, five baths and a kitchen that looked fine to him and had had Lilah sighing.

Standing in a tree-dappled patch of shade, Lilah looked at him. "What do you think?"

Both women were watching him, but Reed's gaze met Lilah's alone. "I think it'll work."

The Realtor laughed sharply. "Work? It's a fabulous piece of property. Completely redone two years ago, from the roof to the flooring. It's only been on the market for three days and it's priced to sell and—"

Never taking his gaze from Lilah's, Reed held up one hand for silence and hardly noticed as the Realtor's voice faded away.

Lilah grinned at the woman's reaction to his silent command. "I like it."

"Me, too," Reed said, and spared a glance for the Realtor. "I'll take it. Have the paperwork drawn up and delivered to me at the Monarch this afternoon—"

"This afternoon? I don't know that I can get it all done that quickly and—"

Now he shot the woman a look he generally reserved for hostile witnesses on the stand. "I have every confidence you will. And, while you're working, you should know there's a nice bonus in it for you if you arrange for a seven-day escrow."

"Seven—"

"And," he continued as if she hadn't interrupted, "since I'll be paying cash for the house, I'd like the keys in five days. Furniture has to be delivered and arranged so that we can move in at the end of the seven days."

"That's highly irregular…"

He watched Lilah turn and walk across the yard, as if she'd done her part and didn't feel it necessary to be in on the haggling. Well, he'd rather talk to her, so he wrapped this up quickly.

"Ms. Tyler," he said quietly, firmly, "I doubt you come across many cash clients and so the regular rules may not apply in this situation. Why don't you take care of this and make it happen?"

"I'll do my best, naturally," she blurted, adjusting the fit of her bright red jacket.

"Twenty percent of the asking price as a bonus above your commission."

Her eyes went as wide as the moon and her jaw literally dropped. Not surprising since he was sure she didn't receive that kind of bonus very often. But it was worth it to him.

He didn't like waiting. He didn't mind paying for what he wanted. And Reed knew that money could pave over obstacles faster than anything else in the world. In fact, the only person he'd ever come across who couldn't be bought—or even rented—was Lilah Strong. Just another reason she intrigued him.

He walked past the stunned-into-silence Realtor and moved toward Lilah. Besides, what was the point of being rich if you didn't use the money?

"I'll get right on this," the Realtor called out when she could speak again. "I'll, uh, just wait outside in my car. Start making calls. You and your wife take your time looking around."

He didn't bother to correct the woman, though the word *wife* gave him a quick, cold chill. Instead, he walked slowly across the lawn to join Lilah as she stared out at the view.

"It's done."

She turned. "What?"

"I bought the house."

She laughed and shook her head. The wind lifted her hair and flew it about her face until she reached up and plucked a long strand out of her eyes. "Of course you did. Moving in tonight are you?"

His mouth quirked. "No, I didn't want to rush. Next weekend is soon enough."

Now she laughed and the sound was surprisingly sexy. He moved in closer and caught her scent. Different today, he thought, and realized she now smelled like cinnamon apples. Lemons yesterday, apples today. As if the woman herself wasn't distraction enough.

"You know," she said, "it took me three months to find my house, then it was another month to arrange for a loan, buy it and gain possession and then move in. Most people don't manage it in a week."

"I'm not most people," he said with a shrug.

"That I agree with." She turned, leaned against the chest-high wall and looked at the back of the house. "It is beautiful."

He never took his gaze from her. "It is."

As if feeling him watching her, she turned her head to briefly look at him. The air seemed to sizzle between them. "What're you doing?"

"Just stating the obvious," he said with a half shrug.

She took a deep breath and looked back at the house, ignoring the flash of heat. That irritated. It was there. A hum of something hot, something potent, and she seemed determined to pretend it wasn't.

"Rosie will love having this yard to play in." She sounded wistful. "I'm glad the pool has a fence around it."

"If there hadn't been," he said flatly, "I would have had one installed before we moved in."

She shot him a glance. "In less than a week."

He winked. "Of course."

"Of course." She nodded, sighed. "We should get back to the hotel and check on Rosie."

"She's fine. Andre personally vouched for the hotel babysitter. Apparently she's the grandma type, great with babies."

"I know. He told me."

"But you don't trust anyone but yourself with the baby."

"I didn't say that," she pointed out. "I just don't know her."

"You don't know me, either," Reed said, studying her features. The sun and shadow played across her face, danced in her eyes, highlighting the worry gleaming there. "So how will you handle leaving her with me?"

"Honestly?" She pushed her hair back with a careless swipe of her hand. "I don't know. But, I don't have a choice in that, do I?" She shifted her gaze back to the sea. "I have to do what Spring asked me to, even if I don't like it."

He watched her for a long minute, the set of her chin, her blue eyes narrowed against the glint of the sunlight on the water. Getting back to the hotel, the waiting Realtor out front, left his mind in favor of staying right there, talking to Lilah, finding out more of who and what she was.

"If you hadn't found the letters from Spring, would you have kept Rose yourself?" He already knew the answer, but he wanted to hear her say it.

"Yes," she said firmly. "I'd have adopted her. I would have done anything I had to, to keep her. I already love her like she's my own."

"I noticed," he said, giving her a brief smile when she

looked at him. "It's impressive…letting go of what you want to fulfill Spring's wishes."

"I'm not trying to impress you."

"Another reason why I am impressed," he admitted. "So tell me. How did you and my sister become such good friends?"

Her gaze followed the clouds racing across the sky. A reluctant smile curved her mouth and for a moment or two she seemed lost in her own thoughts, memories. When she spoke, her voice was soft. "She came to my shop, looking for work."

Still having a hard time realizing his sister had had a *job*, Reed chuckled a little at his own memories. "The first and only job Spring had that I know about was at the movie theater the summer she was sixteen." He smiled at the images his mind showed him. "My father had said something about her being unemployable since all she knew how to do was spend his money."

"That was nice," Lilah muttered.

"Yeah, he's a charmer all right. Anyway, Spring decided to prove to our father that she could make her own money." He shook his head, remembering. "She loved movies and thought it would be a great way to see all the new ones when they came out. With the added benefit of making our father eat his words." He sighed a little. "But she worked the candy counter and hardly had the time to see a movie at all. Plus, she hated what she called the 'ugly' uniform. She didn't last a month."

"People change," Lilah said quietly.

"Not in my experience," Reed countered.

"Well, Spring did." Lilah set her hands on top of the wall, rested her chin on them and looked out at the ocean as if looking back in time. "Her husband had just left her. She was pregnant and alone—" she shot him a quick look "—or so I thought. She needed a job and was willing to do anything I needed."

He frowned. "What kind of shop do you own?"

She laughed at the obvious worry in his voice. "It's called Lilah's Bouquet. I sell artisanal soaps and candles."

Did that explain all the different fragrances that seemed to cling to her? Probably.

"And what did Spring do at your shop?"

"Everything." Lilah smiled to herself. "Hiring her was the best decision I ever made, I swear. She was great with customers. Always seemed to know what they'd like and helped them find it. She took care of the stock, kept track of what was selling and what wasn't. Honestly, she was wonderful. Before long, I made her the manager and that gave me more time to spend in my workshop, making up the soaps and candles to stock the shelves."

It was as if she was describing a stranger. Manager? Spring? Frowning, Reed tried to imagine it and came up short. His younger sister had never been the dedicated sort—or at least that's what he'd believed. But it seemed that he hadn't known Spring as a mature adult at all. And now he never would.

"There's a small apartment over the shop," Lilah was saying. "I lived there myself until I could buy a house. So Spring and Rose moved in and it worked well for all of us. The baby charmed every customer who came through the door and Spring didn't have to worry about leaving Rose with a babysitter. Everything was great, until…" Her eyes went dark with grief and memory.

A sharp stab of pain sliced at Reed's heart. He didn't want to think about his sister's death any more than Lilah wanted to talk about it. So instead, he focused on the life she'd been living away from her family. "It sounds like she was happy."

Lilah's gaze lifted to meet his and a sad smile curved her mouth. "She was. She loved our little town and being a part of it. She had a lot of friends."

Reed tried to picture it. His sister, born in London, raised there and in New York. She had gone to the best boarding school in the city and hung out with the children of rock stars and princes. So it was a little hard to picture her happy in a shop apartment in some small town in— "Where?"

"What?"

"Where do you live? Your shop? Your small town? You didn't say."

"You're right. I haven't. There's just been so much going on. It's Pine Lake, Utah. About an hour north of Salt Lake City, up in the Wasatch mountains."

Reed shook his head and chuckled again. "Sorry. Just hard to imagine Spring in the mountains. She was always more for the beach."

"People change."

One dark eyebrow lifted. "Yeah, you've said that before."

She smiled a little. "Must be true then."

"For some people."

She tipped her head to one side and looked up at him through serious eyes. "People can surprise you."

"That's usually the problem," he mused, then took her arm. "We should go. Ms. Tyler's probably sitting out in her car wondering what we're doing back here."

"Right. I want to get back to Rosie, too."

He steered her across the yard and through the open

back door. With his hand at her elbow, they walked through the house that would be his home in a little more than a week, and Reed told himself that sometimes, change happened whether you were ready for it or not.

Four

The next week was a busy one. She hardly saw Reed, who made himself scarce whenever she and the baby entered a room. He spent most of his time at work and she had to wonder if that situation was normal or if it was simply that he was trying to avoid her completely.

On the other hand, Lilah was really going to miss Andre.

She didn't know what she would have done without him the past several days. Life in a hotel wasn't ideal, but the amazing butler could have made her a believer.

Snooty accent aside, Andre was always ready to help. And though he was loathe to gossip, he had let a few little nuggets of information about Reed drop over the past couple of days. So now she knew that his family rarely visited, he almost never had guests—translation: women—in his suite and that he was a generous tipper.

Which told Lilah that either Reed was a determined loner or he was lonely and that he paid attention when people helped him and made sure to show his appreciation. It wasn't much, but it was more than she'd learned from Reed himself.

Andre cleared his throat to get her attention. "I've prepared another list of furniture shops you might want to check," he said, producing said list from the inside pocket of his immaculate three-piece black suit. Handing it to her, he winked. "I've marked the ones most useful I believe for what you're interested in. As you've already ordered Rose's things, I believe Mr. Hudson's study is the last room on your agenda."

"How do you remember that?" Lilah asked with a laugh. "I can barely keep up with it myself."

"Oh," he said, bending at the waist to wipe a smudge of banana from the corner of Rosie's mouth, "I believe in being thorough, miss."

His hair was steel gray but his eyes were that of a much younger man. She supposed he could have been anywhere between thirty-five and fifty. He stood at least six feet and was the epitome of a British butler.

"Why are you working in a hotel, Andre? Shouldn't you be in London with royalty or something?"

He laid one hand on Rose's head in a loving pat, then looked at Lilah. "I did serve an earl several years ago, but frankly, I grew tired of the cold, gloomy weather in London." He winked again. "It's a lovely place to be *from*, if you understand me."

"Yes," Lilah said with a smile. "I think I do."

"I get back often to visit friends and family and enjoy myself completely on those trips." He folded his hands in front of him and gave a heavy sigh. "Though I must say, I do miss a good pub now and then."

"And I'm going to miss you, Andre," she blurted out, and before she could lose her nerve, came around the table and gave him a hug.

For a second, he went stiff with shock, then relaxed enough to give her a friendly pat on the shoulder. "I shall miss you, as well. Both you and Miss Rose. But this is best for all of you. A child shouldn't grow up in a hotel, after all."

"No, she shouldn't." Lilah looked down at the baby, then thought that Reed shouldn't be locked away in the impersonal suite, either. It couldn't be good for anyone. And that thought brought her back to the day of shopping stretching out in front of her.

She shifted her gaze to the list Andre had given her. "I don't know the stores here at all, so it would be a big help to me if you could tell me which of these is your favorite."

Clearly pleased to be asked his opinion, Andre pointed to the third name on the list. "Lovely leatherwork at that shop. I believe Mr. Hudson would approve."

"Okay, that just got easier. Thank you again," she said as he bowed and turned to leave. She stopped him by saying, "One more question?"

"Of course, miss." He waited patiently.

"I know it's none of my business, but how did a British butler come by the name of Andre?"

A smile flitted across his features quickly, then disappeared. "My mother's father was French. I'm named for him. Caused me quite a bit of trouble as a child, I'm not ashamed to say."

"I'll bet you handled it just fine."

"I like to think so, miss." He bowed again. "Do enjoy your shopping."

When he left, Lilah turned to Rose again. "Oh, yeah, really going to miss him."

A couple of hours later, she was at the furniture shop Andre had recommended and she could silently admit he'd been absolutely right. Reed probably would like what she got here and if he didn't he had no one but himself to blame.

That one brief moment of closeness with Reed at the back of the new house hadn't been repeated and maybe, Lilah told herself, that was just as well. She was caught in a trap—she had to honor her friend's last wish, to have Reed raise the baby, but she wanted Rosie for herself. Basically, she and Reed were standing on opposite sides of a wall and any attempt to breach it—except for dealing with the baby—would be a waste of time.

As if he knew it, too, Reed had been avoiding her as much as possible. It wasn't easy, since they were sharing a hotel suite that, despite its size, seemed to shrink daily. He left for work early every day and didn't get back to the hotel until later in the evening. Usually about the time Lilah was tucking Rose into bed. Accident? Or design? She was willing to bet that Reed deliberately chose to arrive late enough to miss the whole bath time ritual. Then he could claim since the baby was now tucked in and asleep, he wouldn't go in and wake her.

And in spite of all of this? The attraction Lilah felt for him stayed at a slow simmer. The man was clearly uninterested, yet she couldn't seem to convince her body to stop lighting up whenever he walked into a room.

Lilah found it almost impossible to get a read on him.

It was as if he'd accepted his duty in taking Rosie in, but he wasn't going to put any more into it than he absolutely had to.

Not since that first night when he'd scooped Rose out of Lilah's arms to cuddle against his chest had he even once touched her. Held her. Talked to her. Lilah couldn't bear thinking about the kind of life Rosie would have if Reed were simply unable to love her as she needed to be loved. But how could he, when it was clear from everything she'd learned that he and his siblings had grown up without that kind of affection.

Her heart torn, Lilah went through all the motions of what she was supposed to be doing—helping Reed prepare for Rosie being thrust into his life. But furniture and houses and all the money in the world wouldn't make up for a lack of love. She didn't know what she could do, though. She couldn't fight him in court for the baby. Not only was he as rich as Midas, he was a *lawyer*. She wouldn't stand a chance.

So the only hope she had was to somehow break through the wall of ice he'd erected around himself.

"Shouldn't take more than ten or twenty years," she assured herself.

"I'm sorry?"

Lilah flushed, caught talking to herself while her mind wandered. Smiling at the store clerk, she said, "Nothing. Are we about finished here?"

In the past week, with the assistance of the ever-helpful Andre, Lilah and Rose had visited every store she needed to furnish a house she wouldn't be living in. Of course, she had no idea what kind of furniture Reed might prefer, but since he hadn't bothered to give her direction, she'd picked what *she* liked.

Except for one room, a study that would be Reed's territory, Lilah had chosen comfortable furniture, soft colors, all of it coming together to build a warm, safe spot for a little girl to grow up in. Alone, but for a man who wouldn't allow himself to love her.

At that thought, Lilah's heart felt as if it were being squeezed in a cold fist. Soon, she'd be leaving, going back to Utah. She wouldn't be the one taking care of Rosie. Wouldn't be the one to see her walk, hear her first words. She wouldn't be there to dry her tears or hear the baby's giggle first thing in the morning.

She felt the sting of tears in her eyes and quickly blinked to clear them. If she started crying now, the clerk selling her a matching set of twin leather chairs and a sofa for Reed's study would think she was worried about the price. And truly, for the first time in her life, she hadn't even looked at the price tag on any of the furniture.

Normally in this situation, she would have been searching out the best bargain and mentally calculating just how far she could stretch her savings. But with Reed's insistence on blank-check shopping, it was going much faster than it would have ordinarily. Except for a kitchen table and Rosie's room, she was pretty much finished.

"Yes, I'll just print out a receipt for you and delivery instructions for our crew." The man stood and practically danced toward the back room. "I'll only be a minute or two."

"It's fine," she said, glancing down at Rosie, who was two-fisting her bottle.

No wonder the salesman was happy. His commission was no doubt going to be spectacular. With the chairs, sofa, tables, lamps, bookcases and rugs she'd purchased, he could probably take the rest of the month off.

As good as his word, Reed had wangled the keys out of the Realtor just as he said he would. There had been deliveries scheduled every day for the past few days and tomorrow would see the last of them, when this order was taken out to the new house. Beds for the master and three guest bedrooms had already been set up and Rosie's new crib and furnishings would be delivered that afternoon.

By the next day, they would all be living in that house overlooking the ocean. And that, Lilah thought, would just give Reed even *more* room to avoid her and the baby. She had to put a stop to it. Had to ensure that Reed spent time with Rosie. Got to know her. To love her. And if he couldn't?

She didn't have an answer.

Closing her eyes, she winced as instantly a familiar image of Reed flashed into her mind—just as it did whenever she tried to get some sleep. Reed, as he was that first night. Dark hair rumpled, broad, tanned chest naked in the moonlight, drawstring pants dipped low on his hips and bare feet—*why* were bare feet suddenly so sexy? Oh, God. She rubbed the spot between her eyes, hoping to wipe away images she was pretty sure had been permanently etched into her brain.

He was arrogant and bossy, no doubt. Gorgeous and sexy, too. Which only made all of this more difficult than it was already.

It would be so much easier if she could just hate him. But how could she when he had instantly moved to fulfill his late sister's wishes? He had bought a house for Rose. He was changing his life for the baby because it was the right thing to do. Hard to hate a man who could do all that.

But if he didn't open his heart to Rose, did anything else matter? God, it felt as if her mind were on an automatic loop, going over and over the same things, day after day with no solution. The man was taking up way too many of her thoughts and that just had to stop.

Lilah gave a quick glance at the clock on the wall. She had to get moving. There were still things like pots, pans, dishes, glassware, throw pillows, comforters and a million other, smaller things to arrange for.

And oh, how she wished her friend Kate was in town to help with all of this. Kate Duffy was an artist, with the kind of eye for decorating that Lilah lacked. Kate would have mowed through every art gallery, department store and lighting shop and, in a blink, would have seen exactly what should go where in the beautiful house on the cliff. But, Kate was on her long-delayed honeymoon with a military husband finally back from deployment.

So, she was in this alone.

A clatter of sound interrupted her thoughts and Lilah looked at Rose in her stroller, happily slamming her bottle against the tray in front of her. The tiny girl grinned and babbled wildly.

Laughing, Lilah leaned over, kissed the baby's cheek and whispered, "You're absolutely right. I'm not alone at all, am I?"

"All right then, Ms. Strong…" The salesman was back, full of bright cheer that spoke of the giant commission he was about to make. "Paperwork is right here. If you'll sign at the bottom…"

She quickly read over the receipt, then signed her name. "Everything will be delivered tomorrow?"

"Between one and three."

"Okay, thank you."

"Oh, my pleasure." He dipped into the breast pocket of his jacket, pulled out a card and handed it to her. "If you need anything else…"

"Thanks again." She took the card, dropped it into her purse, then left, pushing Rosie's stroller out onto the sidewalk.

June in Southern California could be either gloomy or beautiful, and today was definitely one of the pretty ones. The sidewalks were crowded, and the narrow streets were packed with impatient drivers tapping horns as if doing it could clear traffic. Flower-filled baskets hung from old-fashioned streetlights and teenagers with surfboards tucked beneath their arms bolted across the street toward the ocean.

It was all so far from the familiar, Lilah felt a pang of homesickness that was wiped away by the sound of Rosie's crow of delight. What was she going to do in her quiet house when there was no Rose to shatter the silence? How would she handle being so far away from the baby who felt like her own?

"Problems to face later," Lilah said, deliberately shoving those troubling thoughts aside to get on with her day. There were still so many things to do and she was running out of time.

While Lilah shopped like a woman on a mission, Reed pushed through his own commitments. He filed divorce papers with the court, settled his bill with the hotel and arranged for people to pack and move his stuff to the new house. And now, he had to spend some time reassuring Carson Duke.

"Have you talked to Tia?" Reed asked, following the other man with his gaze as he paced the confines of his suite at the Monarch.

For the first time, Reed noticed that one suite was pretty much like the other. Yes, his own was much bigger than this one, but the furnishings were very similar. And Carson looked ill at ease as he moved through the slash of sunlight pouring through the glass terrace doors.

"No," Carson muttered, shoving one hand through his hair. "Haven't talked to her since I moved out of our place a month ago."

"Keep it that way," Reed advised. He'd dealt with divorcing couples for enough years to know that even a split that started out amicable could turn into a battle. And then the case would be judged in the media, fueled by stealthy camera shots taken by the ever-hungry paparazzi.

Carson stopped, shoved both hands into his jeans and nodded. "I know that's the right strategy. But I can't help feeling that if we could talk—"

"Did talking help either of you the last few months?" His voice was deliberately impatient. If he offered sympathy here, his client wouldn't be able to do what was best for him. Better to be firm with his advice.

He frowned. "No. No, it didn't."

Reed took a sip of coffee, then set his cup down on the low glass table in front of him. "I know this is hard, but it's what you've both decided to do. You're better off not speaking with Tia until the court proceedings are done. With your prenup in place, this should be a painless situation to resolve."

"Painless."

Reed nodded. He prided himself on getting his clients through the end of a marriage with as little pain as possible. "Not completely, but this should move along with few complications."

"That's good, I guess," Carson said with a wry smile. "Didn't imagine I'd be in this position, I've got to say."

"No one does," Reed assured him.

Carson snorted. "Maybe. I do know that not growing up in Hollywood made me believe that people can choose to stay together. To work at it. Hell, my own parents have been married forever. They're still happy."

And Reed couldn't help wondering what that was like. Naturally, in his business, he didn't run into long-term marriages. He had no personal experience with it, either. How had it felt to grow up, as Carson had, with one set of parents? Hell, Reed had so many official and honorary grandparents, he couldn't keep track of them all.

The extended Hudson family hadn't exactly been the "norm" or even close to ideal. But it was what he knew.

"So, when can I expect to be a free man again?"

Reed looked at Carson. "Well, you've been married less than two years, and have no children, so that makes things less complicated."

"Happy to help," the man muttered.

Reed understood what Carson was feeling, so he simply went on, "You do own property together..."

"Yeah," Carson said. "The Malibu beach house and a cabin in Montana."

Nodding, Reed said, "Once Tia signs the papers as well, I'll meet with her attorney and we go into what's called *discovery*. That's laying out all jointly held properties and bank accounts and so forth..."

Carson swiped one hand across his face, but nodded solemnly. "And then?"

Smiling, Reed said, "*Then* we prepare a marital settlement agreement and if you both agree with the terms, you'll sign and six months after that, you'll be single again."

"Will we have to go to court?"

"Depends on how the settlement agreement goes. We could end up in a mediator's office, or be seen by a judge."

"Right." Carson coughed out a laugh and shook his head. "I swear, I just never thought Tia and I would end up this way." He shot Reed a look. "You probably hear that all the time."

"Not really," Reed said. "People don't come to divorce lawyers wanting to talk about how good their relationship is."

"Guess not." Carson turned to look out at the ocean. "I thought we'd be different. Thought we'd make it. Hell, Tia even loves my parents." He shook his head again. "Don't know how we ended up here."

"You may never know," Reed said, and stood up. "And trying to dissect the whole thing won't give you peace."

Carson turned his head and looked at him. "What will?"

Reed gave him a grim smile. "If I find out, I'll let you know."

"Right. Okay. Look, I appreciate your bringing me the papers…"

"No problem. I live here, remember?"

"Yeah, but I don't, so I'll be leaving this afternoon." He blew out a breath. "I've got to get back to Hollywood.

Have an early call Monday and there are a few things I have to do over the weekend."

"New movie?" Reed asked.

"No, just a few reshoots on the last one," Carson said. "Back to make-believe and pretense. Today I'm just a guy, Monday morning I'm a Viking again. Weird way to make a living."

"There are weirder." Reed didn't remind the other man that essentially, at its core, he made a living dissolving people's lives. In Reed's book, that made for much stranger than pretending to be a Viking. With that dark thought circling his brain, he buttoned his suit coat and said, "If you need anything, you know where to reach me. Otherwise, I'll be in touch."

"Right."

"And steer clear of Tia," Reed said again, knowing the warning was necessary.

"Yeah, I will." Carson flashed the grin he was famous for. "If I'd done that a couple years ago, I wouldn't be in this mess, right?"

"True." Harsh, Reed knew, and he saw that single word slam home with Carson. But the simple reality was that divorce was the main reason to avoid marriage in the first place.

If that point hadn't been hammered into him watching his own family's near legendary divorce battles, then it would have been over the past several years. Leading his clients through sometimes messy and always miserable dissolutions. Hell, watching Carson Duke right now was just one more reinforcement of the decision Reed had made long ago to remain single.

"Thanks," Carson said. "For everything."

"Just doing my job," Reed told him, then headed out to take care of the mess his own life had recently become. But with any luck, he was about to smooth some of those choppy waters.

An hour later, he was at the new house and had to admit that Lilah had done a good job of furnishing the place. It looked…settled, he supposed, as if everything had been in place for years, not days. *Years*. Damn, that sounded…*permanent*. If he concentrated, Reed would probably be able to actually *feel* roots sprouting up through the floor of the house to wrap around his ankles like chains. Which was exactly why Reed had never bought a house before this. He hadn't wanted to be tied to anything. Along with avoiding marriage, he'd avoided commitments to *places*, as well.

He'd always kept his options open, so that even if he'd never packed up and left town at a moment's notice, he'd always known that he *could*. But now, that was over. He was a homeowner. Or would be by tomorrow. He would have roots for the first time in his life, and that thought felt almost like a noose slowly tightening around his neck.

Hardly surprising, since between boarding schools and vacation homes and the change of address every time his parents remarried, Reed had never had a childhood "home." At least not one where memories were made. He didn't have a particular love of any one place due to a connection to the past. He lived in a hotel so he could leave whenever he wanted to. And now…well, that was over.

The house itself, though, was fine. Glancing around

the great room, Reed approved. Lilah'd promised color and she hadn't lied, but he had to admit that the overall effect was, he supposed, homey. There were heavy rugs in deep jewel tones and oversize furniture covered in soft colors of cream and pale blue. There were lamps and tables and even some of his own art from the hotel hanging on the walls. Odd, he hadn't even noticed them missing from the suite, yet somehow Lilah had managed to have them boxed, moved and hung.

He heard the rumbles of conversation floating to him from different areas of the house. Movers were there, setting up the nursery, and the surprise he'd arranged for was no doubt getting acquainted with Lilah.

He had to give her full points. She'd done a lot of work in very little time. She would absolutely have been worth the money he'd offered to pay her. He still couldn't believe that she'd refused a hundred thousand dollars. Especially when he knew she could use it.

Reed had done some research on his own. He'd looked into her business—you could find anything if you knew where to look. Lilah's Bouquet was a small company with a few employees and a well-laid-out website for online business. Who knew there were so many buyers for pretty soaps and candles? She owned a home with a reasonable mortgage, a ten-year-old car and was, as far as he could tell, well liked and respected in her incredibly small hometown. No family but her parents, and a year or two after her father's death, her mother had remarried a millionaire, so maybe that was the reason behind Lilah's turning down money from him.

Whatever lay behind it, though, he knew she was staying not because he'd asked it of her, but because she was looking out for Rose. Hard to blame her for that. In fact, he appreciated it. He just didn't like being in anyone's debt.

And until he had this new situation locked down and sewed up, he would owe Lilah Strong.

Five

She came into the room just then as if thinking of her had conjured her. A wide smile was on her expressive face, and her eyes were shining. That amazing hair of hers tumbled in waves and curls and bounced with her every step.

"Okay, she's wonderful," Lilah said.

Satisfaction welled inside him. The surprise he'd arranged had gone off better than he'd thought it would. If he had to say it himself, he'd had a stroke of genius in coaxing his mother's former housekeeper-slash-nanny out of semiretirement.

Connie Thomas was in her early sixties, loved kids and had the organizational skills of a four-star general. For more than twenty-five years, Connie had been the one constant in Reed's life. She'd stayed with them through his mother's many marriages and even more frequent moves. Connie was the one the kids in the family went to when they were in trouble or lonely or just needed a sympathetic ear. She'd finally decided to leave, though, when Reed's mother decided her youngest son, at seven, didn't really need to come home from boarding school for the summer.

His mother wasn't the most maternal woman in the known world, and even as he thought it, Reed felt a pang of guilt. She loved her kids, he knew, but in an abstracted way that didn't necessarily require her children's presence. In fact, Selena Taylor-Hudson-Simmons-Foster-Hambleton had never understood how Connie Thomas had so much patience for kids.

"Rosie is already crazy about her," Lilah was saying. "So of course I am."

He nodded. "I suspected you'd approve."

"How could I not?" Lilah was smiling up at him, and it bothered Reed just how much he liked it. "Connie and the baby hit it off instantly." Taking a deep breath, she went on, "And you should know that Connie loves her suite of rooms off the kitchen. She told me you've arranged to have her things delivered here tonight."

"No point in waiting, is there?"

A short chuckle shot from her. "Not for you—and apparently not for Connie, either. Right now, she's taken Rosie upstairs to 'supervise' the movers setting things up in the nursery."

He wasn't surprised to hear that. Connie wasn't one to sit back and let things happen around her. She liked to have her hand in things.

"She'll drive the movers crazy, but she'll be satisfied with their work before she lets them leave."

"You make her sound like a drill sergeant," Lilah said, tipping her head to one side to look up at him.

"She could be," he admitted, then smiled, remembering. "She was the one who made sure baths were taken, homework was done and teeth were brushed. She also kept the cookie jar filled with her magic chocolate chip bars."

"Magic?" Lilah asked quietly.

"Seemed like magic at the time," he said. "Never had anything taste as good as those cookie bars did." Funny, a few minutes ago, he'd been thinking that he really had no memories of a *home*. But now, his mind filled with images of Connie, making cookies, playing board games with the younger kids in the family. Showing them how to make their own beds and expecting them to do it by reminding them all that the maids worked for their parents, *not* for them.

All the kids in the house had known they would find sympathy, understanding and honesty in Connie's kitchen. Reed had benefited more than once from the woman's no-nonsense view of the world. He couldn't imagine his childhood without her. Smiling, he said, "Yeah, those bars were magic."

"Can't wait to try them." Lilah tipped her head to one side and watched him. "There's more than cookies to your memories, though, isn't there?"

Frowning, he realized she was reading him and he didn't like it. "She's a good person. That's all."

"Uh-huh."

"Look," he said, trying to counter the patient expression on her face, "I'm not looking to learn and share and grow here. There is nothing to this beyond Connie being the most logical solution to our current problem."

"There it is again," Lilah said softly. "Rose isn't a problem to solve."

He stiffened a bit under the criticism. "Her care is."

"So now that Connie's here, you're off the hook in the care department?" Lilah cocked her head and stared up at him through eyes that seemed to have a laser focus. "Is that how it works?"

How the hell had he gone from a hero—bringing Connie here—to the bad guy, for the same damn reason? Beginning to be seriously irritated now, Reed countered, "If you've got something to say, say it."

She shook her head. "Where to begin?"

"Just start," he said, voice clipped. Folding his arms across his chest, he stood in the center of his brand-new living room and waited.

"Fine." She took a deep breath, looked him square in the eye and said, "In the week Rosie and I have been here, you've hardly spent any time at all with her."

He snorted. "In case you haven't noticed, I do have work."

"Oh, hard not to notice," Lilah said. "You're always gone. And on the rare moments you are around, you keep a very real distance between you and Rosie."

Truth hit home, but he didn't feel the need to defend himself against it, either. "There is no distance, for God's sake. I'm her uncle. She's my sister's daughter. I just bought her a *house*. I think it's safe to say that I'm inserting her into my life."

"Why does she have to be inserted?" Lilah asked.

"Because she's never been here before?" Reed countered, his voice lowering to a growl.

"That's not what I meant. You can't just shove her into your old life. You and she need to build a *new* life together." Waving her hands a little as if to encompass the living room, she said, "Buying a house is great. But if that's all it is, it's not enough."

Irritation spiked into a sizzle of resentment that caught and burned at the base of his throat. Since this woman and the baby had walked into his life a week ago, everything he knew had been turned inside out. But apparently, that wasn't enough for Lilah Strong.

Reed gave her the cold-eyed glare he usually reserved for hostile witnesses or clients who tried to lie to him. "She's eight months old. What more does she need? A car? A boat?"

"A *home*."

"What the hell is that supposed to mean?" The tight rein on his temper was strained. He knew that Connie, the baby and the last of the deliverymen were just upstairs. Damned if he'd have an argument the whole world could listen in on.

"It means, buying a *house* doesn't make it a *home*."

"Unbelievable." He shook his head. "You're wasting your time making fancy soaps. You should be writing poems for a greeting card company."

"This isn't funny." Her voice was as cool and flat as his own.

"You got that right." He expected her to back down, to smooth over and try for cool reason. He was wrong.

She moved in on him and he could see actual *sparks* flashing in her eyes. "*Your* life isn't the only one that has been 'disrupted.' Rosie has lost her mother. I have lost my friend. I'm a few hundred miles from home and doing my best to keep Rosie safe and happy."

"I get that," he interrupted.

"Not finished," she continued, taking another step closer. "You've avoided me and Rosie all week."

His back teeth ground together. Yeah, he had, but he hadn't expected her to notice. After all, he was a busy man and God knew she'd had plenty to do. "Not avoiding—"

"Ignoring then," she said quickly. "Comes to the same thing. The point is, a house won't be enough. Connie, as great as she is, won't be enough."

Sunlight slanted over her hair, picking up the gold in the red and making it shine. Today she smelled like orange blossoms, and that scent was clogging his throat and fogging his mind. That was the only explanation for him standing there taking a lecture as he hadn't had since he was eighteen and had displeased his father.

"She needs love. Affection. A sense of belonging."

Shaking his head, he felt the first tiny thread of worry begin to snake along his spine. "She'll have everything she needs."

"How can she when you haven't so much as looked at her since that first night?"

"I don't need you to teach me how to take care of a child." And even if he did need the help, damned if he'd ask for it.

She took a deep breath and tried to calm herself. He could almost hear her thinking, *Yelling at him is no way to get through to him.* She'd be right about that.

"All I'm trying to say is," she said, voice patient enough to spike his irritation meter, "I'm staying until I know Rosie is safe and loved and happy. That's not going to happen until you start interacting with her."

"She's a baby," he said tightly. "She's happy if she's fed and dry."

"She needs more than that—she needs family, a sense of belonging. I don't see that coming from you."

Reed wasn't used to being questioned. Doubted. His clients all believed in him. His family turned to him for every crisis imaginable, trusting him to take care of things. Hell, he'd lived his life accepting responsibility and doing everything he could to make sure the world rolled on in an organized way.

Did she really believe an eight-month-old baby would defeat him? His tone was patient and he gave himself points for that, since inside, he was seething. "Rose will get everything she needs."

"From Connie?" she asked.

"Yeah, from Connie. I brought in the one woman I *know* will do right by her. How is that a bad thing?" He took a deep breath and instantly regretted it since that orange scent clinging to her seemed to be invading him.

"It's bad if you depend solely on her to care for Rose."

"I didn't say I would."

"Actions speak louder than words," she pointed out. "And what you're doing is ignoring me and Rose."

"I'm not ignoring the baby. I'm ignoring *you*."

"Why?" she demanded, tossing both hands high.

Could she really not see what it cost him to avoid her company? Was she clueless about the attraction sizzling between them? Well, if so, Reed thought, it was time to let her know exactly what was going on here.

Her scent reached for him, surrounded him and he threw caution out the damn window. "Because of this."

He grabbed her, pulled her in close and kissed her as he'd wanted to for days.

Lilah hadn't expected *this*.

He'd moved so fast, pulled her in so close, held her so tight.

And, oh, my God, his *mouth*.

Reed kissed her with a hunger she'd never experienced before. And for one split second, she was too stunned, too shocked, to do anything more than stand there. But when that second passed, she was kissing him back.

Her body jumped into life, as if she'd somehow been electrocuted. There was a hot jolt of...*everything* blasting through her. Lilah's arms linked around his neck, she leaned into him and parted her lips beneath his. The sweep of his tongue took her breath and sent even more jagged slices of lightning through her body.

A hot ball of need settled in the pit of her stomach and even lower a throbbing ache awoke, and breathless, she knew she wanted, needed, *more*.

His big hands swept up and down her back, pulling her closer, until she felt as if she wanted to simply melt into his body. He cupped her behind and held her tightly to him until she felt the hardness of his body pressing into hers. The need jangling within jumped into high gear, sending her heartbeat into a thundering gallop. Tingling head to toe, Lilah could have stayed exactly where she was for, oh...eternity.

But even as she thought it, other sounds intruded through the buzzing in her ears. Voices, getting louder. Footsteps, coming closer.

And in a rush, her brain suddenly shrieked a warning, reminding her that the house was filled with moving men, not to mention Connie and Rose.

It took every ounce of control she had for Lilah to break away and take a long step back from temptation. Struggling to catch her breath, she knew what she must look like—eyes wide, hair tangled from his busy fingers running through it, mouth swollen from a kiss like no other. There was nothing she could do about that, though, so she instead fought to slow her heart rate and get her body back under control. Not easy since it felt as if every single cell in her body was wide awake and sending up skyrockets in anticipation.

It had been way too long since she'd been with a man. That had to be the reason she'd…overreacted like that. Running her own business didn't give her much time to look for and develop a love life. At least that was the excuse she usually gave herself. But the truth was, she simply hadn't found a man she was interested in enough to make a try at a relationship.

Not that Reed was the one for her. She already knew that was going nowhere, although, after that kiss, she had to admit that maybe he felt something for her whether he wanted to or not. But even if he did, he was rich and lived in California, while she lived in a tiny mountain town and was substantially less than wealthy. They were from completely different worlds and one kiss—no matter how amazing—wasn't enough to bridge the gap. Best to remember that.

"All finished," a deep voice announced as three moving men walked into the main room.

"Just in time," Lilah muttered. She glanced briefly at Reed, saw the flash of banked lust in his eyes then told herself not to look at him again. At least not until the fire inside her had died down. Shouldn't take more than a week or two.

Oh, God.

Things had just gotten so much more complicated. Maybe it would have been better for him to go right on ignoring her. But it was probably too late to go back now.

They were going to have to talk about this, Lilah told herself. Come to an agreement that there would be no more kissing, and wasn't that a sad thought? But Rose had to be the priority. For both of them.

"Right, I'll just go and check everything," she said, taking the excuse the movers had handed her and running with it.

Connie was just walking into the room, a happy, babbling Rosie on her hip. The baby held out her arms to Lilah and in response, she scooped her up and kept walking. The warm, solid weight of the baby in her arms was the perfect antidote to the still-pulsing need she felt inside. Rose was the reason she was here. The *only* reason. Her happiness was paramount.

In the newly setup nursery, Lilah did a quick inspection, made sure the furniture had all been put together and set where she'd told Connie she wanted them. If she took a couple of extra minutes to cool down, who was to know? Finally, though, she headed back to the main room.

There, she found two of the movers had already gone out to their truck. Since Reed had no idea what furniture she'd purchased, Lilah was the one who signed the delivery and setup sheet the remaining mover held out to her. When she was finished, she closed the door behind him and took a slow, steadying breath before heading into the great room to join Reed and Connie.

"Everything all right in here?" the woman asked, her gaze darting from Reed to Lilah and back again.

"Yeah, fine," Reed said, scraping one hand along his jaw.

"Dandy," Lilah agreed, keeping her gaze locked on the baby in her arms.

"Uh-huh," Connie said with a shake of her head. "You two are terrible liars."

She walked over, plucked Rosie from Lilah's grasp and headed for the kitchen. "I'm just going to give this sweet baby a snack. While we're busy, the two of you can talk about whatever it is that's not happening."

Alone with him in the great room, Lilah listened to the silence for a couple of long minutes before finally giving a sigh and muttering, "That's just great."

"What's the problem?"

She looked at Reed. "Really? You kiss me brainless and then your housekeeper takes one look at me and knows what's been going on and you wonder what the problem is?"

He shrugged. "It was just a kiss."

"Yeah. And Godiva is just chocolate." She pushed both hands through her hair then faced him. She didn't mean to stare at his mouth, it just…happened. God. They really did need to talk. And it looked as though it was going to have to be her opening the conversation.

She lifted her gaze to his and asked, "Why?"

He waved the question off. "Why not?"

Well, didn't she feel special? Then something occurred to her and Lilah inhaled sharply, narrowed her eyes on him. "Did you kiss me just to shut me up?"

Now his green eyes flashed and a muscle in his jaw ticked. "What?"

"We were arguing," she reminded him and warmed to her idea as she kept talking. "You were losing, so you wanted me quiet."

Reed laughed shortly and shook his head. "Again, I'll remind you I'm an attorney. I argue for a living. I wasn't losing."

"Oh, please," she said, giving him a satisfied smile. Connie was right. Reed really was a terrible liar. Which meant she was, too, but that wasn't the point right now. "We both know I was right. You've been ignoring Rosie, avoiding me. I called you on it and you didn't like it. So to end the argument, you kissed me."

He took a step closer and Lilah just managed to not take an equal step back. She wasn't afraid of him or anything. She just didn't know if being too close to him right that moment was the best possible idea. Yet backing up would make him think she didn't trust herself around him. Which she didn't—but why let him know that?

"I don't have to kiss a woman to win an argument. I make a lot of money by winning arguments." His gaze moved over her features before meeting her eyes again. "You want the truth? I kissed you because I wanted to. And like I told you once before, when I want something, I go get it."

Well, that was both insulting and flattering. For a week now, she'd been fighting her attraction to Reed, knowing it couldn't go anywhere. Knowing it would just complicate an already out-of-control situation. And boy had she been right.

In her own imagination, a kiss between them would have been hot, leaving them both uncomfortable. In reality, the kiss was well beyond hot and had left them both…wary. Plus, now she couldn't help wondering what sex with him would be like. But as soon as that thought jumped merrily into her mind, she pushed it back out again. As hard as it would be, she was going to forget all about this kiss and the way he'd made her feel for a few shining moments. It was the only way to survive being around him.

"I'm not a prize you can grab off a shelf, Reed. And if I don't want you to kiss me again, you won't, believe me."

"Not much of a threat." His voice was a dark rumble that seemed to settle along her spine and vibrate. "Since you already want me to kiss you again."

Lilah took a deep breath and let it slide from her lungs on a long sigh. She could lie, but what would be the point? He'd felt her reaction to his kiss. He could probably look into her eyes right now and still see the smoldering embers of the inferno he'd started inside her.

"Fine. Okay, maybe I do want you to kiss me." He moved in on her and this time she *did* skip backward out of reach. If she let him touch her right now, he'd set off a chain reaction within her that would quickly flare up out of control. If she was going to draw a line in the sand, then it had to be here and now. "But unlike you, I don't go after something just because I want it."

A barely there smile touched one corner of his mouth. "Is that right?"

She squared her shoulders, lifted her chin and told herself she was doing the right thing. "Absolutely. We don't always want what's good for us."

He laughed shortly, tucked his hands into his pockets and nodded. "Truer words," he mused.

Lilah's eyebrows arched. She was pretty sure she'd just been insulted. "Thanks very much."

As if he could read the tension spiraling through her, he took a step back, then another. "Look, I've told you my father doesn't want the baby and Spring's mother says she simply can't do it because she would miss Spring too much, though she also pointed out she's not interested in being a grandma. So I'm keeping Rose. Raising her."

"Loving her?" Lilah had to ask. Had to make him see that money and a roof over her head would not be enough to give Rose the whole, complete life she deserved.

He frowned at her. "What is this obsession you have with love?"

"Obsession?" she repeated. "What is your fierce opposition to it?"

"I've seen too many people crushed because love was taken away. Or denied. Or tossed aside. Love," he said, voice dark, deep, "is the root of every misery in the world."

"That's a sad attitude."

"And I earned it," he told her, shaking his head, walking across the room to look out the window at the neatly tended front yard.

He didn't speak again, but Lilah was intrigued enough by his silence to follow him. To try to find the first chink in the wall he surrounded himself with. "How? How did you earn the right to say that love is worthless?"

Glancing at her, he said, "I've had a front-row seat my whole damn life to the show of my parents constantly looking for and never finding this mysterious 'love.' They discard wives and husbands like most people change cars and never once have they found what they're looking for.

"My brothers, sisters and I were caught up in the resulting chaos." He turned to face her. "So no, I can't promise love. And I'd like to say that I really don't require your approval for how I raise my niece."

"I know," she said, though those two simple words left a bitter taste in her mouth. "But this isn't about only you, Reed. This is about what's best for Rosie."

"I know that, which is why you're still here." He loosened his tie, then shrugged out of his suit jacket and tossed it behind him to the arm of the sofa. When he looked at her again, he said, "You've got some idea of what my life with Rose should be. News flash—no kid has a perfect life. I've got a demanding job with long hours. Doesn't leave a lot of time for building a nest, for God's sake."

"You don't have to—I already have," she said, sweeping one hand out to encompass the living room and the rest of the house besides. "But you will have to make some changes for Rose's sake."

He laughed shortly. "I'd say we're both standing in the middle of a pretty damn big change."

"Yes, but—"

"And Connie's here now." He glanced past her toward the hall that led to the kitchen. "Trust me when I say Rose couldn't have a better person taking care of her."

"I believe that," Lilah said, since spending just a few minutes with Connie had convinced her that the woman was a born nurturer. "Okay, yes, Rosie will get plenty of care and affection from Connie. But you're her father figure."

He scowled at her.

She saw the flicker of what might have been panic in his eyes and actually felt better seeing it. "You are the man in her life and you have to *be* in her life—not just some ghost who drifts in and out."

She watched a muscle in his jaw twitch and flex and she knew how hard this was for him. There probably weren't many people in Reed Hudson's life who were willing to stand toe-to-toe with him over anything. And maybe she wouldn't have been either, ordinarily. But this was about Rose's future, so she was willing to do what she had to. Didn't seem to matter that her mouth was still buzzing from that kiss or that her nerves were still tangled together in slippery knots.

"You know," he said, "I don't much like taking orders."

"I didn't mean—"

"Oh, yeah, you did," he said and loomed over her, maybe hoping to intimidate her. But Lilah just met him glare for glare.

Seconds ticked past and the silence stretched out between them.

"Why do you smell different every day?" he murmured, and the irritation in his eyes shifted to something hotter, more intimate.

"What?" The abrupt shift in conversation had her shaking her head, trying to catch up.

"Your scent," he repeated, moving in and drawing a deep breath. "It's oranges today." He laid both hands on her shoulders and then skimmed his hands up along her neck to cup her face in his palms.

God, she felt the heat of him sliding down into her system, again, and she shivered with the rush of it. This was not a good idea. Hadn't she *just* told him that he wouldn't be kissing her again. Ever? And here she was, sliding into that puddle of want just because he touched her.

"It's driving me crazy," he admitted, his voice no more than a whisper now. His gaze locked on hers. "Every day, there's a new scent clinging to you and I wake up wondering what it's going to be. Then I have to get close enough to you to taste it. And," he added, as he dipped his head to hers, "once I'm close I don't want to be anywhere else."

"It's my soaps," she whispered, amazed that she could talk with his mouth no more than a breath from hers. With the golden sunlight streaming through the window, wrapping them both in a slash of light that seemed to glow with warmth.

"Yeah," he said, "I figured that out. And now I know that when you're rubbing that scent all over you, you're wet and naked."

She took a long, slow breath and her stomach did a quick spin. He was going to pull her in again, she knew it. He knew it. Maybe she'd stand a chance against him and what he made her feel if she turned and sprinted from the room. But she wasn't entirely sure her legs would support her. So she had to try for reason instead.

"Okay, maybe we should just stop…"

"Yeah," he agreed. "Maybe we should. But we're not going to."

"No, I don't think we are."

Six

A tiny voice in the back of Lilah's mind shouted that it would be much better for this situation if they could keep their distance. But she'd never felt anything like this incredible heat, this indescribable need, so she silently told that logical little voice to be quiet and go away.

This was ridiculous. She knew it. But she couldn't help the wanting. Her heart hammered in her chest. Breath caught in her lungs and her body felt as if she were on fire. This man had way too much power over her. One touch from him was a storm of sensation and the need for more clamored inside her.

"This isn't solving anything," she managed to say.

"Yeah, I know." He took her mouth again and instantly Lilah's thoughts dissolved into a murky puddle.

She met him eagerly, wrapping her around him, holding on as her body trembled and quaked from too many sensations pouring in at once. His hands dropped from her face to explore her curves with a rough sense of urgency that felt like gasoline being poured on a fire. Up and down her spine, down to her bottom and back up to cup her breasts, his hands seemed to be everywhere at once. She groaned and even that small sound was muffled by the roaring in her ears.

The house was quiet, only adding to the feeling of intimacy. And though it felt as if they were alone in the house, they really weren't, and a moment later, both of them remembered it.

The baby's wail shattered their kiss and broke them apart in an instant.

"What the hell?" Reed demanded, clearly horrified. "It sounds like she's being tortured."

"No." Lilah choked out a laugh and pushed her hair back from her face with shaking hands. "She's just past her nap time."

"Good God."

The appalled look on his face brought another short laugh from her. He was clearly clueless about babies and now was as good a time as any to start his education. Still a little unsteady on her feet, Lilah reached out and patted his chest. "I'll be right back."

She left him, headed for the kitchen. A few deep breaths helped her steady herself, though she figured her stomach would be jumping and her heart racing for quite a while yet. Once inside, she found Connie patting Rose's back and murmuring to her. Glancing up at Lilah, she said, "She's tired, poor thing."

"It's way past her nap time," Lilah agreed. "If we had food and any of her things already here, we could just put her down upstairs. But we'll get her back to the hotel."

"Good idea," Connie said, handing the baby over. "While you three are gone, I'll get groceries and things and have everything ready for all of you to settle in to-morrow."

Rose dropped her head on Lilah's shoulder, but the crying didn't stop. Sliding her hand up and down Rose's back, Lilah gave Connie a grateful smile. "I'm really glad you're going to be a part of Rose's life, Connie."

"Me, too," the older woman said, already beginning to bustle around the model-home-perfect kitchen, making it her own. "Retirement's for old people. I was bored stiff to tell the truth." Humming to herself, she set about rearranging the cupboards and didn't even notice when Lilah and Rosie left the room.

"It's okay, sweetie," Lilah crooned, giving the baby a soft jiggle as she walked down the hall back toward the main room where she'd left Reed.

The comforting, warm weight of Rose's small body pressed to hers made Lilah's heart sigh with love—even while she tried to imagine living without it. That thought was dark enough to make her eyes sting, but she blinked back tears that wouldn't do her any good. The house was cozy, in spite of its size, and she knew that Rose would love living here. Lilah only wished that she could be there, to watch Rose grow, to be a part of her life.

Walking into the great room, she watched Reed turn at the sound of Rose's sniffling cry. His eyes were shining, but wary.

Perfect, Lilah thought. She knew he wasn't immune to Rose. She'd seen him that first night, after all, when he'd cuddled her close. And she could understand the caution she sensed in him. But until he let himself truly care for Rose, that wariness would always be with him.

It was part of the wall he'd built around himself. He'd already told her about what growing up with a very different family had been like for him. So she couldn't really blame him for being suspicious of love. But wasn't it long overdue for him to put his past behind him?

"Is she all right?" he asked.

"She's fine," Lilah said, still stroking the crying baby's back. "Just tired."

"Then we should go." He grabbed his suit jacket off the sofa and shrugged into it. "Give me the keys to your rental. I'll bring it around to the front and you can strap her in for the drive back to the hotel."

"Yeah." She walked up to him and plopped Rose into his arms, giving him no choice but to hold the tiny girl. "I'll bring the car around, then you can strap her in."

He looked like a man caught in a trap. Shifting the baby to his shoulder, he looked at her. "I don't—"

"Look," Lilah interrupted. "She's even stopped crying for you." *Good girl, Rosie*, she thought. "Won't take me a minute to get the car."

She hurriedly left the room, but paused at the threshold long enough to glance back. Reed and Rose stood in a slash of sunlight, each of them staring at the other as if discovering a new world. And maybe, she thought as she left the house, that's exactly what they were doing.

They settled into the house with hardly a bump.

Reed spent every day buried in paperwork, hand-holding clients and thinking about the woman currently living in his house. For the first time in his memory, his concentration was shattered. Reed went through the motions, going to court, meeting with mediators and advising his clients, yet there was one corner of his mind not focused on the job at all. Instead, it was centered on Lilah Strong and what she was doing to him.

Memories of kisses that never should have happened continued to bubble and burn at the back of his mind, tormenting him during the day and torturing him at night. He couldn't sleep, and even work didn't have the same draw for him as it had before.

His life had been thrown into turmoil and there was only one way to get everything back into order. Lilah wouldn't leave until she knew that Rosie would be happy. So, the way to make her go the hell home and let him get back to his normal life was to prove to her that he and Rose would get along without her.

And fine, he could admit she'd had a point about getting to know Rose. He couldn't stand back from a child he'd agreed to raise. Even not counting the problem of Lilah, Reed had to get comfortable with the baby who was now a part of his life.

Which was why he was bent over a bathtub, getting just as wet as the infant sitting in a few inches of warm, bubble-filled water.

"She doesn't think we can do this." Reed kept one cautious hand lightly against Rose's back as she splashed gleefully in the tub. Her tiny feet kicked up a storm, making frantic waves while she laughed and turned her shining eyes up to him.

Unexpectedly, Reed's heart gave a hard *thump* in his chest as he looked down into her bright green gaze. Until tonight, she'd been more or less a shadow to him. He knew she was there of course, but their interactions had been limited—purposely. He'd deliberately avoided contact with her because he hadn't wanted to *care*. Caring was an open doorway to misery, pain, fear and all kinds of dark possibilities.

And as his heart continued to squeeze in his chest, he realized that he was in it now. A few minutes alone with a child who looked up at him as if he was her personal hero was enough to start him down the road he'd managed to sidestep most of his life.

She was so small, yet already, Rose was her own little person with a grin that caught at your heart and a temper that could set off a screech strong enough to peel paint off walls. Weirdly, Reed liked knowing she had that strong personality. She wouldn't be a pushover, that was for sure. She'd stand up for herself.

But he'd be there, too. His course was set and whether Lilah believed it or not, Reed knew his life was never again going to be what it had been. "I'll make sure you're safe, Rose."

The baby giggled, and that deep, rolling, straight-up-from-the-gut sound settled into his chest and gave his heart another hard squeeze.

"You're going to tear me up, aren't you?" He smoothed the soft washcloth over her back, and then around to her narrow chest while she slapped the water, sending droplets flying to splatter his shirt and face.

"Yeah, you are. You're a heartbreaker. It's in your eyes and you're already working on me." He sighed a little as the baby laughed and then gently ran the flat of his hand over her damp curly hair.

It had been inevitable, he told himself. From the moment Lilah had carried Spring's daughter into his office, he'd been headed exactly *here*. Somewhere deep inside, he'd known that Rose would be able to breach his defenses. He'd spent most of his life with the determination to keep from caring too much about anyone. He loved his brothers and sisters of course, but even there he maintained a distance. Just enough to protect himself. But this one baby with her happy smile and trusting eyes could undo him. Reed blew out a breath and tried to accept his new reality. But if he was still fighting it just a little, who could blame him?

"Time to get out," he said with a sudden laugh as Rose kicked and slapped all at once and splashed water into her own face. Her tiny features screwed up, the smile disappeared and she blinked frantically. "Not as much fun when you're the one getting splashed, is it?"

She looked up at him, her mouth turned down, and he knew he was about to be deafened by a screech. Quickly, he snatched her up out of the water and, using only one hand, wrapped a towel around her as he cuddled her to his chest. "Hey, you're okay. It's just water."

She sniffled and watched him as she seemed to think it over for a minute or two. Then, apparently the crisis passed, because she smiled and patted his face.

God. She already had a hold on him with those tiny fingers of hers. His heart did another slow tumble and Reed told himself to be careful. To not be drawn in so deeply he wouldn't be able to defend himself. Maybe the answer here was to show Lilah he could and would care for Rose, but to hold enough of himself back that he wouldn't eventually have his heart crushed.

He stood in the bathroom, looked into the mirror and saw his own rumpled reflection, holding a tiny wet baby. Bath time should definitely prove to Lilah that he was willing to involve himself with Rose, right? And that was good, wasn't it? Lilah would leave when he and Rose had "bonded" and then he could get back to the way life should be lived without constantly thinking about a woman he shouldn't be thinking about.

Reed wondered if he was losing his mind. His sharp, cagey brain was fogged a lot lately and he had the feeling it was all because of Lilah. Desire was eating away at his logic. *Bonded.*

"Stupid word, isn't it, Rose?"

"What's stupid?" Lilah spoke up from the doorway.

He groaned inwardly. See? Another example of foggy brain. He hadn't even heard Lilah approach. Shaking his head a little, he met her gaze in the mirror. She looked good, of course. Even in faded jeans and a pale blue T-shirt, Lilah Strong was enough to make a man's mouth water. No wonder he was foggy. With her around, he would challenge *any* guy to keep his mind on the mundane. Not like he could tell her that, though. So he did the first thing he could think of and lied.

"Nothing. Rose was just telling me she thought USC would beat UCLA this fall and I told her that was stupid. Nobody beats the Bruins."

"Uh-huh." Lilah's fabulous mouth curved. "Big football fan, is she?"

"Who isn't?"

She studied him and he realized he could get lost in those blue eyes of hers. The color of summer skies, or clear lakes. Her red-gold hair was a constant fascination to him, and now that he'd had his hands in that heavy, silky mass, all he could think about was doing it again. Her lips were full and shaped into a slight smile that made a single dimple wink in her cheek, and all he could think about was getting another taste of that mouth.

He was in deep trouble here, and when he took a breath and dragged the scent of lilacs into his lungs, he almost groaned aloud. Seriously, couldn't the woman pick *one* scent and stick to it? The changeup was making him crazy.

"Are you okay?" she asked.

"What? Yeah. Fine." Perfect. His poker face had almost completely dissolved now. Somehow, this one woman managed to always keep him off guard—which was another good reason for her to get back to her own life as soon as possible and leave him to his. "Did you want something?"

"Just to tell you your sister Savannah's here."

"Here?"

"*Right* here, actually." Savannah stepped up behind Lilah and grinned.

The huge master bath was beginning to feel like a broom closet.

"Well," Savannah said, still smiling, "here's something I never thought I'd see. Reed Hudson bathing a baby."

He sighed at his sister's teasing. Savannah's short black hair hugged her scalp and her eyes were the same shade of green as his own. He, Savannah and their brother James were the first batch of Hudson siblings, and they were all close.

Though he was surprised to see Savannah, he shouldn't have been. A few days ago, Reed had sent out an email blast to the entire family giving them his new address. It had been only a matter of time before they started trickling in to see him, demanding help with one thing or another.

"What's up, Savannah?" He kept his gaze on his sister, since she was far too observant, and if he chanced glancing at Lilah, his sister would no doubt see more than he wanted her to. He was less and less sure of his ability to mask his thoughts since Lilah had entered his life. After all, if she could read him after knowing each other only two weeks, his sister would probably be able to pick thoughts right from his brain.

"Nothing much." Savannah lifted one shoulder in a shrug. "Just wanted to see your new place, see Spring's baby and—"

"And?" He waited, knowing there was a real reason for her visit. None of the siblings came by or called unless they needed something.

"Okay," she said with a laugh, "I want to use the family jet and the pilot won't take off without your say-so."

He frowned. "Where are you going?"

"Just Paris for a week or two. I need a change," she said and gave him the pout that had always worked on their father. It didn't have the same effect on Reed, because he knew she used that poor-little-me look as her most effective weapon. "I broke up with Sean and I need some me time. You know how it is, right?"

The last, she directed at Lilah, who had been watching the byplay silently. "Um…"

When she got no support from Lilah, Savannah turned back to her brother. "Come on, Reed. Be a sport. You're not using it in the next day or two, are you?"

"No," he said, jiggling the baby a little when she began to squirm.

"So what's the problem?" Savannah turned and said, "Lilah, right? You're with me on this, aren't you? I mean, you know what it feels like to just need a break, right?"

Lilah smiled and shook her head. "I don't know. When I take a break from work, I drive to the city. I've never been to Paris."

"Oh, my God." Savannah looked at her as if Lilah had confessed to being a serial killer. "Seriously? You've *got* to go. Make Reed take you. Well, after my trip," she added quickly. "But you should definitely go. There is this amazing little street café right near Sacré-Coeur…"

While his sister babbled on about the wonders of the City of Lights, Reed jiggled the baby nestled against him, trying to keep her happy. That's when he felt a sudden warmth spread across his chest.

"Oh, man." He looked down at the naked baby in his arms and realized he really should have put a diaper on her right away.

"What's wrong?" Lilah asked instantly.

"Nothing," Reed muttered. "She just—"

Picking up on what had happened, Savannah laughed in delight. "She peed on you! God, Spring would have laughed so hard right now…"

As soon as she said it, silence settled over the three of them like a cold blanket. In the harsh bathroom light, Reed could see the signs of grieving that his sister had tried to conceal with a bright smile. Even as he watched her, Savannah sobered and she looked from Reed to Lilah. Shaking her head, she swallowed hard, blew out a breath and whispered, "I can't believe she's gone. Not really, you know?"

"I feel the same way," Lilah said softly, reaching out one hand to lay it on Savannah's arm. "Spring was a good friend to me, but she was your sister and I'm so sorry."

Lost in the face of his sister's pain, Reed was grateful for the sympathy in Lilah's gaze and voice. Helping Savannah or any of the others deal with Spring's death was especially hard for him since he hadn't actually dealt with it yet himself.

"That's why you really want to go to Paris, isn't it?" Reed asked.

"Yes," Savannah admitted on a sigh. "Sean was just another ship in the night, but Spring…" She winced a little. "We went to Paris together five years ago, remember?"

Reed gave her a tired smile and said wryly, "I remember getting a late-night call from a gendarme asking me if I was willing to pay bail for you and Spring after you went swimming in a public fountain."

Savannah laughed and lifted one hand to cover her mouth. "That's right. I'd forgotten about that. God, we had fun on that trip. Now… I just want to go back. Remember."

Reed looked into her eyes and saw the misery just beneath the surface and he understood her need to go back, retrace her steps with their lost sister. Try to relive the joy to ease the pain. Though none of their parents would win any awards for their skills at nurturing, all of the siblings had managed to stay close.

He had no doubt that Savannah was thinking of a trip to Paris as a sort of wake for the sister she would miss so much. Hell, he knew how she felt. He felt it, too. Here he stood, holding his sister's child, and the baby girl would never remember her mother. Reed would never see Spring again. Never hear that raucous laugh of hers, and it tore at him that the last time he'd seen her, they'd parted angrily. He'd never get that moment back. Never be able to rewrite the past.

Too many *nevers*, he told himself. Too much left unsaid, undone, and now, too late to change a damn thing.

"If it helps to know it," Lilah was saying, her voice breaking through his thoughts, "Spring was really happy with her life. She had a lot of friends."

Savannah looked at Lilah for a long minute, then finally nodded. "It does help. Thank you. And you should know that whenever I talked to my sister, she told me about how kind you were. How much she loved her job."

Now Reed was surprised. Savannah had known about Spring actually working? Was he the only one his sister hadn't confided in?

Turning to her brother again, Savannah said, "I'm so glad I came here in person instead of calling. I like seeing you with the baby and I think Spring would get a real kick out of it, too."

"Yeah," Reed said, still holding the squirmy, wet baby close to his chest. "You're right. She would."

He looked from the baby to Savannah to Lilah and realized that he was surrounded by women—and that wasn't even counting Connie, who was off in the kitchen. Yeah, Spring would have loved seeing him like this. And the thought made him smile.

How his life had changed in a couple of short weeks.

"So?" his sister prodded. "Can I use the plane?"

Nodding, he said, "I'll call the pilot. Let him know you're coming."

Lilah looked up at him, gave him a wide, approving smile, and for some reason, Reed felt as if he'd just won a medal.

"Savannah seemed nice," Lilah said later as she shared tea and some of Connie's magic chocolate chip bars with the housekeeper in the kitchen.

And, she thought as she took another bite and gave an inner sigh, Reed was right. They were "magic."

Lilah loved this room. As with any house, the kitchen really was the heart of things. And this one was amazing. It could have graced the pages of any magazine. The walls were cream colored, the miles of quartz counter were white with streaks of gray marbling. Upper cabinets were white, lowers were a dark gray and the floor was a wide-plank dark walnut. Tucked into the nook where a bay window offered a view of the backyard, the two women sat at an oak pedestal table. A silver pendant light that looked like an old-fashioned gas lamp hung over the table and provided the only light in the otherwise darkened room.

"Oh," Connie said with a laugh, "that Savannah has a good soul but a wild heart. She's always up to something." Chuckling now, she added, "Always had a plan cooking in that quick brain of hers. She spent many a night in my kitchen washing dishes for some transgression or other."

Lilah smiled in response. "Reed told me that you were their real parent."

Flushing with pleasure, Connie shook her head, took a sip of tea and said, "Not really, but I'm sure it felt that way to them from time to time. Anyway, it was good to see Savannah even though it was a quick visit."

Quick indeed. Reed's sister had left almost immediately after he'd called the airport to okay her flight to Paris. As for Reed, once he'd dressed Rose in her pj's and got her into bed, he'd shut himself up in his study. He hadn't so much as poked his head out in hours.

And Lilah had had to force herself to leave him to his solitude. But there'd been a look on his face when

Savannah had rushed out—as if he wished she'd stayed longer. But he hadn't said anything. Hadn't asked her to sit down for a while and have a cup of coffee, and she wondered why. It was as if the distance he tried to keep with Rose was simply the way he treated everyone he cared about.

Had he always been so closed off? Or was it a self-defense mechanism? And if it was, what was he protecting himself from? She had more questions than answers and Lilah knew there was one sure way to get some insight into who exactly Reed Hudson was. Talk to the woman who'd raised him.

"Reed didn't seem surprised to have his sister dash in and out."

"Oh," Connie said, taking a sip of tea, "he's used to that. All of the siblings come and go from his life regularly." She set her cup down and continued, "They love each other, but every last one of them has a *loner* streak. I suppose that's to be expected, since their parents really did leave them to their own devices more often than not. And, ever since he was a teenager, the others have turned to Reed to solve problems."

Lilah's heart ached a little for the loneliness he must have felt as a child. Lilah's own childhood had been great. With two parents who loved each other and doted on her, she'd never been left on her own.

"But he was just a kid, too."

Connie laughed a little. "I think Reed was born old. At least, he has an old soul. Never a single day's trouble out of that boy. Always did what was expected of him, never made waves. He had his own…*code*, I guess you'd say. His own rules for living, even as a little boy. To tell the truth, I used to wish he would rebel a little. But he's always had the maturity that the rest of the family—" she broke off and scowled "—including his parents, lacked."

Now Lilah had the mental image of a little boy, carving out a set of rules so he could keep the world around him safe. Was that what his private wall was about? Keeping out people who might disturb his sense of order?

"Really?" Lilah had already realized that a one-word question would be enough to keep Connie talking.

"Oh, don't get me wrong," Connie said, and the halo of light from the pendant fixture overhead gilded her hair and shone in her eyes. "His parents aren't evil by any means. They love the kids, they're just…careless. Careless with what means the most and the sad thing is, they won't realize it until it's too late to change anything.

"One day they'll be old and wondering why their children don't come to visit." She nodded to herself and gave a little sigh. "They've no real relationship with their own children and that's a sad statement to make, I think."

"It is," Lilah agreed. She couldn't imagine the kind of childhood Reed and his siblings had had. But it still didn't give her insight into the man. And she found she wanted to know him.

"Does he see a lot of his family?"

"Well, now," Connie admitted, "I've not had a chance to see it on a daily basis for the last couple of years. But when the kids come to visit me, they often talk of Reed."

"They visit you?"

"Sure they do," Connie said, laughing. "I'm the one who smacked their bottoms, dried their tears and took care of them when they were sick, aren't I?"

His parents might not have been worth much, Lilah thought, but he'd had Connie and somehow that made her feel much better both about his childhood and Rose's situation, as well. With Connie in her life, Rosie would get plenty of affection and care, Lilah told herself.

"Reed's told me how much you meant to all of them. To *him*."

Connie smiled, clearly pleased to hear it. "They're all good people, every last one of them. And I know how they'll all miss Spring." She took a breath and slowly turned her teacup on the counter in tiny circles. "But I think it will hit Reed hardest—once he finally allows himself the chance to mourn her. He was always the one who took charge of the others. And losing her hurt him. I can see it in him."

"I can, too," Lilah mused. More tonight than ever before. It was seeing him with Savannah, she thought. The brother and sister having that sorrow-filled moment over their sister. While Savannah's pain had been obvious to anyone looking at her, seeing that same anguish in Reed took more effort. But Lilah had seen his brilliant green eyes go momentarily soft and she'd read the regret in those depths. Her heart hurt for him and she was surprised by the strength of her compassion.

When she'd arrived here, she'd expected to hate him on sight. To resent him for taking Rose away from her. Now she was beginning to feel for him, understand what drove him.

"The others now," Connie said after a moment, "they come and go from Reed's life. Each of them will pop in from time to time, usually when they need something, then they disappear again until there's a new need. He'd never say it, but I imagine that bothers him."

"It would bother anyone," Lilah said and she found herself offended on his behalf. Did his siblings appreciate him only for what he could do for them?

"Reed's a strong one. He's made himself so." Connie lifted her cup for a sip. "But there's a fine line, I think, between being strong and being hard. I worry that he doesn't see it."

So did Lilah. The wall he'd built around himself was so solid, she had thought it impenetrable. But there had been one or two times when she'd sensed a chink in his armor.

"Well," Connie announced, "morning comes early, so I'm off to bed. Just leave the teacups here on the table, Lilah. I'll take care of them in the morning."

"Okay. Good night." She watched Connie walk to her suite and for a minute, Lilah just sat there in the kitchen, listening to the silence. The refrigerator hummed and ice thunked into the bin. She checked the time and told herself to go to bed. It was already eleven o'clock and Connie was right, morning would come early. Rosie wasn't one for sleeping in.

But Lilah wasn't ready for bed. She felt…restless.

She stood, then turned the lights off, plunging the room into darkness as she left and headed down the hall. Her mind was busy, rehashing that scene with Savannah, then the conversation with Connie. Which turned her thoughts to Reed. No surprise there, since he'd spent a lot of time front and center in her brain over the past couple of weeks.

But now, along with the attraction she'd felt from the start, there was also…admiration and a tug of—not sympathy, she assured herself. He didn't need her pity and wouldn't want it even if he did. But she could feel bad for him that his family came to him only when they needed something from him.

The more she thought about him, the more she wanted

to see him. Talk to him. Assure herself he was okay and not sitting in a dark room feeling sad or depressed or… Oh, hell, she just wanted to see him. Before she could talk herself out of it, Lilah marched up to the closed study door and knocked.

Seven

"What is it?"

He didn't sound happy and Lilah almost changed her mind, but then she remembered that look in his eyes when he and Savannah were remembering Spring. Nope, she wasn't going to leave him alone until she knew he was all right.

She opened the door, poked her head inside and asked, "Are you busy?"

She could see he wasn't. The room was dark, but fire-light spilled out into the shadows, creating weird images that danced across the ceiling and walls.

Rather than sitting behind his desk, he was on the other side of the room in one of the wide leather chairs pulled up in front of the wide, stone hearth, facing the fire. Those shadows moved over his features as he half turned to look at her. There was a short glass of what she guessed was scotch sitting on the table beside him.

She noted his usually tidy hair looked as if he'd been stabbing his fingers through it repeatedly. He wore a short-sleeved black T-shirt that he'd changed into after bathing Rose and a pair of worn jeans that looked as good on him as his usual uniform of elegant suits. He was barefoot, legs kicked out in front of him, and again, she had to wonder what it was about bare feet that had become so sexy all of a sudden.

"Good, I'm glad you're not busy," she said, walking over to sit down in the chair beside his.

He scowled at her. "Who said I wasn't?"

"I did. You're having a drink and staring at a fire. That's not busy. That's brooding."

"I'm not brooding," he argued. "I'm busy thinking."

"About?"

His scowl deepened and, weirdly, Lilah found it sort of cute. He probably thought it was intimidating, but he was wrong. At least, as far as Lilah was concerned.

"You're damn nosy," he mused, gaze fixed on her.

"If you're not, you never find out anything," she argued, then picked up his glass and took a sip. Instantly the fire of the expensive liquor burned a line down her throat and settled into her stomach to smolder.

"Please," he said, waving one hand. "Help yourself."

"No thanks, one sip of that is plenty. How do you stand it?" Firelight danced in his eyes and shadows chased each other across his features.

Smirking a little, he said, "Hundred-year-old scotch is an acquired taste. I acquired it."

He was probably hoping that if he was surly enough, she'd leave. But wrong again. She glanced around the room, pleased with how it had turned out. There were bookcases behind his desk and along one wall, with paintings and framed awards hanging on the opposite wall. The stone hearth took up a third side of the room, while floor-to-ceiling windows made up the fourth. It was male, but cozy.

"Your sister seems nice."

He snorted and picked up his glass for another sip. "Savannah is a force of nature. Like a hurricane. They're rarely nice."

Lilah saw more than she suspected he wanted her to see. He loved his sister, that had been clear. And though he sounded dismissive now, he was just doing the whole don't-get-too-close thing. "Do you see her often?"

He slanted her a look. "Writing a book?"

"Keeping secrets?" she countered, smiling to take the sting out of her accusation.

He sighed, turned his gaze back to the fire and said, "She drops in from time to time."

"When she needs something?" Lilah asked, wanting to see his reaction.

"Usually." Frowning, he turned his gaze back to her. "Why do you care? And why are you asking so many questions?"

"Like I said, if you want answers, you have to ask questions." She ran her fingers over the edge of the table. "I just wondered if you and your brothers and sisters see much of each other."

His brow furrowed, he asked, "Why does that matter?"

She couldn't very well tell him that she was worried that his siblings were taking advantage of him, so she lied instead. "I want to know if Rose will have lots of aunts and uncles coming over all the time."

He took another sip of scotch and drained the glass. "I told you I'd take care of her."

"I'm not arguing that," she said, and wished she'd come up with a better lie. She hadn't come in here to argue with him. She'd wanted to…talk. To make sure he was okay. And that sounded just pitiful, even to her.

"Well, that's a first." Reed pushed to his feet, walked to the wet bar in the corner and refilled his glass. "You've been arguing with me since the first day I met you."

She supposed that was true, but their *relationship*, if that was what it was, hadn't exactly started out friendly, had it?

"To be fair," she said, standing up to walk to him, "you did a lot of that, too."

He studied her through eyes that suddenly looked as dark and mysterious as a forest at midnight, and something fluttered into life inside her. What was it about Reed Hudson that turned her insides to jelly and made her want to both argue and comfort at the same time? Lilah took a breath and steadied herself, for all the good it would do. Being this close to him, having his eyes pinned on her, was enough to unsettle any woman's balance.

"And now what?" he asked. "We're friends?"

"We could be," she said, though a part of her doubted it. There was too much underlying tension simmering between them for a friendship. She didn't have any other "friend" she imagined naked.

"We won't be," he said and set his glass down with a click.

He turned to face her and Lilah's stomach did a slow spin as her heart gave one hard lurch. Nerves jangled into life inside her, but she paid no attention. The night was late, the room was dark but for firelight simmering in the shadows. There was closeness here and she didn't want it to end.

Stupid, her brain warned and Lilah didn't listen. She didn't want to think too much about what was going on between them right now, because she didn't want this quiet, intimate moment to end. Not yet. "Why not, Reed?"

"Because I don't want to be your *friend*, Lilah. What I want from you has nothing to do with being pals."

She took another breath, but it didn't help. Her balance was dissolving and she didn't care. Staring into those green eyes of his was mesmerizing. She couldn't have looked away if she had tried. And she didn't want to try. Lilah wanted to look into his eyes until she discovered everything about him. Until the wall he hid behind fell crashing to the ground.

"My friends don't smell as good as you do," he said quietly. "They don't have hair that looks like gold and feels like silk."

Lilah shivered. She'd known when she knocked on the study door that *this* was what she had been heading toward. For two weeks now, her mind had been filled with nothing but thoughts of Reed Hudson. Even her dreams had been pushing her here, to this moment in the darkness with him.

"What if I don't want to be your friend, either?" she whispered.

"Then I'd say we're wasting precious time standing here talking," Reed said, moving in on her, "when we could be doing something far more interesting."

Awareness roared to life inside her and Lilah felt every single cell in her body wake up and jostle each other with eagerness. She gave him a slow smile that belied the nerves boiling in the pit of her stomach. "Is that right?"

He stepped up so close, their shirts brushed against each other. She felt heat pumping from his body and knew that her own was sizzling, too. Bending his head toward her, he inhaled sharply and murmured, "Vanilla today. I like it."

"Show me," she said and met his mouth in a kiss that lit up every inch of her body. Just like the first time he kissed her, spontaneous explosions of desire, need, hunger were set off inside her, one after the other. She was rocked by the force of them, stronger than before, as if her body had just been waiting, biding its time until it could finally let loose.

He pulled her in tight against him, his hands running up and down her spine, curving over her bottom, holding her close enough she couldn't miss his body's reaction to the kiss. And knowing that he felt the same throbbing need she did only fed the fires licking at the edges of her soul.

The core of her throbbed and pulsed in time with the beat of her heart that was so fast it left her nearly breathless. But then, she thought wildly, who needed air?

He didn't let her go as he moved forward, with Lilah backing up until she bumped into the edge of his desk. Their mouths still fused together, Lilah's tongue tangled with his as he swept inside her mouth to explore, to taste, to torture.

It had been a long time since she'd been with a man and even then, she'd felt nothing close to what she experienced with Reed. This was something brand new. Exciting. Amazing. The man had talented hands and his mouth was downright lethal.

He suddenly tore that mouth from hers and dropped his head to the curve of her neck. His lips, tongue and teeth made a trail along the length of her throat and Lilah groaned as she tipped her head to one side, giving him better access. Silently asking for *more*.

As if he heard her, he lifted both hands to cup her breasts and even through the fabric of her shirt and the lace bra beneath, she felt the heat of him. Her nipples pebbled and every stroke of his fingers sent a shooting star of sensation slicing through her. She gasped, letting her head fall back as her breath whipped in and out of her lungs. Staring at the ceiling, she blindly watched the fire-lit shadows shifting, pulsing in the darkness.

All she felt was him. Every last, hard inch of him pressing her into the edge of the desk. His muscular thighs aligned with hers and she held on to his waist to keep from falling. She wanted him on her, in her, over her. She wanted to feel his body pushing into hers, and easing the ache that only seemed to grow more frantic with every passing second.

He was tall and strong and really built. That one wild thought careened through her mind even as his fingers began to tug at the buttons of her blouse. Impatient now, for the feel of his hands on her skin, she tried to help, but only fumbled and got in his way.

"I've got it," he whispered harshly, his voice straining over every word. "Don't help."

"Right, right." She nodded, grateful he could still move since she seemed to be nearly paralyzed with her body's insistent demands, which clutched in her chest, her gut and, oh, so much lower.

Then he had her blouse undone and was pushing it off, down her arms to land on the desk behind her. The air in the room was cool in spite of the fire and she shivered a little. But then his hands were back on her breasts and heat spiraled up out of nowhere, delivering a different kind of shiver.

His nimble fingers flicked the front clasp of her bra and then her breasts were free and being cupped and stroked by those amazing hands of his. His thumbs and forefingers circled her nipples, tugging, pulling gently. He kissed her again, a sweep of his tongue across her lips, as if offering her a small taste of something incredible.

"Oh, boy," she said on a sigh and caught his satisfied smile.

"Only getting better from here," he promised, and Lilah could hardly wait. She'd never been like this before, her mind whispered. Never felt so much, wanted so much. No man before him had emptied her brain and filled her body so quickly, so completely.

At the core of her, she trembled and ached, and dampness filled the heat at her center. She was more than ready for whatever would come next and she let him know just how eager she was, by reaching up, cupping his face in her palms and dragging his mouth to hers.

Again and again, they claimed each other, breath sliding from one to the other as they delved into a pool of unbelievable sensations. And still it wasn't enough. Not nearly.

She reached beneath the hem of his T-shirt and flattened her palms against the hard planes of his chest. She felt the definition of sculpted muscles and nearly whimpered with the glory of it.

He hissed in a breath, then ripped his shirt off before pulling her tight against him again. Skin to skin, heartbeat to heartbeat, they clung together, relishing every brush of their bodies as the flames around them flashed higher, stronger.

"That's it," he said thickly. "We're done here."

"What? *What?*" She shook her head. Was he stopping? Was he going to say good-night and leave her like this? Needy? Desperate?

"My room," he said shortly, snatching up her blouse and laying it around her shoulders. "We're going to my room. To a bed."

Lowering as it was to admit, she didn't want to wait that long. Oh, she was in serious trouble. "Don't need a bed."

"There're condoms in my room." He looked at her. *Duh.* "Right. Of course. Do need those." She held on to her blouse with one hand as he grabbed her other hand and tugged her in his wake. They left the shadow-filled room and walked down a darkened hallway, following the dimly lit path provided by the night-lights plugged into wall sockets. His long legs were hard to keep up with, but Lilah managed, driven by the growing hunger chewing at her.

He pulled her into his bedroom and the only light there came from the slant of moonlight streaming through the windows to lay like silver across his king-size bed. The navy blue comforter looked as wide and dark as the sky. And when he picked her up and dropped her onto it, she felt as if she was flying into that dark expanse.

Moonlight gleamed in his eyes as she stared up at him, and when she lifted her arms to him, he went to her, sliding his body up and along hers. The incredible brush of his skin felt electrifying. He kissed her again and she felt herself drowning in his taste, in the heat of him.

She tossed her blouse aside then shrugged out of her bra and tossed it, as well. Lilah didn't want anything coming between them. She wanted, needed, and she didn't want to wait. For the first time in her life, Lilah was spiraling out of control.

He grinned as if he knew what she was thinking and completely agreed. "Now the jeans," he muttered and reached for the snap on her pants, but Lilah was too fast for him. She had them undone in a blink and then he was sliding them and her panties down off her legs.

If she was thinking right now, she might have felt a little embarrassed, uneasy, being naked in his bed, the cool night air kissing her skin, the fire in his eyes warming her. But she didn't want to think. She only wanted to *feel*.

"Now you," she demanded and wasn't willing to be patient about it, either. It had been a long two weeks, Lilah told herself, filled with bristling tension and heightened awareness until she'd hardly been able to sleep at night.

She kept her gaze on him while he quickly stripped, and she was really glad she did. He was beautiful. His broad chest was leanly sculpted muscle. Narrow hips, long legs and…her eyes widened and her heart gave an almost painful jolt in her chest. Oh, my.

He grinned again and Lilah said, "You have to stop reading my mind."

"But it's so interesting," he countered, joining her on the bed, dropping a kiss on her flat belly, then moving up to take first one nipple then the other into his mouth.

Lilah came up off the bed, digging her heels into the mattress as she arched her back, instinctively moving closer to that amazing, talented, wonderful mouth of his. She held his head to her breast and watched as his tongue drew lazy, sensual circles around her nipple.

"God, you taste good," he whispered against her breast, giving her skin another long lick.

"It's my soaps," she said on a sigh. "Organic. You could eat them if you wanted to."

"Your scent's been driving me crazy for two weeks," he admitted, looking at her briefly before slowly trailing his mouth down her body again. "Every night, I lay there wondering what you're going to smell like in the morning. Lemons?" Kiss. "Oranges?" Kiss. "Cinnamon?" Kiss.

And now he was close, so close to the throbbing, aching center of her. Everything in her clenched in anticipation, expectation. She held her breath as he shifted on the bed, as he moved to kneel between her legs. As he bent his head to—

"Oh!" Her hips rocked helplessly as his mouth covered her, as his tongue slipped over one sensitive nub of flesh. His hands squeezed her bottom, then moved over her body, sliding up to cup her breasts again, tweaking her nipples while his mouth worked her body into a frantic mass of raw nerves.

Lilah reached down, tangling her fingers in his hair, never wanting him to stop what he was doing—even though she wanted him inside her, filling her, easing the empty ache that hammered against her with every beat of her heart.

His tongue stroked, caressed, his breath dusted her skin and she moved with him, chasing the building need, trying to ease it, trying to make it last at the same time. Tension coiled, tightened until every breath was a victory. Her mind fogged over, her body took charge, racing toward the completion that remained just out of reach.

He pushed her higher, faster, never letting the pressure ease. She both loved and hated him for it. Her head whipped from side to side on the mattress. Her hips continued to move against him. She had no control, wanted none. All she wanted was... The first ripple began and Lilah braced for what was coming.

But there was simply no way she could have prepared herself for the conflagration that erupted inside her. Her head tipped back, her eyes closed and her body bucked and shivered as he sent her flailing over the edge of reality into a skyrocket-filled fantasy.

"Reed... Reed..." She gasped for air and groaned his name, when he moved away from her. But while the last of the tremors were still rippling through her, she heard a drawer open and snap closed.

Moments later, Reed covered her body with his and thrust himself deep inside her. Lilah gasped again at the absolute completeness she felt. He was big and strong and his body felt as if it was meant to be a part of hers.

"You're beautiful," he whispered. "I love watching you shatter."

She choked out a laugh followed by a gasp as he thrust deeply inside her. "Then pay attention, it's about to happen again."

Chuckling, Reed dipped his head to her mouth and tangled his tongue with hers. He stroked one hand along her body, up and down and then back up to cover her breast as he moved in and out of her with a wild, possessive rhythm that stole her breath and made sure she didn't care.

Lilah's legs came up, wrapped around his hips and clung there as her hands grasped his shoulders, nails digging into his skin. Again and again, he took her breath away. Staring up into his emerald green eyes, she lost what was left of her sanity. All she knew was the feel of him moving within her, the brilliant stab of his gaze and the delicious friction of his skin moving against hers.

And then the tension coiled in her belly suddenly spilled throughout her system. She rushed to meet what she knew was coming. Moving with him, rushing together toward that pinnacle, she cried out his name as new, fresh waves of pleasure washed through her. And while her brain fogged over, she heard him groan, felt his body tremble and Lilah held him as they both fell from the sky.

What could have been minutes or hours later, Lilah stirred halfheartedly. She was content right where she was, with Reed's body pressing her into the mattress. But her legs had lost all feeling—unless it was hysterical paralysis.

She wouldn't have been surprised.

Reed Hudson was something she never could have prepared for. He was, in a word, astonishing. She shifted a little beneath him and stroked one hand down his back.

"I'm squashing you."

"Are you?" she asked, a smile of pure female satisfaction curving her lips. It was a powerful thing for a woman to bring a strong man to such a state that he couldn't move. "I hadn't noticed."

Rather than reply, he rolled to one side, but kept her with him, dragging her on top of him. "Better," he said.

Since she could breathe now, she had to agree. Smoothing his hair back from his forehead, she said, "Well, that was worth waiting for."

"Yeah." He looked into her eyes. "I guess it was."

Idly, he traced his hand down her back to her behind and caressed her in long, lazy strokes.

When he closed his eyes and simply let his arm lay across her waist, Lilah took the chance to study him. Always when they talked, when they were even in the same room together, he maintained a closed expression and wariness in his eyes. Seeing him like this, unguarded, tugged at her heart.

But the minute that thought entered her mind, she discounted it. This had been about lust, not love. There were no hearts involved here and if she was smart, she'd keep it that way.

As spectacular as their little interlude had been, it hadn't really changed a darn thing. If anything, she'd only complicated matters by sleeping with him. Not that it hadn't been worth it, but Lilah was a big believer in never making the same mistake twice. So as much as she hated it, there couldn't be a repeat performance and now was as good a time as any to break the news.

"Reed…"

He didn't answer, and she frowned. "Reed."

Still nothing. Stunned, Lilah realized that while she had been doing some soul-searching and coming to a hard, but reasonable conclusion… Reed had fallen asleep.

"Well, I guess our little talk will have to wait, won't it?" Shaking her head, she rolled off him, stretched out on the bed and turned her head on the pillow to look at him. He didn't look young and innocent in his sleep. He looked exactly what he was… A strong, powerful man at rest. And for some ridiculous reason, she felt another hard tug on her heart. Oh, Lilah thought, that was probably not a good thing.

Easing out of the bed, she picked up her discarded clothes and left his room. But on the threshold, she couldn't resist glancing over her shoulder for one last look at him.

He slept in the moonlight and looked so alone, she almost went back to him. Almost. Before she could give in to an urge she would only come to regret, she stepped out of the room and carefully closed the door behind her.

By morning, Reed had worked out exactly what he would say to Lilah. He figured that she would be just like every other woman he'd ever encountered—assuming that sex was a natural gateway to a "relationship." Not going to happen.

Naturally, though, Lilah had thrown him for a loop again. Not only hadn't they had "the talk," she hadn't even been home by the time he walked into the kitchen looking for coffee. Connie had explained that Lilah had taken Rose for an early morning walk and he'd had to tell himself that talking to her about what had happened the night before would just have to wait until he got home after work.

Home. The house was quickly becoming home. More of Lilah's influence. She'd furnished it so that every time he stepped inside, he relaxed as he never had in the impersonal, starkly modern hotel. Hell, he'd even been thinking about redecorating the office lately because he didn't like all the chrome and black.

Her influence.

She was seeping into every corner of his life—and he knew he'd never be able to sleep in his bed again without remembering what the two of them had shared there.

Okay, yes, it had been the most incredible experience of his life, but that didn't mean anything, really. Of course sex with Lilah had been mind-blowing. He'd done nothing but think about and fantasize about her for the past couple of weeks. Finally getting her into his bed was…staggering. Okay, fine, he could admit the sex was great. But that didn't mean he was interested in anything more.

He had spent a lifetime building a controlled, organized life. With his extended, wildly passionate family, he'd learned to maintain a certain emotional distance. Mainly because if he allowed himself to be drawn into every crisis his family brought to him to solve, his own life would end up as convoluted as those he worked to keep out of trouble.

So control had been a part of his personality for as far back as he could remember. Reed kept his thoughts and emotions to himself and showed the world only what he wanted them to see. That control had allowed him to build a fortune, a career and a reputation he was proud of and to avoid messy entanglements like the rest of his family.

But since Rose and Lilah had walked into his life, that control had been slipping. He didn't like it, but there was no point in lying to himself about it.

The truth was, Rosie had already wedged her way into his heart. That tiny girl had a grip on him he wouldn't have thought possible. Then there was Lilah.

He sat back in his desk chair, spun it around to look out at the sun-splashed ocean and instead of seeing the Pacific, he saw Lilah. Her eyes. Her hair. Her smile. He saw her tending to Rose, laughing with Connie and sitting beside him in the firelight.

But damn it, mostly he saw her in his bed. Naked,

writhing, calling his name as her body erupted beneath his.

Before Lilah Strong, his life had rolled along as it should. Okay, maybe it had its boring moments… Fine. He was bored. Work didn't hold the same appeal it had years before. Reed watched his brothers and sisters having adventures and, yes, screwing up so he had to ride to the rescue, but still. They were *living*.

While he, like an old man at a party, complained about the crowds, the noise and the irritations.

When had he turned into an old fogy?

"I'm not," he muttered, as if he'd needed to hear it said out loud for it to be true. "I can have a good time. I just choose to live my life responsibly."

Groaning at the thought, he frowned at the buzzer on his phone when it sounded. Stabbing the button, he asked, "What is it, Karen?"

"Ms. Strong is on the phone. She insists on talking to you."

Just thinking about her could conjure her—if not in person, then on the phone. Well, hell, maybe "the talk" they should have had that morning would be easier if they had it on the phone. He wasn't looking forward to it. She'd probably cry, tell him she loved him or some such thing. But he'd be cool. Detached. And set her straight. "Fine. Put her through."

"Reed?" Her voice sounded low and worried and instantly he responded.

"Are you okay? Rose? Connie?"

"Everything's fine," she whispered. "I don't like bothering you at work, but—"

Thoughts of "the talk" had faded from his mind. Now

all he could think about was what must have happened at the house to have Lilah calling him.

"What's going on?"

"There's a little boy here."

"What?"

"A little boy? Male child?" Even whispered, he caught the sarcasm. "He says he's your brother Micah."

Reed jumped to his feet. "Micah's there? He's supposed to be in school."

"Well, he's in the kitchen eating everything Connie puts in front of him and he says he'll only talk to you."

"I'm on my way." He hung up, grabbed his suit jacket and on the way out the door could only wonder when he would have the time to be bored again.

Eight

Lilah liked Micah Hudson.

He was twelve years old, had Reed's green eyes and a shock of dark hair that continually fell into those eyes. He also had quite the appetite. He'd already mowed through two sandwiches, a half a bag of chips, three of Connie's chocolate chip bars and three glasses of milk.

And through it all, he managed to maintain a guarded look in his eyes that she'd noticed in Reed's way too often. Lilah thought no child should look so wary and it tore at her to see him sitting there waiting for the proverbial ax to fall.

"Reed's on his way home," she said as she sat down at the kitchen table opposite the boy.

"Okay, good." Micah looked up at her and bit down on his bottom lip. "Did he sound mad?"

"No," she assured him. Surprised, yes. Angry, no.

She'd seen Reed in action dealing with his sister Savannah, so she hoped he was just as understanding and patient with this boy who looked so worried and anxious. "He did say you're supposed to be in school."

Instantly, Micah slumped in the chair until he looked boneless. His head hung down so that his chin hit his chest and he muttered, "I don't want to be there. I wanted to come see Spring's baby." He looked at Rose, who gave him a wide, drooly smile, and Micah couldn't help but smile back. That expression faded when he looked back to Lilah. "They wouldn't let me come. Said my father had to sign a paper to *allow* me to go and he wouldn't."

For a boy who had at first insisted he'd speak only to his brother, once Micah started, he couldn't seem to stop. He picked up another cookie bar but instead of eating it, he crumbled it between his fingers as words poured from him in a flood.

"I called Father to tell him I wanted to come here but he said I couldn't come and see the baby because I had to stay at the school and be *supervised*." He added about six syllables to that last word for emphasis, then kept right on talking, his eyes flashing, and a stubborn expression settling on his features. "But Spring was my *sister*," he argued, eyes filling with tears he blinked back. "She *loved* me and I loved her. And now she's *dead*. I should get to see Rose, right?"

"I would think so," Lilah hedged, on his side, but wary about criticizing his father. That didn't keep her from reaching out to briefly lay one hand over his clenched fist.

"That's what I thought," Micah said, nodding as if to remind himself he'd done the right thing. "So, I had some money and I walked out of the school and bought a bus ticket and here I am."

She couldn't imagine a child just hopping a bus and taking off on his own. "Where do you go to school?"

"Arizona," he muttered and watched as cookie crumbs drifted like brown snow down to the plate in front of him. "And it sucks."

Arizona to California was a long bus ride for a little boy on his own, and Lilah took one silent moment to thank the universe for protecting him on his journey. Now that he was safe, Lilah could admire the courage it must have taken for him to go off on his own, and still, his eyes looked wounded, nervous.

Once again, Lilah was reminded of just how idyllic her own childhood had been. She'd never been forced to run away because she'd been miserable where she was. She'd never once gone to her parents with something important only to be turned away and ordered to basically sit down and shut up. She thought of what Connie had said about the Hudson parents and had to agree.

They were careless about the important things. Their children. Couldn't Micah's father hear the misery in the boy's voice? Had he even taken the time to help the boy grieve for his sister?

Oh, she really hoped Reed was kind when he showed up to talk to his younger brother. Micah didn't look as though he could take another dismissal of his feelings. But until Reed arrived, Lilah could only keep the boy talking, try to ease his fear and help him relax.

"Don't like Arizona, huh?" Lilah asked the question lightly, not letting him know how horrified she was that he'd taken such a chance by running. She handed Rosie a slice of banana that the tiny girl immediately squished in one small fist.

"It's not Arizona I don't like. It's my stupid school," Micah muttered.

He looked caught between childhood and adulthood. His face was still round and soft and would hone down over the years, making him a handsome man one day. But right now, he looked like a little boy, unsure of himself and the world around him. He wore black slacks, black shoes and a white shirt with a red-and-blue crest on the left pocket. The uniform had probably been starched and ironed when he began his trek. Now it looked as rumpled and stained as its wearer.

Lilah couldn't believe a twelve-year-old boy had just walked out of his private school and hopped on a bus. What kind of school was it that didn't keep better track of its students? And what kind of parent, she wondered again, couldn't see that a child was sick with worry and grief and misery? She felt sorry for the boy, but at the same time, she knew he'd been lucky to make the trip safely.

Rose, in a high chair alongside Micah, picked up a fistful of Cheerios and tossed them at the boy. Surprise flickered in Micah's eyes, then delight.

"I think she likes me," he said and his smile briefly chased the darkness from his eyes.

"Why wouldn't she?" Lilah told him, then stood up to answer the phone when it rang. Still smiling at the kids, she said, "Hudson residence."

"This is Robert Hudson speaking. Who are you?"

The gruff, hostile voice came through so loudly, Lilah lifted the receiver from her ear slightly. Reed's father? she wondered. "I'm Lilah Strong and I'm here to—"

"I know why you're there. You brought Spring's baby to Reed." There was a brief pause in that silence. Lilah heard a distinct tapping as if the man were slapping something against a tabletop in irritation. "Is my son Micah there?"

"Well," she hedged, not wanting to rat the boy out but unwilling to let his father worry any longer—if he *was* worried. She glanced at the boy, who was watching her through anxious eyes. "Yes, he is."

"I want to speak to him. Now. I've been handling phone calls from his school," he snapped, "and I knew damn well he'd make his way to Reed. I demand to speak to him now."

"Wow," she murmured and slid her gaze to where Micah sat, watching her. He had to have heard his father through the receiver. The man's furious voice was only getting louder. But as much as she wanted to shield Micah, she couldn't keep his father from talking to him. "Hold on, please." She cupped her hand over the phone and said, "It's your father."

Micah's smile was gone and his eyes looked haunted. Pushing himself out of his chair, he dragged himself across the floor like a man heading for the gallows, then reluctantly took the phone. "Hello, Father."

Instantly, the older Hudson started shouting even louder than before.

Lilah didn't mean to eavesdrop, but unless she actually left the room, she simply couldn't help it. She shot a worried glance at Connie and saw the older woman's scowl. But it was Micah's expression that tore at Lilah. As she watched, the boy seemed to shrink into himself as his father ranted like a crazy person.

A few words stood out from the stream. *Irresponsible. Brat. Selfish. Reckless.*

Lilah's temper simmered into a froth that nearly choked her. Seeing that sweet boy reduced to tears was just more than she was going to take.

"Give me the phone, Micah," she said.

The boy gaped at her, but handed it over. Lilah smiled at him, and ignoring the spiel pouring from the receiver, told the boy, "Why don't you go finish your cookies and sit with Rosie?"

He was looking at her wide-eyed as if he couldn't decide if she was brave or crazy. She was neither, Lilah thought. What she was, was going to defend a boy against a man who should know better than to rail against a child. He was still shouting.

"Mr. Hudson," Lilah spoke up and paused for the tirade to fade away in stunned shock at having been interrupted.

"Where's Micah?"

"He's having milk and cookies."

"Who the hell—"

She cut him off again and maybe it was small of her, but she enjoyed it. Now Lilah understood why Reed's siblings came to him when they had a problem. She couldn't imagine anyone would run to Robert Hudson for help. The man would no doubt throw a fit of humongous proportions and solve absolutely nothing.

Shaking her head, she had to admit she also had a whole new respect for what Reed had to deal with on a daily basis. Juggling so many different personalities had to be exhausting.

When Robert Hudson's voice finally trailed off, she spoke up.

"I'm sorry, but Micah's busy right now," she said and heard the man sputter on the other end of the phone. Smiling, she could silently admit that she sort of enjoyed knowing she'd thrown him for a loop. "But please call back as soon as you've had a chance to calm down."

"I beg your pardon?"

She almost smiled. "Goodbye, Mr. Hudson."

When she hung up the phone, Connie applauded. Lilah winced and laughed a little uneasily. Sure, the housekeeper might be pleased, but Lilah had just hung up on Reed's father. Not that she regretted it, she told herself when she looked at the boy staring at her with stars in his eyes. There was just no way she could have stood there and done nothing.

"That was so cool," Micah said quietly, awe coloring his tone. "Nobody but Reed talks to our father like that."

Hmm. "Well, maybe more people should."

Micah's gaze dropped and so did his voice. "Reed's gonna be mad at me, too, isn't he?"

Lilah really hoped not. She didn't think the boy could take much more right now. He looked beaten down after a few minutes of his father shouting at him. If Reed came in furious, it would only add to the boy's misery. Instantly, she thought back over the past couple of weeks and though she could remember a few times when Reed had behaved like a stuffy old man, she couldn't bring up one instance of him really being furious. And she had to admit, he'd had so many things thrown at him lately that he could have blown a gasket at any point. So maybe he'd be exactly what Micah needed.

"Reed will be happy to see you," Connie put in, stopping to give the boy a hard hug. "Just like I am."

"Thanks, Connie," he said, then shifted his gaze to

Lilah again. "Will you talk to Reed for me like you did to my father?"

She smiled and got him another glass of milk. That much at least, she could promise. "If you need it, sure."

"Okay." As settled as he could be, Micah focused on the baby and visibly tried to relax.

When Reed arrived a few minutes later, he came straight to the kitchen and Lilah's heart broke a little as she watched Micah straighten in his chair and go on guard. She really hoped Reed could see beyond the boy's bravado to the frightened kid inside.

Shrugging out of his jacket, Reed loosened his tie and glanced from Micah to the two women in the room watching him. Not for the first time, Lilah wished she could read his mind. It would be good to know if she'd have to jump in front of Micah or not.

But she told herself that how Reed treated his little brother would give her an idea of how he would deal with Rose in the years to come. Would he be patient or angry? Understanding or dictatorial? Nerves pinged inside her. She was sure there was a warm man beneath the cold, detached shell he showed the world. But what if she was wrong?

"Got any coffee, Connie?" he asked.

"Since I'm breathing, yes." She waved him at the table. "Go sit down. I'll bring you some along with a couple cookie bars."

He gave her a wink. "I should come home early more often." Glancing at Lilah as he walked to the table, he asked, "So you've met my brother. What do you think?"

Micah's gaze snapped to hers and she read worry there. She smiled at him. "I think he was very brave to ride a bus all the way from Arizona by himself."

"Yeah. Brave." Reed sat down, reached out and gave Micah's arm a slight punch. "Also stupid. You were lucky you got here all right."

Micah frowned. "I'm not stupid or anything."

"No, not stupid," Reed agreed, "but walking out and making the school panic enough to call Father wasn't the brightest move."

"Yeah, I know. He already called." Micah looked at Lilah. "She told him to calm down and then she hung up on him."

Lilah actually felt herself flush as Reed turned an interested gaze on her. "Is that right?"

"He was shouting at Micah and I couldn't stand it," she said, throwing her hands up. "Shoot me."

"Hell, no," he said, smiling, "I only wish I'd been here to see it."

Lilah grinned at him. So far so good.

"It was awesome," Micah admitted.

When Connie brought the coffee and cookies, Reed turned his gaze back to his brother. Lilah felt Micah's nerves and knew he was as anxious as she was.

"I don't want to go back," the boy said, his voice hardly more than a whisper. "I hate it there, Reed. They make you wear this dumb uniform and somebody's always telling you what to do and the food sucks, it's all healthy and you can't even eat when you want to—"

He said that last as if he were being force-fed twigs and grass.

"And Mom said I have to stay there this summer, too, and there's only me and two other kids in the whole place over the summer and it's really creepy at night when it's so empty and—"

"Take a breath," Reed advised softly and pushed the cookies toward the boy.

Tears stung the backs of Lilah's eyes. Sunlight glanced in through the windows and lay across the kitchen table in a puddle of gold. Rosie smacked her hands on the food tray, and Connie came up to stand beside Lilah, as if they were building a wall to defend one lonely little boy. The question was, would they need it?

"You can stay here," Reed said, and Micah's gaze lifted to his, hope shining as brightly as the sun.

"Really?" One word, said in a hushed awe that held so much yearning Lilah's heart broke with it.

"Yeah, I hated boarding school, too," Reed said, shaking his head. "It is creepy at night, especially when most of the other kids are gone. We've got plenty of room, so you can spend the summer here and we'll figure out what to do about school in September."

"Really? I can stay?" Micah's voice broke and he wiped his eyes with the backs of his hands.

Lilah released a breath she hadn't even realized she'd been holding. She should have known Reed would come through. Hadn't she seen enough evidence over the past couple of weeks that he wasn't nearly as detached as he pretended to be?

Reed ruffled the boy's hair, then took a sip of his coffee. "I'll clear it with Father and your mother. On one condition…"

Wary now, the boy asked, "What?"

"You have to get rid of that ugly uniform and start wearing jeans and sneakers."

Micah's bottom lip trembled, his eyes went shiny and in a rush of gratitude, he jumped out of his chair and hugged his brother. Lilah's heart swelled as she watched

Reed hug him back, and she shared a smile with Connie. Then Reed caught her gaze over Micah's head and she could have sworn she saw another piece of his personal wall break apart and shatter.

God, she was falling in love. Reed Hudson wasn't a cold man, she thought, he had just been protecting himself for so long, it had become a way of life. His gaze bored into hers and even at a distance, she felt the heated stare right down to her bones.

Yep, she thought. *Love*. There was no future in it. There would be no happy ending. Oh, she was in serious trouble—and the only way out was pain.

A few hours later, Reed reasoned with his father. "Micah can stay with me. He hates that stupid school so why keep him there if I'm offering an alternative?"

A part of him wondered *why* he was offering, but the more sensible part knew exactly why. He had been in Micah's shoes and the memories were still clear enough that he understood just how the kid felt. Sent off to boarding school, allowed home only at Christmas and sometimes during the summer. Otherwise, ignored and endured until school started up again. There was no reason for Micah to go through it any longer.

Besides, the memory of the kid's tears had been burned into Reed's mind and heart and damned if he'd send his brother back to a place that made him miserable.

"We'll spend the summer together and if he's happy, he can go to school here," Reed continued firmly, using the only tone of voice his father respected. "There's a good school just a few blocks from here." He'd made a point to check out the schooling situation *before* confronting his father.

"Even if I'm willing to let him stay, Micah's mother will never agree," Robert Hudson muttered.

"Come on, Father," Reed said with a laugh. "You know Suzanna will be fine with anything that keeps Micah out of her hair."

His father huffed out a breath. "True. I don't know what I was thinking when I married her."

Neither did Reed, but that wasn't the point. Although he would admit that his father had wised up fast. He'd been married to Suzanna only a little more than a year. Then, the money-grubbing woman had disappeared from their lives. Thank God. "So you're okay with Micah staying with me?"

"It's fine," his father said after a long minute. "I'll call the school tomorrow, tell them he won't be back. Then I'll let Micah know."

"Good." Relief that he hadn't had to make a bigger fight of it filled Reed. He'd been willing to go to battle for his younger brother, but the fact that he hadn't had to made everything much easier. "How's Nicole doing? Baby news yet?"

His father sighed. "She's fine, but the doctor says it could be another two weeks."

Hard to believe his father was still out creating children he never seemed to have time for. But Robert kept marrying much younger women who always insisted on having a family of their own.

"Tell her I said hello."

"I will." His father's voice softened. "Thank you. I appreciate it. And on another subject," he continued a moment later, "who told that woman she could hang up on me?"

Reed laughed. "Nobody tells Lilah what to do. She

came up with that solution on her own when you were ranting."

"Huh. Well, I liked her. She's got spine."

Amused, Reed thought that his father had no idea. After he hung up, he sat back in his desk chair and glanced to the corner of his desk. Just last night he and Lilah had been right there, wrapped up in each other, tearing at each other's clothes, mindless to anything but what they were feeling. Instantly his body went hard as stone as memories flooded his brain. He groaned, shifted in his chair and steered his brain away from thoughts of Lilah to focus on his new set of problems.

Last month, he was living in a hotel and had nothing to worry about but his clients and the occasional call for help from a sibling. Now he had a house, a housekeeper, a baby and a twelve-year-old to think about. There was just no way Connie would be able to take care of the house *and* two kids. He was going to need a nanny. And until he found one, he'd need Lilah to stay on.

Though his body liked that idea, his brain was sending out warning signals. But it wasn't as if he had a choice here. He had to work and there were two kids who needed looking after. Surely she'd see that and understand why she had to stay longer than she might have planned.

With that thought firmly in mind, he left his study, headed down the hall to Lilah's room and quietly knocked at the door. The hall was dark but for the night-lights. Rosie's bedroom door was cracked open, but Micah's room was closed up tight. The house was quiet, almost as if it was holding its breath. Just like him.

She opened the door and the first thing he noticed was the scent of strawberries. Her hair was still damp from a shower and lay in waves atop her shoulders. She wore no makeup at all and she was still more beautiful than any woman he'd ever known.

His heart jolted in his chest as his gaze met hers. She wore a bright yellow nightgown, the hem stopping midthigh. It had a scooped neck, short sleeves and was covered in pictures of puppies. All different kinds of puppies, from poodles to German shepherds. For a second or two he couldn't even speak. Finally, though, he lifted his gaze to hers and asked, "Like dogs?"

"What? Oh." She glanced down at herself, then shrugged. "Yeah, I do." Then she frowned. "Is something wrong? The kids okay?"

"Everything's fine," he said quickly, easing the worry that had leaped to life in her eyes. He probably should have waited to speak to her until morning. But it was too late to back out now. "We have to talk, Lilah."

A sinking sensation opened up in the pit of her stomach as soon as she heard those words. Never a good way to start a conversation, she thought, stepping back and waving Reed into her room. Lilah had one instant to wish he hadn't seen her in her puppy nightgown, then that thought fled in favor of other, darker thoughts. She'd known this talk was coming.

Ever since the night before when they'd shared some truly spectacular sex, Lilah had been waiting for Reed to take one giant step backward. But it was all right because she'd already decided that the only way for her to deal with her new feelings for Reed was to leave. As quickly as possible.

She'd seen him in action now, not only with Rose but with Micah, and she could believe that though he maintained safe distances from most people, he wouldn't be cold to children. His gentleness with Micah coupled with his willingness to let the boy move in with him had been the cherry on top of her decision. No one that understanding and kind would be anything less to the baby who'd been left in his care.

Reed paced the confines of the guest room as if looking for something. He raked one hand through his hair and then turned to look at her. "We never talked. About last night, I mean."

"I know. But really," she said, "there's not much to say, is there?" Now that she knew she loved him, Lilah really didn't want to listen to him tell her how there could be nothing between them. How it had just been sex—no matter how life altering. That he wasn't interested in a relationship.

Why not just set the tone right from the beginning? She would be the one to say that she didn't want anything from him. That she had no expectations. Just because her heart would break when she left him didn't mean he had to *know* that.

"Seriously?" He looked surprised, both eyebrows winging up. Then he laughed shortly and shook his head. "Of course you would be different from every other woman I've ever met."

"What's that supposed to mean?" It had sounded like an insult, but he looked almost pleased as he said it.

"It means—" he paused, pulled the curtains at the window back and let the moonlight flood the room "—that every woman I've ever spent the night with woke up with diamonds and wedding bells on her mind."

Lilah laughed a little at that. Well, good. She was happy to be the one different woman in his life. At least, she thought, he'd remember her. If her private dreams were more romantic than she was letting on, they weren't something she was going to share, anyway. Lilah had known going in that there was no future for her and Reed so why pretend otherwise? Why give him the slightest indication that she was disappointed? That she'd miss him? No, thank you. She'd keep her own pain private.

"You're completely safe," she said. "I promise. It was an amazing night, Reed, and I'll never forget it, but it was one night."

Frowning, he said, "Right. I just—never mind. Doesn't matter. So, if we're both clear on last night, there's something else I need to talk to you about."

Lilah sat on the edge of the bed, pulled the hem of her nightgown as far down as she was able and said, "Go ahead."

"The thing is," he said, "I'm going to need you to stay a while longer."

"Oh." She hadn't expected that. Especially after last night, she'd half thought he'd hand her a plane ticket this morning and wave bon voyage from the porch. Which was, she could admit privately, why she had gotten up early and taken Rosie for a walk. She hadn't wanted to hear him explain why he didn't want her.

He walked closer until he stopped right in front of her. Lilah had to tip her head back to meet his eyes. In the moonlight, with his face half in shadow, he looked dangerous, mysterious and so very good. She took a breath and tried to rein in what was no doubt a spill of hormones rushing through her bloodstream. But it wasn't easy, especially since now she knew what it was like to be with him. To have his hands on her, his mouth. She shivered and took another breath.

He scraped one hand across the back of his neck and said, "The thing is, now that Micah's going to be staying here, I can't expect Connie to watch over both kids and take care of this place all by herself."

"True." Lilah's mind started spinning. She really hadn't stopped to think about the logistics of everything. But he was right.

"I'm glad you agree. So look, I need you to stay—"

Her foolish heart leaped.

"—until I can find a nanny."

And then it crashed to the ground.

Oh, God, for her own sake, Lilah knew she should leave. Not only had she left her business alone long enough, but if she stayed on here with Reed, her heart would only get more and more involved. And that would only make eventually leaving that much harder.

"So?" he demanded impatiently.

Lilah smiled. "You really need to work on your patience chakra."

"What?"

"Nothing." Why was it, she wondered, that the man could look so completely irresistible when he was standing there staring at her as if she were speaking Martian? Everything about him appealed to her. From his gruff exterior to the tender lover, to the kind and understanding man he was to his siblings. Lilah was toast and she knew it.

She sighed and stood up, but kept a good foot of space between them. She wouldn't leave him in the lurch. No matter that it might end up costing her, she had to at least help him find the right nanny—for the kids' sakes if nothing else. "Okay, I'll stay."

He blew out a breath and grinned, never knowing

what the power of that smile could do to her. "That's great. Okay."

"But…"

"Always a *but*," he muttered, giving her a wary look. "What is it?"

"I've already been away from my business for two weeks." Lilah had been spending two or three hours every day, checking online and then getting her employees to go into the store to fulfill orders. Her emergency system was working fine, but she'd feel better if she at least checked in, in person. "I need to fly home for the weekend, check on stock and have a meeting with my employees."

He frowned thoughtfully, then said, "All right. How about this? We'll all go."

"What?" Laughing now, she looked up at him in surprise.

"I'm serious." He shrugged. "Micah, Rosie and I will go with you. We can take the family jet this weekend— it'll be more comfortable."

Undeniable, she thought, since she hadn't been looking forward to the flight home even if it was only an hour and a half.

"You can show us the mountains," he was saying, "see your place. Then we'll all come back together."

"You don't have to do that," she said, though she loved the idea of him coming to her town, seeing where she lived. Maybe it would be a way for her to remember him with her once this time with him was over. God, she really was a sap. Having memories of him in her tiny hometown would only make living there without him that much harder. And yet…

"I'd actually like to see the shop where you make all

of the amazing scents that are always clinging to your skin," he murmured, and lifted one hand to sweep her hair back from her face.

She shivered at his touch and held her breath, hoping he'd do more.

"Strawberries tonight." He moved in closer, bent his head to her neck and inhaled, drawing her scent inside him. When he looked into her eyes again, he said, "I like strawberries even more than vanilla."

Her stomach did a slow slide into happy land and her heartbeat jumped into a racing, thundering crash in her chest. Whatever her brain might be worrying over, her body had a whole different set of priorities.

"Do you really think this is a good idea?" she whispered when his mouth was just a breath from hers.

"Probably not," Reed answered. "Do you care?"

"No," she admitted and let him pull her down onto the bed.

His kiss was long and deep and demanding. His hands swept down to snatch up the hem of her nightgown and she trembled as he cupped her breast and rubbed her hardened, sensitive nipple. His tongue dipped into her mouth, tangling with hers in an erotic simulation of just what he wanted to do with her next.

And foolish or not, Lilah was all for it. If she had to give him up, then she might as well enjoy him while she had him, right?

She wrapped her arms around his neck and held on when he rolled them over until she was sprawled on top of him. Then she broke their kiss and looked down into misty green eyes that she would see in her sleep for the rest of her life.

"You're amazing," he whispered, stroking his fingertips along her cheek, tucking her hair behind her ear.

Her heart felt as if a giant fist were squeezing it tightly and the ache was almost sweet. These few moments with him were all she would have. She wanted to remember everything. Every touch. Every sigh. Every breathless word.

When he bent to kiss her again, Lilah moved to meet him, parting her lips, loving the slide of his tongue against hers. The soft sigh of his breath mingling with her own.

Moonlight flooded the room, silence filled the air and—a long, plaintive wail erupted from the baby monitor on the bedside table. Lilah broke the kiss and leaned her forehead against his. Rosie's cry continued to peal into the quiet and Lilah smiled sadly. It was like a sign from the universe.

"I think someone somewhere is trying to tell us something." She gave him a sad smile and rolled off him to stand beside the bed. "I have to go to the baby and you should probably just…go."

"Yeah." He sat up with a resigned half smile on his face. "I'm going to head to bed myself."

They left the room together, each of them going in different directions. A metaphor for their lives, she thought. And even though she would still be with him for a while longer, she knew that tonight signaled an end.

At the threshold of Rosie's room, Lilah paused and murmured, "Goodbye, Reed."

Nine

Reed hated LA.

But there was no help for it. At least once every couple of weeks, he had to bite the bullet and make the trek into the city.

Today, he had a lunch appointment with a federal judge he'd gone to law school with, followed by a meeting with a prospective new client. Which almost took the sting out of the drive in California's miserable traffic.

Of course the constant stop-and-go on the freeway gave him plenty of time to think, too. Mostly what he was thinking about was that interrupted night with Lilah. He loved Rose, but the baby had lousy timing.

He loved that tiny girl.

Funny, he hadn't really considered that before. He'd spent so much of his life avoiding the mere mention of the word *love*, the fact that it had just popped into his head surprised the hell out of him. But it shouldn't, his ever-logical brain argued. He wasn't a robot, after all. Reed loved his brothers and sisters—it was just the so-called *Love* with a capital *L* he had no interest in.

And wasn't he lucky that Lilah was such a sensible woman? He smiled and nodded to himself, remembering their talk and how well it had gone. Reed couldn't remember a time when he and a woman had been so in sync. So why did he have an itch between his shoulder blades? His satisfied smile faded and became a thoughtful scowl. She could have been a little more reluctant to let go of what they had. Hell, *he* was reluctant.

He'd never in his life been dismissed so completely by a woman. Especially one he still wanted. Reed was usually the one to call a halt. To back off and remind whatever woman he was with that he didn't do forever. That chat never went over well. Until Lilah, he silently admitted. She didn't seem to have a problem walking away and he should be happy about that. Why wasn't he happy about that?

"Even when we're not together she's driving me crazy," he muttered and cursed under his breath when a Corvette cut him off. Still talking to himself, he said, "Now, she's so focused on the kids it's as if she's forgotten I'm even in the house."

For the past few days, he'd hardly seen Lilah. Micah was settling in, making friends in the neighborhood, playing with Rosie and apparently adopting Lilah. The three of them were cozy as hell, with Connie rounding out their happy little group and Reed being drawn in whether he liked it or not.

The hell of it was, he *did* like it. He'd never imagined himself in this situation—a house and kids—but surprisingly enough, it worked for him. The hotel suite had been impersonal, convenient. The house was loud and messy and full of life. There were no empty corners or quiet shadows there and it struck him suddenly how much of his life had been spent in lonely silence. It was only after it had ended that he could actually see *how* he'd been living. Not that it hadn't worked for him. Could still work, he reasoned. It was just that now he knew he liked a different kind of life, too.

What really surprised him about all of this was just how much Reed hated the idea of Lilah leaving. It wasn't about him wanting her there, of course. It was more for the sake of the kids that he worried about it. Though he had to admit that now, every time he thought about the house, he heard Lilah's voice, her laugh, he imagined one of her amazing scents trailing through the air.

Somehow his life had been yanked out of his control.

When his cell phone rang, Reed answered gratefully. Anything to get his mind off Lilah. A moment later, he realized the truth of the old statement "be careful what you wish for."

"Hey, Reed I need a little help."

He rolled his eyes. His half brother on his mother's side hadn't called in a few months. Reed should have known he was due. "Cullen. What's going on?"

A deep, cheerful voice sounded out. "I just need the name of a good lawyer in London."

"What did you do?" Reed's hands fisted on the steering wheel even as his gaze narrowed in concentration on the traffic around him.

"It wasn't me," Cullen said, innocence ringing out proudly in his tone. "It was my car, but I wasn't driving it."

Reed counted to ten, hoping for patience and thought maybe Lilah had had a point about working on his chakras, whatever they were. "What. Happened?"

"A friend was driving the Ferrari and took a bad turn is all."

"A *friend*?"

"Yeah. You'd like her. She's great. Not much of a driver, though."

"Anyone hurt?" Reed clenched his teeth and held his breath. Cullen was the most irresponsible of the whole Hudson/everyone-else bunch. And, he had the habit of going through a long song and dance before finally reaching the bottom line. Cullen was twenty-six and destined to follow his father, Gregory Simmons, into the banking world. God. Reed shuddered to think of Cullen in charge of anyone's money.

"No injuries, the only casualty was a bush."

"What?" He frowned and shook his head, sure he hadn't heard that correctly.

"Juliet mowed down a hundred-year-old shrub and a patch of dahlias." Laughing now, Cullen said, "To hear the woman who lived there going on, you would have thought we'd murdered her beloved dog, not a bloody bush."

"Damn it, Cullen—" Reed's head ached. Sometimes it was a bitch being the oldest.

"Hey, no speeches," his brother interrupted, "just the lawyer, okay?"

Grateful that he wouldn't have to deal with Cullen and the remarkable Juliet, Reed ran through a mental file, then finally said, "Tristan Marks. Call Karen at my office she can give you his number."

And he hoped Tristan would forgive him for this.

"Great, thanks. Knew I could count on you. If I need anything else, I'll call you at home tomorrow, all right?"

"No," Reed said tightly, "it's not all right. I'm going away for the weekend."

Cullen snorted. "Another fascinating law conference?"

"No," Reed said, even more pleased now that he wouldn't be home to deal with anything else Cullen came up with. "I'm taking a couple days off."

There was a pause that lasted long enough that Reed thought for a moment the connection had been lost. Then his brother spoke up again.

"I'm sorry. I think I must have had a small stroke. You said you're taking two days *off*?"

Reed put his blinker on, then changed lanes, preparing to exit. "What's so hard to understand about that?"

"Oh, nothing at all. Miracles happen all the time."

"You're not as amusing as you think you are, Cullen."

"Sure I am," his brother said with a laugh. "So tell me, who is she?"

"She who?"

"The incredible woman with the power to get Reed Hudson away from his desk."

"Go away, Cullen. Call Karen." He hung up with the sound of his brother's laughter ringing in his ears.

Incredible? Yeah, he thought, Lilah really was all of that and more. Just what the hell were they going to do without her?

Utah was prettier than Reed thought it would be. There were a lot of trees, a lot of open space on either side of the freeway and most amazing of all, hardly any traffic. He actually enjoyed the drive from the airport to the mountain town of Pine Lake.

The flight was short and he'd had a rental car waiting for them, complete with car seat for Rosie. It amazed Reed just how much *gear* was necessary when traveling with kids, though. Good thing they'd taken a private jet. They would have been waiting for hours at baggage claim otherwise.

"So do you ski and stuff?" Micah asked from the backseat.

"I do," Lilah said, half turning in her seat to look at him. "You'll have to come back in the winter and I'll take you up the mountain myself."

"Cool!" The kid's face lit up. "Can we, Reed?"

He glanced in the rearview mirror at the eager smile on his brother's face. "Maybe."

How could he say yes? Lilah was talking about the winter and Reed knew she wouldn't be a part of their lives then. If that thought left a gaping hole in his chest, he didn't have to acknowledge it.

"Turn left here," Lilah said. "We can stop at my house first, unload everything, then go to the shop."

Reed glanced at her and realized she looked as excited as Micah. Clearly, she'd missed this place, her home, her *life*. She'd already given him more than three weeks. How much more could he ask of her? Hell, he was going to owe her forever, and he didn't like the sound of that.

Following her directions, he finally turned into the driveway of what looked like an oversize box. As first impressions went, he could only think how small it was. The house was a perfect square, with black shutters against white siding and a porch that ran the length of the house. The yard was wide and deep, with the house sitting far back from the road. There were at least a dozen trees shading the property and Reed thought that somehow the house fit Lilah.

She jumped out of the car, grabbed Rosie and headed for the house, with Micah close on her heels. Reed followed more slowly, watching her, enjoying the view of her backside in black jeans. Once inside, he saw the place was as small as it had appeared, but it also had a cozy feel to it. There were warm colors, soft fabrics and plenty of windows to let in the light.

"Micah, you and Rosie will share a room tonight, okay?"

"Sure." The boy shrugged and picked up his backpack. "Where?"

"Top of the stairs on the right."

Reed watched him go, silently marveling at the change in his little brother. Just a few days away from the boarding school and the boy had relaxed and smiled more than Reed ever remembered him doing.

When he was alone with Lilah, Reed said, "I like your house."

"Thanks," she said, turning a grin up to him. "I know it's tiny, but it's all I've ever needed. I've got the kitchen and the mudroom set up as my workshop and that's worked pretty well up until now. But I may have to add on at some point."

Nodding, he couldn't help thinking that there was plenty of room at his house to build a huge workshop for her where she could make all the soaps and stuff she wanted. But, his brain reminded him, she wouldn't be there to use it, would she?

Scowling now, he paid attention when she went on.

"The house is still a work in progress and it's only

got two bedrooms, so Micah and Rosie aren't the only ones who'll have to share a room…"

One eyebrow arched. Things were looking up. "Really? Well, now I like your house even more."

Wryly, she said, "I thought you might feel that way."

After they got settled in, they all walked to the center of town and Reed had to admit there was something about the place that appealed. He'd never thought of himself as a small-town kind of guy, but walking down the main street, with its bright flowers tumbling out of half barrels, old-fashioned streetlights and buildings that looked at least a hundred years old, he could see the charm of it. And when they got a tour of Lilah's shop Reed was definitely impressed.

The shop was bright and clean and so tidy, there wasn't a thing out of place. Shelves were lined with the famous soaps in a rainbow of colors, many of them wrapped together by ribbon to be sold as sets. There were candles as well, and tiny bottles filled with lotions in the same scents as the soaps.

Lilah had built something good here, Reed thought, and he felt a stir of admiration for her. When her employees hurried in for a spontaneous meeting, he watched Lilah's happiness as she listened to all the latest news and he realized just how much she'd given up to stay with him and help with Rosie. These were Spring's friends, the town his sister had called home, and Reed listened to stories about her that made him smile and wish again that he and Spring hadn't been at odds when she died.

The rest of the afternoon passed quickly, with exploring the town, stopping for dinner and then walking to a lake so Micah could throw bread to overfed ducks. It was the first time in years that Reed had actually slowed down long enough to enjoy the moment. And being there, walking through a soft night with Lilah and the kids, brought him a kind of peace he'd never known before.

That worried him. He was getting far too used to Lilah. And that was a bad move. She wasn't staying with him. There was no future waiting for them. There was only now.

"Are you okay?" Lilah's voice came softly, since the kids were asleep in the room across the hall.

"Yeah, why?"

"I don't know, you seem…distracted."

"It's nothing. Just thinking about work."

She laughed and climbed into bed. "Let it go, Reed. You're allowed to *not* work once in a while, you know?"

"You're right," he said, looking down at her. "You want to guess what I'm thinking about now?"

She smiled, a slow, deliberate curve of her mouth that sent jolts of lightning spearing through him. "That's too easy."

He joined her in the bed and pulled her in close, holding her body pressed along his length as he dipped his head to kiss her. That first taste spiraled through him and the jagged edges inside him softened. This moment was everything, he realized. Thoughts, worries, problems could all wait. For now, all he wanted was her.

She moved into him and he slid one hand down her body to explore her heat, her curves, the luscious lines of her. She was so responsive, it pushed him higher and faster than he'd ever been before. She scraped her hands up and down his back and he felt every touch like tiny brands, scoring into his skin.

They moved together in silence, hushed breath, whispered words, quiet movements. When he entered her body, there was almost a sigh of sound and the rhythm he set was slow, tender. He looked down at her and lost himself in her eyes. She touched his face, drew him down for a kiss and he swallowed her moan of pleasure as she reached the peak they were each racing toward. A moment later, he joined her, bending his head to hers, taking the scent of her with him as he fell.

In the quiet aftermath, lying in the dark, entwined together, Reed heard Rosie stirring. A few minutes more, he knew she'd be howling, waking Micah up, as well.

"I'll be right back," he whispered and walked naked from the room. When he came back, he was carrying the sniffling baby, who lit up like Christmas when she saw Lilah.

Reed lay down in the bed and set Rosie down between them.

The baby cooed and clapped and giggled, happy now because she wasn't alone in the dark.

"When she falls asleep, I'll put her back in her bed," Reed said, dropping a kiss on the baby's forehead.

"That might take a while," Lilah answered, while Rosie played with her fingers.

"We've got time." Not much, he told himself, but they had right now.

As he lay there, watching the woman and child communicating in smiles and kisses, Reed realized that it felt as if they were a family. And he scowled into the darkness.

"I have some bad news," Reed said, dropping his briefcase onto the nearest chair. He gave a quick glance around at the Malibu beach house Carson Duke had been living in since splitting with his wife. The place was bright, lots of white and blue, and it sat practically on the sand. With the French doors open, he could hear the rush and roar of the sea.

Carson turned to look at Reed, worry sparking in his eyes. "Tia? Is she okay?"

Amazing, Reed thought. Even though they were in the middle of a divorce, the man reacted as if they were still lovers, still committed to each other. Fear came off Carson Duke in thick, fat waves until Reed assured him, "She's fine. But she wouldn't sign off on the property issues, so we'll be going to mediation in a judge's chambers."

Carson actually slumped in relief, then gave a shaky laugh and scraped one hand across his face. "Thank God. The mediation doesn't matter. As long as she's okay." He turned, walked through the open doors onto the stone terrace and tipped his face into the wind. Reed walked outside to join him and took a moment to look around.

Despite the gloomy weather, there were dozens of surfers sitting on their boards, waiting for the next wave. And laid out like elegant desserts on a table, women in barely there bikinis draped themselves on towels in artful poses.

Reed stared out at the slate gray water. "If you don't mind me saying so, you just don't sound like my regular about-to-be-ex-husband divorce client."

One half of Carson's mouth quirked into a humorless smile. "Guess not. I told you before, I never expected Tia and me to end up like this." He frowned at the ocean. "I can't even tell you where things went to hell, either." Glancing at Reed, he asked, "I should know, shouldn't I? I mean, I should know *why* we're getting this divorce, right?"

Normally, Reed would have given Carson the usual spiel about how he was getting a divorce because he and his wife had agreed it wasn't working. But somehow that sounded lame and generic to him now. Oddly enough, Reed and Carson had sort of become friends through this process and he felt he owed the man more than platitudes.

"I don't know, Carson." Reed tucked his hands into his pockets. "Sometimes I think things just go wrong and it's impossible to put your finger on exactly when it happened."

Carson snorted. "Thought you said you'd never been through this. You talk like a survivor."

"I am, in a way," he said thoughtfully. "My parents love being married. Repeatedly. Between them I have ten siblings with another due anytime now."

Carson whistled, low and long, whether in admiration or sympathy, Reed couldn't be sure.

"I had a front-row seat for way too many divorces as a kid and I can tell you that neither of my parents would be able to say *why* they got those divorces." To this day Reed had no idea why his parents jumped from marriage to marriage, always looking for perfect, never satisfied. Sadly, he didn't think they knew why, either. He only knew that they'd made themselves and their children miserable. If that was what love looked like, you could keep it.

"You're in this now, Carson," he said quietly. "And even if you can't recall the reason for it, there *was* one. You and Tia both want to end it, so maybe it's better if you just accept what is and move on."

The other man thought about that for a long minute or two, then muttered, "Yeah, logically I know you're right. But I know something else, too. Acceptance is a bitch."

"Thanks for coming, really. I'll call the agency when the decision's been made." Lilah smiled and waved the third nanny candidate on her way, then closed the door and leaned back against it.

Honestly, these interviews were awful. She hated talking to a steady stream of women all vying for the opportunity to take care of the kids *Lilah* loved. How was she supposed to choose? Young and energetic? Older and more patient? There was no perfect nanny and there was absolutely *no* way to guarantee that the women would even like Micah and Rosie. Or that the kids would like them.

Pushing away from the door, Lilah threw a glance at the kitchen, where Connie was giving Rose her lunch. Lilah should probably go back there, but she wanted a few minutes to herself first.

Plopping down into an overstuffed chair in the living room, she pulled her cell phone out of her pocket and scrolled to the photo gallery. Flipping past image after image, taken last weekend in Utah, she smiled. Micah feeding the ducks. Rosie trying to eat a pinecone. Micah and Reed riding a roller coaster at the Lagoon amusement park. Rosie trying her first ice-cream cone, then "sharing" it with Reed by smacking him in the face with it.

Lastly, Lilah stared down at the image of all four of them. She had asked a stranger to take the picture, wanting at least one with them all grouped together. They were all smiling. Lilah's arm hooked through Reed's, Micah holding Rose and leaning into Reed. "A unit." That's what she felt when she looked at the picture.

For the length of that weekend, it had felt as if they were a family, and for a little while, Lilah had indulged herself by pretending. But really, they weren't a family at all.

Her heart hurt. That was the sad truth. Lilah looked at these pictures, then imagined leaving them all and a sharp, insistent pain sliced at her. How was she supposed to walk away? She loved those kids. But more, she loved *Reed*. The problem was, she knew he wouldn't want to hear it.

"Well, maybe he should anyway," she told herself. Wasn't she the one who'd said people change? Reed had already changed a lot as far as she could see. He'd taken Rosie and Micah into his life and was making it work. Why not welcome *love* into his life, too?

She scrolled to a picture of Reed, smiling at her, sunlight dancing in his eyes. Trailing one finger over his face, she whispered, "Even if you don't want it, you should know that I love you."

Sighing, she stood up and tucked her phone back into her pocket before heading to the kitchen. Connie was at the table, feeding Rose, who happily slapped both hands on her tray. Stopping long enough to pour herself some coffee from the always-ready pot, Lilah then took a seat opposite Connie.

"So," the older woman asked, "how was contestant number three?"

Lilah sighed and cupped her coffee between her palms. "She was fine, I guess. Seemed nice enough, even if she did keep checking her phone to see if there was something more interesting going on somewhere else."

Connie clucked her tongue and shook her head. "Cell phones are the death of civilization."

Smiling, Lilah said, "She's young—so she'll either learn to not text during interviews or she won't find a job." Taking a sip of coffee, she glanced out the window at the backyard. "Where's Micah?"

"Down the street playing basketball with Carter and Cade."

"Good." She nodded. "He needs friends."

"And what do you need?" Connie asked.

Lilah looked back to her. "World peace?"

"Funny, and nice job of dodging the question."

"I don't know what to do," Lilah said. "I haven't found the right nanny, I can't stay here indefinitely and—" Since they'd been back in California, Reed had spent so much time at work she hardly saw him. A reaction to the closeness they'd shared in Utah? Was he silently letting her know that the family vibe she'd felt in Utah wasn't something he wanted? Was he trying to convince her to leave without actually saying it?

"I know," Connie said softly. "It's the *and* that's the hardest to live with."

Reacting to the sympathy in Connie's voice, she said, "Yeah, it is."

"Well, I can't do anything about that." Connie took a baby wipe, cleaned up Rosie's hands, then, while the tiny girl twisted her head trying to avoid it, wiped her mouth, too. Lifting the tray off, she scooped Rosie up, plopped her down on her lap, then looked at Lilah. "I do have something to say on the nanny front, though."

"What is it?"

"I'm a little insulted, is what." Connie waved a hand when Lilah started to protest that she'd never intended to insult her. "You haven't done a thing, honey. If Reed Hudson thinks I can't ride herd on one twelve-year-old, look after a baby who's as good as gold and take care of a house, well, he's out of his mind." Connie jiggled Rosie until the little girl's giggles erupted like bubbles.

Smiling, the woman continued, "Am I so old I can't watch over two kids? I don't think so. We don't need a nanny. What these kids need is a mom. And until they get that, they have a Connie."

Mom.

Lilah's heart squeezed again. Like the prospective nanny she'd just said goodbye to, she'd been interviewing for the job she wanted but would never have. She wasn't Mom. She wasn't going to be. Unless she took a chance and told Reed how she felt. At this point, she asked herself, what did she have to lose?

"Good point, Connie," Lilah said, with another sip of coffee. "I know Reed was trying to make your life easier…"

"When I need that, I'll say so."

Lilah chuckled. "I'll tell Reed you said so."

"Oh, don't you bother," the other woman assured her. "I'll tell him myself, first thing. I've been biting my tongue and it's past time Reed got an earful."

It was, Lilah thought, past time that Reed heard a lot of things.

Later that evening, Reed was shut up in his study, going over a few of the details for several upcoming cases. Focus used to come easily. Now he had to force himself to concentrate on paperwork that had once fascinated him. Organization had always been the one constant in his life. Even as a kid, he'd been the one to know where everyone was, where they were going and what they were doing once they got there. Now his life was up in the air and his brain was constantly in a fog.

At the knock on his door, Reed gave up trying to work and called, "Come in."

Lilah stepped into the room, smiled then slowly walked toward him. She was wearing white shorts, a red T-shirt and sandals and somehow managed to look like the most beautiful thing he'd ever seen. Hell, he could watch her move forever, he thought. She had an innate grace that made her steps seem almost like a ballet. Her hair caught the lamplight in the room and seemed to sizzle with an inner fire. Her eyes, though, were what caught and held him. There were secrets there and enough magic to keep a man entranced for a lifetime.

A lifetime?

Reed took a breath and told himself to ease back. This wasn't forever. This was *now* and there was nothing wrong with living in the moment. He'd been doing it his whole damn life and he was doing fine, wasn't he?

"Am I interrupting?" she asked.

He glanced down at the files on his desk and the one open on his computer monitor, then shrugged. "Not really. Can't seem to concentrate right now, anyway. What's up?"

"I have something for you." She held out a picture frame and when he took it, Reed smiled.

"The one the man with the snow cone took of the four of us at the amusement park."

She came around the edge of the desk and looked

down at the photo with him. "Yeah. I printed it out and framed it for you. I thought maybe you might like it for in here or at the office."

The weekend in Utah seemed like a long time ago, but looking at the picture brought it all back again. Micah laughing and forcing Reed onto every roller coaster at the park. The kid was fearless so how could Reed not be? Even though a couple of them had given him a few gray hairs. And Rosie so happy all the damn time, clapping at the animals at the zoo, eating ice cream for the first time and doing a whole-body shiver at the cold. His mouth quirked into a smile as he remembered that one perfect day.

Then his gaze landed on Lilah's smiling face in the photo and everything in him twisted into a tangle of lust and heat and...more. The four of them looked like a family. At that thought, he shifted uneasily in his chair. "It's great," he said, looking up at her. "Thanks."

"You're welcome." She perched on the edge of his desk and her bare, lightly tanned leg was within stroking distance. He didn't succumb. "Connie wanted to talk to you about—"

He held up one hand. "The nanny thing and yeah, she's already let me know where she stands on the whole situation."

Lilah smiled and her eyes twinkled. "She was pretty insistent that she can handle two kids and a house."

"I have no doubt about it," Reed said with a wince as he remembered the housekeeper giving him what for just an hour ago. "By the time she was finished with me, I felt like I was ten years old and about to be sentenced to washing dishes again."

Her smile widened. "She really loves you."

"I know that, too," he admitted wryly. "I was only trying to make life easier on her but now she's convinced I think of her as some useless old woman, though I think she was making that up to get her way, which she did, obviously."

"So no nanny?"

"No." He couldn't really argue with Connie when she'd hit him with one question in particular. *"Didn't you have enough of nannies in and out of your life when you were a boy? Do you really want to do the same damn thing to those kids?"* And no, he didn't. If Connie wanted to handle everything, then he had no problem with it.

"Well, then," Lilah said quietly, "that brings me to why I'm really here interrupting your work."

Reed swiveled his desk chair around so that he was facing her. Her eyes seemed dark and deep and for some reason, the back of his neck started prickling.

"I was only staying on to help find a nanny," she was saying, "and, since you're not going to hire one..."

She was leaving. She'd come in here, smelling of—he took a breath—green apples, and looking like a summer dream to tell him she was leaving. His stomach fisted, but he held on to his poker face for all the good it would do him.

"You don't have to go," he said before he could talk himself out of it.

She blew out a nervous breath. "Well, that's something else I wanted to talk to you about."

He smiled slowly, hoping she was about to say that she didn't want to leave. That she wanted to stay there with them. With him.

"I love you."

As if a bucket of ice had been dumped in his lap,

Reed went stone still. He didn't have to fake a poker face now, because it felt as if he'd been drained of all emotion. "What?"

Her eyes locked on to his and heat and promise filled them.

"I love you, Reed. And I love the kids." She reached over, picked up the photo and showed it to him again as if he hadn't been staring at it a moment before. "I want us to be the family we look like we already are." She reached out and gently smoothed his hair back from his forehead. Reed instinctively pulled back from her touch.

She flinched, fingers curling into a fist.

Jumping up from the chair he couldn't sit still in a moment longer, Reed took a few quick steps away then whirled back around. "This wasn't part of the plan, Lilah."

She pushed off the desk and stood facing him, chin lifted, eyes shining. Tears? he wondered. "Falling in love with you wasn't in my plan, either, but it happened."

He choked back a sound that was half laugh and half groan. *Be a family.* Instantly, the faces of clients, hundreds of them, flashed through his mind. Each and every one of them had started out in "love." Built families. Counted on the future. None of them had gone into marriage expecting to divorce, but they all had. And that wasn't even counting his own damn family.

"Not gonna happen," he said shortly, shaking his head for emphasis—convincing her? Or himself? "I'll never get married—"

"I wasn't proposing."

"Sure you were," he countered, then waved one hand at her. "Hell, look at you. You've got white picket fence all over you."

"What are you—" Her eyes flashed in the lamplight and it wasn't love shining there now, but a building anger that was much safer—for both of them.

He didn't let her talk. Hell, if he'd known this was what had been cooking in her brain, he'd have cut her off long ago. "Yeah, I like being with you and the sex is amazing. You're great with the kids and they're nuts about you. But that's it, Lilah.

"I've seen too much misery that comes from love and I'm not going to get pulled into the very trap that I spend every day trying to dig other people out of."

He saw hurt tangle with the anger in her eyes and hated being the cause of it. But better for her to know the truth than to hatch dreams that would never come true. It tore at Reed to lose her, though—and then an idea occurred to him. Maybe, just maybe, there was a small chance they could salvage something out of this.

"You could stay," he blurted out and took a step toward her before stopping again. "This isn't about love, Lilah. I won't get married. I won't be in love. But I do like you a hell of a lot. We work well together and the kids need you. Hell, I could pay *you* to be their nanny, then Connie would get the help she needs without being offended."

"You'd pay me…"

He took another step. "Anything you want. And I'll build a workshop onto the back of the house. You could make your soaps and lotions and stuff in there and ship them to your store in Utah. Or hell, open a store here in Laguna. We're a big crafts town. You could be a franchise." Another step. "And best of all, we could be together and risk nothing."

Lilah shook her head and sighed heavily. Sorrow was

etched into her features and the light in her eyes faded as he watched.

"If you risk nothing," she said softly, "you gain nothing. I won't be your bought-and-paid-for lover—"

Shocked, Reed argued, "I didn't say that. Didn't think it."

"Paying me to stay here while we continue to have sex amounts to the same thing," she told him.

"That's insulting," he said tightly. "To both of us."

"Yeah," she said. "I thought so. I'm going home, Reed. I'll leave tomorrow. I want to see the kids and say goodbye, then I'll go."

Though she hadn't moved a step, Reed thought she might as well have been back in Utah already. He couldn't reach her. And maybe that was best. Whatever it was they'd shared was over and was quickly descending into the kind of mess he'd managed to avoid for most of his life.

Turning, she headed for the door and he let her go.

It was the hardest thing he'd ever done.

Ten

The next month was a misery.

Lilah tried to jump back into her normal life, but there was another life hanging over her head and she couldn't shake it. She missed Rosie and Micah and Connie.

And being without Reed felt as though someone had ripped her heart out of her chest. Every breath was painful. Every memory was both comfort and torture. Every moment without those she loved tore at her.

"Are you sure you did the right thing?"

Lilah sighed and focused on her mother's concerned face on the computer screen. Thank God for video calls, she thought. It helped ease the distance while her mother and Stan were off on their never-ending cruise. Of course, the downside to video chats was her mother could see far more than she would have on the phone.

The ship had just made port in London and since it

was her mother's favorite city, Lilah knew that as soon as she was through with this chat, her mom and Stan would be out shopping and sightseeing. But for now, Lilah was telling her all about Rose and Micah and, most especially, Reed.

"I really didn't have a choice, Mom." Lilah had thought through this situation from every possible angle and there just had been no way for her to stay and keep her pride. Her dignity. Her sense of self.

If she'd given in to her own wants and Reed's urgings, she would have eventually resented him and been furious with herself for settling for less than they both deserved.

"No," her mother said softly, "I suppose you didn't. But I think, from everything you've told me, that the idiot man *does* love you."

Lilah laughed a little and it felt good. It seemed as though she hadn't really smiled or laughed since she left California. Behind her mother, Stan came up from somewhere in their suite, bent over and said, "Hi, sweetie! I'm going to have to go with your mother on this one. He does love you. He's just too scared to admit it."

Frowning now, Lilah said, "Nothing scares Reed."

Stan grinned and she had to smile back. He wasn't exactly the image of a millionaire businessman in his short-sleeved bright green shirt and his bald head shining in the overhead lights. It was impossible to not love Stan. Especially since his one desire was to make her mother happy.

"Honey, real *love* scares every man alive." He kissed the top of her mother's head. "Well, except for me. By the time I met your mom, I'd been alone so long that one look at her and I knew. She was the one I'd been waiting for. Looking for. And when you're alone all your life, you grab hold of love when it comes along and you never let it go."

"Oh," her mother said, turning her head to kiss her husband's cheek. "You are the sweetest man. For that, we can go to the London Imperial War Museum again."

Stan winked at Lilah, then grinned again. "I'll let you two talk, then. Just don't give up on the guy, okay, honey?"

Sighing a little, Lilah promised and then when it was just her mother and her again, she said, "I'm glad you've got Stan."

"Me, too," her mom answered. "Even when the ship docks in London and I'm dragged through that war museum again. But that's something for you to remember, too. Your father was an amazing man and I was lucky to love him for all those years." Smiling, she leaned toward the screen and said, "But, he was scared spitless to get married. He even broke up with me when it looked like we were getting serious."

Surprised, Lilah said, "You never told me that."

"You never needed to hear it before now. *Forever* is a big word and can shake even the strongest man. Your dad came around—but not until he got the chance to miss me."

Lilah thought about that and wondered.

"If you need me all you have to do is say so, honey. I'll catch the first flight out of Heathrow and catch up with Stan and the ship later."

Because her mother absolutely would throw her own life to the winds to support her daughter, Lilah realized again just how lucky she was. In spite of the turmoil in her life right at the moment, she had stability and love. And that was more than Reed had ever had.

"Thanks, Mom. But I'm fine." She straightened in her chair and nodded. "I've got the shop and my friends and…it'll get better."

"It will," her mother promised. "You are the best daughter ever and you deserve to have the kind of love that fairy tales are made of."

Tears stung her eyes but Lilah blinked them back.

"I *know* this will all work out just the way it's supposed to," her mother continued. "And like Stan said, I wouldn't give up hope yet. After some time to think and to really miss you, I'm willing to bet that Reed Hudson is going to realize that life without Lilah just isn't worth living."

Reed had made it through the longest month of his life.

He wasn't sure how, since thoughts of Lilah had haunted him day and night. *I love you.* Those three words had echoed over and over again in his mind. He heard her voice, saw her eyes and felt again his own instinctive withdrawal.

I love you.

No one had ever said that to him before. Not once in his whole damn life had Reed ever heard those words. And the first time he did, he threw them back in her face.

"What the hell…" Scraping one hand across his face, Reed pushed everything but work out of his mind. He didn't have any right to be focusing on his own life when someone was *paying* him to focus on his.

"You okay?" Carson Duke asked in a whisper.

"Yeah," Reed assured him, "fine. Look, we'll just get through the mediation and we'll be back on track. The judge will keep everything on track, you and Tia will decide how you want things done and it's over."

Nodding, Carson inhaled sharply, then exhaled the same way. "Gotta say, best thing about this mediation is seeing Tia. It feels like forever since I've been close to her."

Reed knew just how the other man felt. He hadn't seen Lilah in a month and it felt like a year. It hadn't helped that the kids were complaining, missing her as much as he was. Well, Micah was complaining, demanding that they go to Utah and get her, while Rosie just cried, as if she were inconsolable. Then there was Connie, who took every opportunity to sneer at him and mention how lonely the house felt without Lilah's laughter.

He was being punished for doing the right thing.

How did that make sense?

But if letting her go was the right thing, then why did it feel so wrong?

"Tia." Carson shot out of his chair and turned to face the woman walking into the room beside her lawyer, Teresa Albright.

Reed knew Teresa well. She was a hell of an attorney and had always been a good friend. But today, her sleek red hair only reminded him of Lilah's red-gold waves and he found he resented Teresa for even being there.

"Carson," Tia said as she stepped up to the table. The legendary singer had long black hair and big brown eyes. Those eyes as she looked at her husband were warm and her smile was tentative. "How are you?"

"I'm all right," Carson answered. "You?"

Reed watched the byplay and could feel the tension in the room. Hell, Carson looked as if he was ready to launch himself across the table, and the way Tia was wringing her hands together made it seem she was doing everything she could to keep from reaching for him. Reed was relieved when the judge showed up and they were forced to take their seats.

"Everyone here?" the judge asked as he walked into the meeting room at the courthouse and settled into the chair at the head of the table. At the nods he received in answer, the man said, "All right, let's get this show on the road. Why don't we start with the houses and work from there?"

The Hollywood Hills house went to Tia and the lodge in Montana to Carson. No arguments slowed things down and Reed wondered why in the hell they were even there. The two people appeared to be willing to work together, so why hadn't Tia just signed off on everything in the first place?

"Concerning the Malibu house and its contents," Teresa was saying, "my client wants Mr. Duke to retain possession."

"No," Carson blurted out, glancing first at Reed, then to Tia. "You should have that place," he said.

"No, I want you to have it," Tia argued.

Both Teresa and Reed tried to shush their clients—it was rarely productive for the parties involved to get into conversations. Best to leave it to the attorneys. But this time, no one was listening.

"You love that house," Carson said softly.

Tia nodded and bit her bottom lip. "I do, but you do, too. Carson, you built the brick barbecue on the terrace by hand. And you laid the stone terrace."

"*We* laid the stone terrace," Carson reminded her, a half smile on his face. "Remember, we started out in the afternoon and refused to stop until it was finished?"

Tia smiled, too, but her eyes were teary and the sunlight spearing in through the windows made those tears shine like diamonds. "I remember. We wouldn't quit. We just kept going, and we finally laid that last stone at three in the morning."

"We celebrated with champagne," Carson said softly.

"Then we lay on the patio and watched a meteor shower until nearly dawn," she said sadly.

"Damn it, Tia, why are we even here?" Carson stood up and planted both hands on the table, leaning toward his wife. "I don't want this. I want *you*."

"Carson..." Reed warned.

"No." He glanced at Reed, shook his head and looked back at the woman he didn't want to lose. "I love you, Tia."

"What?" She stood up, too, in spite of Teresa's hand at her elbow trying to tug her back into her seat.

"I love you," Carson repeated, louder this time. "Always have. Always will. I don't know how the hell we got to this ugly little room—"

"Hey," the judge complained, "we just had the place redecorated."

"But we don't belong here," Carson said earnestly, ignoring everyone but his wife. "I made a promise to you. To love you and cherish you till the end of my life, and I don't want to break that promise, Tia. Just like when we built that damn terrace, I don't want us to quit."

"Me, either, Carson," she said, smiling through the tears already spilling down her cheeks. "I never wanted this divorce. I'm not sure how this even happened, but I've missed you so much. I love you, Carson. I always will."

"Stay married to me, Tia." He was talking faster now,

as if his life depended on getting his words right, and maybe it did.

"Yes. Oh, yes." Her smile brightened, her eyes sparkled in the overhead light.

"Hell, let's take a couple years off," he said. "We'll go to the lodge in Montana and lose ourselves. Maybe make some babies."

She grinned at him. "That sounds wonderful. I don't want to lose you, Carson."

"Babe, you're never going to lose me." He slid across the table, swept his wife into his arms and pulled her in for a kiss that would have sent their fans into a deep sigh of satisfaction.

Hell, even Reed felt as if he was watching a movie unfold. When the happy couple left the office a few minutes later after abject apologies for wasting their attorneys' time, Reed thought about everything that had happened. He'd never before lost a divorce to marriage and he found himself hoping that Carson and Tia really could make their life together work.

Carson had taken a chance, fought for what he wanted—and he'd won. Hell, Tia and Carson had *both* won.

A *promise*. That's what Carson had called his marriage vows. Giving your word to someone, promising to be faithful. To be there.

As if an actual lightbulb flashed on in his brain, Reed suddenly understood. Marriage wasn't a risk if you trusted the person you were going into it with. Giving your word, keeping it? Well, hell, Reed Hudson had never gone back on his word in his life. And he knew Lilah was the same.

Love wasn't the misery. It was the heart of a promise that could change a life.

Now all he had to do was hope that the woman he wanted would be willing to listen.

Lilah's Bouquet was doing a booming business. Her new shop manager, Eileen Cooper, was working out great and though Lilah still missed Spring, life marched on. Being able to count on Eileen, letting her move into the apartment over the shop, had actually helped Lilah get through—not *over*—Spring's loss.

Plus, burying herself in work had helped Lilah survive a different kind of loss. Her dreams of a happy-ever-after with Reed and the kids were gone and their absence created a dark, empty space inside her that ached almost continuously. So keeping busy also left her little time to wallow.

The past month hadn't been easy, but she'd made it through and every day she got that much closer to maybe someday finding a way to get over Reed. She laughed to herself at the idea. Good luck getting over someone you couldn't stop thinking about, or dreaming about.

She was even thinking of buying a new bed. One that didn't have memories of sex with Reed imprinted into the fabric. Probably wouldn't help, though, because the man was etched into her mind and heart permanently.

"This is wonderful," Sue Carpenter said, shattering Lilah's thoughts, for which she was grateful. The woman hustling up to the counter held a soap and lotion set in one of Lilah's newest scents. "Summer Wind? Beautiful name and I absolutely love the scent. Makes me feel like I'm at the beach!"

"Thanks, Sue," Lilah said, taking the woman's things

and ringing them up. "I really like it, too. Makes me think of summer." And Laguna, and a house on the cliffs where everything she loved lived without her.

"Well, it's wonderful." Sue had no idea that Lilah's thoughts had just spun her into a well of self-pity. "Will you be making candles in that scent, too?"

Lilah forced a smile. Sue was one of her best customers and a great source of publicity for the shop since she told everyone she met all about Lilah's Bouquet. "You bet. I'll have some ready for sale by next week."

"Then I'll be back, but for now, I need a few of the lemon sage candles and might as well get three of the cinnamon, as well." She grinned. "I like to give them to my buyers with the sale of a house."

"That's so nice, thank you." More publicity, since the name of Lilah's store and the address were on the bottom of every candle. Once she had Sue's purchases bagged, she said goodbye and walked over to help another woman choose the right soaps for her.

"I just can't make up my mind," the woman said, letting her gaze sweep around the crowded shop. When she spotted something in particular, though, she murmured softly, "Never mind. I've decided. I'll take one of those. To go."

Smiling, Lilah turned to see what the woman was looking at and actually *felt* her jaw drop. Reed was walking into her store, looking through the crowd, searching for her. When he spotted her, he smiled and a ball of heat dropped into the pit of her stomach. Lilah's mouth went dry and her heartbeat jumped into a fast gallop. What was he doing here? What did it mean?

Oh, God, she told herself, *don't read too much into*

this. Don't pump your hope balloon so high that when it pops you crash back to earth in a broken heap.

But he was walking toward her, sliding in and out of the dozen or so female customers as if he didn't even see them. Lilah's gaze was locked with his and for the first time since she'd met him, she couldn't tell what he was thinking. That poker face he was so proud of was in full effect. But for the smile, his features were giving nothing away. So by the time he reached her, nerves were alive and skittering through her system.

"God, you look good," he said and the warmth in his voice set off tiny fires in her bloodstream. "Damn it, I missed you."

"I missed you, too," she said softly, not even noticing when the woman she'd been assisting slowly melted away. It was as if there was no one else in the shop. Just the two of them.

August sunshine made the store bright and she told herself that's why her eyes were watering. Because she wouldn't be foolish enough to cry and let Reed know how much it meant to see him again.

"What're you doing here?" she asked, when he only continued to stare down at her and smile.

"I came for you," he said simply.

Somewhere close by, a woman sighed heavily.

"Came for me?" Lilah asked. Did he think she'd go back to California with him just because she'd missed him so much her heart ached every day and night? She couldn't. Wouldn't. Loving him didn't mean that she was willing to set aside who she was for the sake of being with him.

"Reed…" She shook her head and tried to tamp down

the oh-so-familiar ache in the center of her chest. "Nothing's changed. I still can't—"

"I love you," he said, gaze locked with hers.

She swayed unsteadily. He loved her?

"That's a huge change for me, Lilah. I've never said those words before. Never wanted to." His gaze moved over her before coming back to her eyes. "Now I never want to stop."

Lilah gasped and held her breath, half afraid to move and break whatever spell this was that had given her the one thing she had wanted most.

He moved in closer, into her space, looming over her so that she had to tilt her head back to meet his eyes. Laying both hands on her shoulders, he held on tightly as if worried she might make a break for it. Lilah could have told him that even if she wanted to, she didn't think her legs would carry her. As it was, she locked her knees to keep from dissolving into a puddle at his feet.

"I've done a lot of thinking in the last month," he said, scraping his hands up and down her arms to create a kind of friction that seemed to set her soul on fire. "In fact, all I've really done is think about you. And us. And how much I need you. The truth is, the house is empty without you in it."

"Oh, Reed," she said on a soft sigh.

"Noisy as hell and still empty," he said, giving her a half smile that tugged at her heart and made her want to reach up and cup his face in her palms. But she didn't. She needed to hear it all.

"The kids miss you—"

"I miss them, too," she said, the pain she felt staining her words.

"And Connie's so furious with me she keeps burning dinner. On purpose."

Lilah laughed, though it sounded a little watery through the tears clogging her throat. "So they made you come?"

"No," he said, shaking his head and smiling at her as his gaze moved over her face like a caress. "Nobody *makes* me do anything. I came because I don't want to live without you anymore, Lilah. I don't think I can stand it." His eyes burned, his features were tight with banked emotion. "And I finally realized that I don't *have* to live without the woman I want. The woman I love."

"What are you saying?" Lilah's question sounded breathless, anxious.

"That I figured it out," he said, tightening his hold on her. "A couple of days ago, I watched one of my clients back out of a divorce because he was willing to fight for what he wanted. And I realized that the problem isn't that divorce is easy—it's that marriage takes work. It takes two people who want it badly enough to fight for it."

"Reed—"

"Not finished yet," he said, his eyes boring into hers. "No one in my family is a hard worker, which explains the marital failures in the Hudson clan. But I *do* work hard and I never quit when I want something. I'm willing to do whatever it takes to make sure we succeed. The only thing I'm not willing to do is live without you. Not one more day, Lilah."

Her heart was pounding so hard, it was a wonder he couldn't hear it. He was saying everything she'd dreamed of hearing. And as she looked into his eyes, she realized that now the decision was hers. He'd come to her. Told her he loved her—which she was still hugging close to her heart—and he wanted her. But uprooting her life wouldn't be easy. Her business. Her home.

As if he could read her mind, and hey, maybe today he could, he said, "You can open a new shop in Laguna. Or you can just keep this one and we'll all come to Utah every month so you can stay on top of things. We'll add on to your tiny house of course. But we all loved being here in the mountains. And we all love you. I love you."

She'd never get tired of hearing that, Lilah thought.

He held on to her and pulled her a bit closer. "I swear to you, Lilah, I will be the husband you deserve." His voice dropped to a husky rasp. "I will give you my word to be with you always. And I never break my word."

Husband? She swayed again. "You're proposing?"

He frowned. "Didn't I say that already? No. I didn't. I swear, just looking into your eyes empties my brain." He grinned now and her heart turned over. "Yes, I'm proposing." He dug into his pocket, pulled out a small black velvet jewelry box and flipped it open to reveal a canary yellow diamond ring.

"Oh, God…" She blew out a sigh and looked up at him through tear-blurred eyes.

"Marry me, Lilah. Live with me. Love with me. Make children with me—they'll grow up with Micah and Rosie and we'll love them so much they'll never doubt how precious they are to us.

"Between us, we'll build a family so strong, nothing can tear it apart." He bent, kissed her hard, fast. "I just need you to take a chance on me, Lilah. Risk everything. With me."

Lilah inhaled sharply and tried to ease the wild racing of her heart. But it was impossible. Her heart was his and it would always race when she was with him.

Finally, she lifted her hands, cupped his face in hers and whispered, "Love isn't a risk, Reed. Not when it's real. Not when it's as strong as our love is."

He turned his face and kissed her palm.

"I love you more than anything," she said softly. "Yes, I'll marry you and make children with you and love you forever. And I swear, we'll never get a divorce because I will *never* let you go."

He sighed and gave her another wide smile. "That is the best news I've ever heard."

Pulling the ring from the box, he slid it onto her finger, then kissed it as if to seal it into place. When she laughed in delight, he did, too, then he pulled her into his arms and kissed her, silently promising her a future, a life filled with love and laughter.

And all around them, the customers in the little shop applauded.

* * * * *

While he drove, he thought about Sierra Benson.

Blake had been startled by their chemistry. He had overreacted by offering so much money, but when had a woman ever set his pulse pounding by merely saying hello?

Her stay at his ranch should be interesting. Maybe their attraction was something that only happened at a first meeting and wouldn't happen again. But with the smoldering chemistry between them, he couldn't keep from dreaming of seduction.

Dream on, he thought.

She was wrapped up in saving the world. She looked at everything through rose-colored glasses and saw everyone as filled with a basic goodness—which was not reality. This was a lesson he had learned early in life. Eventually, Sierra would learn that not everyone could be saved and all her sweet talk would be a memory. *That* was human nature.

No, she was not his type in any way—except for that hot, intense, mutual attraction. A scalding attraction he intended to pursue in spite of their differences.

* * *

Expecting the Rancher's Child is part of the Callahan's Clan series: A wealthy Texas family finds love under the Western skies!

EXPECTING THE
RANCHER'S CHILD

BY
SARA ORWIG

MILLS & BOON

First Published in Great Britain 2016
By Mills & Boon, an imprint of HarperCollins*Publishers*
1 London Bridge Street, London, SE1 9GF

© 2016 Sara Orwig

ISBN: 978-0-263-91867-0

51-0716

Our policy is to use papers that are natural, renewable and recyclable products and made from wood grown in sustainable forests. The logging and manufacturing processes conform to the legal environmental regulations of the country of origin.

Printed and bound in Spain
by CPI, Barcelona

Sara Orwig lives in Oklahoma. She has a patient husband who will take her on research trips anywhere, from big cities to old forts. She is an avid collector of Western history books. With a master's degree in English, Sara has written historical romance, mainstream fiction and contemporary romance. Books are beloved treasures that take Sara to magical worlds, and she loves both reading and writing them.

Many thanks to Stacy Boyd,
Charles Griemsman and Tahra Seplowin

Thank you to Maureen Walters and Tess Callero

With thanks also to Jon Craig for answers for
That Night with the Rich Rancher

With love to my family

One

Eagerness gripped Sierra Benson as the time arrived for her appointment with Blake Callahan.

She had done interior design for him, but that had been nearly two years ago and she'd never actually met him. Since she'd finished that job, and received a personal note of thanks from him, she'd changed careers. She was now director of Brigmore Charities of Kansas City, Kansas.

She hoped he'd asked to meet with her to make a contribution.

She'd read enough about him to know he was thirty-four, six years older than she was, a Texas multimillionaire, a hotel mogul and a rancher with interests in commercial real estate. Excitement bubbled in her to think their nonprofit might be getting a sizable donation.

Breaking into her thoughts, her assistant, Nan Waverley, announced her visitor's arrival.

"Send him in, please," Sierra said, as she stood and gave a pat to her light brown hair, pinned at the back of her head. She smoothed her straight brown skirt and looked up as Nan opened her office door.

"Thank you, Nan," she said—or that's what she hoped she said, anyway. Coming face to face with Blake momentarily took her breath.

She had seen pictures of Blake Callahan and knew he was nice looking, single and had an active social life, but she wasn't prepared for the dynamic man who, without one word, seemed to charge the air with energy as he entered her office. Even more startling, she was caught and held by brown eyes so dark they looked black. With their gazes locked, a sizzling current rocked her.

An even bigger surprise shook her when she noticed a flicker in the depths of his eyes. His chest expanded with a deep breath—he appeared jolted by the same magnetic charge that captured her. With an effort, she gathered her wits and turned away, ending the eye contact. She crossed the room to shake hands with him.

"Mr. Callahan, I'm Sierra Benson, and it's nice to finally meet you," she said, trying to regain her poise.

The handshake was a mistake. The instant his warm fingers closed over hers, the same riveting current jumpstarted again, only stronger this time.

Snagged by another exchange with his mesmerizing gaze, she stood breathless, aware of the physical contact, even more conscious that he was as immobile as she. How long did they stand in silence, held by a handshake and eye contact?

She slipped her hand out of his.

"It's Blake and, I hope, Sierra," he said easily in a deep voice. His tone sounded casual, friendly, but his look was probing, as if trying to find something that would explain why they were caught in an invisible current.

"Fine," she answered, striving to get a firm note into her tone. "Please, have a seat. I missed meeting you at the grand opening of your hotel because of a family emergency. Decorating your hotel was an exciting project."

Blake sat across from her, with her ancient hardwood desk between them. In an impeccable navy suit and a shirt with French cuffs that revealed gold cufflinks, Blake could have been a model—except he conveyed the signs of a man accustomed to more physical activity. He moved with an ease that indicated a high degree of fitness.

She suspected he had not been in any office in his life that was as run-down as hers. In his elegant clothes, he looked out of place in the eighty-three-year-old building that had not been maintained well. Tattered, faded books lined her shelves. The wooden floor had long ago lost its luster. Gusts of March wind rattled the aging windowpanes behind her.

"You did the best job on that hotel of any interior designer we've ever hired," Blake said.

"Thank you," she answered, pleased to hear that kind of praise.

"I was surprised to discover you've left the business when you have a natural talent for design."

"Thanks again. Helping others is my first love, so when this opportunity arose, I took it. We do a lot of good for people, which I'll be happy to tell you about. I assume that's why you're here." She settled back in her chair.

When he shook his head, her spirits plummeted. "No? Your response is an immense disappointment," she admitted. "If you're not here to make a donation, why are you here, Mr. Callahan?"

"It's Blake," he reminded her with a smile that momentarily made her forget business. It was warm, disarming and added to his appeal. She tried to focus and pay attention to what he was saying.

"I'm building a new wing on my ranch house in Texas. You're the best at interior design, and I'd like to hire you."

"I'd hoped you were here to learn about our charities and to possibly help in some way. I appreciate the job offer, but I have to decline," she answered as her disappointment increased. "I'm sorry you wasted time and effort to come talk to me in person." She smiled at him. "I wish you'd give me some time and let me tell you about all we do here to help those who need a lift."

"We have a problem," he said, studying her with those riveting eyes that scrambled her thoughts. "If we try, perhaps we can do both—I'll help with your charities and you consider my ranch job," he answered pleasantly, but she knew he was telling her he would listen if she agreed to what he wanted.

"I appreciate your offer. It's flattering, but I'm not leaving this work. It means too much to me. This was the work my grandfather loved, and before he died I promised to continue it."

"If you'd take this job, which would only be short-term, I could make it worth your while," he said, as if he hadn't heard her last remarks.

She smiled. He obviously did not take refusal easily.

"My interests are here," she replied. "You can find talented interior designers who can do your new wing," she added, wondering when he would give up trying to persuade her to do what he wanted.

They sat in silence a moment before he took out a checkbook and wrote. She suspected he would try to offer her more than the usual amount to do the decorating job for him. That aura of confidence surrounding him indicated he was a man accustomed to getting what he wanted. The money would be tempting, but she could find money elsewhere.

Certain he would offer an exorbitant sum, she watched as he wrote a second check.

Now he leaned forward, stretching out a long arm to place the two checks on her desk. "One of these is for your work on the new wing at my ranch. You'll have to live there to get the job done, but it shouldn't take more than a few weeks. The other check is a donation to this agency, and if everything is satisfactory, I'll make the same donation annually for at least three years."

Stunned, she looked at two identical checks, each for half a million dollars. For a moment she was speechless, trying to digest his offer.

"Why would you offer me so much money? There are other excellent decorators."

"I don't know them or their work. You're the best choice for the job. Besides, now that we've met, I'd like to get to know you."

Yes, there was chemistry between them—she couldn't deny it. But his admission that he'd like to get to know her only increased her reluctance about the job. She hoped to avoid ever being in a situation like her last job—where her boss tried to bribe her into his bed.

Staring at the checks on her desk, she forgot the past. She couldn't ignore the money Blake would pour into her nonprofit, and she couldn't stop thinking about the good that could be accomplished by his incredibly generous donation. And the promise of more donations to come. Her head spun with possibilities, dreams they had for the charity to grow. The kind of money Blake offered would take years to accumulate.

"You would really do this?" she whispered, looking up at him. "Just to get my design services?"

"Yes. And if it works out well, you'll get more donations," he said with a coaxing smile. As she looked at the check again, he sat in silence.

There was no way she could turn down such a dazzling offer that would put so much money into Brigmore Charities. It was thrilling to think how many people they could reach. Without looking up, she considered the man sitting across from her. She had seen his picture in society pages, Texas magazines and occasionally on television. He had an active social life, and a lot of the pictures had shown him escorting beautiful women.

"You actually live and work in Dallas most of the time, don't you?" she asked.

"One week out of each month I'm in Dallas, unless something important interferes. The ranch is where I prefer to be."

Realizing she might have to deal with him on a daily basis, she considered the job. In spite of his remark about wanting to know her, she could ensure they had no contact with each other socially. She suspected he received few rejections from women, but his sexual interests would not involve her. In spite of his personal remark, he would want her to concentrate on the job he had hired her to do.

The money he offered danced in her thoughts, with possibilities of how to use it to do the most good. There was no way she could turn him down, which she was certain he knew.

She nodded. "You win. I accept your offer. This is a marvelous, breathtaking contribution."

"It may be breathtaking, but it isn't solely a contribution—it's also payment for your work," he corrected with a slight smile, causing creases to bracket his mouth and making her pulse flutter. She had to admit he was appealing. Briefly, it occurred to her again that the huge sum might carry expectations of seduction, but she immediately dismissed the worry. He had enough beautiful society women in his life who were willing to keep him happy.

"I'll want to hire at least two people to assist me, and I'll pay them out of the check you've given me."

"No. I'll take care of their salaries. Just give me the bill."

"How soon do you want me to start?" she asked, still shocked by the sudden change in her schedule and the huge windfall.

"As soon as you can manage. Next week would be great. I'm anxious to get this wing finished."

She pulled her calendar close, though she knew she could start Monday. He couldn't be any more anxious to finish than she was, because as soon as she was done she could focus her full attention on Brigmore Charities' projects—and now she would have the funds to accomplish some of the agency's goals.

Years ago, the agency, started by Clyde Brigmore, one of her grandfather's friends, had almost gone under until her grandfather got involved, and with the support of her dad's church and her grandfather's hard work, the agency went from running a very small homeless shelter to supporting a larger shelter as well as a children's shelter. In the past year they had opened an animal rescue branch. Now many churches in Kansas City helped support the agency, along with individual donations, and most of her work focused on acquiring funding. It was work she loved, and through it she felt close to her grandfather.

She realized Blake was talking and she needed to pay attention. She tried to focus on Blake Callahan.

"Would you like that?" he asked, and she felt her cheeks flush with embarrassment.

"I'm sorry. It's difficult to get my mind away from

the changes in my life and the fabulous contribution you just made. What did you say to me?"

His dark eyes twinkled with amusement. "I'm glad you're pleased with our deal. I'm very pleased with it. What I asked was about transportation. If you'd like, I have a private jet. I can have you flown to Dallas, where a limo will take you to the ranch, which is about an hour and a half away from the airport."

"Thank you. I'll accept that invitation. If I start Monday, I'd like to arrive Sunday and get settled."

"That works. I'll be at the ranch, and I'll show you around."

She nodded, unable to keep from looking again at the spectacular checks.

"Then we have a deal?" he asked.

She looked up into black, fathomless eyes that seemed to hide his feelings. "We have a deal," she replied, feeling a tingle.

For a fleeting moment she wondered what she had gotten herself into. What would it be like working with him daily, staying in his home, having him constantly close at hand? The questions made her pulse race…but then common sense said he would turn supervision of the job over to someone and go on with his life.

In a languid manner, he stood. "If you have any questions, feel free to call me. Here's my business card and another number that's private. If you'll let me know your preference for what time of day you'd like to leave Kansas City, I'll let you know about the flight arrangements."

"Thanks. I can tell you right now, I'll be ready to leave after twelve Sunday."

"How should I contact you?"

She took a card off her desk and held it out to him. "My cell number is there, and you can always get me that way." As their fingers brushed, she had another flash of physical awareness of him.

She shrugged away the feeling as ridiculous. She couldn't understand the tingly reaction she had to him— that had never happened with any other man, but it was meaningless at this point in her life. She wasn't dating because she was focused on her work. This was a business arrangement, and she intended to keep her relationship with Blake Callahan professional.

She walked him to the door where he turned. This time she avoided offering her hand. Even so, as she stood looking up at him, dark eyes searched hers for a few seconds as they stood in silence. "This should be good for both of us," he said in a husky voice that heated her.

"I hope so," she said faintly.

He opened the door and stepped out before turning again.

"I'll text the flight arrangements and have a limo take you to the plane. The chauffeur will pick you up wherever you want."

"Thank you. That's a huge convenience. Until then, thank you for the donation, and the job and for having so much faith in me."

"I've seen the results of your work," he answered. He turned to leave and paused at her assistant's scarred desk, which had one leg missing and was propped up with bricks. He told Nan that he was glad to have met her, and then, smiling at Sierra and her assistant, he left.

When he had disappeared from sight, she turned to her assistant. "I'm going to take some time off. He's hired me to do a decorating job at his ranch."

"Mercy! I'd take that job, too. That's the most handsome man to ever walk through this office. Don't tell Bert I said that."

"Don't worry, I won't," Sierra said with a smile, thinking about her assistant director, Bert Hollingsworth, who was six years older than she was, with sandy hair he never could get totally under control and gray eyes that held a perpetual worried look. She had been friends with him since the moment they were introduced. Unlike her response to Blake Callahan, Bert had never once evoked any physical reaction in her.

Reassuring herself once again that she would see little of Blake once she was on the job, she tried to shove him out of mind.

"Will you please call Bert and then both of you come to my office? We have some things to discuss."

Giving her a quizzical look, Nan nodded and picked up a phone, repeating Sierra's instructions to Bert.

Sierra left her door open as she hurried to her desk and sat, taking the checks in hand to stare at them again in amazement. All that money—her head spun at the thought. She had promised her grandfather she would continue his hard work and help people when they needed help.

She had been raised to believe in the good in people,

and every week she had proof of that goodness from one person or another. Blake Callahan couldn't understand why she'd left interior design, but her career in nonprofit work was about what really counted in life. She had great faith in the ability of the human spirit to overcome adversity.

Shortly, Nan and Bert entered her office, Bert with his usual smile. "How'd the meeting go?"

"That's the reason I wanted to talk to you. He's hired me to do the interior design for a wing he's built onto his ranch house. I'll have to take a leave of absence."

"I thought you gave up that career," Bert said, frowning slightly.

"I thought so, too, but he gave me two payments—one for my work, and one as a donation to this agency. Here are the identical checks—each one for half a million." She passed the checks to Bert, who shared them with Nan. Bert stared open-mouthed while Nan read the amounts again. Nan's eyes were wide as she looked at Sierra.

"All that money to our agency," she whispered.

"Saints above." Bert shook his head, his eyebrows raised in surprise. "I knew the man was wealthy, but this—I never dreamed we'd get this kind of donation."

"I'm surprised you didn't faint," Nan said. "You don't even have to share that with your old design firm."

"No, but I'll share my personal check with Brigmore Charities. I'm also going to share with Dad and his church. Just think what good we can do with all this money."

"*I* may faint," Bert said. "No wonder you took the job. How could he want you that badly?"

"He thought I did a good job on his hotel. I turned him down at first, but I don't think the man is accustomed to hearing no. And there's more. If I do a good job, he will make an annual contribution of this amount to Brigmore Charities for the next three years."

Bert shook his head as if in denial.

"Is he single?" Nan asked.

Sierra bit back a smile. "Very. When I worked for him before, I heard gossip that he doesn't have serious relationships."

"I think you ought to use a little of that money for a background check on him. He wants you too badly," Bert said.

Sierra smiled and shook her head. "I don't think a background check is necessary. Look him up on the internet and look up his business. He can afford this check without thinking about it. His father is a billionaire, and Blake Callahan is wealthy on his own. There are a lot of women in his life. He has no need of me, except as a decorator."

"Want me to come with you?" Bert asked, a frown creasing his brow. Sierra held back another smile.

"Thanks, Bert. I don't think that's necessary."

"If for any reason it becomes necessary, you call me and I'll be right there."

"I will," she said, appreciating his offer, though it seemed ridiculous. "I won't be alone. I'm hiring two people to help me. He'll pay their salaries, and they'll live on the ranch with me part of the time."

"That's good," Bert said.

"If you need a secretary, don't forget me," Nan said, smiling.

For the next half hour they talked about depositing the check and presenting the donation to the Brigmore Charities' board of directors.

Finally, Nan rose to go back to her desk. Bert came to his feet, he closed the door and returned.

"I want to talk to you."

She sat behind her desk and waited.

"I don't think you should take the job or accept the check."

"You have got to be kidding," she said, staring intently at him. "Why on earth not?"

"He's up to something. That's too much money."

She held back a laugh. "I'll repeat—Blake Callahan will never miss this money."

"Why didn't he go to the New York agency he hired when you first worked for him?"

"He should have, but he said I did the best job he'd ever seen. He's accustomed to getting what he wants. He's flying me there in his private jet. Stop worrying, and start thinking about the best use for this money."

Bert shook his head and stood. "All right, but at the first sign of trouble, promise you'll call me. Let me know where this ranch is."

"I'll be fine," she said, smiling at him, knowing Bert had perpetual worries even when everything was rosy.

"If you're okay...what a windfall for us. This is going to help a lot of people. Our buildings are old and need repair—the homeless shelter was the original charity and it needs a new roof, new plumbing—all sorts of things. We have a waiting list for the orphaned children and their building and grounds need work."

"Plus the four-footed friends. Don't forget our dog and cat shelter. This will buy a lot of chow, and we can run some great ads. Maybe we can get a bigger place because what we have is so tiny we can only take a few animals at a time."

"True. I'll get busy."

"Good," she said and watched him go, leaving her door open behind him.

She knew Bert's worries were unnecessary, but there was only one threat from Blake Callahan.

That sizzling attraction that flared the first second they looked into each other's eyes. Never again would she get involved with an employer—yet how well could she protect herself from Blake's sexy appeal?

Late Friday afternoon Blake flew home to Dallas, where he had a small plane waiting to fly southwest to the tiny airstrip at Downly, Texas. At Downly he climbed into his waiting car and headed west to his ranch.

While he drove along a county road devoid of traffic, he thought about Sierra Benson. He hadn't met her when she did the hotel job, so he had been startled when the air sparked with a chemistry that he suspected she felt as much as he did.

Some of the most beautiful women he'd dated had never caused that kind of reaction in him. When he had taken Sierra's hand, the impersonal contact had had the impact of a blow to his middle, a tug on his senses that made him want to get to know her. His reaction to her had blown his intentions to hire her all out of proportion.

He had wanted her to handle the decor of his new wing because she was the best at interior design and decoration he had ever met. Add the intense physical appeal to her business skills, and he wasn't about to let her disappear out of his life. He had overreacted by offering so much money, but when had a woman ever set his pulse pounding by merely saying hello? Or shaking hands with him?

Her stay at his ranch should be interesting. He knew he had acted impulsively, and in what was an uncustomary manner for him, but he didn't want her to say no and disappear out of his life before he got to know her. He wanted to hold her, to kiss her. The thought set his heart racing.

Maybe their attraction was something that happened at first meeting and wouldn't happen again. With the smoldering chemistry between them, he couldn't keep from dreaming of seduction.

Dream on, he thought. She was wrapped up in saving the world and would probably be earnest, wanting marriage if there was a relationship.

They were from two different worlds—her whole aim in life was helping others, a commendable ambition, but not practical. At some point reality would hit, and she would give it up. Right now, it seemed ridiculous for her to toss aside a career she had a tremendous talent for to do charity work. She could have had her own design firm! Instead, she looked at the world through rose-colored glasses and saw everyone as filled with a basic goodness—which was not practical.

This was a lesson he had learned early in life when his father abandoned him. There was nothing good about a man who would dump his wife and small child, cutting them permanently out of his life. He never gave time or attention, and they had been hurt repeatedly by his indifference. Eventually, Sierra would learn that not everyone could be saved.

He'd learned about the realities of human nature at an early age, watching his father be honored for his philanthropy only to turn around and lie to get what he wanted, cheat on his wife and abandon his children.

Sierra would soon be like the rest of the world— as out for herself as the next person, and all her sweet talk about saving souls would be a memory. *That* was human nature.

No, she was not his type in any way—except for that hot, intense, mutual attraction.

A scalding attraction he intended to pursue in spite of their differences, because it was obvious she felt it too. He intended to clear his calendar and spend some time at his ranch while she was there.

He had planned on being at the ranch this week, anyway, so it would work out well with her starting Monday.

Then he would find out if that mutual attraction was a first-meeting fluke—or something more.

* * *

Sunday afternoon Sierra watched from her window as the plane lifted from the tarmac and gained altitude, revealing Kansas City spread below. Her gaze traveled around the plush interior of the aircraft with its luxurious reclining leather seats, tables between them, a magazine cabinet, a television screen and a laptop. The plane circled the city and headed south.

As she flew, she checked again to see that she had the phone numbers for two people she had worked with who now had their own New York agency. They had accepted her offer to work on Blake's ranch house, and they would start Monday.

Eli Thompkins was a quiet presence and excellent at interior design. She had admired his work before she graduated and gotten into the business, and she would be happy to work with him.

Lucinda Wells had started as an interior designer at the same time as Sierra. She was talented, specializing in contemporary design. Eli and Lucinda would look for art, paintings and sculptures, as well as furnishings. Sierra had already given them a few suggestions.

She'd taken care of the donation details with Bert before she left. She tried to focus on all the wonderful improvements and opportunities Blake's money would provide, but nothing could distract her from the tingly anticipation of seeing him again. Would she have the same sizzling reaction to him?

She hoped not, because that would complicate her job. Blake was far too cynical; his dismissal of her current work was proof of that. It was as if he was unable to see the goodness in others. She couldn't understand his outlook on life, and he didn't seem to understand hers. She needed to keep him out of her thoughts.

What was even worse, she hadn't slept well because of dreams that included Blake—dreams she definitely didn't want.

Had he felt anything when they'd met? Or had she imagined his response?

She suspected that by tomorrow morning she would have her answers.

Right on schedule, they touched down at Love Field in Dallas. She thanked the pilot and departed, crossing to the waiting white limo for another luxurious ride.

When they finally turned onto the ranch road, they passed beneath a wrought-iron arch with the name BC Ranch.

As they approached Blake's house, she saw barns, out-buildings and a sprawling two-story stone ranch house that had to have cost a fortune. Slate roofs glistened in the sunlight, and she could spot the new wing because of construction equipment still in the yard. In front of the house sprinklers slowly revolved, watering the lawn and beds of early spring flowers bordering the porch.

As she remembered Blake's midnight eyes and black hair, butterflies danced in her stomach. She hoped when they greeted each other she felt nothing except eager-ness to start this job and gratitude for his donation.

The limo drove around the house, pulled beneath a portico and stopped. Blake stepped out and approached them. In jeans, a navy Western-style shirt and black boots, he looked like the successful rancher he was.

The driver opened her door and she stepped out of the limo. When she looked up into Blake's brown eyes, she realized this job would not be as easy as she had hoped, because a sizzling current rocked her to her toes.

How was she going to work with this tall, handsome man without giving in to this attraction?

Two

On a windy March afternoon, Blake watched Sierra Benson step out of the limo. She wore deep blue slacks and a matching shirt, her hair tied back by a blue scarf.

Taking a deep breath, Blake walked over and extended his hand. He wanted to find out if he had the same sensual reaction he'd had when he first met her, or if that had been his imagination. The moment his hand enveloped hers, he had his answer.

He felt the same sparks, and he saw the same surprise flicker in her big, blue eyes.

He never dated anyone he worked with, and she was not the type of woman he would be friends with. Even as he thought of the reasons he should keep his relationship with Sierra impersonal and professional, he was caught in those blue eyes and didn't want to look away.

Far from it. When his gaze lowered to her full red lips, he inhaled, trying to ignore a flash of curiosity. What would it be like to kiss her?

With a mental shake, he tried to get a grip on his thoughts. For all he knew she was engaged, deeply in love with someone at home and totally off limits.

"Welcome to my ranch," he said with a smile. "Come inside, and I'll have someone bring in your things while I show you around."

"Thanks," she said, slipping her hand out of his and falling into step beside him. "You have a beautiful home. It looks very big already, even without adding a wing to make it larger."

"It's home—a haven for me. I wanted a larger bedroom suite, something in a contemporary style, and there are three more large suites in the new wing. I wanted an entertainment room, an exercise room and a casual living area—so I'll have all that in the new wing, too."

"It's a huge place for one man."

He smiled. "I have a staff to take care of it and relatives on Mom's side of the family. They're scattered across the country, and she likes to have them here during Christmas—they'll fill both wings. I have three half brothers who visit and one of them, Nate, is married with a baby girl. Cade and Gabe—heaven knows if and when they'll marry. I have friends who come to fish or hunt or for a party or just to visit. I don't intend to rattle around alone. Would your family fill the space?"

Her eyes widened. "We could fill a lot of the bed-

rooms. Growing up, we always had kids sleeping on
air mattresses and sofas because of the company we
brought home."

He saw her looking at the heavy crystal-and-brass
chandelier hanging over the circular entryway filled
with potted palms. There were also oil paintings on
the walls. The entryway ceiling was two stories high,
and on both sides of the hallway the rooms were open,
with Corinthian columns instead of walls on the side
facing the circular hallway.

"I have an office you can use on the second floor.
It's next to your suite." He motioned toward a sweeping staircase with iron railings.

On the second floor he directed her down a wide
hallway. They passed a bedroom and then stepped into
a living area. "This suite will be yours. If you need
anything, just let me know." He saw amusement curve
her mouth slightly. Tempting lips that looked soft and
enticing.

Mildly exasperated that she stirred unexpected
feelings in him, he shifted his thoughts to the present.
"What's amusing you?" he asked.

"How could I possibly want anything in all this luxury?" she asked. "You've seen my office."

"Yes, I have. I suspect you didn't do the decor for it."

She smiled, and a warm feeling filled him. Her smile
was contagious, as inviting as sunshine. "No, there is
no decor in my office. Very plain vanilla, and we have
buckets for rainy days."

"You should have enough money from my check to
fix the roof."

"Probably, unless things come up that are more urgent."

Surprised, he glanced at her, realizing again that he didn't have any acquaintances like her. Neither his friends nor his family would put a charity project over repairing a leaky roof. She was a marvelous interior decorator, but he couldn't fathom her views of the world, her preferences. Again, he wondered how long this career would last for her. She would discover the reality of human nature and return to her old career. She would change, he had no doubts, but until then, her rosy view fascinated and confused him.

Hot chemistry or not, she was definitely not his type, and he knew with absolute certainty he wasn't hers. He needed to stop thinking about her lips.

"You have an adjoining bedroom and bath, and if you'll come with me, next door is the office."

She laughed softly. "It's bigger and better equipped, and far nicer than mine at the nonprofit. I might not go home." He saw the twinkle in her eyes and smiled at her.

"Nice office or not, I suspect you'll be ready to go when the time comes. Some who have a city background don't like the ranch after a few days. Or sooner—it's too quiet and isolated for them. Wear boots or take care when you're outside—we have rattlesnakes."

He waved his hand. "You have four computers with extra-large monitors, a copy machine, scanner, fax, a laptop, an iPad, a drawing board. If you need anything else, let me know."

"I think that covers what I might need, and I brought my own iPad." She turned to face him. "Blake, I want to look at the rooms we're talking about so I have an idea what I'll be dealing with. I've hired two talented people. When I unpack I'll give you their cards and a brochure about their agencies. Right now, they'll work out of New York, but they'll fly out here as we get to the later stages. That will mean they will need to stay nearby—"

"They can stay right here. There is plenty of room in this house and there are two guest houses. If you need or want anything, just tell me, or if I'm not here, tell Wendell."

A man knocked lightly on the door. He wore a black shirt, jeans and Western boots as he entered with her carry-on and a small bag.

"Perfect timing, Wendell. Sierra, this is Wendell Strong, who keeps the house running. Wendell, meet Ms. Benson, our decorator for the new wing."

After they exchanged greetings, Wendell set down her things. As he did, Blake added, "Wendell does a lot of jobs—butler and valet, but basically he's my house manager. With the exception of the cook, he manages my house staff and the gardener. His wife, Etta, is my cook."

"I'm glad to meet you, and thank you, Wendell, for getting my bags," Sierra said, smiling at him as he nodded and left.

"Have dinner here with me tonight," Blake said. "Etta has cooked all afternoon, so I hope when the time comes, you're hungry. I thought you might want to settle in now and catch your breath after the flight and drive. If you'll come down about six, we can have a drink and relax a bit before dinner. After dinner I'll show you the new wing."

"Sounds good, Blake," she replied. "One other thing—we have a big picnic at home Saturday, so I'm flying back to Kansas City on Friday afternoon."

"Sure. I'll take care of the flight arrangements for you." He walked to the door and managed not to turn around and take one last look.

As Sierra unpacked her few belongings, she couldn't keep from comparing the ranch house to her condo, which was large enough to be comfortable for her, but not too big, and she thought about the home where she grew up with her five siblings.

Her family's two-story house had been large enough for her big family, kid friendly and nothing fancy. Always a place any of them could bring their friends, their house was usually filled with company. Many meals had included twelve to fifteen around their table.

Now, because of her work with Brigmore, she interacted daily with people who needed help, and helping them seemed so much more important than jobs like this one for Blake. They were good people who had had misfortune—illness or just bad luck. He was cynical, yet ironically, his money would be such a help. Most people would appreciate the help, and use it to make their lives better, something Blake didn't seem to believe.

She needed to get this job done and get back to Kansas City. She was attracted to Blake to a degree she had never been attracted to another man before. He hadn't done one thing to cause the attraction other than be himself, but she knew he felt it as much as she did.

His handsome looks and sexy appeal took her breath. While he seemed laid-back and easygoing, his air of supreme confidence was so strong it was almost tangible. He was sure of himself, accustomed to getting what he wanted, and it showed in his attitude, his demeanor and his walk. His assurance was obvious when he entered a room.

To her relief, he had been impersonal, businesslike, since her arrival. She hoped that didn't change. She appreciated him not flirting or trying to charm her. She hoped she could stay businesslike, too.

Yes, she'd agreed to dinner tonight, but after this getting-to-know you session, she hoped to spend as little time around him as possible. When she thought of the enormous check he had given her to get her to take this job, a staggering amount, she had to wonder what was behind that offer. Why had he wanted her that badly? She might have once been good at interior decorating, but so were others.

Feeling suspicious about his motives, she hoped he had paid that much for purely business reasons. She couldn't keep from thinking about the CEO she'd worked for previously. She had been an executive ready to move up when he had propositioned her, promising to make her a vice president if she would become his mistress. She hadn't seen that coming from him and he had held no sexual appeal.

His startling offer had shaken her judgment in men and angered her. Unlike with her CEO, a physical attraction had existed between her and Blake from the first second they had met.

She would have dinner with him tonight, get the lay-out of the new wing and find out what he wanted and then, hopefully, he would go on about his business. He didn't look the type to hover.

She showered and changed, dressing in a skirt, a matching red silk shirt and high-heeled pumps. She tied her hair behind her head with another silk scarf and went downstairs to meet him at six.

As she walked down the curving stairs, she saw him stop at the foot to wait. And watch her.

His dark gaze made her tingle. Taking him in at a glance, she smiled at him. He had changed, too. He wore jeans, boots and a different short-sleeve shirt that em-phasized his dark, handsome looks.

"You don't look as if you've traveled most of the day. You look as fresh as the proverbial daisy," he said.

"Traveling in your private jet and a limo was not dif-ficult or tiring. Both were about as comfortable as one can get," she said, falling into step beside him .

"Want to look around a little, or wait until later?" he asked.

"Now's fine so I'll have some idea where things are located and what kind of house you have."

"Let's go to the formal living area. It's rarely used, but I felt I needed it, and I know my mother would have been unhappy if we didn't have it."

"Does she entertain here?"

"Never on her own, but she's been hostess for me a few times. More in the past, when I first moved out here. This is it," he said, and she walked through double doors into a room with a marble floor, elegant furniture and chairs upholstered in deep blue antique satin and brocade. Ornate, gilt mirrors and original oils of landscapes hung on the walls. The vaulted ceiling was two stories high, and floor-to-ceiling glass comprised a wall of windows overlooking the front drive.

"This is beautiful, Blake."

"Thanks. The formal dining room adjoins this room," he said, motioning toward more wide double doors that were open. They entered a room with a large ornate crystal chandelier centered over a gleaming fruitwood dining table that could easily seat two dozen people.

Silver candelabra sat on a buffet with a sterling tea set. The stone fireplace and hearth were flanked by paintings of hunting scenes.

"This is another beautiful room."

"This one has been used more than that front room. I seem to have more dinner parties, although most of them are casual, the patio and backyard type. Much easier for everyone, and the food is still Etta's cooking."

"I think the cooking is what everyone remembers," she said.

They moved through a study, a library filled with books that he had not read, and she laughed with him over his plans to read them someday. He showed her a downstairs bedroom that had more ancient, beautiful furniture—old-fashioned, heavy pieces, hand carved and made of mahogany, including a four-poster bed.

"This is absolutely gorgeous, Blake."

"I think it's time for a drink, and later we can continue the tour. I have three more bedrooms on this floor, an office on the ground floor and another smaller one adjoining my bedroom upstairs. Let's go to the sitting room across the back. There's a bar and it's more comfortable."

She walked beside him into a room filled with light thanks to more floor-to-ceiling glass. It overlooked a patio, a garden and a kidney-shaped swimming pool of crystal blue water with a waterfall.

When he crossed to the bar, she scooted onto a stool across the counter from him.

"This is quite a contrast to your Dallas life," she said, gazing outside and seeing unending fields beyond his fenced yard.

"I love this place, and I need the ranch life. You've switched from New York City to Kansas City—still cities, but that's a switch."

"It's quieter, and I love my work now far more than what I was doing."

"I don't see how you can. You could have opened your own design firm, but now all your energy goes to people who won't thank you for it. You'll see. These people you help will just want more help again—no one really changes. This," he said, motioning to the expanse of his ranch home, "is where you can do something that will really last and be appreciated. You seem to have deep beliefs about how good people are—I'm sorry to say, you'll be disillusioned eventually."

"Blake, you're a cynical man. Look for the goodness in people. Believe in it, and you'll find it."

He smiled at her indulgently.

"You're looking at me as if you're going to pat me on the head and try to set me straight on what people are really like."

"That's a thought." He laughed.

She watched his hands as he poured drinks. He had fine, strong hands, which were probably good for ranch work. Maybe the isolation of this spread was what he preferred because he had a warped view of the world and a poor opinion of people in general.

When he held out a glass of pale white wine, she reached to take it, her fingers touching his lightly. He looked up, his gaze meeting hers. "Thanks," she said, taking her drink and sliding off the bar stool to cross the room and look at his pool. But she didn't see the water as questions swirled in her thoughts. Why did she have this intense reaction to him? Worse, why did he feel the chemistry, too?

"Running away from me?" he asked in a deeper tone as he joined her.

Startled, she met his probing gaze and wondered how long this reaction to him would continue. She didn't want to try to guess what he was thinking at the moment. It was impossible to miss the blatant look of desire in the depths of his brown eyes.

"We better stick to talking about business," she replied, wishing she didn't sound so breathless. How could she have this reaction to him when he wasn't doing anything to cause it, and when they held such opposing views of the world?

"Blake, we're not going there," she whispered.

Suddenly, he looked mildly amused, which shattered

the intensity of the moment. "Not going where, Sierra?" Exasperation pricked her.

"You know where. I don't know why we have this chemistry between us, but we need to ignore it, avoid it and hope it will go away because I'm sure you don't want to feel it any more than I do."

"I'm hurt," he teased, his eyes twinkling. "I didn't know I was such an ogre that you don't want to find me attractive."

"Right now, you're moving into an area where neither of us should go," she snapped, losing her usual good nature and patience. She was on edge because of her reaction to him, and his sudden flirting was only adding fuel to the fire.

He laughed softly. "Relax, Sierra. I know our relationship is a professional one, but while you're living here, we might as well indulge in some unbusinesslike moments."

With an effort, she smiled and tried to bank her impatience with him. He had made light of that intense moment, and she was certain it had meant nothing to him. She wanted him to feel that it meant nothing to her, too. She had no intention of letting him know the extent of the edgy, sharp physical awareness she had of him as a sexy, attractive male.

She suspected a man like Blake did not need any coaxing to entice him into a physical relationship. She was certain he had attracted females from a young age and was fully aware of the effect he had on women.

"If that big check you gave me included anything

besides the design work you described in my office, then the deal's off."

Instantly the amusement left his expression. "Hey, Sierra. Absolutely not. My teasing was in fun and meant nothing."

She realized her reaction had been too strong. Her past biased her. She tried to relax, getting them back on a casual, friendly footing. "I don't know you well at all. Just making sure we understand each other," she said, smiling at him.

"Good. Have a seat. Etta is in the kitchen, and Wendell is helping her get dinner on the table. I'll introduce you to her. She's a fantastic cook, which always makes it easy to come home."

"You think of the ranch as home," she said a few moments later, after they'd stepped outside and were sitting in chairs facing his patio.

"I told you that I love it here. This is my haven. I can come out here and enjoy the total silence. Sometimes you hear the wind, and sometimes you don't even hear that. For a few minutes I can imagine the whole world is at peace. Even if it's not, my little corner of it is." He grinned. "Obviously, I like the ranch and I'm happiest here."

"You're fortunate. Far luckier than you give much thought to. I work with people daily who don't have a haven, not even a tiny one. Then, there are those who surprise me—one would think they couldn't possibly feel at peace because they own nothing, but they have an inner sense of a haven. That's resilience, and it's amazing."

"You really like working with those people, don't you?" he asked, looking more intently at her. He sounded surprised.

"More than anything. It's the most wonderful feeling in the world to help someone, or rescue an animal and find it a loving home, or make someone's life easier. That's the best possible reward."

"That's commendable, but in my experience people don't change. You can work your fingers to the bone and not make a difference. With the career you had, there were some very tangible financial rewards and lasting legacies. You could have built your own business instead of working with people who will disappoint and deceive you."

"You have a cynical view of the world. Expect more from people, Blake. There's a deep-rooted goodness in most people. Look for that and believe in it."

"I'm just puzzled. You've tossed over a spectacular, successful career, a fabulous reputation and a hefty income for something that will take infinite patience, probably have low financial returns and be a lot of hard work that sometimes goes unappreciated and unrewarded."

"Wow, Blake. That's strong. You're only looking at the downside of what I do."

"Just looking at it honestly because I can't understand your great faith in the goodness of human nature."

"I don't know what you've experienced, but I have seen that people are good and can live up to high expectations, or occasionally exceed them. Look at you.

You don't need money, yet you work hard to build your hotel business."

He looked away and was silent a moment. She noticed a muscle flex in his jaw and wondered why her question caused him to tense up.

"I want to know that I can be a success in the business world as well as in the ranching world. We all have our goals."

Wendell appeared, wearing a white apron over his jeans. "Dinner is served."

"Thank you." Blake stood. "Leave your wine. There will be some poured at the table."

She walked with him toward the front of the house, and then they turned into the wide hall. In minutes Wendell directed them to a kitchen that was big enough to hold her Kansas City apartment, but the tempting smell of beef assailed her before she ever stepped inside. Doors stood open to reveal stainless steel appliances and state-of-the-art cookware that, when not in use, would be out of sight behind the elegant dark wood. A tall, slender woman with her brown hair clipped at the back of her head, smiled. Etta wore a white apron over a black uniform.

"Sierra, this is Etta Strong, my cook. Etta, this is Ms. Benson, who is here to plan the decor for our new wing."

"So what's for dinner tonight?" he asked as soon as the women had greeted each other.

"Tossed salad with chunks of lobster, slices of avocado on the side and French dressing. Prime rib, asparagus hollandaise, mashed potatoes and gravy and buttermilk biscuits. With homemade peach ice cream," Etta answered.

"That sounds like a fabulous banquet," Sierra remarked.

"When you're seated, I'll get you started."

As Sierra walked with Blake to the adjoining informal dining area, she had another view of gardens and his irrigated yard, and marveled at the luxury of his lifestyle. She was thankful again for his check, and after their earlier conversation, she knew he needed to see some of the good his money would do.

They sat at a table that could easily seat ten. Wendell came with a bottle of red wine and one of white. He asked Sierra her choice and tipped red into her glass before pouring Blake's.

Etta set the prime rib in front of Blake for him to carve. She returned with a bowl of steaming asparagus that she served.

After the first bite of prime rib, Sierra sipped her wine and smiled at Blake. "I have to agree—you have a fabulous cook. This is delicious."

"Wait until you try her homemade ice cream. Wendell helps her with that."

"No wonder you like the ranch so much."

He smiled. "The food is the best, but there's more than food. Have you ever been to a rodeo?"

"No, I haven't."

"Actually, one of the best is in New York City, the Professional Bull Riders at Madison Square Garden," he explained.

"Do you ever participate locally?"

"Sometimes—not as much now as I used to. I have ridden bulls a couple of times, but not seriously. That's a bit rougher than I'm up for."

"Aw, shucks," she said, smiling. "So I won't see someone I actually know in a rodeo. The pictures I've seen look wild."

"That's the thrill of it," he said, and she laughed.

Through dinner, he was charming, keeping the same professional manner as if they were at a business dinner in Kansas City. Even so, there was an undercurrent of sensual awareness, and every minute spent in his company drew her closer to him and heightened his appeal.

As Wendell removed her dinner plate, she smiled. "My compliments to the chef. That was one of the most delicious dinners I've ever eaten. I don't know which was best—that prime rib or those fantastic biscuits."

"Thank you," Wendell said, smiling as he started toward the kitchen. "I'll tell Etta."

Sierra looked at Blake. "I meant every word of that. What a marvelous cook you have."

"I do everything I can to hang on to both of them. Etta has a reputation throughout the county—and probably farther than that. If she decided to leave, she would have so many offers, I don't know how she would decide."

The peach ice cream was served with white chocolate chip cookies, and they lingered over coffee, which Sierra barely touched. Once again, she thought about the homeless people at the shelter and how they often lived with hunger. Blake's check would provide food for so many, and again, she felt enormous gratitude for his donation.

"Etta should open a restaurant—talk about natural talent for a job."

"Don't put ideas in her head," he teased.

"Did she cook for your family before cooking for you?" she asked. For a fleeting second, she saw a hard look cross his features. It was gone so quickly, she thought she must have imagined it.

"No. The family she cooked for decided to move to South Texas and sell their ranch. I was friends with her son growing up. We're the same age and went through school together. He's a great guy. After graduation from high school, he went to the Air Force Academy and now flies fighter jets. He's stationed in Europe. They have four other kids who are scattered except for an older, married daughter who has four kids. She lives in Dallas, and the grandkids come out here a lot and stay with Etta and Wendell. They're cute kids, and we have horses for them—except the little one, who's too young to turn loose yet."

"That's great. Were you born and raised in Dallas?" she asked. This time she had no doubt about the shuttered look she received.

"Yes. My father divorced my mother before I was a year old. He severed all ties with us, so I grew up without knowing him. He has never been a part of my life. If he's ever spoken to me, it was before I was old enough to remember. I don't know why, but my mother has never remarried."

He spoke in a flat voice, and she realized she had

touched on a sensitive area. "I'm sorry, Blake," she said, meaning it, unable to imagine how devastating it would be if her father had rejected her. She thought about her generous, loving dad who had always been a big part of all his children's lives.

Blake's voice dropped, and she heard a note of amusement. "Sierra, don't ever play poker. You look like you'll start crying over me any minute. Of course, if you want to hold me close and try to console me for being abandoned—"

"Forget it, Blake," she interrupted, laughing at him. "I see you survived and grew up quite well."

"I'm friends with my father's other sons, my half brothers, now because the oldest one and I went to school together. He's a little younger, but we played football together in high school. Enough said on that subject. Where are you from? New York?"

Still thinking about his abandonment by his father before the age of one, she shook her head. "No. I'm from Kansas. That's why I came back to work in Kansas City. My dad's a minister, and I have a big family with a lot of contacts in the city. My mother is a retired teacher, and most of my family is involved in charity projects related to my job. Mom and two of my sisters volunteer at our animal rescue shelter. Dad runs some programs to help people from the shelter get to church. He has free breakfasts at his church every morning… I could keep going. There are six kids in my family, fourteen grandkids and a foster grandchild—soon to be adopted. I'm the one with no kids."

"That's a big family. It's a very different lifestyle

from my background, where I grew up with just two of us at home—Mom and me."

"We were always free to bring our friends home with us, so we constantly had a house filled with kids," she said, unable to imagine a home of just two.

"Don't look at me like I was left by myself on the street," he said with a grin. "I'm not one of your charity projects, although that might be interesting."

She smiled in return. "There is no way I could see you as a charity project at any point in time. I suspect your mother showered you with love, and you had friends galore."

"I always thought so," he answered easily. "Let's move and let Etta and Wendell clean up and go home."

"Sure. I want to step into the kitchen and tell Etta how wonderful dinner was. I can't imagine having someone like that cook for you all the time."

"It is another draw the ranch holds, although if I had to live in Dallas year round, I'd try to get her to move with me. Wendell, too, of course."

Blake waited while she went to the kitchen to tell Etta and Wendell again how wonderful dinner had been. She returned to find him leaning one shoulder against a door jamb and looking at her legs. His gaze flew up to meet hers, and there was no mistaking the blatant sexual speculation in his expression.

Trying to ignore the unguarded moment, she crossed the room to join him, and they walked into the big living area overlooking the patio and pool.

"Tell me when you're ready, and I'll show you the new wing. We can take a quick look tonight and go over the rooms in detail tomorrow—or we can skip anything related to work tonight and let you relax."

"I can relax while I work. If you care to, you can show me around tonight. I don't mind at all."

"Come on and we'll look," he said and they headed for the stairs. "Tomorrow I'll give you blueprints and pictures, so you'll know what I want. The workmen aren't completely finished with construction, but they're far enough along that they'll finish this week. By the time you're ready for the actual work, they'll be gone.

"I told you about the additions earlier. Also, I had an elevator put in because my grandmother visits, and she is getting less enthusiastic about stairs. Mom has her own one-story house on the property, but she rarely spends time there. She's in Patagonia, sightseeing with friends now, or I would have had her join us for dinner. Here we are—we'll walk through, and then if you have questions, fire away."

As they strolled down a wide hall, she was more aware of the tall man beside her than of her surroundings. Their footsteps in the empty, unfinished wing created a hollow sound. When they entered the first suite, she saw that the rooms would be light because of the abundant windows.

She could smell sawdust and new lumber. She was equally aware of the faint scent of Blake's aftershave, the scrape of his boot heels on the new hardwood floors, of his nearness when he opened doors for her and stepped back to hold them.

Thankful she wouldn't be working with him on a daily basis, she couldn't shake the acute awareness of him. As they stood in the large living area of the suite, he turned to her. "Downstairs in the older part of the house I showed you some of the rooms. They all have formal French-style furniture, European antiques, plus one suite holds two-hundred-year-old furniture I bought at an estate sale in New Orleans."

"The rosewood furniture that's ornate and elegant. It's beautiful, Blake," she said.

"Thanks. I think so. I did that mostly for my mom because she loves that kind of furniture, and she was influential in the selection of the earlier furnishings. Up here, I'd like a change in decor. I'd like these suites to be contemporary with sleek lines, open spaces. That's more my style."

"That's popular now, and there are some beautiful furniture designs available," she said, walking through the empty rooms while he followed. "You'll have plenty to choose from."

"Whoa," he said. "Sierra, I'm turning this project over to you. I want you to make the decisions about the decor—that's your field, and I trust you totally. From here on, you take charge. Do your stuff, get it lined up and then show me. I do not want to be too involved."

"Suppose you don't like it?" she asked. "People usually want to see some of the early planning. You had people who checked on what I was doing at your hotel."

"That's because you'd never worked for us before. Now the early stages will be your deal. I've told you contemporary, and we'll set an upper limit for the cost.

I don't want to be consulted until you've made some selections and have sketches showing how it'll look."

"That's flattering, and you're the boss," she said. "At least you know what you want."

"Damn straight," he said quietly, his voice acquiring that husky note that indicated furniture was no longer on his mind. "I know exactly what I want," he said.

"All right, Blake. I'll see if I can please you," she flung back at him. Her pulse raced as she turned to walk away. When she did, her back tingled, and she felt his gaze on her. Telling herself that it was probably her imagination, she had no intention of turning to see if he was studying her.

The suites in the new wing were roomy, each unique, one with arched, wide windows giving a panoramic view of his lighted pool.

As she turned, she once again caught Blake gazing at her with a lustful look. She met his gaze and the moment intensified, her surroundings disappearing, leaving only the tall, handsome man facing her.

Her heart pounded as she left the room. "I'll move on," she said over her shoulder without glancing back.

They had only started looking and had the rest of the wing to finish. She drew a deep breath, determined to keep her mind on business. Not so easy when she was beside him or when she caught him looking at her with unmistakable desire.

Again, she was grateful that he didn't live on the ranch full-time.

They looked at suites with large rooms, lots of glass and open spaces, big walk-in closets and bathrooms large enough to hold several pieces of furniture besides the usual bathroom equipment. She could envision some beautiful suites.

"You'll have a hotel when you finish," she said, amused. "This would even be big for my family."

He smiled. "I like plenty of room. I do have company, and I have family now, thanks to Cade and my other half brothers. When they come to visit they need their own space. I told you before, Nate is married. He's two years younger than Cade. He has a beautiful wife and a beautiful little baby daughter who is about two months old. They are back east right now, visiting her parents."

"Is Cade the one close to your age?"

"Yes. Cade is the Callahan I know best. He's the oldest of the three. Gabe is the youngest."

While they talked, she gazed into his dark brown eyes. She was aware of how close he stood, and she considered initiating conversations only when standing across the room from him. This intense reaction was unique, disturbing and something she couldn't understand. She turned to walk away, reminding herself to keep a professional distance between them.

"That's it," he said finally when they finished. "It's early. Let's go downstairs and talk for a while. You'll live and work in my house temporarily, so we might as well get to know each other."

She knew now was the moment to politely decline, but looking into his midnight eyes, she couldn't. "For a while," she said, unable to resist accepting his invitation. What was it about him that held so much forbidden appeal?

As they walked downstairs, he asked, "Want anything to eat or drink? We have desserts, more ice cream and an after-dinner liqueur. What would you like?"

"Just a glass of ice water, please," she said.

They went to the sitting room at the back of the house, and he stepped behind the bar to get ice water for her and a beer for himself.

As she sat in a straight wingback chair, he sank down on a large brown leather chair facing her, sipped his beer and set it on a table. "Do you plan to stay with the nonprofit, or will you go back to decorating someday?"

"I plan to stay where I am. A project I have dreamed about is finding foster parents for homeless kids—now with the funds you provided, maybe we'll be able to start that program. You would have room to take one," she teased.

He gave her a startled look and then smiled, the corner of his mouth lifting a fraction. "That's commendable, but a little kid right now wouldn't fit in with my lifestyle."

"Nonsense. You can hire nannies, maids and tutors, whomever you need."

"I think you're yanking my chain. If I take in a child, it won't be to turn them over to staff to raise."

"I'm glad to hear that," she said, not telling him he surprised her. He didn't look the type to be interested in child care. "My brother and sister-in-law have a two-year-old foster child right now. They've already started adoption proceedings, and the agency is helping them. She's a precious baby."

His black eyelashes were thick, slightly curly and

added to his handsome looks. Was it going to be difficult to work for him? Even if he weren't her boss, his cynicism didn't fit her worldview. Perhaps his dad's rejection had brought about Blake's sour opinion of people. She couldn't expect any of her arguments to change his mind. Because of that, she didn't want to get involved with him, no matter how intense his physical appeal.

"Is this your brother's first child?"

For an instant she stared at him blankly, and then remembered their conversation. "No, she isn't. They have three other girls and a boy."

"That's overwhelming."

"Not really. They wanted a family, and they have one they shower with love, but they feel they have room for another baby." She paused. "You said you're not planning on marriage anytime soon…"

"Not even remotely. I'm wound up in my career, and I'm not a family man at this point in my life." He paused as if lost in thought while he shook his head. "Right now I don't want a serious relationship. If I ever get romantically involved, I'll have to give it a lot of thought and time before I make even a small commitment. You don't sound as if you're into serious relationships, either."

"That's right. I suppose for the same reasons as you. I'm immersed in my job and want to build our agency. Since I'm single, I can devote a lot of time and energy to getting things going. Also, with the money from you, we can get our programs on more secure footing and increase our outreach. You should try my profession sometime," she said, half in jest.

He was too cynical about people to get involved in the details of helping others, but maybe she could make him see the good she was doing, the good his money would be doing. "You've already helped, but you could help more, maybe even on a small scale. You could easily start a program on your ranch for homeless kids, and you wouldn't have to involve yourself any more than you'd like to get involved."

He gave her another crooked smile. "Don't try to talk me into saving the world. That isn't my thing. I give in plenty of ways."

"How much do you give of yourself, Blake? Try just once, and maybe you'll see why I feel the way I do. Maybe you'd see the goodness in people."

"Money will be a bigger help than my presence."

"Blake, I've never known anyone so cynical."

"Call it cynical. I call it realistic."

Her gaze lowered to his mouth. What would it be like to kiss him? When she glanced up, his brown eyes were intent on her, as if he could guess her thoughts. She felt her cheeks grow warm. As she turned away, she heard a clock chime. "My word, it's one in the morning," she said, picking up her empty glass. "I need to say good-night."

Standing, he grinned. "You don't have to be anywhere at any specific time. You're in charge of the schedule. As for me, I'll be up and out of here before dawn, and then I'll come back to answer any questions you have about getting started."

"Thanks for your confidence in me. You're leaving lights on," she said as he walked beside her.

"I can turn them all off from my room when I turn on the alarms."

As they climbed the stairs, they talked about the new wing. He stopped with her in front of her door and turned to face her. He stood close, once again holding her full attention. She forgot the hour, the place, everything around her. She forgot the incredible differences between them. All she was aware of was the handsome man facing her with an expression that made her heart race.

He reached behind her head, moving languidly, his fingers working at the silk scarf knotted behind her neck. Each faint brush of his warm hand against her nape stirred tingles. He tugged lightly, and her hair fell free with long strands tumbling slightly below her shoulders.

Sinking in brown eyes, she couldn't get her breath and her heart drummed. *Step away...step away...*repeated steadily in her thoughts, a silent warning that she couldn't possibly heed. His mesmerizing eyes sent another message. He intended to kiss her.

Never before had she crossed that invisible line between business and pleasure, but she couldn't back away now or even dredge up a protest.

"I don't know why we have this volatile chemistry between us," he said in a husky voice, "but we do. It's impossible to ignore. Sooner or later, I'm going to kiss you. I figure it might as well be sooner and get this attraction settled," he said as he slipped an arm around her waist.

Why couldn't she walk away right now—set the right

precedent? Common sense whispered that now was the time. This was what she had intended to avoid, yet she couldn't pull away.

Her heart clamored for his kiss. Curiosity made it inevitable. With the hot attraction between them, what would it be like to kiss him?

She couldn't answer her own question. She had to take the risk to find out.

Three

Immobilized by his declaration, Sierra felt her heart thud. She placed one hand lightly against his forearm, feeling the hard muscles that indicated physical labor. He definitely did not spend most of his time in his Dallas office.

He stepped closer, and then leaned down as she finally managed to whisper, "We shouldn't—"

He brushed her lips with his, a faint, feathery touch that stirred a longing for more. Her insides heated while her heart pounded faster.

"We shouldn't," he whispered, "but we're going to." He kissed her before she could say anything else.

For a second she stiffened, and then she slipped her arm around his shoulders and placed her hand at the back of his neck while she kissed him in return. With his tongue stroking hers, he drew her tightly against him. He was solid, flat planes of rock-hard muscle against her softness.

She tumbled into heart-thudding passion. For a moment all caution vanished, replaced by yearning for more of him. She wanted to touch and kiss him, to forget all her warnings to herself. She longed to let go and make love. What chemistry did they have that set this sizzling desire burning between them?

His kiss stopped logic and caution, and made Blake the most desirable man she had ever met. It created a bond between them that she couldn't easily—if ever—forget.

How long did they kiss? She didn't know, but finally common sense resurfaced.

Gasping for breath, she stepped back. He was also breathing heavily, gazing at her as if he had never seen her before. A sinking feeling enveloped her. She had opened the proverbial Pandora's box.

"We have to forget that happened," she whispered.

"There's no way in hell I can forget that kiss," he replied.

"You'll have to. We're working together. The dinner was wonderful. Good night, Blake," she said, then stepped into her suite and closed the door.

Her heart pounded. How was she going to work with him? How could she keep from falling in love with him? She had left her last job not only to pursue her dreams but also to get away from a sexual situation with her employer. Now she had taken a job where she had a far bigger problem with her employer—she wanted him.

The fleeting thought of quitting was gone as fast as it had come. His donation was too big, the possibilities too great to turn him down.

She would just use caution and stay away from him. He was a busy man with many interests and friends, including women who should be far more appealing to him than Sierra was.

Taking a deep breath, she walked through her suite to get her cotton pajamas and get ready for bed. She couldn't imagine sleeping. Every inch of her body tingled. An intense longing to be in his arms was paramount and hopeless to try to shove out of her thoughts. Her lips still tasted of him, and it was as impossible to forget his kiss as it was to ignore the electrifying attraction between them.

Could he sleep? Or was he tied in knots with desire too?

She couldn't think about what Blake felt—that would only make the situation worse. She hoped he realized they both needed to back away. Blake was a charmer, but his deepest feelings and views on life were the opposite of hers. He was hard, cynical and didn't believe in the goodness of others. During dinner he had talked about his feelings on commitment and the career she'd left behind. He didn't understand her views at all.

For her own good, she had to stop this before it went any further.

She had hoped to avoid ever getting into a sticky situation with a boss again. Yet going against all logic and planning, she had kissed Blake—but she had no intention of letting that kiss escalate.

There had been attraction with her last boss, Alex Deagens, too, but it had been more about friendship. She'd liked Alex—until the night their relationship changed.

They had worked late at the office and were the only people there. Alex had kissed her. When he paused, holding her, he'd told her he would get her a fancier apartment and promote her to vice president if she slept with him.

Shocked and betrayed by his proposition, she'd refused and left in haste.

Feeling gullible and foolish, she'd spent a sleepless night. First thing at the office the next day, she turned in her resignation. Within the hour she was told by someone from Human Resources that her resignation had been accepted immediately and she did not have to stay the rest of the month as she had offered.

That experience with Alex shook her judgment about men, and afterward she had backed away from getting involved with anyone romantically. She didn't accept dates.

Even so, she still believed anyone could change. Her new career allowed her to focus on the good in people, and occasionally provided the chance to offer life-changing acts of kindness. That absorbing work, plus moving back to Kansas City to be close to her family, kept Sierra too busy to miss not having a social life outside of her family. But now she was here with Blake. This was a man for her to avoid. Already she knew any emotional entanglement with him would only end painfully. By placing monetary success above helping the less fortunate, he missed out on the best parts of life.

She thought about his father abandoning him when Blake had been a baby—a hurt that had to have left permanent scars. No little child could understand a father who walked away. That had to have been devastating, and perhaps was the reason Blake seemed to be tough and hard. Again, she was thankful for her loving father, a man who had always been a part of his children's lives.

She needed to get this job done and get home, away from Blake and the consuming attraction that resonated between them.

Business and pleasure didn't mix well. He was her boss, albeit a temporary one, and she needed to remember that. She had to stay professional, get the work done and go home where she could forget him.

And forget their kiss. Hopefully Blake already had.

Blake left for his gym and indoor pool. He swam laps, hoping the activity, the cold water and the lateness of the hour would combine to drive Sierra out of his thoughts and cool his body.

The hot chemistry they'd felt since the first moment seemed guaranteed to fulfill its promise of passionate, raw sex—at least as far as their kiss was concerned. He still burned with longing to make love to her. Kissing her had not eased his desire for her at all. Instead it set him on fire with need for more. If she was responsive with a kiss, what would she be like in bed?

The thought tied him in knots and promised a night of little sleep.

Of all the women he had known, she was the most unlikely to generate lusty longings. She was the daughter of a minister, a lifelong do-gooder whose goals were foreign to him. How could she give up a brilliant, successful career for one with so little return? Her income would be only a fraction of what it could have been. Why would she want to live that way and make such unnecessary and thankless sacrifices? He knew too well the bad blood that could arise between people, the lasting hurt that could be caused. The only thing he trusted was his bank account—something that gave solid returns, including power and a fortress against hurt from trusting the wrong people.

He didn't need or want a future with Sierra. All he wanted was to seduce her, to get her into his bed and make love for hours, to find out if that sizzling chemistry would take them all the way.

Thinking about her, about their kiss, aroused him. Never in his life had he experienced the same intensity of attraction, and it made no sense to him.

With a groan he swam faster, trying to get her out of his thoughts, to wear himself out and cool the hot longing that tormented him.

As much as he wanted to make love to Sierra, he knew the sensible thing would be to stay away from her. Let her do her job and go back to her charity work. That was the intelligent thing to do because she would want commitment. This was not the woman for him, not even for one wild night of making love. His body wasn't listening to his brain, though. In spite of knowing what he should do, he still wanted seduction.

He continued swimming until he was exhausted. After he showered and dressed in the gym, he ran five miles on the treadmill. Hoping he had done enough so he would drop into bed and be asleep in two minutes, he returned to his suite.

He passed her door and remembered both kissing her and her response with vivid clarity. He had a sinking feeling sleep was a long way off.

Blake slept a couple of hours and woke long before sunrise. He dressed, grabbed a bite of breakfast and left the house as if chased by goblins. He needed hard, physical labor, or at least to be outdoors and moving around, to work with others who would take his mind off Sierra.

As he walked his land by the light of the moon, he wondered whether she had slept. Would she be able to concentrate on work? He had to laugh at himself. His kiss might not have unnerved and aroused her to the same extent as it had him. She might have slept peacefully and right now be working away without a thought about him.

"Pompous jackass," he called himself quietly. "Forget her."

She was an employee, and he needed to keep a professional relationship with her. Actually, he needed to stay the hell away from her. He had already paid her a ridiculously exorbitant sum and committed himself to donating to her agency for the next three years—he should have left her office and pulled his wits together before he wrote those checks. He could imagine his accountant's questions. The only honest reason Blake had paid such princely sums was because he wanted to see more of her. There wasn't any other way to explain it. If he kept pursuing her, what other mistakes would he make?

Blake swore quietly. She had jumbled his thought processes—something he couldn't recall happening with any other woman. He couldn't understand himself and the reaction he had to Sierra. She was a gorgeous, appealing woman, but he was friends with more than a few who fit that description. And she was definitely not his type.

But if she was so much not his type, why couldn't he shake her out of his thoughts?

Later that morning, Blake drank coffee and ate a muffin, leaving the house and intending to find some kind of ranch work that was so demanding, he wouldn't think once about Sierra.

Shortly after 9:00 a.m., he returned, showered and went to find Sierra so they could go over the blueprints for his new wing.

When he knocked lightly at the open door of her suite, he saw her standing in the office. Smiling, she motioned him to enter.

"Come in."

"Good morning," he said.

With a lurch to his insides, his gaze swept over her, taking in her hair pinned high on her head. Her pale blue shirt and coordinating slacks heightened the blue of her eyes. He wanted to cross the room, wrap his arms around her and kiss her into a frenzy of desire.

Instead, he paused at the door of her office, glancing beyond her to see the monitors showing the floor plans of various rooms in his new wing.

"You're already at work," he said. "Did you have breakfast?"

"Oh, yes. Etta was in the kitchen and I had a delicious breakfast—eggs Benedict, melon and berries, and orange juice. I assume you were out working."

"Yep, I was. How's it coming here?" he asked.

"We're just getting started. Let's look at each suite and you tell me if there's anything I need to know," she said, walking to the computers and pulling a chair close so they could look at the same monitor.

He still intended to let her make the decisions, but he sat beside her because he wanted to be close to her, and this was the only way. He caught a faint whiff of her perfume, something light, barely discernible, yet enticing. Everything about her was enticing and he inhaled deeply, trying to focus on what she was saying to him. He looked at her long, slender neck, fighting the urge to run his fingers lightly over her skin and trail kisses under her ear.

With an effort he studied the computer screen and tried to squelch all lusty inclinations—a hopeless ambition when he sat only inches from her. The chemistry between them shook him.

With grim determination he stared at the monitor and tried to forget that she sat beside him. She seemed unaware of their attraction this morning, but he wondered what would happen if he brushed her hand with his or leaned closer when he asked her a question.

Unable to resist, he decided to find out. "Shift to the west bedroom," he said.

When she paused to find the one he was talking about, he placed his hand over hers and moved the mouse. "There," he said. He pointed to a balcony off one of the bedrooms. "This is on the west, and I've ordered an awning for it. Out here in summer that afternoon sun will be fierce."

He was barely thinking about what he told her. He had heard her quick intake of breath and knew she was responding to the physical contact, just as he had.

The knowledge was electric. He wanted to forget business and kiss her again, but he could not and would not.

For the next hour he maintained a professional manner, keeping his distance. She managed to be just as cool and detached, and if he hadn't heard her deep breath when his hand covered hers earlier, he would think that she barely noticed him as anything other than her client. They would not have a lot of time together before she would be working on her own and then going back to her Kansas City office. Once the job was over, he wouldn't see her at all.

He turned to her. "While you're here, you might as well see a little bit of Texas, some local life. Do you eat barbecue?"

Smiling, she nodded. "Yes, and I imagine Etta is as good at cooking barbecue as she is at cooking prime rib."

"She is, but this time it won't be Etta's cooking.

There's a rustic barbecue restaurant in a small town near here. I want to take you. How about this Thursday night, since you said you're leaving Friday?"

Something flickered in the depths of her eyes, and there was a few seconds' hesitation that made him think she would refuse, but then she nodded. "Barbecue Thursday night sounds great," she answered cautiously.

It had been a spur-of-the-moment invitation, but now his anticipation grew because she had to have debated with herself whether or not to turn him down—and she had said yes.

"Eli and Lucinda will arrive tomorrow afternoon and fly back to New York Wednesday."

"They can have suites here. I'll tell Wendell so everything will be ready for them."

It was midmorning, and he was already eager for the evening.

He knew he should leave her alone. But he couldn't help thinking that maybe, this time, there would be more than a kiss between them.

After a quail dinner that night, Sierra went to the kitchen to compliment Etta. When she turned to leave, Blake took her arm lightly, another one of those casual contacts that she shouldn't even notice, much less want. Now was the time to tell him good-night and get out of his presence, except she wanted to stay with him.

"Let's sit on the patio. It's a perfect night. There's no wind, and it's pleasant and quiet."

"Sure. That was a marvelous dinner. It's the first time I've eaten quail."

"Etta knows how to cook game birds."

"Blake, this is lovely," Sierra said, enjoying the cool spring evening, the pool with a splashing fountain and beds of red and yellow tulips in bloom in front of a backdrop of pink japonica and yellow forsythia. "Do you sit out here a lot?"

She saw a crooked smile as he shook his head. "Only with company. Otherwise, I always feel too busy. I expect to take the time, but I don't ever get around to it."

"That's dreadful. You're missing wonderful, peaceful evenings. What about when you and your brothers get together on holidays?"

A cold look filled his eyes, and he shifted his gaze away from her, looking over his yard. "We're getting together more and more, but still not always on holidays. Growing up, until I was in high school, I was never part of their family. Our mothers were never on friendly footing, and my mom and I were cut off from even knowing them all the years I was a little kid."

"I'm sorry," she said, meaning it.

He smiled. "I had a good childhood. You look as if I'm one of the big disasters you need to help."

"I know better than that, but I'm sorry about your family. Family is the biggest part of my life."

"Mom showered me with love and kids accept life as it comes."

"Oh, yes, they do. I just thought you and your half brothers were close from the way you spoke of them."

"We are now, thanks to Cade. If our father comes to Texas, I stay away. He and I don't speak—or, to put it more accurately, he doesn't acknowledge me," Blake said, and this time she heard the flat tone of his voice that she guessed hid anger and hurt.

She thought of her own big, close-knit family, and realized that while Blake was enormously wealthy, he didn't have some of the simpler things in life that were far more important to her.

"How did you ever get to be friends with Cade if you grew up without associating with him—or am I asking too many questions?"

"No, you're not," he answered, his voice remote and casual. "I think I mentioned we both played football in high school so we were thrown together a lot. We got to be friends, and he introduced me to his brothers. All of us played ball. Our parents were out of the picture a lot at that age, and we all became friends. When we got to know each other, none of them had any hostile feelings toward me, and I didn't have any toward them."

"That's great, Blake," she said, glad that he'd found those relationships even though his father hadn't acknowledged him. "I think your father made a huge mistake when he cut you out of his life."

"I certainly thought he did," Blake said lightly, smiling at her. "Enough about the dad I don't even know. So who's the guy in your life, Sierra? Do you have anything serious?"

"Nothing serious, and there's really no guy right now. Since I moved back and started working with the nonprofit, I'm so busy. I have a few friends who go out together on Saturday nights, but most of my time is spent with family. There's no one special. There sort of isn't time right now."

"I can understand that," he said, stretching out his long legs. "Ditto for my life. I have friends, but I'm busy and I travel for work. I figure someday that will all change, but right now, I'm deeply involved in my business. These are the years to build a career."

She smiled. "I think that last is a bit of advice directed at me in particular."

"I try not to lecture, but yes, it is. I'll never understand the choices you've made. You could have invested your time, energy and money in a business that would grow and hold value. Instead, you've invested in people—you'll never know if they've done the right thing with what you've given them. They may not even be grateful."

"I don't feel that way about my work. I guess you don't understand mine and I don't understand yours," she said lightly, but meaning every word. "So you have the biggest and best chain of luxury hotels. Will they keep you happy when you're not working? Will they entertain you? No family, no love, no companions, no laughter and fun. All you have are hotels and money. Makes no sense to me."

"I told you—this won't go on forever. I'm young, energetic and ambitious, and I want to build my chain of hotels now. There's time for love and laughter later when I have a fortune. I have moments when I enjoy myself and the others in my life. I know how to have a good time. Let's take last night for instance—"

"Never mind," she interrupted hastily and shook her head, smiling. "I remember last night without you bringing it up again. No matter how much we talk about our views, I doubt we'll ever understand each other."

"Maybe not," he stated, leaning closer and lowering his voice. "But that doesn't mean we can't have a great time together or become friends. There are times when I enjoy life to the fullest, and I suspect you do also."

Tingles raced through her as she saw the hot desire blazing in his brown eyes.

"I'm amazed you took tonight off from work and social appearances," she said, knowing he had a very active social life that was chronicled in papers and Texas magazines.

"I can forget completely about work when I want to," he said quietly, his voice dropping another note. He stood and closed the distance between them, grasping her wrist lightly to pull her to her feet.

Startled, she gazed up at him as his arm circled her waist and he leaned close to kiss away what she had been about to say.

Her heart thudded the instant his mouth covered hers. For a fleeting moment she started to push against him and step away, but then she was lost in sensation, spiraling away in a kiss that made her heart race.

Hot kisses made her want more as she ran her hands across his strong shoulders. When his palm drifted lightly over her breast, she gasped with pleasure and strained for his touch.

She didn't know how long they kissed. She was lost in him, his hands moving over her until she felt his fingers tugging at her blouse. Holding his wrist, she looked up at him. "Let's back up," she whispered, trying to catch her breath while she stepped out of his embrace. "This isn't why I'm here."

"You're the one who told me I'm missing out. That I need to learn how to really enjoy life. I can't think of a better way to enjoy it."

She walked away from him, straightening her clothes. Then, with space between them, she turned to face him. "Let's enjoy the conversation tonight. We can get to know each other."

"You're ending some of the sexiest kisses I've ever experienced. Or maybe you don't find them so sexy."

"I'm not answering that because you're pushing me into more kisses."

"It was just a statement—nothing more."

"Do we sit and talk, or do we say good-night and I go to my suite?" she asked.

"We sit and talk," he answered, taking a deep breath. "As a matter of fact, let's get a cold drink. What would you like?"

"I'll have iced tea," she said, and watched him move to a bar and fix her drink. She crossed to perch on a barstool as he worked. She felt as if they both needed a moment to get away from the past few minutes. "So tell me more about who you see staying in these rooms in this new wing?"

He smiled, and she knew he guessed her efforts to shift their attention back to business. "I see myself staying there. It could become easy to see you staying if you wanted. Would you like that?"

She laughed softly. "I will not be staying in your new wing and you know it. If you don't want to talk about that, tell me about your newest hotel."

"A twenty-story tower in Orlando," he said, opening a beer for himself and walking around to motion to her. "Let's go sit where it's comfortable. C'mon, we'll go inside now. It's chilly this evening."

When she sat in a tall, brown leather chair, he pulled another closer to her. They had a small table between them. He took a sip of his beer. She drank some tea, and then turned slightly toward him.

"The hotel in New York that I was hired to do was close to one of your father's hotels. I'm surprised to hear you don't see or talk to him, because your hotels are so close. I figured you worked together, or even each owned a share of the other one's chain. That must not be the case."

"No, it definitely isn't," he said so quietly that a chill went down her spine. A subtle change came over him, giving him a hard, cold look.

"Your father's hotel was older, so it was built first," she said.

"Yes, it was." As he gazed at her, she realized he had built near his father's hotel on purpose.

"Do you have any other hotels close to your father's?"

"Yes, as a matter of fact. And yes, I've built by his hotels on purpose."

Shocked, she stared at him. "That sounds as if you are competing. Is this a battle between the two of you? Does he ever build close to a hotel you already have?"

"No, he doesn't."

"So, it's only you building where you will give him competition," she said, looking at him intently. "He's so successful—aren't you making it more difficult for yourself? Competition goes both ways."

"I hope I've done a better job than he has, and frankly, I hope I've made a dent in his hotel business. My hotels are bigger, newer, have more amenities and are more luxurious, so I'm sure you've got the picture—I intend to put my father out of the hotel business," Blake said quietly. "I'm building an empire that I want to make larger than my father's. It is a competition I intend to win."

She stared at him. "You're doing this because of the past—because he left you when you were a baby," she said, unable to imagine that life mission. "You're out for revenge." He intended to get even with his father for old wrongs. The idea was so removed from her way of life, she could only stare at him as if she had never seen anyone like him.

"You're bent on revenge—the absolute opposite of all that I hope to accomplish," she whispered without realizing she had spoken aloud. "You'll ruin your life, Blake."

Four

"Nonsense," Blake answered easily. "My father has billions. I won't hurt him, because he has other endeavors and a fortune that I can't possibly diminish significantly. Nor do I want to."

"Then what's the purpose? Why would you spend millions, your time and your energy in pursuit of something destructive that can't possibly help you or him?" They viewed the world so differently. She realized again that she would never understand Blake.

"I want him to know that he has a son who exists, who is a good businessman and who can do a better job at some things than he can. Hotels are only one part of his fortune. My chain isn't a big deal to him, though they are good business for me."

"That makes it seem even more futile and a waste of your time."

"No. My hotels are making a tidy sum for me. My hotels will pay your salary."

"I'm glad there's something besides revenge as a motivation," she said, still shocked to discover his purpose.

Her gaze swept over his thick black hair, straight nose, penetrating eyes, firm jaw and wide mouth. Her heart skipped a beat as she recalled their kisses last night. He was so handsome, so appealing, yet so very wrong in seeking revenge.

She knew that no matter what was happening between them, after this job, she would tell him goodbye, go back to her routine and never see him again. They had no common ground, no part of their lives they could share. Sexy appeal and hot kisses were not the foundation of solid relationships.

Though her body might try to convince her differently, this was a man she did not want in her life. As she studied him, he leaned closer, moving his chair until their arms touched. Blake brushed her cheek lightly with his warm fingers. She shivered, momentarily forgetting their differences, responding to the feathery contact.

"See what I can do," he said softly. He placed his fingers lightly on her throat and raised his eyebrows. "This between us goes beyond our differences. When we touch, the world and our differences don't even matter."

"Yes, they do. Maybe for a short time we can forget

them, but they're real and stronger than thrills from kissing." She took a deep breath, trying to recall why she needed to pull back from him. "I thought you said you're close to your half brothers. You'll hurt them if you hurt your father."

Blake smiled at her. "No, I won't. They know what I'm doing and they know I will never do any real damage to my father. It's a point of pride. And, frankly, my hotels are making money for me. Our father has ignored all his sons to some degree. They all know what I'm doing, and they don't care. He's hurt them, maybe more than he's hurt me, because he gave them more hope that he would be in their lives."

"Is he close with their mother?"

"They're friendly. They speak. My mom and dad are definitely not friendly. He cut her out of his life abruptly when he cut me out. She hasn't spoken to him since I was three or four years old," he said, taking a pin out of Sierra's hair.

"He has remained in Cade's life, and in the lives of his other sons and sees them once or twice a year, but he was never much of a father. Financially, he provided for them, but they all went to boarding schools and got little of his attention or time."

"That's entirely different from my family or how I grew up," she said, catching his hand where it was wrapped in her hair. "You probably shouldn't do that," she whispered, aware of his fingers and the slight tugs on her scalp, of his dark gaze on her.

"Be thankful you didn't grow up the way we did," Blake said in a cynical tone. "All his sons—all of us—

are wealthy in our own right, and my half brothers will inherit more wealth from him. I'm not taking any of that away from them. What I'm doing is like a flea bite on a dog—annoying, yet meaningless to my father. It only means something to me."

"Perhaps, but you're aiming all your energy at revenge," she said, horrified by the current goal in his life, and how readily he admitted it. "We're total opposites," she said, thinking about what he was telling her while at the same time aware of his fingers moving in her hair, taking it down, letting her locks tumble over her shoulders.

"I suppose we are, and I guess that's why it's so difficult for me to understand why you gave up your interior design career. You have a master's degree. How can you toss that aside? That took you years, and a lot of work, to achieve. You could make a fortune, make a name for yourself—why throw that away?"

"Because what I'm doing now is more important to me. There are people in the world who just need a little help. There are animals that are abandoned and hurt. That's what's important to me."

"I think you'll have regrets."

She shook her head. "I don't think so. I'm just amazed at the choices you've made. Maybe someday you'll rethink what you're doing."

He leaned close. "Maybe I will, or perhaps you can convince me to do so," he said in a sexy, coaxing voice that made her think about hot kisses and forget all about careers and revenge. "Want to take a shot at reforming me?" he whispered, brushing his lips over her ear, fanning her desire.

"I can't convince you to do anything," she whispered.

"You'd be surprised how easily you can convince me to do some things," he whispered back, leaning a fraction closer while his gaze dropped to her mouth. She could barely get her breath.

"Blake, stick to business." Could he tell her heart was pounding? She should move away from him, but she was immobile, held by light kisses and feathery caresses. "Blake…"

His mouth covered hers, and his fingers combed into her hair, pulling her closer as he kissed her—a hot, passionate kiss that drove everything from her thoughts except desire. She wound her arms around his neck, forgot her resolutions to keep her distance, no longer cared if he sought revenge on the father who abandoned him. For the moment, heat poured into her and she wanted his arms holding her tightly against him.

Blake picked her up, placing her in his lap. He leaned over her, shifting to cradle her against his shoulder while he continued to kiss her senseless.

Her fingers played over him, running across his broad shoulders, down his thick biceps, across his broad chest. How could he turn her world topsy-turvy, making her forget reason and toss aside caution, causing her to risk her heart when he could so easily break it to pieces? She knew she should stop him. But it was long past the time to say no.

Instead, she held him tightly, kissing him wildly, pouring herself into kisses and caresses while she trembled with the need that he built as he caressed her in turn.

As he tugged at her buttons, she wriggled away and stood, gasping for breath. He came to his feet. His shirt was undone, open to reveal his sculpted chest.

"We should say good-night, Blake."

"I'll go with you to your room," he said.

"No. I have some reading to do, and I want to get my notes in order."

He leaned close to whisper in her ear. "You're scared to stay down here with me for another hour tonight. You won't work on your notes."

She laughed softly. "You might be right. You're a physically appealing man, Blake Callahan—something I didn't consider when I took this job."

"Physically appealing," he repeated. "That may keep me up all night, as well as the thought of more kisses."

"It's been an interesting day and evening, and the dinner was grand. Thanks."

"You're welcome. I'm enjoying having you here."

"I'm enjoying being here. You have a beautiful home."

"It's going to be even more in line with what I want when this wing is finished. I'm ready for a change."

"Have you thought about a change that might go deeper than rooms and furniture? Perhaps turning your energy and focus in another direction?"

"I do believe you are trying to reform me," he said, looking amused as he ran his fingers lightly over her shoulder and smiled.

She couldn't resist, and smiled back. "Doesn't hurt

to try. Have you ever thought about just calling your father and trying to make peace? You're a grown man now. He might be happy to meet you and talk to you. Have you spoken to him since you became an adult?"

Blake tugged a lock of her long hair gently and then curled it in his fingers. "You're trying to reconcile me and my dad. That won't happen at this point in my life. I've tried to talk to him only once. I was three or four, and he had to talk to my mother. A limo waited, and when he came out, I tried to get his attention. My mother stepped out, carried me back into the house and closed the door. He never said a word to me that I remember."

"Blake, that's dreadful. He missed out on so much that he can never get back."

"That isn't how he saw it, I'm sure. The court left my mother financially well off, so I had a good education, but my father was never any part of my life. What's worse, he was only a small part of his other sons' lives, even though he definitely played dad to them. I told you, I knew where I stood. They didn't. They kept hoping for more from him. By the time I was five, I knew better than to expect even a hello."

"That's sad," she said, thinking again about her father and how much a part of his children's lives he had always been, and now how good he was with his grandchildren. "Your father cut so much joy out of his life."

Blake smiled at her. "You live in a rosy world, Sierra."

"No, I don't. I see people every day who are hurting and have needs—health, income, relationships—their situation isn't rosy. Children adapt, so all of you accepted not seeing him as part of your lives, but he cut himself off from love from all of you."

"How did we get back on the subject of my dad? Damn. There are better things to talk about. And a lot better things to do," he said in a thicker voice as his gaze lowered to her mouth.

Her heart drummed. She wanted his kiss, even after spending the past hour learning that he was a man bent on revenge.

She shouldn't kiss him. She shouldn't even stay the rest of the week on his ranch. She could work from her office in Kansas City. She was set up here with all kinds of electronic equipment and could work all week undisturbed, but here she would see Blake. With the attraction that burned between them, she should be packing her bags now.

If only she could remember how opposite they were and not be dazzled by hot kisses, flirting and sexy smiles.

If only she didn't respond to his slightest touch, to just being near him. A week and then they'd part—surely for one week she could keep her heart and head intact.

As she looked up into midnight eyes, she knew she was making promises to herself she couldn't keep.

She lowered her gaze to his mouth and then looked back up to his brown eyes.

"Sierra," he said quietly, sliding his arms lightly around her waist and leaning down to kiss her.

Standing on tiptoe, she kissed him in return, shutting off all thoughts of packing and leaving. She just let go and enjoyed his kiss.

Soon enough they would say goodbye permanently, and a few kisses tonight wouldn't matter at all.

His arms tightened as he leaned over her and his kiss deepened, becoming more passionate. He ran one hand through her hair, down her back and then over her bottom, under the hem of her skirt and along her thigh.

His warm hand, barely stroking her, drifted up along her leg and then moved between her thighs. Gasping, she clung to him while she thrust her hips against him. He was aroused, hard and ready.

"Blake, slow down. We're going too fast for me."

"We have something here, and we both like it," he replied gruffly.

"Kisses aren't enough," she whispered, clearing her throat. "Goodnight, Blake." She stood on tiptoe to brush a kiss on his cheek.

"Sure you don't want to come to my suite, have another drink?"

She laughed. "I'm sure, but good try. Such a subtle approach," she added, shaking her head.

He grinned. "I keep waiting and hoping you'll ask me into your suite. I'm good company at night."

She laughed. "I'm sure you're fabulous company, and I know you have the best kisses this side of the Atlantic Ocean, but I have to say good-night." Smiling, she brushed his cheek with another kiss and went up to her room.

Picking up her phone, she saw two messages from Bert. He had worked late, which wasn't unusual. Far more than any of her family, Bert worried about her constantly, and she had answered half a dozen text messages since she'd landed on Sunday. Sending him another reassuring text, she placed her phone on a bedside table and hoped she didn't hear anything more from him until tomorrow.

Long after she went to bed, she lay in the dark, thinking about all Blake had told her about his dad. There was a tough, hard side to Blake. She could see why. She didn't think he had chosen the right way to deal with his father, but she could understand his anger.

She sighed because she was certain Blake would have no part in calling his father or doing any such grown-up thing. He was bent on revenge, and she couldn't sway him. She had no intention of sticking around to try, either. Blake was not the man for her, so with their wild chemistry, she was running risks every time she was with him.

Finish this job for him, go home and never look back. That's what she needed to do. She didn't want a broken heart, didn't want to fall in love with a man who would spend his life on revenge, a cynical man who was set on getting even with his father instead of trying to seek reconciliation.

Tossing and turning through the night, she tried to get Blake out of her thoughts. For the majority of the night, though, she was unsuccessful.

On Tuesday Lucinda and Eli arrived, and Sierra spent a busy day working with them as they took measurements and discussed possibilities.

That night Blake returned from his work out on the ranch and met with them in the informal sitting room, where he served glasses of wine and they talked. She was surprised when Eli and Blake found they had favorite artists in common: David Hockney and Gerhard Richter. They discussed art, architecture and furniture design. Eli left to get a portfolio to show Blake. It surprised her how attentive and engaged Blake was throughout the evening. Blake even asked about Lucinda's husband and three-year-old daughter.

During another delicious dinner of salmon, green beans, a salad and hot rolls, Blake smiled at Lucinda as he passed a crystal bowl of strawberry jam. "Next time you come—and Sierra said you and Eli will be back later in the project—we'll have barbecue. I'm taking Sierra Thursday night to eat at a place that has some of the best."

"I've been to Texas before and I love barbecue," Eli said. "I'll be counting on that."

Blake was charming with his new guests. This polite, friendly evening was so different from her first evening with him. Again, she wondered at the response they stirred in each other, something she had never experienced with anyone else.

With Lucinda and Eli present, there was more talk after dinner about various artists and buildings that Blake liked, and they all looked again at the new wing.

When they said good-night and thanked Blake, Sierra went to her room, turning in early and going over notes she had made during the day.

On Wednesday, Lucinda and Eli flew back to New York. Sierra returned to poring over catalogues.

Blake continued to charm her, talking about suggestions Eli had made that he liked. After dinner they returned to the new wing while she went over some of the suggested changes. Throughout it all they managed to remain professional.

On Thursday she couldn't keep her mind on her work. She had agreed to go to dinner with Blake tonight. Tomorrow she would fly home for a family picnic that had become a spring tradition, growing in size each year. But tonight…

Sierra stopped work at four to get ready for the evening out. The minute she had accepted Blake's invitation to eat barbecue, she'd complicated her life more. She should've turned him down, but the words wouldn't come. She *wanted* to go out with him.

In spite of all her warnings to herself, she spent more than an hour getting ready to go, finally settling on jeans, boots and a red cotton shirt. As she dressed, she felt eager to spend the evening with Blake, knowing she would have a good time and a fabulous dinner.

And later—her thoughts stopped there. She wouldn't think about his kisses, or how she should resist them. After brushing her hair vigorously, she let it fall free. She picked up a white Resistol, and with one final look in the mirror, she left to find Blake.

When she entered the library, her breath caught. Looking more handsome and sexier than ever, Blake stood across the room. He wore a brown Western shirt that complemented his good looks. His tight jeans fit slender hips and long legs, and the cowboy boots added to his height. The instant her gaze met his, she was hopelessly lost, dazzled by the prospect of a fun evening out with him.

"Wow, lady, you look great," he said, enthusiasm filling his husky voice as his gaze swept over her again. "Every guy in the county will want to meet you."

"You wanted me to meet the locals."

"Yeah, so I did," he said, still studying her and sounding as if he was thinking more about something other than his answer. "Ready? Let's go get one of the best barbecue dinners you'll ever eat."

As the sun cast longer shadows, Blake drove to Marvina, a small town that looked only half a dozen blocks long. In the center of what had to be the main street was a restaurant with a red neon sign declaring the place to be Barney Jack's Bar-B-Q.

Inside they were seated in a booth in a dark corner. There was a dance floor, but no musicians yet, and no dancers as people talked and ate, and busy wait staff scurried back and forth with trays heaped with baskets of shoestring fries, wrapped sandwiches and bottles of beer or frosty mugs of iced tea.

"If this barbecue is as good as it smells, then it will live up to all you said."

"It's the best ever."

"You lived in town, so when did you get this love of ranching and the cowboy life?"

"My maternal grandfather was a rancher. I inherited his spread. I spent a good part of my childhood there and I loved it. I loved him," Blake said. In the dim light she couldn't see any difference in his expression, but his tone of voice changed, and she suspected his grandfather had been important to him.

"So, you did have family who loved you in addition to your mom."

"Yep, my mother's parents meant a lot to me. I never met my paternal grandparents, and both died when I was in high school." As Blake talked, she watched two men step up on the stage. As they spread out to start playing a fiddle and bass, couples moved to the dance floor and in seconds dancers circled the floor in a brisk two-step.

A waiter appeared to take their order, and as soon as he left Blake slid out of the booth and held out his hand. "Let's dance," he said.

She started to protest, listening to the music and watching the few dancers. But she took his hand and stood up. In seconds they were on the dance floor, keeping time with the music. For a few minutes, it was fun to stop thinking about problems and differences and tomorrows—to just enjoy the moment dancing with a tall, sexy rancher who set her heart fluttering and would kiss her later.

For tonight, she intended to enjoy life, enjoy the Texas barbecue and enjoy Blake.

After one more dance, he said, "We should have our dinner."

"I can't wait," she answered, smiling at him, aware of her hand still enclosed in his. He took her arm as they walked back to their table where their meals waited.

The inviting smell made her mouth water in anticipation. Taking the first bite, she closed her eyes. She opened them to find him watching her. "Blake, that is the best barbecue. I didn't think any could be as good as in Kansas City, but that's right there with it. It's fantastic."

"So now you have a brand new experience—the night I introduced you to Texas barbecue."

She laughed. "Thank goodness you did."

"Hey, bro," came a deep voice as a tall, dark-haired man slid into their booth beside Blake.

They shook hands while the newcomer looked at her and smiled with a flash of straight white teeth.

"Sierra, meet my half brother Cade. Cade, this is Sierra Benson, the fabulous interior designer."

She laughed as she shook hands with Cade Callahan. "I don't know about fabulous, and that isn't my career now. I'm with a nonprofit, Brigmore Charities."

"Very good, Sierra. Maybe you can reform this guy."

She laughed with him, thinking there was a strong physical resemblance in their black hair, straight noses and prominent cheekbones. Cade's broad-brimmed black hat was pushed to the back of his head. He wore black boots and a black shirt, the top buttons undone. His wavy hair was a tangle, falling onto his wide forehead, and he had a streak of mischief in his blue eyes that made her feel he might be more fun loving and less serious than Blake.

"Have a beer with us," Blake urged.

"Will do," Cade said, smiling at Sierra. "I hear you're the best interior designer in the USA."

She laughed, and he grinned along with Blake, who

shrugged. "Yes, she is. She's modest, so I'll answer for her. Wait until you see the new wing on my house and you'll agree with me. We can make a bet on it now," Blake said. "Best interior designer out there."

"Will both of you stop," she said, smiling at them as they grinned. "I'll tell you what's best—it's this barbecue and these curly fries."

"We'll all agree on that one," Blake said. "Where's our baby brother?"

"He's around here someplace. He'll join us. Ah, here he is," Cade said, and stood to face another tall, dark-haired Callahan who also had blue eyes.

"Sierra, meet our baby brother, Gabe Callahan. Gabe, meet the famous interior designer, Sierra Benson."

"I'm glad to meet you, Gabe Callahan," she said, smiling at him as he shook her hand. She noticed that she didn't have that same volatile reaction to any other Callahan that she'd had with Blake, which was a relief.

They sat and talked, including her in their conversation until Cade stood. "It's dance time. Sierra, would you care to dance?"

She nodded, and she and Cade slid out of the booth.

On the dance floor, she turned and they began circling, doing the two-step.

She danced the next time with Gabe, and then Blake was her partner again.

He danced her around the floor and gazed into her eyes. She was caught and held, her heartbeat accelerating, desire fanning to life. She wanted to be in his arms. She wanted his kisses, even when she shouldn't. This was her last night with him for a while. She'd be going home and then to New York; he'd be leaving the ranch for Dallas. This was the last time for kisses.

It was after midnight when they climbed back into his truck. She turned slightly to watch him drive. "I had fun tonight, Blake. I haven't been out like that in a long time. And dinner was fabulous."

"I thought you'd like that barbecue. It was fun. It's unusual that both my brothers were there. I think they wanted to meet you. They didn't want to miss the opportunity to meet one of the world's best interior designers. Particularly the opportunity to dance with you after they found out you are definitely the world's best-looking interior designer."

She laughed. "That is all ridiculous, but I was glad to meet them. I'm amazed how much alike all of you look, having different mothers. It's great you're so compatible."

"We weren't always. Before Cade and I became friends we used to fight. Then we both realized how ridiculous that was, because we really didn't have any reason to dislike each other. Cade doesn't have any more control over how our father treats him than I do. He's just fortunate to be in better favor than I ever was."

"I'm amazed they're understanding about your competition with your father in the hotel business. I looked up some information on the web about your hotels and about his. You have more of them, plus they're bigger, fancier and definitely more luxurious."

"I intend to run him out of the hotel business," Blake said in a quiet voice that carried a cold tone. "I told you, Cade, Gabe and Nathan understand, and they don't ob-

ject. It won't really hurt our father, but it'll annoy the
hell out of him because he's competitive. He doesn't
like me and never has."

"You said he abandoned you when you were a baby.
How could he not like you when you were so young?
That doesn't make sense."

"It was my mother he didn't like, and I was part of
her," Blake answered flatly.

She stared at him in the darkened pickup and thought
again about how different their lives were. She couldn't
understand his drive to get even for something during
his childhood, something that seemed behind him now.
All his efforts were such a waste of energy and talent.
She couldn't keep from thinking about all the people
he could help if he put that energy and those resources
to good use. With the money he used for hotels to com-
pete with his father's, he could instead build shelters,
start reading programs and hire tutors—so many easy,
constructive ways to help less fortunate people.

Blake couldn't understand her way of life, and she
couldn't understand his.

He parked at the rear of his house and stepped out
of the pickup to come around and open her door. His
hands closed on her waist, and he swung her out of the
truck. For an instant he held her up easily as she looked
down into his eyes, and the moment changed. Desire
ignited, hot and intense, as Blake lowered her, pulling
her close and wrapping his arms around her.

They walked into the wide entryway together, moving into a sitting room. Light spilled into the darkened
room from the hallway, and through the floor-to-ceiling

glass they could see the lighted swimming pool. But all she was aware of was Blake, who drew her closer.

Her heart thudded. Her hands were light on his shoulders as she gazed up at him. She was held by a look that made her pulse race. Locked into another electric moment with him, she wanted his kiss.

"This is crazy, Blake."

"It's been a fun night, and it doesn't have to end yet. There's more I want, and so do you," he said softly, his arm circling her waist and pulling her close against him. She slipped her arms around his neck even as she knew she should be pulling away.

All evening Blake had been sexy, fun and appealing. Desire had tugged on her senses for days. Each night their kisses made it impossible to avoid thinking about sleeping with him.

His appeal was physical. They didn't have an emotional connection. With his drive for revenge, he was a man so much the opposite of all she believed in, she couldn't imagine an emotional connection forming between them.

She could have this one night and not lose her heart.

Five

Sierra stopped reasoning with herself as she gazed up at him. Desire was blatant in his dark brown eyes, making her pulse jump. Standing in his arms, she trembled with longing. His arm tightened around her and he leaned closer, his lips brushed lightly, and then his mouth settled, his tongue going deep.

With the first brush of his mouth, her heart thudded. Slipping her arm around his neck, she closed her eyes as she returned his kiss. Passion blazed, making her lean closer. She relished his hard body and his solid muscles against her softness. Why was she so responsive to him and him alone? How could he make her melt with only a glance? Or a brush of his fingers on hers?

Wanting him, too aware they'd be parting soon, she tightened her arms around his neck, letting go of restraints and reason. She pressed against him, wanting to seize the moment. They had an electrifying chemistry that made every glance, every moment together breathtaking and exciting.

He was aroused, ready to make love. With one arm he held her close while his hand roamed down her back, over her bottom and along her thigh. She gasped with pleasure as she ran her hands along his back, tugging his shirt out of his jeans to slip her hands over his bare skin.

She shifted to give him access to the buttons on her shirt, and he twisted them free while he kissed her. She returned his kiss equally passionately.

Showering feathery kisses on her throat, he pushed open her blouse to unfasten her bra. He cupped her breasts, which filled his large hands as he rubbed each nipple. She moaned softly with pleasure. Need for more of him built with each touch. Her hands played over him, unfastening his belt, freeing him.

She ran her fingers over his warm belly, touching his manhood. Her first caress, so faint, made him gasp and shake with loss of control.

As his fingers tugged at her jeans, she leaned back to look at him. His dark gaze consumed her with a need so intense that she shivered. His touch was light and tantalizing, making her want him desperately. Swamped by desire, she wanted his kisses on her, his hands on her, his hard body against her, his heat inside her.

"Blake," she whispered, running her fingers through his hair. "Kiss me," she whispered again, touching her lips to his jaw, feeling the stubble of his beard. She continued, trailing kisses down his chest as her hands moved lower, grasping him to stroke and tease.

"Blake, I'm not protected."

"I'll take care of you," he answered, kissing away her words while he stroked her, his hand caressing her breasts.

He picked her up and carried her to his bedroom, standing her on her feet by the bed and yanking away the covers. As she caressed him, running her hands over his sculpted chest, he opened a drawer to withdraw a condom and put it on before picking her up and placing her on the bed, moving between her legs.

He was hard, breathtakingly handsome with a fit masculine body that was muscled and strong. She arched her hips, wrapping her long legs around him. He came down, his mouth covering hers.

She felt him shift beside her, and then he trailed more kisses down her throat, across each breast, taking his time, his tongue circling first one nipple and then the other before he moved lower. His hand caressed her thighs and moved between her legs.

Kissing her again, he stroked her, driving her to want him more than she had thought possible. Every touch was magic, fiery and building their desire to a feverish pitch. He shifted, his tongue following his fingers, and she cried out in need and pleasure.

"I want you," she whispered, not caring whether he heard or not, just having to say it. "I want you more than anything," she added, barely aware of what she said as his hands rubbed and stroked her, building her need.

She sat up, pushing him down. "You're driving me

wild." She trailed kisses across his belly until she took him in her mouth.

His fingers wound in her hair while his other hand caressed her breast with the lightest of touches. He groaned, sat up and rolled her over as he moved above her. She watched him lower himself to finally enter her slowly, withdrawing as her hips arched beneath him and he thrust into her, filling her, hot and hard.

Sensations rocked her, need consuming her as she moved with him.

He withdrew again, moving slowly, filling her. Her legs locked around his narrow waist while she drowned in sensation.

They moved together wildly, pumping fast in heart-pounding need. She pressed against him, crying out as she reached the pinnacle of her release.

He thrust hard and fast, climaxing with another gasp of pleasure, finally slowing while holding her close.

She clung to him, hot, damp with perspiration and happiness as they slowed. Gasping for breath, their hearts pounding together, she held him tightly. For a few moments she was in a special world, locked in his embrace.

She wanted to hold him tightly and keep the world shut away for the night.

When they were still, she ran her fingers slowly through the crisp, short hair on the back of his neck while he brushed kisses on her throat.

"I don't think I will ever forget this night," she whispered, being blunt and truthful. When he continued with his light kisses, she decided he hadn't heard her.

She knew that she would never forget their love-making, and yet she also knew she had made another mistake with him. She should not have opened herself to this man whose view of the world was so different from hers.

One night of love should not cost her heart. No matter what bond they'd forged with intimacy, she had to forget this night and she should forget him. She hoped she could do that quickly—as soon as this job ended.

She shoved aside her worries and relished holding him while he caressed her in return.

She held fast to the moment. This night was special, and their differences in priorities and philosophies didn't matter right now.

In the light of day, reason would set in and they would go on with their jobs and their lives, and she would eventually get past this night.

When he shifted, she gazed into his dark eyes, which were filled with curiosity.

"Are you sure you have to go home tomorrow?"

"Yes. This picnic is a big deal—it used to be mostly family, but it's grown. Now we invite a lot of people I've worked with, plus people—and children—from one of the shelters."

"Children? As in abandoned?"

"As in orphaned, mostly. Some were runaways and have no home to go back to, and some are from broken homes whose families can't keep them at this time, but they hope to get them back in the future. We sponsor a children's shelter."

She combed a few locks of his hair away from his

face. "Come home with me. See how we live—maybe you'll understand what I do if you'll come meet people."

"I'll be in the way," he said.

"Nonsense. There's no such thing as a stranger."

"Little Miss Do-Good."

"Scared to accept, Blake?"

He gave her a crooked smile. "Why the hell would I be scared to go to a picnic?"

"You might be afraid it will change your lifestyle," she said, teasing him, but also wondering why he wouldn't accept her invitation. "You have time to go. Come home with me. Sunday you can fly back here. C'mon. It won't hurt you to meet my family, the people I work with and the kids. It will broaden your outlook a bit."

She waited while he toyed with long locks of her hair. "Okay," he said, and satisfaction flowed through her. She smiled at him. "You can fly back to Dallas with me and leave from Dallas Monday morning to go to New York. You can fly in my private jet. I have to be in Chicago, so I'll go that far with you. You do that, and I'll go home with you this weekend," he said, studying her. "I want one more night with you in my arms," he whispered, his breath warm on her throat.

As with all his invitations, she was torn between what she should do and what she wanted to do. What was the appeal that Blake held? She had never been attracted to another man the way she was to him—it was purely physical, sexual, lustful—and she couldn't understand it.

"You're arguing with yourself. C'mon, Sierra. This

is a brief moment in your earnest, do-good life. Live a little, darlin', and stay. You'll get me for the weekend, and you can show me some of what you do. I'll see how you live, and you'll be back here to see a little more about how I live. One more day together won't be earth shattering."

She had to smile at him. "You're wicked, Blake. The proverbial bad boy all grown up into a wicked man."

"Then save me. You stay, and I'll go home with you for the weekend, and maybe the visit will transform me into an everlasting do-gooder," he said.

"It would serve you right if that is exactly what happens," she said, staring intently at him. "All right. I'll fly back to Dallas Sunday night, and Monday morning, I leave Dallas for New York. That means canceling my commercial flight."

"You'll get a refund," he said.

"There won't be any privacy at my house," she warned him. "Not only that, everyone will be busy getting ready for the picnic."

"We might find a moment alone. Tell me you don't want more kisses," he said, shifting to look at her mouth and causing her heart to lurch. The joking and lightness of the moment vanished.

His arm tightened around her, pulling her against him while his mouth came down on hers. He kissed her, his tongue stroking hers while his free hand played along her hip and then between her thighs.

Moaning softly, Sierra kissed him in return. She wanted to tell him that he wasn't fair. He had to get his way about everything, but words were lost, and in minutes her thought processes scrambled. All she wanted was Blake—his hands, his mouth and his body. She wanted his kisses, caresses and his lovemaking. She wanted him inside her, thick, hot and hard. With a gasp, she shoved him down on the bed and shifted over him, straddling him, shaking her head to get her hair away from her face.

His warm hands cupped her breasts, and his thumbs drew lazy circles over each taut bud.

"Ah, darlin', you set me on fire," he said.

Barely hearing him, she showered kisses on his throat, feeling his hands moving over her bottom and down the backs of her thighs. Tingles radiated from his touch and desire flashed into a raging need. She wanted him—his arms, his hard body, his energy.

"Where you're concerned, I don't have a backbone," she whispered, wondering how she could possibly be so attracted to someone so wrong for her.

"I thought you had a backbone," he whispered. "Let me see." His fingers slid down her spine, and then his hand spread lightly as he rubbed her bottom and she gasped, thrusting her hips against him.

He rolled her over, moving on top while he kissed her, and she was lost to his lovemaking for the rest of the night.

Friday afternoon Blake gazed out the window of his private jet at the broad channel of the Red River as they flew north toward Kansas. A silver ribbon of water followed the curving banks.

Blake figured the weekend would be spent meeting

people and watching Sierra chat with those she had helped. Tagging along was fine with him if it meant she would return to Texas with him. She'd promised only Sunday night, but that was better than telling her goodbye in Kansas City and each of them going different places.

At the thought of another night in bed with her, his pulse jumped. For a night with Sierra, he could easily sit through a family picnic.

He still couldn't understand the hot attraction that burned between them, but he wasn't questioning it any longer. He wanted her in his bed, and he thought about her constantly when he wasn't with her. Of all the women he had ever known, he would have guessed that she would have been one of the least likely to generate this fiery, irresistible appeal.

Not only were they complete opposites, he couldn't understand her outlook on life or her lifestyle any more than she could understand his. She actively disliked his way of thinking, and he thought she was throwing away her talent and her future by taking a low-paying, thankless job that would be endless work with few rewards.

Next to him, she gazed out the window. She took his breath sometimes. When he had danced with her, just a two-step, she'd had a sway to her hips that was tantalizing. He wanted to kiss her slender throat. She responded to any touch, even the most casual kiss.

He was ready for Sunday night in Dallas.

To get his mind off the temptation of Sierra, he tried to think about her family and get their names straight. He couldn't imagine growing up the way she had—a house filled with kids who brought other kids home with them. And providing for a family on a minister's salary had to have been a struggle, but Sierra never sounded as if it had been and she didn't particularly care about money. She was truly indifferent to Blake's wealth, which was something he couldn't say for any other woman he had met.

Yes, Sierra was different. She had him willing to meet family and spend the weekend in separate rooms just for one more night with her.

Once during the evening, when the noise level was high, Blake gazed at the chaos around him. Three toddlers played with blocks while kids ranging in age from elementary school to middle school were occupied with electronic gadgets. Women bustled in the kitchen, getting big platters of food cooked and ready for Saturday. The delicious smell of baked beans was enticing, even after a big dinner.

He helped her dad and two brothers load games, balls, rackets, bats and equipment into two pickups. Her family amazed him. They worked together and they had a good time, getting things done without tempers flying in spite of kids needing attention and toys breaking.

Most of all, he noticed her mother and dad, who worked efficiently at their jobs. Watching them, it was obvious they cared deeply for each other and had a strong marriage. They were constantly aware of each other and worked as smoothly as two trapeze artists high above an audience. And they were amazingly polite to each other and all around them. It made him realize that he had never been around an older couple who were in love and happily married.

He hadn't ever seen a family like this one. Blake's half brothers had a mother who loved them, but she had divorced their dad. She was often gone, and when she was home she seldom had male guests.

Some of Blake's friends had two parents who seemed happy with each other, but they didn't have the warmth and love that radiated in subtle ways from Sierra's parents.

In this big family, everyone seemed to love and care about everyone else and be genuinely welcoming to their guests.

Blake began to see why money was not of the utmost importance to Sierra. She had a supportive family. They were all there for each other, and she was grounded in that assurance. His gaze shifted to her as she came out of the house, her arms loaded with equipment. He hurried to take it from her, his hands brushing hers.

"I can get this stuff. This is heavy. I'll come get the next load."

"That's it for now," she said. "Thanks for helping."

"You have an interesting family," he said, wishing they were alone so he could give her a hug. "They're all very likable people."

"Thank you. I think they're great, and we'll all have fun tomorrow. You'll see."

A little boy came around the corner of the house, crying loudly.

"Someone is unhappy," she said. "I'll go help." She

went to pick him up. Blake had no idea which child he was or to whom he belonged.

As he continued to help load the truck, he watched Sierra wipe away the child's tears, set him on his feet and hold his hand. Whatever she told him brought a smile to his face, and together they disappeared into the house.

By ten o'clock that night, when most of Sierra's family had said good-night and gone to their own homes, he sat alone with her in the big family room of her parents' two-story house. He smiled at her and shook his head. "I'll never get all the names. We'll go back to Texas before I have half of them figured out."

She smiled at him—an enticing smile that flashed with warmth. "You're being modest. You did pretty well tonight. You were a hit with my dad, talking about the early days of the railroads—he loves trains and has a library of train books. I'll show you tomorrow. Right now, I just want to sit and relax."

"We can't do what I want to do, but sitting and relaxing will be okay."

"I'm not asking what you want to do, and don't tell me."

"I didn't tell you, but I think you know. I just wanted to hear you say you want to do the same thing."

She narrowed her eyes. "You're shameless."

"No, I'm fun," he answered, and her smile widened as she shook her head. "You were a hit with them tonight—even the youngest. He followed you around. I'm surprised. You've said you're never around kids."

"I have the magic touch with kids and dogs and beautiful women. Come sit closer and I'll show you," he said, having fun flirting with her.

"I'm staying right where I am. The 'magic touch with kids,' huh? When are you ever around kids?"

"Tonight," he answered. She shook her head.

"You'll be around them tomorrow. That's for sure. We'll have a lot of people at the picnic."

"You had a lot of people here tonight. Too bad Cade couldn't spend an evening like this with your family. He needs to see a family like yours and know that love and harmony are possible."

"Cade? He seems happy enough."

"All his life, Cade has vowed he will never marry because our father inflicted so much grief on so many people. He wasn't a good father to his children or a good husband to his wives. He had a string of mistresses, and I know some of them were as unhappy with him as his ex-wives were. Financially, he was an enormous success, and that's what you read about him, but with close friends and family he was a dismal failure. Cade is scared of ending up like him."

"That's ridiculous because Cade is such a nice person. At least, he seemed nice when I met him."

"He is nice, and I've told you he has a warped view of marriage because of our dad. I can't convince him. Seeing your family might. I don't know how your folks cope with all the commotion."

"This was just a regular weekend night, except for cooking and packing stuff into the pickups to get ready for tomorrow."

"I'm surprised you ever left here for New York."

"I was ambitious, eager to see what I could do in interior design—it was an exciting time. I accomplished a lot until finally I reached a point where I wanted to be here and work here. Life changes."

Relaxing, he stretched out his legs. He wanted to sit close beside her, but he knew she would prefer he stayed right where he was. To his surprise, he enjoyed just sitting with her the way they were now. Twice he heard the deep chimes of a grandfather clock from the hallway, and he knew the hour was growing late, but he didn't want to leave her.

When she stood, he came to his feet. "It's late, and tomorrow will come early."

He helped her switch off lights until there was only the dim glow from the stairs. He grasped her upper arm and turned her to face him. "Come here just a minute," he said, wrapping his arm around her to draw her close and kiss her before she could protest.

The moment his mouth covered hers, she melted against him. He held her tightly, kissing her, wanting her and wishing they were alone, back on his ranch.

When she stepped out of his embrace she was as breathless as he was. Her big blue eyes were wide, filled with so much desire that he couldn't get his breath and had to struggle to control the urge to take her upstairs.

He wanted to kiss her again, but he let her go. He couldn't understand the reaction he had to her. Seeing her family, her background, should have emphasized their differences and how foreign her life was to him. With her positive view of the world, she shouldn't have been able to hold his interest more than a few hours. Instead, she not only held his interest, she set him on fire and had ruined his sleep for nights.

"It's late," she said softly, walking away. He caught up with her and walked in silence to her bedroom door, where she faced him.

"Goodnight. I'll see you shortly after sunrise." She stepped inside and closed the door without waiting for him to reply.

Blake lay awake in the dark for a long time in a room that had to have been shared by both of her brothers because it still held high school trophies and memorabilia. He couldn't sleep. He wanted Sierra in his arms. How long would it take him to forget her after she finished the job for him and went home?

If he had asked himself that question two weeks earlier, he would have thought it would take a day to move on, take someone else out and forget Sierra. He knew better than that now. In her quiet way, she had ensnared him. For the first time, he realized he had finally met a woman who might be difficult for him to say goodbye to.

Maybe if he could get his fill of sex with her, it would be easier to walk away. He'd be happy to test that theory when they returned to Dallas.

Saturday was a warm spring day. Sierra walked into the kitchen as her mom checked on biscuits in the oven and her dad scrambled eggs. Dressed in cutoffs and a blue knit shirt, her sister Ginger set the table, while her sister Lenora helped her niece, two-year-old Penny, with her oatmeal. To Sierra's surprise, Blake poured orange juice into glasses on a tray to carry to the table. As he looked up, she drew a deep breath. In tight jeans that emphasized his narrow waist and long legs, Blake made her pulse jump. His brown knit shirt revealed muscles hardened from ranch work.

"Good morning. I'm here to help," she announced. As his gaze swept over her, she was suddenly aware of her cutoffs and clinging red knit shirt. She tried to ignore the tingles his one glance caused.

"Great," her dad said, holding out a spoon. "Come stir these eggs, and I'll see about the strawberries."

From that moment on, she had little chance for more than a "good morning" to Blake, but she was acutely aware of him as he moved around the kitchen helping with breakfast.

"Where are the guys? Are they still asleep?" she asked. "Blake, why are you the only male besides Dad who is cooking?"

"Rita and Damon's car broke down, and your brothers have gone to help them," Homer Benson said, slicing washed strawberries. "One of the pickups has a flat, and Roger and Jason are changing it. Blake volunteered to go help, and they told him to stay to help me."

"Well, aren't you nice," she said, smiling at Blake. "Thank you."

"Happy to help," he said, his words friendly even though his dark eyes held unmistakable desire.

She stirred fluffy yellow eggs, and they soon had breakfast on the table as her other nieces and nephews began to appear. They sat to eat breakfast, and Blake held a chair for her, his hands brushing her lightly as he helped her before sitting next to her.

All through breakfast, she was aware of him at her side. The family included him in their conversation as they always did with any visitors. Soon her brothers, sister, brothers-in-law and more kids joined them.

Sierra was busy the rest of the day, but she searched for Blake in the crowd, hoping he was enjoying himself. At one point, he had joined in helping with games, participating with the kids. He seemed to truly care about the children and the people around him. His actions were so different from what he said in their conversations. Maybe making money wasn't his sole focus in life. But that knowledge didn't make it easier to resist his appeal. In fact, she was getting more involved with him.

She'd hoped he would get a glimmer of what his money was doing. She hoped this weekend would interest Blake in the agency, in her father's church and in the people whose lives he could change. And he could so easily contribute. She was certain he supported charities, but she was equally certain his support was simply writing checks and letting others handle the donations for him. She wanted him to get up close and personally involved with the kids and people his money helped.

They hadn't been at the picnic five minutes when Bert appeared with Nan beside him. "We're so happy you're here for this picnic," Nan said. "And you brought Blake Callahan. That's great."

"I think he'll enjoy being here."

"How's the job going, Sierra? Do you think you're halfway through yet?" Bert asked. "We miss you here."

"The job is going well, but I miss the agency. No, I'm not halfway through yet, but I'll be home for good before you know it. Bert, will you set this basket on the long table with the red plastic cover? Nan, you can come help me over here."

"Sure," Nan said, smiling broadly. "Bert worries all day, every day about you," she said as soon as they walked away. "Nothing new there. I want to say hello to Blake."

"Say hello and whatever else you want," Sierra said, smiling at her assistant, aware Blake had local women and some of the teenage girls fluttering around him. In minutes, Nan stood talking to Blake while Sierra carried another basket of food to a table.

Along with all her family, Blake helped cook burgers. By two, soccer, badminton and baseball were in progress.

Mid-afternoon found her and Blake helping with scorekeeping and coaching kids playing baseball. Between innings, Blake paused beside her. "There's a kid sitting over there who doesn't play. He's one who hasn't played anything so far, and he doesn't engage with the others. Is there a physical reason, or something else? He's sitting on the bench with the kids, but he doesn't talk to them, and they leave him alone, too."

"That's William. Maybe you can relate a little, although he's on a different financial level. His dad abandoned them at birth, and his mom was killed in a car wreck when he was five. He's eight now, and he lives in the shelter because he doesn't have relatives."

"What do you do with a kid like that?"

"Just be friends with him. I'm not a social worker, though there is one who works at the shelter. William doesn't make friends like some kids do."

She patted Blake's wrist. "See, this is where some of your donation will help. We may be able to get more resources for these kids."

"I think he needs more than what money can buy."

"I won't argue that one," she said, surprised Blake would acknowledge that truth.

"One item your money bought is the automatic batting machine the kids are enjoying today. It sends the ball straight to them, and they have a better chance of getting a hit because when little kids pitch, the ball is all over the place. You see their smiles? We have lots to thank you for."

"Sure," he said, gazing solemnly at her before shifting his attention back to the boy who sat on the bench, scuffing his toe in the dirt. "I hope the money helps get more than a batting machine," Blake said.

He walked away, and when she looked again she was surprised to see him sitting beside William. Blake had a bat in his hands and seemed to be talking to William about playing ball.

She was busy with kids and watching third base, cheering for each child who could get a hit or run in for a score. By the end of the inning, she looked around and saw Blake showing William how to hold the bat.

The next inning, William stepped up to home plate.

She asked someone to take her place and walked over to Blake.

"I see William is going to play. That was fast work."

"He hasn't said a dozen words to me, but he listened and he agreed to give this a try. I told him that people get better when they try and when they practice."

"Whatever you told him, you got through to him. That's pretty good, Blake. I'm impressed."

"I'll be back in a few minutes. I want to move closer where I can coach a little," he said.

"I thought you said Blake had never been around kids," her mother said, stopping beside Sierra.

"He hasn't until today—that's what he told me."

"Well, then I'm glad you invited him. If he just helps one child, it'll be really good. Did you tell him that some of his donation went for the batting machine and some of the sports equipment?"

"Yes, I did. If he helps William, that'll be a small miracle, but in some ways, Blake can relate to William and vice versa."

"It's a stretch, but both of them having no dad is a common bond," her mother said as they watched William swing and miss. Blake talked to him. When William swung again, the ball glanced off the bat and was a foul. On the third swing, the bat connected and the ball bounced away while she heard Blake yell for William to run. The boy on third scooped up the ball and threw it wide, and William touched first base. He turned to Blake and grinned while kids and adults clapped.

"Maybe two lives were changed a little this afternoon," her mother said. "Blake's a nice guy, and I'm glad you took the job with him. He's going to help so many people here. Dad is already making plans about what he can do with the money you've given him."

"I'm glad."

"Here comes Justin with a skinned knee. I don't see his mother, so I'll go help him." Her mother moved away to take care of one of her three-year-old grandsons.

In minutes Sierra was busy clearing tables, and she didn't talk to Blake the rest of the afternoon. She saw him with her brothers as they joined a bunch of kids of all ages in a tug-of-war over a narrow part of the winding creek.

They had a cookout for dinner, wanting to send everyone home with a hearty meal. It was eleven when quiet settled at home, and she finally stood at her bedroom door to tell Blake good-night.

"Thanks for all your help today."

"It was interesting. I'm sure you wanted me to see what you're involved in, and you wanted to stir my sympathy. Well, you succeeded."

"Some of those kids have a tough deal."

"Are you sure Bert isn't a relative of yours? He quizzed me about how long you'll have to be in Texas, that sort of thing."

"Bert worries and he hovers, but his intentions are good."

"I don't think his intentions toward me are so good," Blake remarked.

She smiled at his joke. "He worries about me. He worries about Nan. He's a good guy. You don't have to go with all of us to church tomorrow if you'd rather not."

"I'll go and see what life is like for you," he replied.

"That will please Dad. He is always happy to have someone come hear him preach," she said quietly, looking up at Blake. Beard stubble shadowed his jaw, and his black hair was tousled. Her heart drummed because she wanted to be in his arms, wanted his kisses. She had seen another side to him today, a really good side. His helping her family, caring about people and kids, particularly William, drew her to him in ways that were even stronger than their physical attraction.

This one weekend wouldn't make him a different man. He was still bent on revenge. But it had changed the way she saw him. There was so much to him that was good.

She would soon have to tell him goodbye. She suspected it would take a long time to forget him, but the sooner they parted, the sooner she would start.

On Sunday Blake joined Sierra and her family for church and another delicious meal with so many people that he marveled at how well her mother handled everything. After dinner a lot of her family played volleyball, and he joined them, laughing and helping the little kids who joined in.

It was sundown when he told everyone goodbye. Sierra drove as they headed for the airport and his private jet. Relaxed and friendly, he occasionally brushed her fingers lightly, or her nape, or moved a lock of her hair—tiny touches that shouldn't have even been noticeable, but instead steadily built a longing in her for more.

When they landed, a limo waited to take them to

his Dallas home. Following the winding drive, the car stopped in front of a palatial three-story home with lighted grounds. Inside, as soon as he switched off an alarm, closed the door and locked it, he turned to embrace her.

Surprised, Sierra looked up into midnight eyes that conveyed his intent. Her heart thudded.

Six

"This is Sunday night, and we haven't kissed since Friday," he said in a husky voice as his arm circled her waist and held her against him.

While her heartbeat raced, she gazed at him in silence. She had always wanted a marriage like her parents' because they truly loved each other and their family. That seemed the best possible situation to her. There was no hope of that if she fell in love with Blake. He didn't know what a loving relationship was. He had no role models, no examples. He didn't even seem to want that in his life. Right now his goal was revenge—a chilling ambition.

Blake was a solitary person and probably had been for so long that he didn't even realize he was different from a lot of people. She had seen a good side to him this weekend, but it would be foolish of her to expect him to give up his drive for revenge or his lifelong feelings of resentment about his father. The sooner she and Blake said farewell and parted ways, the better off she would be. She had to cut ties with him…

But it would be after tonight.

Even as she reminded herself of all these things, she was mesmerized by Blake's brown eyes, breathless because of the intent they conveyed.

Wisdom whispered to walk away while desire shouted to put her arms around him and kiss him in return.

She followed the longings of her body, of her heart. Tomorrow she would be in another state, away from Blake. She would no longer have temptation to struggle with. She'd go on with her life and let Blake Callahan become a memory.

She wrapped her arms around him, winding her fingers in the hair at the back of his head. Holding him tightly, she kissed him, wanting to excite him as he did her, to rock his world as much as he had rocked hers.

While he continued kissing her, Blake swung her up in his arms and headed for a bedroom. As he did, her heart drummed and she clung to him tightly.

Tonight, she wouldn't think about tomorrow. Tonight she wanted to make love. Would she ever be able to forget him?

Hours later, she sat with her back against him in a large tub. His arms were around her while he showered light kisses on her neck. She was warm and satisfied.

For the moment, happiness filled her. She thought about the weekend and William.

Had Blake really been interested in William, or had his attention to the boy been meant to impress her? She didn't know Blake well enough to know what he truly felt about William. No matter what the motive, he had helped the boy, and for a short time at least, thanks to Blake, William had broken out of his shell, enjoying life and the kids around him.

"This is perfect, Sierra."

"I have to agree. I'm glad you went home with me. You may have made a big difference in William's life. Sometimes kids, even adults we work with, think they're the only one something has happened to, and William may be one of those. Although he knows there are other kids at the shelter who don't have anyone."

"How does he do in school?" Blake asked. He massaged her shoulders, rubbing lightly, his hands warm and soothing.

"I have no idea, but I can find out. My guess is average, or I would have heard otherwise," she answered quietly, scared to hope that Blake would really get involved in William's life.

"Check and see. Too bad they don't have a ranch for some of those kids who are old enough. They could learn to care for a horse, to ride, to help out and do chores. It's a good life for a kid who is willing to work."

'We're doing good to have shelters in the city. We don't have the staff or facilities to have horses and land."

They were both quiet, letting the warm water lap against their skin.

He broke the companionable silence to say, "You have a nice family. And your folks have a good marriage." He combed her long hair back from her face.

"My parents have the best of marriages. They're very happy."

"My family had more money—your family had more love. Too bad things can't balance out."

"We're all there for each other. When I quit my New York job and came home, I had everyone's support." She paused. "Blake, I'll ask again—have you ever thought about talking to your dad as an adult? It might be different now. You might find out that you really don't want to pursue a course of revenge."

"Don't try to reform me," he said, brushing light kisses on her neck, his breath warm against her.

"I wouldn't think of it. I imagine you're way too stubborn for me to reform," she teased. He wound his arms around her and cupped her breasts gently, caressing her, making her close her eyes and gasp with pleasure.

"You're starting something again," she whispered.

"I hope I am," he answered.

"Please remember I have to get up early tomorrow to fly to New York."

"Yes, ma'am," he answered in a polite tone of voice that made her smile briefly, until he twisted her around. When he looked into her eyes, his teasing expression vanished. He pulled her up to kiss her hard and then reached for a condom before he moved her over him. She straddled him as he held her hips and thrust into her, filling her, making her cry out with pleasure while she moved with him until they were in a frenzy of need.

When she climaxed, ecstasy shaking her, she held him tightly and felt his wild, thrusting response as he shuddered with his own release.

She didn't know how much time passed before he spoke softly. "When you finish this job, I want to see you again."

"When that time comes, I'm guessing you'll change your mind," she whispered, her head against his shoulder. "We'll say goodbye. You'll see."

The words were easy to say when they were locked in a warm embrace after loving. At the moment, telling him goodbye didn't seem to loom in the near future, but she knew parting and not seeing him again was reality.

When he didn't answer, she assumed he agreed with her.

It was early morning when she slipped out of bed and went to the shower. She glanced back once. Blake was sprawled in bed, one muscled arm flung across a pillow and the sheet around his waist. His hair was a tangle.

For a moment, she longed to go back and kiss him awake, but she had a flight to catch. Two hours later, as he drove her to the airport, out to his waiting private jet, she wondered again how long it would be before she forgot him. She knew time would give her the answer.

When Blake opened the car door and she stepped out, he moved close and wrapped his arm around her waist.

"This isn't very private," she said, watching a breeze tangle short locks of black hair above his forehead.

"I don't care about that. I want to hold you close."

"You still don't want to be involved in all the details?"

"I still don't," he said, smiling. His gaze lowered to her lips, and her heart beat faster at the desire in his eyes.

"I may not take another job with an alpha male."

"That would suit me just fine," he said, smiling again. "I'd have you all to myself." Their smiles faded as she gazed up at him. "I'm going to miss you," he said, his voice lowering a notch as his gaze shifted to her mouth.

She forgot their surroundings. She was telling him goodbye, and it might be a long one. His arm tightened and he leaned down to give her another possessive, fiery kiss that made her want to get back in the car with him and go back to his house.

"Don't stay away too long," he finally said as he released her. He was breathing hard, looking at her intently with desire clear in his warm brown eyes.

"Hurry back, darlin'," he whispered. The endearment shook her because he didn't say it often. She reminded herself that he meant little by it.

"Goodbye, Blake," she said, a chill sweeping her.

"Not yet. No goodbyes until the end of the job," he said. "I'll be around when you come back. We can say our goodbyes later. A farewell kiss would be good. Then we'll have a hello kiss when we're together," he said. He leaned down and kissed her again.

She finally turned and boarded the plane where she sat to watch him drive away. She wondered if he had plans to be at the ranch when she returned.

* * *

For the rest of the next week Lucinda, Eli and Sierra worked together in New York, looking at furnishings and artwork, getting together at the office to go over the day's selections, plus the changes, the sketches and suggested purchases.

Sierra worked long hours looking at sketches, plans, catalogues and pictures of furnishings. During the day she spent time in art galleries, searching for the right pieces, wondering all the time if Blake would like what she did.

She missed him and thought about him constantly. She tried to convince herself it was because she was working on the design for his new wing. Late at night he usually called, and they talked for a long time about nothing important.

The more she missed him, the more she worked. Late on Wednesday night she fell asleep at her desk. Her phone woke her, and when she heard Blake's voice, she came fully awake. She was glad to talk to him. She sat back, listening to him, telling him about paintings she had selected, and sending him pictures from her phone of what she had chosen that week, even though he had said he didn't want to be consulted.

To her relief he listened, made suggestions and, even better, liked what they had picked and what they planned to do.

"Tomorrow I'll call the contractor and set up a time for all of us to meet at your ranch. We've talked on the phone and I've sent plans, so he already knows a lot about what he'll need to do."

"What I'm interested in is when you'll be here at the ranch to stay, and we can be alone."

She laughed. "You lusty, lusty man. Eli and Lucinda will be with me when I come back. Eli is excellent in dealing with contractors, and I'm turning some of that over to him. I don't know if you and I will be alone much."

"That's not what I want to hear. I'll work on that one. This is a big house. We'll put Eli and Lucinda in the guest houses. They might enjoy the privacy."

"Actually, they might enjoy the peace and quiet. However, do not make plans for me to move in with you when I'm busy, and so many people are working in your house."

"I wouldn't think of asking you to move in with me."

"Oh, yes, you would, and I'm sure you were planning exactly that," she remarked, amused and certain she was right.

"Well, I'll admit the thought crossed my mind."

Smiling, Sierra continued talking with him for another hour before finally telling him goodbye.

During the week she called Nan to ask about William. Sierra hoped Blake would really care about the kid. He had cared enough to give William some attention when they were in Kansas, but that had been easy. Now, when Blake was back in Texas, it would be a bigger task. Part of her hoped Blake would make the effort.

For the rest of the week she got a call late every night from Blake, but then he had meetings in California and the calls stopped. She knew he was busy with his commercial properties, and he was deeply involved in his work. And she also knew that she should get used to living without his conversation or company.

Sooner or later she'd have to let go because they had no future together.

Blake's schedule was packed, partially because of things he had put off doing when Sierra was at the ranch, and partly because he worked at finding ways to keep busy to try to forget her.

She was not his type, and the sooner he went on with his life, the better off he would be. All sensible thoughts, but not a solution. He missed seeing her. He wanted to go out with her again, and he wanted her back in his bed.

Blake called old friends, accepted party invitations, kept busy and resisted calling Sierra. His father had just built a new luxury hotel in Florida, and Blake had already bought nearby land and made arrangements to start construction. Blake flew out to look, staying in his father's hotel to check it out, something he did about once a year. His hotels were taking more business than ever from his father's.

But even that work made him think of Sierra. He remembered their conversations about his father. She didn't understand his motives because she had never been hurt the way he had. She had grown up insulated by the love of her family.

He had seen the latest figures on the hotels. He had cut into his dad's business so much that he expected him to sell his properties.

In years past that small success would have brought

more satisfaction than it did now. Was that Sierra's influence—or was Blake tiring of trying to get a bit of revenge for the years his father had refused to acknowledge him?

Blake thought about the kid at the picnic, William, who didn't know his father and had lost his mother. There ought to be some way to help the boy beyond sticking him in a shelter. The shelter was better than the street, of course, but there must be something that would give him a better chance in life. Blake made a note to have someone look into it.

That was definitely Sierra's influence, he thought.

How could she have had such an impact on him in such a short time?

In early April, Sierra flew to Dallas to meet with Blake and his contractor, and make arrangements to commence work. She was jittery, and not sure if it was because she was presenting their final plan for Blake's approval or because she would be seeing him again.

When she stepped out of the rental car, he was waiting on his porch. Tall and handsome, Blake looked like the Texas rancher he was with his jeans, boots and tan shirt. He came down the steps to sweep her into his embrace.

The moment his strong arms closed around her, she forgot her mission and lost all her apprehension. She clung to him tightly and kissed him.

She felt as if she'd come home.

All that she had intended to say was forgotten when he took her into his arms. After a moment, she moved out of his embrace. "Blake, you hired me to finish this job for you, and it will never get done if we don't stop kissing."

He grinned. "So? I can live with that."

Laughing, she shook her head. "Eventually, you wouldn't want to. You paid me a lot of money for this. You might as well have your new wing finished, and I've bought some expensive artwork."

"All right. I'll listen."

"I want you to look at what we've done. After I change, I'll get things set up in the office you said I can use."

It was late afternoon before she emerged from her shower, dressed in stone-washed jeans, boots and a blue knit shirt. She left her hair loose and went to find Blake.

She brought him into the office where she had sketches spread on a long table along with 3D designs on her iPad. Blake studied them quietly. "Look through the iPad for pictures of how the artwork, sculptures and furniture for each suite will look. Go ahead." She stood by the table, watching for his reaction.

"This is perfect, Sierra," he said, pointing to a sketch of a bedroom. "This will be my room." He closed the distance between them to place his hands on her shoulders. "I knew you'd do the best possible job."

Warmed by his praise, she smiled. "Thank you! I'm thrilled you're happy with it, and I'll let Lucinda and Eli know because they deserve as much credit. They are really good at this."

"This is just perfect," he said, studying her. "I don't know how the hell you can leave a career you're perfect for. Do you know how many people would like to have half the talent you do, and they're in the business? You selected what I would have selected," he said, turning to look at her intently. "That's interesting, Sierra, because we don't see eye to eye on anything else in life. Well, maybe a few things."

She ignored his flirting. "Thank Lucinda and Eli. They found a lot of those pieces. They took note of what you like when we toured your house."

"That they did. These are perfect. I'm glad I hired you."

Her gaze ran over him. She could still feel her heartbeat speed up when she looked at him or thought about kissing him.

How could she be so drawn to him or find him so exciting when they were totally different?

Memories tugged at her senses, and she gulped for air. She wanted to be back in his arms, and she suspected she would be soon.

The next day Lucinda and Eli arrived, and Sierra stayed in her own suite that night. For the rest of the week and through the one following, workers were coming and going, goods were delivered to the ranch and there was constant activity from early in the morning until about nine in the evening. Blake left for business in Dallas and they talked each day, but she didn't see him.

The next week Blake went to California. Sierra, Lucinda and Eli stayed at the ranch to be available for the contractor and make sure everything was going well.

They all worked hard to get everything finished by the deadline.

On a weekend trip home to Kansas City, Sierra's worries and priorities shifted as a new concern emerged—one she'd never dreamed she would have.

She could not ignore her body—she might be pregnant with Blake's baby.

A few hours later, Sierra stood staring at the results of the pregnancy test. Blake had taken precautions, always. But she knew that condoms were not always effective, even when used appropriately. Apparently, this was one of those times.

Her head swam, and for a moment she felt faint. She sat in a chair, putting her head down, hoping the dizziness would pass.

Looking again at the results of her test, she shook her head. "No," she whispered. She couldn't be pregnant.

What would she do? What would Blake do?

She had no answers to those questions. All her life, her family, her friends, her school, her activities, her jobs—everything had been harmonious, satisfactory, even fantastic. She had a big, loving, happy family. She'd had success. She had wonderful friends, and she was in a second great career. An unwanted, unplanned pregnancy, being tied to a man she wanted and yet couldn't have—how would she cope?

She placed her hand on her flat stomach. She was carrying Blake's baby.

Panic gripped her, and she felt light-headed again. She had planned her life in the usual manner—marriage then children. It had never occurred to her that her life would not follow that pattern.

She wanted a doctor's confirmation in addition to the pregnancy test.

With a sigh, she calmed down only slightly. Deep in her heart, she knew the test wasn't mistaken. She was going to have Blake's baby.

But he was a man who planned to remain single. A man who didn't know anything about being a dad, about families or about children. He didn't even want any.

He was also a man who definitely did not want a long-term relationship right now. And she didn't want to marry him. They wouldn't be compatible—not beyond the bedroom.

He would probably give her a generous sum of money to support his child, though.

She thought about Blake at the picnic, sitting and talking to William, then later, coaching the boy when he joined the ball game. He'd never been around children, and yet he'd taken to William immediately. He'd even asked about the boy in their phone conversations. He cared, even when he pretended he didn't, and common sense told her that Blake would never abandon his own child.

Probably, he would insist on marriage even though they were not in love. With all the bitterness Blake felt toward his father, he would never make the same mistakes with his own family. Blake would do everything in his power to be a part of his child's life full-time. He'd talk her into getting married, or living with him, no matter how unsuited they were as a couple.

They weren't in love. Yet she was certain he would push, try to bribe her, charm her, or do everything else he reasonably could to win her to his way of thinking. If she did agree to something long-term, it would be a disaster. She held marriage sacred, the vows were lifelong, the outcome of abiding love. She would have none of that with Blake, whether they said "I do" or avoided a ceremony and simply shared a house.

When she broke the news to him, she should be ready for an onslaught of persuasion. She knew Blake was accustomed to getting his way and would not give up easily.

There had been fabulous sex between them, but not love. She thought about her parents and how deeply they loved each other and how it showed in a myriad of tiny ways day after day. That's the kind of love Sierra wanted.

She felt hot tears sting. She had gotten herself into a situation that didn't seem to have a happy solution. Maybe with time and a baby, she and Blake could fall in love.

Wiping her eyes, she stood and took a deep breath. Tears solved nothing. She called her doctor and made an appointment. Then she stared into space, trying to make a plan. How was she going to convince him he could be a great dad without having her in his life full-time?

She definitely did not want to give up her baby, so they would have to share custody. Blake was one-hundred percent alpha male, and he would not take no for an answer, so she needed to figure out how to deal with him.

If he did propose, would it be so bad to be married to him?

Again, she thought of her parents' harmonious marriage, deeply grounded in love and care for each other. If she married Blake without love, they would never have that special union.

Maybe she was jumping to the wrong conclusions. She shouldn't start imagining what he would do and making wild guesses.

She dreaded telling him and having to deal with a strong-willed, determined man who would be set on doing things she did not want to do. She wasn't accustomed to having to deal with someone else on major decisions that affected her life.

When would she tell him? She wanted to wait until she was finished with his new wing. She'd settle up with him and know she could walk away without doing any further work for him. But she'd never be able to keep the secret while living on his ranch, working for him, seeing him every day. She'd have to tell him sooner than that. If they had a fight, a real battle over the future, she would just have to live with still seeing him and working with him.

She felt a little better because she had a plan of action—she'd see a doctor and have the pregnancy confirmed.

The second thing was to finish his new wing.

Then she'd tell him he was going to be a father.

Next week she was staying at the ranch, and Blake would be home from California. Sierra knew with absolute certainty that when Blake learned the news, he would start planning their lives and their future. This would be one dad who would not disappear. She felt certain that, one way or another, Blake would be part of her life for the next twenty years or so. He might not propose to her, but he would not ignore his child.

She ran her fingers across her forehead. She had a doctor's appointment tomorrow. Sunday afternoon at two she would leave Kansas City for Texas.

She had told her parents, and they were as supportive as she had expected them to be. She still needed to talk to her older brothers. They were protective of their sisters in a very old-fashioned way, and she suspected they weren't going to be happy with Blake unless she handled telling them carefully. At least they were in Kansas and Blake was in Texas.

She would see Blake on Sunday—that knowledge kept her pulse beating faster. Part of her was eager to see him, while another part of her wished she could put off seeing him for years. She didn't want to see him while keeping this secret and she didn't want to have to break the news to him because it would turn his world upside down.

She debated what to wear, how to fix her hair and how much to pack. Finally, the next morning, she dressed in a red linen suit with a matching silk blouse and high-heeled pumps. She combed and clipped her hair up at the back of her head.

The commercial flight to Dallas seemed short. Blake was home and knew she was coming, so there was a plane waiting to fly her to the ranch.

All too soon, they landed at the ranch airstrip. As it

taxied to a stop, her pulse beat faster, eagerness now intermingling with dread. She didn't want to tell Blake. In the next few hours his entire future would change, and she didn't think he would be happy about the prospect.

She placed her hand defensively against her stomach. She'd had some time to get accustomed to the fact that she would become a parent. At some point after the initial shock, joy had enveloped her. She was going to have a baby. Another grandchild for her parents. Her family would give her all the love and support she would need.

A baby in her life—the thought was scary, but joyous. She had taken care of her little nieces and nephews, and she loved being with them. She had a great support network and a job she loved. No matter what happened with Blake, she would make her new little family work.

When she stepped out of the plane, a warm, dry gust of wind hit her. Blake stood waiting at a car and walked toward her. At the sight of the tall rancher, her heart thudded.

A black, broad-brimmed hat sat squarely on his head, and as always, boots added to his height that was over six feet. He wore jeans and a blue plaid Western shirt. The sight of him kept her heart racing, and all she could think about was telling him that he would be a father.

She was torn between wanting to walk into his arms and kiss him, or blurting out that she was pregnant with his baby.

Before she reached the last two steps on the plane's stairs, his hands closed on her waist to lift her up and set her on her feet on the ground.

"Someone will get your things. I'll drive you back to

the house," he said, taking her arm lightly and walking back to hold the car door open.

Once inside, he turned to her. "You look gorgeous, Sierra," he said quietly.

"Thank you," she answered.

"I'm glad you're here. When the new wing is finished, I want to have a party. You can invite your family, and I'll invite mine. I want them all to see what a great job you've done."

She smiled at him. "Let's wait and see if it really is a great job."

"Cade wants to have their family home done over. He'll give you a call."

"Blake, I'm out of that business, remember?"

"He's not going to offer what I did, but I think he'll make a generous offer for your Kansas City agency, as well as your fee."

She had to laugh as she shook her head. "I may make more money for the agency by sticking with interior design than I ever did seeking donations."

Conversation went from one topic to another, and she barely paid attention because all too soon she would be home with Blake and she would have to tell him her news.

The minute they walked into his house, tempting odors of hot bread and roast beef reached her. "Etta must be cooking up a storm."

"Etta cooked and has gone. We're alone," he said, turning to slip his arm around her waist and draw her close.

She had promised herself she would show some resistance to him this time, but the minute he touched her and she looked into his brown eyes, she couldn't tell him no. She leaned into him, as he pulled her closer and kissed her.

She was lost in his kiss, swept up in desire that made her tremble. At the same time a pang hit her. If only they had love in their relationship, how wonderful the next few hours would be. The best news in the world was a baby when there was love and a union of two people who wanted to be together the rest of their lives. Instead, the news would be an earthquake hitting his life.

His arms tightened, and he held her close with one arm while his other hand caressed her. He took the clip from her hair, letting it fall over her shoulders.

"I wasn't going to do this," she whispered, not caring whether he heard her or not.

"I was—I've dreamed of this moment since the day I told you goodbye in Dallas. I want you in my arms, in my bed. I want to kiss and touch you, love you for hours. I've dreamed about you every night you've been gone," he whispered, and her heart pounded.

"Why do we have to be so different?" she asked, agonizing over what was coming and the monumental differences between them.

"Differences that dazzle me," he whispered. "You look fabulous. I've missed you," he added. Under other circumstances, his words would have thrilled her, but now she worried his feelings toward her would change with her news. She didn't know how angry or unhappy he might be. She was certain he wouldn't welcome it with joy.

His kiss drove all her worries away. She was swept up in desire, wanting to hold and kiss him, feeling as if this might be the last time. Even so, she knew she couldn't hold in the news any longer.

In minutes she leaned away to look up at him. "Blake, wait a moment. We should talk."

"There isn't anything as important as kissing you," he whispered, brushing her lips with his. She pushed against his shoulders lightly and stepped out of his embrace.

"There is something as important," she said. He stared at her a moment and nodded, and she knew she had his attention.

She had put off telling him as long as she could. Standing by the window as the sun slipped below the horizon, she faced him. He sat in a leather chair, his booted feet on an ottoman as he looked at her. "Something's worrying you. What is it? Can I help?"

"You can help," she said quietly. "Listen to me, be patient and let's try to cooperate."

She saw the flicker in his eyes and knew he realized he was somehow involved in whatever worried her.

"I don't know how to tell you except to just say it— Blake, I'm pregnant, and it's your baby."

Seven

Blake felt as if he'd had the breath knocked from him. Dazed, he stared at her. "I'm going to be a dad," he said. He hadn't meant to say it out loud.

"Yes, you are. We have a long time to sort things out and decide what we'll do, so all you need to do right now is get used to the idea. It's a big, unexpected shock," she said, sitting quietly and letting him think.

"I used a condom every time," he said, more to himself than to her. He had gotten Sierra pregnant. They would be tied together for the next eighteen years. They would never view life the same way, but he was certain she wouldn't want to marry him any more than he wanted to marry her.

But how else would he be the kind of father his own never was?

He raked his fingers through his hair and stood, going to the kitchen and getting a beer, more to move around than to have something to drink. He walked to a window to gaze outside. The daylight was growing dim and night was creeping in, changing the landscape.

He knew he would never forget this moment. He was going to be a father. The idea shook him. He had dimly thought that someday he would marry, someday he would have a family, but it was in the distant future, a fuzzy prospect that had held no reality for him until now.

He was going to have a baby. When he glanced at her, Sierra sat looking at her fingernails, remaining quiet while he absorbed the news.

He was thankful for that. Thankful she wasn't in tears or yelling at him or asking him what they would do. He focused more on her and wondered what she thought. She had already known about this. She looked calm, poised, and she had obviously adjusted to the idea. He thought of her big family and knew she would have their support. Blake realized if he walked away now, her family would be there for her.

Not that he intended to walk away or abandon her. He thought about his father. He would never be a father like the one he'd had. He wouldn't abandon or reject his own child, not ever. There was one way to put himself in his child's life forever—marry Sierra. That seemed to be the only solution to being a real dad to his child.

Blake's gaze shifted back to Sierra who looked up, giving him a level stare.

He crossed the room to face her. "You caught me by surprise."

"I knew I would. There was no way to avoid that."

"You're very calm about this," he said, looking into wide blue eyes, and he realized she had passed the point of shock and was thinking calmly about the situation.

"It won't help to get hysterical," she said.

"Damn straight on that. I'm thankful you're not."

"We'll have to make decisions and work things out, but we don't have to do anything right now except adjust to the idea. I think we should take a little time before we start trying to figure out what we'll do."

"It all looks simple to me."

"Blake," she interrupted, shaking her head. "Don't propose."

"I don't see why not," he said, startled that she wouldn't even discuss marriage. "You know your family will want us to marry."

"None of them will if they know I don't want to. You and I are opposites. I don't like your work, and you don't like mine."

"That's nine to five, and we can get around that," he said, surprised she let their jobs be the reason for rejecting what would be best for their child. "Our jobs will have little to do with life at home," he said.

"For us and our chosen fields, it has everything to do with life at home. I may want to foster kids or find homes for more dogs. We'll work something out, I'm sure, because we're both willing, but it isn't going to be marriage."

Shocked, because she seemed so firm in her refusal,

he stared at her. "I want to be part of my child's life," he said, trying to hang on to his temper.

"You will be. I promise. I want you to be. But that doesn't mean we have to be married."

"Damn, Sierra." Once the idea had presented itself, it hadn't occurred to him that she would reject his proposal, at least not under the circumstances. She sat calmly facing him, her long legs crossed at the ankles and her hands in her lap. She looked composed and determined. He suspected he was going to find out how strong-willed she could be.

"You don't want to marry. You made that clear," she added.

"My life has changed since I said that. I was single and not expecting to become a father. I want to know my baby, to be with him or her every day I'm not away for work. There is no way I'm going to be the father that mine was and abandon my child. I can promise you that," he said, determined that he would not let her stop him from being the father his child needed. "I want to take care of both of you. The easiest way to do that is if we marry. If we try, we can make marriage work."

"This is a knee-jerk reaction, Blake. We don't have to decide today, this week or this month, so let's consider the possibilities. I know you want to be a dad to your child, and I want that. I want to be a mom to our child. We don't have to marry to be parents, or even to be good parents."

"You're not being sensible," he said, his gaze running over her.

"I'm not being sensible?" she snapped, her eyes narrowing. "I'm the one being the most sensible. We're opposites, Blake. Marriage won't work. We're not in love."

"Marriage can be a partnership. It's something we can work at. We can get along. If we share a child, we can probably get along even better than now."

"I can't believe you're saying that," she said. "You've dedicated your life to increasing your fortune because you want to get back at your father. You're concentrating on competing with him just to ruin his business. That's revenge.

"Revenge drives you, Blake. Not love. Meanwhile, I'm trying to save people. I'm not marrying someone who is driven by revenge for childhood hurts. I'm sorry for what you went through, but there's a better way."

"That may seem foolish to you because you had an abundance of love and attention, but having a father abandon you hurts, Sierra, and it's the kind of hurt you never forget. It's not a silly childhood notion."

"I know that, but you're grown now. Move on and do some good in the world," she said.

"I believe you have a very sizable check from me that will do some good. Don't forget that," he said.

She was being stubborn. They had a fabulous relationship, and if she would give it a chance, they could work out something that would give their baby both a mom and a dad.

"I only have that check because it was a bribe. You wanted me for this job, and you wanted me in your bed. You said you were attracted to me, and you wanted to see me again."

"Yeah, I did. And you acted glad to take both checks I gave you, and glad to be in my bed," he said.

Her cheeks grew red, and he suspected she was trying to hold her temper just as he was. She stood and clenched her fists. "I think we should call it a night and cool down. I have a lot to do tomorrow, and you're leaving town. We can talk later, when you've had time to think about this."

"I'll think about it constantly, and I imagine you will, too. You might give some more thought to my proposal before you turn it down. Try to think of the baby—you shouldn't turn down my proposal just because you don't want to marry me. You're not allowing our child to have both a father and a mother full-time, in a home we all share. And think of what I can provide, including my name. Marriage will make raising our child more convenient, more workable. Think about the baby you're carrying before you reject my proposal."

"I'll do that, Blake. I *have* done that. There is nothing about a loveless marriage that would be good for our child! Look at us now—you think this would be good for a child to be part of our squabbling? I don't think so." She took a deep breath. "I think we've talked enough tonight. I'm going to my suite before we say something one of us will really regret."

She brushed past him and hurried into the hall. Her back tingled because she felt his gaze on her as she left the room.

Anger and hurt filled her. Why had she ever been so wildly attracted to Blake? Worse, why had she succumbed to his kisses and then to his lovemaking?

Now there would be no way to forget him. She was tied to him for the rest of her life. Her anger grew. She had tried to be calm and reasonable with him. She had expected him to propose and to insist on her accepting. She had no intention of marrying a man who was building a hotel chain with the sole purpose of getting back at his father. In the privacy of her bedroom she paced the floor, not only angry at herself but that Blake wouldn't stop and think before he started pushing for marriage. Yes, that had been her first thought, too, but if he would give the future some thought, she expected he would come to the same conclusion she had—they were not compatible out of bed, and they shouldn't be married.

By one in the morning, she had given up on getting to sleep. She was exhausted and yet still angry when she thought about Blake's stubborn insistence on marriage before he had really had time to think things through.

It was almost dawn when she fell asleep, and then she overslept. As she showered and dressed in green slacks and a matching cotton blouse, she hoped Blake had already left the ranch.

She soon found out from Etta that Blake had left for Dallas, and she didn't know when he would return. Trying to concentrate on the tasks at hand and put him out of her thoughts, Sierra went to work. The sooner she could get his new wing finished, the sooner she could return to Kansas City.

As she sat at a desk with sketches before her, she paused, staring into space, remembering being in Blake's arms, the laughter they had shared. They had liked being together—it almost made her wish they *could* make a marriage work—but there was no way she could get past his efforts to get revenge. That was a solid wall that would always divide them.

In spite of all common sense and absolute certainty that marriage to Blake would be a disaster, she couldn't keep from thinking about him. He had a forceful personality, and the attraction between them, the electrifying appeal that made him unique, was irresistible. He could certainly turn on the charm, and they'd had a good time together.

With a sigh, she focused on the tasks for the day to try to move on.

Within the hour, she was lost in thoughts about Blake again. Common sense said she would get over missing him. That it was just a matter of time. Her heart was trying to tell her differently.

As the morning progressed, she kept busy, supervising placement of the new furniture and area rugs, the installation of the mirrors and new paintings. Blake was in California, and she talked to him briefly on the phone at night because of questions about the house. Each time she heard his voice, she felt a pang of longing that she tried to ignore. They were cool with each other, remote, as if there had never been intimacy between them, and she suspected when the calls about the house ended, she wouldn't have any contact with him for a while.

Finally, they were finished. Blake was due back on Friday, and Saturday morning she, as well as Eli, Lucinda and the contractor, were going to meet with him to go over the rooms. She was certain any party Blake had planned earlier wasn't going to happen now.

While it wasn't convenient to move her things, she didn't want to stay on the ranch with him after the work was done, so she stayed in the small hotel in town. In her hotel room, she looked intently at herself in the mirror.

At two months her stomach was still flat and her waist had not changed plus her five-ten height might be the reason she didn't see any change. So far, she felt well and had not had any morning sickness.

She had rented a car to drive to the ranch tomorrow. She didn't want to rely on Blake for anything—not transportation, food, lodging, companionship. Her anger with him was a constant feeling. She was certain he had not changed his mind in the least, and he would continue to insist they marry for all the wrong reasons.

It was simply something she would not do.

Friday afternoon in Dallas, Blake met Cade for lunch, sliding into a chair opposite his brother.

"Well, is the house finished?"

"Yes, and it looks great. I'll have a party and you can come see. I was going to have a big party soon—you and the rest of the brothers, if Nathan and family are back, Sierra and her family, friends. I'll have it, but it may be postponed for a time."

"Are you leaving town?"

"Yes, but that isn't why. The job is over, and I don't know how much I'll see of Sierra."

Cade tilted his head. "Are you two dating each other?"

"Yes and no," Blake said. "Yes, we were, but no, we're not currently. But we'll see each other some. We have some problems to work out."

"House problems?"

Blake gazed at his half brother. He felt closer to Cade than anyone else he knew. He had to share his news. "Okay, this isn't for public announcement, but maybe— oh, hell. She's pregnant with my baby."

"Kaboom," Cade said, his eyes opening wide with a startled expression on his face. "Wow. Congratulations, I think. You don't sound like a happy dad. I know you didn't plan to marry this soon, but you said you expected to get hitched sometime. Just move it up."

"That's not the problem. The lady said no. We're opposites in so many ways, and she doesn't think we can ever truly make it work or fall in love. Her parents have this perfect union of like-minded individuals, and that's what she wants. Plus, she is Miss Do-Good and wants me to be the same."

Cade sputtered and tried to bite back a smile. "Sorry. You're a nice guy, but not out to save the world."

"No, I'm not, but I'm not an ogre. It's this deal about my hotels and our dad that gets her."

"Ah, the light dawns. She doesn't know our dad. He's no saint. His people will just dump the hotels and go on to something else, and he may never even know you were behind the loss in revenue."

"Yeah, that's what I'm starting to realize."

"If she won't marry, maybe you're better off. Look

at our dad and all his marriages—all disasters. Sierra's folks are an exception. You may be fortunate she turned you down. She's not going to try to keep you from your baby, is she?"

"Oh, no. She would never do that."

"Well, then. I'd think you'd be a lot happier without a wife. Stop and think about it. With your way with the ladies and your money and success—most women would be screaming for marriage. They would be running to get a preacher before the words were out of your mouth. Be glad, my brother. Besides, she could be right, you know. If the two of you are opposites, why tie your lives more closely together? You can still be a dad, and she'll still be a mom, and each of you will find love with someone else."

"Why did I tell you about this?" Blake asked, frowning at Cade.

"To get some sound advice. Seriously, think about what she's telling you. You may be much better off without her in your life. She's sharing your child, letting you be dad, and that's good. An unhappy marriage isn't great for a kid to grow up watching. I can promise you that because I was caught in one—a little kid doesn't understand. I'd say you've got good advice, so go with it."

"Well, I'll think about what you and Sierra are telling me, but I think I came to the wrong person. You're warped."

"Yes, because of my father's lousy marriages. Need I say more? That proves my point."

"All right, I'll think about it. I don't have a choice.

She seems to have her mind made up," he said, looking at Cade and thinking about how cynical and hard he could be about some things in life. Usually he was easygoing, friendly and upbeat, but he had another side, too. Was it because of their dad? Was Sierra right that they could never make a marriage work?

Cade stared intently at him.

"What?" Blake asked. "Did you say something to me? Sorry, my mind wandered."

"Watch out when you cross the street. If you're that lost in thought about her, you'll get run over."

"I'm not going to get run over, and I'm not lost in thought about Sierra."

"You were a minute ago. You haven't fallen in love with her, have you?"

"No, I'm not in love, but that wouldn't be the end of the world."

"No, but if you've fallen in love, then you won't be able to cope very well with her rejection. Otherwise, live your life, love your child and don't look back. A lot of guys would trade with you in a flash."

"You're just Mr. Wisdom. I may go to a gypsy fortune-teller for advice next time."

Cade grinned. "I'm more interesting, and I know you better. You didn't even hear what I asked you, so maybe you're in love and you don't know it."

"Don't be ridiculous. I'd know it."

"You've got the symptoms. You're lost in a fog. You didn't eat your lunch. You're thinking constantly about her. If you're in love, then that's a whole different disease with different symptoms and a different cure."

"Sometimes I wonder why I talk to you. Under the same circumstances, wouldn't you think constantly about the woman you got pregnant?"

"Sure. Seriously, Blake, reconsider pushing that proposal. You'll get time with your child, and you will be a lot happier."

"You can't rescind a proposal," Blake remarked dryly. "I need to get back to work."

"Okay, bro. Take it easy and come see me. I'll drop by soon to see the new wing. Congratulations on the baby. That's exciting news. Nate's little girl is a doll. I'm scared to pick her up, but she's a cutie. With your baby, I'm going to be a half uncle—how's that?"

"You'll be a full uncle. Wait until I ask you to come help."

"Call someone else. That's not my field."

"No kidding," Blake remarked, shaking his head as they walked out together and parted outside. "The party may not happen until after I'm a dad," he called over his shoulder.

He left Cade and drove back to his office on the fourth floor of a building he owned, away from downtown Dallas.

He needed to give some thought to several things. One was his true feelings for Sierra. He wasn't in love. Were Sierra and Cade right—that the baby would be better off if he and Sierra didn't marry? If that was true, then he should back off and drop his proposal.

After considering it for the next hour, he still thought marriage was the best solution. They could make it work without love. Why wouldn't Sierra give it a chance? He didn't want to examine why the idea of coming home to her as his wife appealed to him.

For the rest of the day, he thought about the baby, Sierra, Cade and the future—and he continued to debate with himself about his marriage proposal. Tomorrow, they would all look at his new wing, and if everything was satisfactory, Sierra, Lucinda and Eli would be done. As far as his relationship with Sierra went, when she left it wouldn't be goodbye. Even if they didn't marry, they would see each other and their lives would be intertwined for years to come.

It was difficult to see how it would be better without marriage, yet both Sierra and Cade thought so.

Anger persisted when he thought how stubborn she was over this issue. She told him to take his time and think about it, but she didn't seem open to thinking about it herself.

This pregnancy was something neither of them had expected, and now they had to work it out some way. He just knew he would be there for his child.

The one thing he wouldn't consider was the question Cade had asked: Was Blake in love with the mother of his child?

On Saturday morning, Sierra dressed in navy slacks and a white silk blouse. Brushing her hair, she let it fall loosely over her shoulders. Eli and Lucinda had flown into Dallas earlier and picked her up on the way to the ranch. She'd be going with the others, the contractor and a photographer Eli was bringing, so she wouldn't be alone with Blake, which suited her. She was certain he hadn't changed his mind, and neither had she.

At his ranch, he opened the wide front door to welcome them all inside.

At the sight of him in jeans and a black knit shirt, she wished she didn't have the same breathless reaction she'd always had. He stepped back. "Come in," he said.

After greeting everyone, Blake stood talking to Eli and motioned to them. "We'll go look at the new wing that all of you have worked on. It's exactly what I hoped I would get—a fantastic addition to my house, and something I could never have come up with on my own. Let's look at all your work."

They entered the open living area with its ceiling that was two stories high. The remaining walls were off-white so the artwork would stand out. The painting over the mantle was an early David Hockney that Eli had managed to find. It was one of Blake's favorites.

Sierra thought the room was beautiful—sleek lines in the furniture, minimal clutter and so different from the rest of the house. Blake sounded sincerely happy and enormously pleased with the finished wing.

As she looked at him, she felt another pang. She wouldn't let herself think of possibilities, wishes that couldn't happen. She wanted love in her marriage, and she didn't think a union without love would benefit their baby, no matter what Blake said.

She missed him, and she wanted to finish this tour, tell him goodbye and start trying to get over him. She needed to get to the point where she could deal with him without it tearing her apart.

As she looked at him, he turned and his gaze locked with hers. Again, she experienced that sizzling current taking her breath. She didn't want to feel it or be held in his mesmerizing gaze. But she was, this time like all the others.

She turned her back to him and moved with the group to the next room. Why, oh, why, did he hold such a volatile attraction for her? They were worlds apart, and a baby wasn't going to pull them together. As far as she could see, marriage would just make things worse.

The last time she was home, she had talked with her mother first and then both parents, and they had agreed with her that marriage without love would be disastrous.

She would have felt better about her decision upon hearing their agreement, except she was certain they would support her in whatever she decided. If she had said she was marrying Blake even though they were not in love, she felt she would have had the same approval from them.

Her sisters were divided on the subject, and her brothers pushed her to marry Blake, but all of them would stand by whatever decision she made, and they would welcome her baby the same as they had all the other children in the family. She already had toys and baby clothes, presents from her family.

When they entered Blake's bedroom, she spent time studying the art, avoiding looking at the king-size bed because it would stir memories of being with Blake, even though it had been in his other bedroom. She wanted out of his house, to get away from the ranch and back to her own world in Kansas, doing the work she loved—and beginning to get over her time with Blake Callahan.

Finally, the tour was over. Wendell served trays of delicious-looking food, and the dining room table held more trays and platters. Since she had come with Eli and Lucinda, she would have to stay until they left, so she drifted around, trying to keep away from Blake, wanting to avoid talking to him.

But then he appeared in front of her. "You don't have anything to drink. We have orange juice, tomato juice, iced tea—all kinds of drinks. Can I get you something?"

"I'm fine, Blake."

"If you'll stay, I'll get you home later and we can talk."

She gazed into brown eyes that hid his feelings. "Thanks, but I have a plane to catch, and I don't think we have anything else to say to each other at this point in time. I still feel the same as I did when we last talked."

"We still might try to work things out."

"We have months to figure things out. I'm not staying."

She could feel the clash between them. Nothing showed in his expression, but she was certain he wasn't pleased. She turned and walked away, stepping into the kitchen to see if Etta was there. Sierra wanted to say hello and compliment her on the food.

"We'll miss you here," Etta said. "You come back." She patted Sierra's arm. "His rooms are wonderful."

"Thank you. A lot of people worked on them."

"Take care of yourself."

"Thanks, Etta," she said, surprised by the last. She couldn't imagine Blake had said anything to Wendell or Etta about the baby, but she couldn't recall Etta saying that to her before.

Finally, Lucinda asked if she was ready to leave, and fifteen minutes later she stepped to the door and turned to Blake.

"I'm sure we'll be in touch."

"Sierra, the new wing surpassed all my hopes and expectations. Eli and Lucinda are very talented. You've got a wonderful eye. Everything in the new wing is perfect. Thank you."

"You're welcome," she said, thinking how polite they were being with each other. She was aware that Lucinda and a few others standing around could hear their conversation.

"Lucinda and Eli have done a fantastic job. I'm glad you like everything. I have to say thank you, too, Blake. Your generosity will help Dad's church and the agency immeasurably. We'll keep in touch to let you know where the money goes. It will do so much to help so many."

"That's good. I'll see you soon," he said, holding out his hand. She had to take it, and the minute they touched she felt an electric current, a deeper awareness of him.

"I'll call," he said quietly, and released her. She joined Lucinda and Eli, who stood beside the rental car. Her back tingled, and she didn't want to turn around and look to see if Blake still stood at the door watching them.

She didn't expect to see Blake again for a long time.

Would he come around to her way of thinking about marriage?

She hurt. And she knew why. She had fallen in love with Blake. Maybe with time it would diminish.

She fought back tears, thankful that Lucinda and Eli were discussing their art purchases.

Once Sierra got her emotions under control, she joined in the conversation, thanking them for all their hard work and complimenting them on so many excellent choices in art and furniture.

Sierra kept her emotions bottled up until she reached home, a house she had rented near her parents. She finally sank into a chair, put her head in her hands and cried. She missed Blake.

She had to admit to herself that she had fallen in love with a man bent on revenge. She couldn't marry a man like that. Even more of a stumbling block was the fact that Blake wasn't in love with her. She never wanted to be in a loveless marriage.

She had gotten pregnant, and she couldn't change that. She would have Blake's baby and they would share their child. She'd have to figure out a way to heal her broken heart.

Eight

Blake sat staring at the phone. Sierra still didn't want to take his calls. They had talked a few times, but they always had the same argument, then she would hang up. He missed her, and it shocked him. There seemed to be a big, empty hole in his life. He couldn't stop thinking about her, wanting to see her, even just to talk to her. He wanted to be with her again.

He still thought marriage was a good idea. Even with their differences, marriage seemed the best solution. Surprisingly, it was something he wanted.

Mostly he just wanted to see her. Why wouldn't she take his calls? They had to talk again.

What would he have to do to get her back into his life? Promise to not mention marriage? He remembered

Sierra urging him to call his dad—would that get her to talk to him again?

If he hoped to ever get Sierra back in his life, he suspected he would have to change his attitude toward his father. He remembered her asking if he had ever tried to call his father and find out more about the man.

Blake hadn't ever gotten past his hurt and anger enough to do so before, but he began rethinking things. A phone call was a simple matter. He had nothing to lose. Having lunch together wouldn't be a big deal, and if his father said no, at least he would have tried. If he called—even if his father wouldn't talk to him—maybe that would soften Sierra's attitude.

He suspected his father wouldn't be one bit more eager to talk to Blake than Blake was to talk to him, but then Blake could tell Sierra he had called his father.

Cade knew how to get hold of the man, so Blake sent Cade a text asking for the number to talk to their dad. He received a prompt reply: Do I need to get an ambulance for you?

He fired back, Not yet.

Staring at the number, he sat a long time, still debating with himself. "So, what the hell?" he finally asked aloud. If his dad wouldn't take the call, so what? That wouldn't be a change from their relationship all of Blake's life. He dialed, and in seconds he heard a voice he didn't even recognize. Taking a deep breath, expecting the connection to be broken within a minute, he knew he had nothing to lose.

"This is Blake Callahan," he said, wondering if the man would even acknowledge him. "I feel that I should address you as Mr. Callahan. I don't know you well enough to call you anything else."

"This is a surprise," said a deep voice.

Through the years, Blake had seen pictures of his father, but none recently. Would he even recognize him? He used to see a family resemblance sometimes.

"I called to see if we can have lunch soon. I think it's time I met you."

The silence stretched between them. "I live in California now."

"I'm working out there, so that's fine. I can meet you wherever you want," Blake said, amazed he was asking his father to have lunch.

"Lunch would be a good idea. Are you familiar with San Francisco? I live in Carmel, but we'll have more privacy in San Francisco."

"San Francisco sounds fine," Blake answered, shocked that this was actually happening.

"Good. There's a restaurant that's popular—Patterson Place. How's that?"

"I'll make reservations for two. How about Thursday at noon?"

"Thursday is good. I'll be there."

"Excellent. I'll see you there." He was tempted to ask how they would recognize each other, but held off. He knew he would at least recognize his father.

The call ended, and Blake wondered whether the man would actually show.

* * *

On Thursday Blake arrived twenty minutes early and ordered iced tea, then settled back to wait. It wasn't as difficult as he thought it would be to recognize Dirkson Callahan. Blake was mildly shocked, because he looked more frail than Blake had expected. He was thin and wrinkled, with white hair around his face and streaking his black hair. He wore wire-frame glasses, which was another surprise—but Blake had been a small child the last time he had actually seen his father in person.

Blake stood when he saw Dirkson survey the restaurant crowd and pass over him without another glance. Blake threaded his way across the room and was halfway to the front before the older man spotted him and waved slightly, coming toward Blake. He headed back to the table.

Continuing to stand, he waited until his father reached him and offered his hand. Blake had wondered if his father would even give him the courtesy of shaking hands. "Mr. Callahan," he said, feeling a strange mixture of emotions that flashed through him like lightning.

In his memory, his father had always loomed as powerful and formidable. In reality, he was not threatening in any manner. Blake could see only a faint family resemblance, and Dirkson didn't give the appearance of wealth or success. He could easily be the wealthiest man in the restaurant, but Blake didn't think anyone who saw him would even remotely guess he had such wealth unless they knew his identity.

To Blake's surprise, he experienced a streak of guilt. Through all his efforts to damage his father's hotel business, Blake had envisioned an opponent who was strong, powerful and invincible, not the elderly gentleman facing him. Dirkson had to have someone handling the media, and he must be using photos from several years back, or touched-up photos.

"Have a seat, sir," Blake said politely, still studying his father intently.

"Blake, please don't be so formal. It's a little late for Dad, so why don't you call me Dirkson? There's no more need for you to address me as Mr. Callahan than there is for me to call you by that name."

Blake had to smile. "Fine. It does seem awkward." As they sat facing each other, Blake continued to study his father, noticing details, curious about this man who was a mystery and a stranger, even though they had the same blood in their veins and might be more alike than either one wanted.

Curiosity nagged at Blake. "Did you drive from Carmel?"

Amusement seemed to lighten Dirkson's features momentarily. "No. I don't drive. The limo will be waiting when I'm through. Rudy brought me here, and when I call him, he'll come back to pick me up."

"Cade said to tell you hello."

Dirkson merely nodded as he opened the menu and read. He closed it within seconds. "I've heard the ahi tuna is good here. So, Blake, you're all grown up now. I know your business is good. You've done well."

Surprised that his father knew anything about him,

Blake smiled. "Thank you. I have done well. My office is in Dallas, and part of the time, when I can, I stay on Granddad's ranch, which he left to me."

"So, it's your ranch now."

"Yes, it is." They paused while a white-coated waiter took their order, and then Dirkson gazed at Blake. "You've done well with your hotels, too." He looked amused, which surprised Blake.

"Yes, sir. I'll admit I had goals in mind when I started the luxury hotels. They've achieved a certain amount of success, and I'm moving on to other things. You won't see any more of my hotels near yours. I'll admit I had a lot of anger stored up."

He looked into his father's dark brown eyes and felt very little for the man who was really a stranger—not even the anger or resentment he'd held on to for so long. He knew very little about this man except what he had read in magazines and newspapers. His mother never talked about him, and even as a small child, he suspected she didn't want to because Dirkson had hurt her badly.

"The years go by and change a person. When I look back, I realize I made mistakes, but that bit of wisdom has come years too late to do any good."

His words shocked Blake, and he wondered what mistakes his father thought he had made and whether he was talking about family relationships.

"You and I have never talked," he continued. "I'm a stranger to you. You called me Mr. Callahan. Well, it's my fault, and at this point in life I have regrets, but I can't undo what I've done and there's no use in trying to win your friendship now. Or in trying to get closer to my other sons."

"It might be too late for us, but there's the next generation. You know you have a granddaughter? Nathan is married and has a baby girl."

"Yes. I have a secretary who keeps up with all of you and keeps me posted. I've seen pictures of Nathan's baby. I've never talked to her mother. But I've opened a trust fund for the baby."

"That's nice, sir," Blake said, wondering if Nathan even cared. "This grandchild might give you a second chance with your offspring. You can try talking to this little baby, and maybe she will at least know you're her grandfather. Twenty years from now she won't address you as Mr. Callahan."

"True enough, but I'm afraid I know little about children."

"You don't have to," he said, remembering Sierra's advice about entertaining kids. "When she gets bigger, get a child's book to read to her. Children are forgiving, and she'll like you if you just give her a little attention and talk to her."

"How is your mother?"

"She's fine. Doesn't know I'm here. She's in Patagonia with friends right now. She travels a lot."

"I admire you for the success you've had and for the competition you gave my hotels. When I realized what you were doing, I was curious to see if you would succeed, and you did amazingly well. That took some gumption and some good decisions."

"Thank you. Any competition from me is definitely

over," Blake said, feeling a hollow sense of victory. He didn't care to try to get to know his father now, after all these years and after such a deep hurt in childhood, but he had lost his anger.

"I'm sorry about the way I behaved with all my sons. I don't know any of you, and I doubt if any of you care about me any longer."

"I can only speak for myself, but after all the years, frankly, sir, no, I don't care."

"That's honest." They paused as the waiter brought their lunches, ahi tuna for his father and a thick, juicy hamburger for Blake.

"Your call was a big surprise, but I'm glad you did. You're an adult, and it's time we met. When all of you were babies, I thought money was so important. It turns out it's not that important at all. It seems that way when you don't have it, or when you're young and trying to acquire it. I wanted money and power and I left my family behind."

"I think in some ways you set an example for us— sort of what not to do."

"If it keeps any of you from feeling the way I do when you're my age, then that's good. You said no more hotels, so what will you do? What's your focus now?"

"Ranching, and I still deal in commercial real estate. I'm not giving up either of those endeavors. I have some good property in this state."

"Yes, you do. I told you—I keep up with my sons. I'm proud of all of you."

"I suppose I need to say thank you," Blake said, surprised at how well this lunch was going.

They ate in silence, and Blake thought of all the years of anger, when he was growing up and as an adult. Now that he was finally with his dad, he could see there was no longer any reason for anger. Pity was the strongest emotion evoked by the man across from him.

Sierra had been right that it was foolish to try to get revenge at this point in life. What else was she right about? Would it matter to her if he told her that he'd had lunch with his dad? Or would she even listen to him if he tried to call her?

They continued to eat in silence, and he wondered if that was really all he had to talk about with his father.

"One more nugget of advice from your elder. Pay attention to what's important in your life," his dad finally said. "I didn't pay attention in my own life, and I can't undo that now. There is no going back."

"Yes, sir," Blake said, thinking about the people who had come into his life in the past month. "Sir, there's a way you can help someone else, and maybe help some little boys who don't have dads. I've been seeing a woman, and she runs a nonprofit agency that helps people. They have a shelter for homeless children. I have her card," he said, thinking about William.

He withdrew his wallet to get Sierra's card and handed it to his dad. "I went to a picnic with her—homeless kids who live in a children's shelter run by her agency attended. Some of these kids don't have either parent. There are kids you could help with a donation.

"I didn't plan this ahead of time, but I thought of it now because of our conversation. I met a little boy at that picnic. William has never known his dad, and his mother was killed. William lives in the shelter, and he has clothes, but nothing else—not a bicycle, not a ball, nothing. You might help him or other kids. It won't be your own sons, but those kids will know someone cares. That would mean a lot to a child."

And Blake knew it was true. All that Sierra had said—about doing good, about helping others—somehow it had sunk in. There was good in the world, sometimes, and he suddenly understood her better than he had before.

Nodding, his father took the card and put it in his pocket. "I'm glad to have talked to you today, glad you called. With the hotels and all, I figured you were really angry."

"I was, but it doesn't matter now."

"You're smart to recognize that. It really doesn't matter. Don't ruin the things that do matter."

"Yes, sir, I'm trying not to," Blake said, thinking again about Sierra. "It was nice to have lunch with you. I have a plane waiting, and I need to go. Can I call the limo for you?"

"Thanks. I'll get it. Good luck, and call again sometime, if you're in town."

"You can't imagine what those words would have meant to me when I was a little kid," Blake said softly. His dad merely nodded. Blake turned away, walking out of the restaurant feeling as if a weight had lifted and some old hurts had been laid to rest. He wondered if he would ever see or talk to his father again.

He had to talk to Sierra. Had she moved on with her life and put all thoughts of him aside? Was she already wiping out memories of their time together? She could never put him completely out of her mind—not with a baby between them. But he wanted more than a child with her. He wanted a life.

But before he could strategize how to win back Sierra, there was currently one person waiting to hear about lunch: Cade. When Blake was seated in the jet, still on the ground and waiting for clearance to take off, he called his half brother.

"Lunch is over and so is the competition. Cade, he's an old man. He told me to call him Dirkson. He says he has a lot of regrets, and I believe him."

"You didn't tell him off for what he did?"

"I'm all grown up. It just doesn't matter anymore."

"I can't believe I'm talking to the same Blake. I haven't seen him in a while, but we've seen him all through the years and you haven't, so you probably notice bigger changes. Well, maybe you'll sleep better now. And maybe he'll sleep worse," Cade said, laughing. "Would serve him right, but he probably sleeps like an old dog in front of the fire."

"That's my cue to stop talking to you. My plane is taking off." He could hear Cade chuckling as Blake ended the call.

He stared at his phone, wanting to call Sierra. He missed her, and he hoped he hadn't permanently ruined his chances with her.

He needed a way to win her back.

He'd tried going out with friends, but even with the most charming ones, his mind wandered until he was lost in memories of being with Sierra. Today, with his father, it had been her voice whispering to him about William and the good he and his father could do for a child.

When he was alone at night, too many times he had reached for his phone to call her. He knew now he would never be able to move on, and he hadn't expected it to be this difficult to figure out what to do next. But then, nothing about her had ever been simple. She still complicated his life, even when she wasn't present and he hadn't talked to her for days.

The thought that he might not kiss her again gave him a hollow feeling. The thought that she might be out of his life, except as his baby's mother, made him hurt.

He hadn't been turned down before by a woman who really mattered to him. Getting turned down by Sierra felt as if he had lost something valuable. He wanted to tell her he had dropped the hotel business, that he was no longer bent on revenge, that he'd even reached out to his father. But he couldn't because she wouldn't even take his calls.

He stared into space and saw her blue eyes and her thick, silky brown hair. He remembered her laughter. He remembered everything about her. With a groan, he shook his head.

He was in love with her.

He thought about his conversation with his father. *Don't ruin the things that do matter.* He couldn't let her go. He couldn't lose her. He didn't want to be like his dad—a man filled with regrets.

Why hadn't he recognized the depths of his feelings sooner? Could he ever win her love after all the things he'd said and done? He couldn't even get her to take his calls!

He picked up his phone to call her—and got her voicemail.

There had to be a way to reach her. And a way to make her listen.

Sierra stared at the papers on her desk without seeing them. Instead she saw Blake's dark brown eyes, his smile and his thick, black hair. She missed him—and with each day she missed him more instead of less.

She couldn't forget him. She couldn't even shake him out of her thoughts. She didn't want to marry him, but this being away from him was terrible. She knew she was in love with him. And that romantic part of her wanted to marry him. But what if they married and he never fell in love with her? Would that kind of one-sided marriage work?

She ran her fingers through her hair and massaged her temples. His revenge plan still chilled her. Hot tears threatened, and she wiped her eyes in hurt and annoyance.

She couldn't concentrate on work, and she didn't think it was healthy to be so glum, but she couldn't see a solution to these feelings she had for Blake. If she could just stop thinking about him…but everything in her life reminded her of him.

How long was she going to cry over him and miss him? Was she making a huge mistake by not saying yes to his proposal?

* * *

Early Wednesday morning, Nan informed Sierra she had a call. Sierra didn't recognize the name, but she took the call anyway.

When the call ended, she stepped into Nan's office. "That was a man representing Dirkson Callahan. He's made an appointment to see me, and he'll be here this afternoon at one."

"Dirkson Callahan? Mercy. Do you think he's here because you're carrying his grandchild?" Nan asked.

Sierra shook her head. "No. Absolutely not. Dirkson Callahan wouldn't even talk to his own son. Why would he be interested in a grandchild? Besides, he has a little granddaughter. Blake's half brother has a little girl and Mr. Callahan has never made overtures to her."

"What would he want to see you about? If he's making a donation, he'd send it in the mail."

"I don't think that's what it is."

"This will send Bert into a frenzy trying to figure out what's going on. Speaking of Bert—when he checked on the children's shelter, he said Blake had sent a bat and three balls—a baseball, a soccer ball and a football—plus a baseball glove and new tennis shoes to William. He also sent new balls and gloves to the shelter so they'll have more equipment."

"That's good news," Sierra said, surprised and pleased.

"Bert said Mrs. Perkins at the shelter told him that Blake Callahan stopped by to see William. Are you still not taking his calls?"

"Yes," Sierra said, shocked and lost in thought. Blake

had taken the time to see William. She didn't want to think about why that made her feel warm and hopeful. "He went by there. So he's been in Kansas City?"

"Sierra, talk to him. You didn't know he was here because you won't take his calls."

"That's amazing that he's been out to see William. Did Mrs. Perkins say anything about William joining the other kids?"

"Yes, she did. He's been making friends. She said once he started talking to the other kids and playing with them, he seemed to like being with them. She said he's changed a lot. He's still shy with her and other adults, but not with kids."

"That's really good news," Sierra said, surprised and pleased. "So Blake did help. I'll tell him how great that was."

"So you'll talk to him?"

"I'll think about it. I'm happy for William. I might just send Blake a text."

Rolling her eyes, Nan left Sierra's office. Sierra turned back to her desk, thinking about William, about Blake being in Kansas City and not calling, and about someone coming this afternoon who was sent by Dirkson Callahan. The last was the most puzzling to her.

At one o'clock, Nan ushered in a man she introduced as J. Wilson Sedgewick, who represented Dirkson Callahan.

Sierra faced a short man with a fringe of black hair and rimless spectacles that were perched on his nose. After she asked him to be seated, he opened a briefcase. "Ms. Benson, I'm here on behalf of Dirkson Callahan.

He wishes to make a donation to this agency, particularly for a children's shelter you have." He handed a sealed envelope to her.

"It is in honor of his four sons, and he hopes it will help some less fortunate children."

"Thank you," she said, astonished, as she looked at the envelope in her hand. She began to open it. "Four sons?" she asked, remembering Cade and Gabe, the married son, Nathan—and Blake had to be the fourth. She opened the envelope and withdrew a folded paper. When she opened it, a check fluttered to her desk.

She read the handwriting scrawled across the page. *In honor of my sons: Blake Callahan, Cade Callahan, Nathan Callahan, Gabe Callahan.*

Dirkson Callahan.

She picked up the check and drew a deep breath when she saw the figures for a quarter of a million dollars.

"This is extremely generous, Mr. Sedgewick," she said, looking at him. "That's an enormous donation, and we'll try to honor it the best way possible. This will help a lot of little girls and little boys, kids that have no families. Please tell Mr. Callahan we'll try to find some way to thank him and honor his sons."

"He does not want publicity for this. I'm sure you can understand. Just some simple recognition to his sons—perhaps a letter from the agency."

"Of course," she answered as he closed his briefcase and stood. She followed him to the front door of the agency and then turned back. Nan stood behind her, and Bert was beside Nan.

"What was all that about?" Bert asked.

"I can't figure it out. Dirkson Callahan never acknowledged his oldest son. According to Blake, he barely was a father to the other three sons. Yet Mr. Sedgewick was Dirkson Callahan's representative, and he gave me an envelope containing a donation to the agency in honor of his four sons. It's a check for a quarter of a million dollars for the children's shelter."

"Saints above!" Bert gasped. "Sierra, what is it with you and the Callahans and all this money?"

"Are you and Blake engaged?" Nan asked.

"No, we're not speaking. At least, I haven't been taking his calls."

"Maybe you better take them now," Nan said.

"I have to agree. Think of what we can do for the children's shelter."

They stared at one another until Sierra passed him the check and headed for her office. "Bert, will you make a copy and get this check in the bank now?"

"Yes, I will," he replied.

"I guess I'll call Blake. I can't figure this one out. How did Dirkson Callahan know about us or about the shelter? He's never talked to Blake, and the other Callahan sons don't know about the shelter."

"Blake had to have told him," Nan answered.

"That's impossible. Blake is actively trying to destroy his dad's hotel business. I can't understand what just happened here."

She heard her cell phone.

"Maybe that's your answer. See if it's Blake."

"No, but I'll take this call," she said when she saw it was her mom.

They talked briefly. After telling her mother what had just happened, she tried to call Blake, but couldn't get him. She stared into space. What had caused the huge donation, and when did Dirkson Callahan start acknowledging his oldest son? Where was Blake, and what was he doing? Why did she miss him so much when she was the one who'd said goodbye?

At six, Sierra closed and locked the office, then drove through traffic to her small house. As she tried to eat a bowl of soup and drink a glass of milk, a car horn sounded.

Looking out, she saw a tall man with a cowboy hat on her porch. He stood with his back to her, but she knew it was Blake.

"Just a minute," she called. She opened the door and her heart thudded. He had on a broad-brimmed black hat, a navy shirt, jeans and boots.

She wanted to walk into his arms. Instead she asked, "What are you doing here?"

Nine

Blake took a step closer as she unfastened and opened the screen door.

"I didn't call to tell you I was coming because you won't take my calls," he said as he closed the door behind him.

Her heart pounded, and she couldn't get her breath. "Blake," she whispered, knowing that she loved him, whatever he did. She was tired of pushing her feelings away. "I missed you."

His eyes narrowed, and he dropped a package from his hand and wrapped his arms around her. He pulled her close, and she clung to him as he kissed her.

She held him tightly, as if she might lose him again.

How could she marry him if he didn't love her?

Yet how could she *not* marry him when she loved him so much?

She stopped thinking. She was in his arms, kissing him, and right now that was all that mattered. When he picked her up and raised his head a fraction, she looked up into dark eyes filled with desire. "Where's your bedroom?"

She pointed and pulled his head down for another kiss. He stood her on her feet beside the bed as he unfastened buttons on her yellow cotton blouse and removed her skirt.

Her hands shook as she undid his jeans. She ran her hands over him as if to make certain he was still there, and she didn't stop kissing him when he picked her up to place her on the bed.

Later, Sierra had no idea what time it was as she lay in his arms, their warm bodies pressed together with her tangled hair spread across his shoulder. His lips touched her temple, her cheek, her ear.

"You haven't taken any of my calls."

"I tried to call you today, and you didn't answer."

He raised his head slightly. "Why did you try to call me?"

She pulled the sheet higher beneath her arm. "Blake, your father made a huge—*huge*—donation to the children's shelter. It was done in honor of his four sons."

Blake stared at her. "I'll be damned. I called him, Sierra. I decided you're more important than old hurts, and having your love is more important than any revenge—"

"You did?" she cried, sitting up and throwing her arms around him to hug him.

"Hey," Blake said, hugging her and laughing. "Yes, I did. Do you want to hear what happened?"

She looked into his eyes and pulled him closer to give him a long, passionate kiss before she listened. "Now tell me."

Looking amused, he settled beside her, pulling her close by his side. She placed her head on his shoulder as she waited.

"I called him and asked him to go to lunch. I told him I wanted to see him. He accepted my invitation."

"You did this for me?"

"Yes, I did."

"Why?"

He gazed at her, his warm brown eyes making her heart race. "I love you and I want to marry you. That revenge thing seemed to be what was in the way. It's gone now, Sierra. Will you marry me?"

Her heart thudded. She didn't know what he'd done, or much about the meeting with his father, but he was telling her he loved her and she knew she loved him.

"Yes. Oh, yes, I'll marry you. I love you, Blake." Tears of joy filled her eyes and spilled down her cheeks.

"Hey, what's this?" he said, rubbing away tears with his fingers. "Why are you crying?"

"I love you so much and didn't realize it until I thought it was too late. I thought you were out of my life."

"I hope not." He kissed her again. "I love you, Sierra. With all my heart. I want you more than anything else."

"I love you so much, Blake," she whispered between kisses. Finally, she lay back and looked up at him. "Now, tell me about lunch, and why he made this gigantic donation to the shelter."

"My father was really a stranger. I could have grabbed a guy off the street and wouldn't have felt any different about him. I was surprised how old and frail he looked. I remembered him as I had as a child, a strong, powerful man. I had already decided to end the competition with his hotels. It seemed pointless and was causing trouble between you and me."

"There really wasn't much of an 'us' earlier."

"There's been an 'us' since the day I met you. Don't tell me you didn't feel sparks flying when we met. I know better."

"I suppose so," she said, smiling at him. "Go back to your dad."

"He was kind of sad. I felt sorry for him. He said he made mistakes, thinking money was the most important thing. He said he didn't know how to be a father. I reminded him he has a new little granddaughter. He said he really never knew how to be a dad, and it's too late now.

"Sierra, I don't ever want to end up like my dad. I told him it wasn't too late, and I gave him your card. I told him about the children's shelter, and that he could be a dad in spirit by helping those kids and making a donation. I guess he decided to do that."

"Oh, my, yes he did. I think Bert was close to fainting. I have the note your dad wrote."

"Because of you, we've made peace."

"I'm thrilled. I'm so, so happy. Thank you. Blake, he sent us a huge check for a quarter of a million dollars for the children's shelter. We can take more kids now, and pay tutors and… I'm thrilled."

"Oh, I have something—just wait. Don't go anywhere and don't do anything while I go get what I brought you."

"A present? The only thing I can give you right now is a dog."

"That's not the only thing," he said, grinning slyly at her. She shook her head.

She watched him walk away and thought about the day she'd had—Mr. Sedgewick, the check, Blake on her doorstep, in her arms, in her bed. He loved her. The best of all possible days.

Blake returned, slipped beneath the sheet and turned to her. "I have to ask your dad for your hand in marriage."

"You know that's an old-fashioned custom that you don't have to do anymore."

"Why do I feel that I would make a better impression on your minister father if I did it?" He placed a long box in her hand. It was wrapped in pink paper and tied with a wide pink silk ribbon.

"For you, darlin'," he said.

Curious, she opened it and gasped as she looked at a beautiful gold chain necklace with a heart-shaped pendant covered in diamonds and a large diamond in the center.

"That, my love, is a gift from me to you because you are having our baby," he said solemnly.

"Blake, that is gorgeous. It's the most beautiful necklace ever. Thank you," she said.

"Turn around and let me put it on."

She laughed. "In bed—that's ridiculous, but okay." She sat quietly while he fastened it around her neck. She looked down at the brilliant diamonds. "Blake, it's beautiful. I love it. Thank you."

He kissed her and she held him tightly, kissing him in return. He shifted and took her hand in his. "This ring is also for you," he said, opening her hand. "Sierra Benson, will you marry me?"

She smiled at him in delight. "Yes, oh, yes, I will. I love you, Blake Callahan," she added.

"Hold out your hand," he said, slipping the ring on her finger. She looked down at a dazzling emerald-cut diamond surrounded by smaller diamonds.

She gasped. "Blake, that is magnificent. My word," she said, sounding breathless and holding her hand out to turn it, letting the diamonds catch the light and create small rainbows. "This is the most beautiful ring ever, in all of history."

He laughed. "It's pretty."

Suddenly her smile vanished. "Blake, what will I do about the agency? I promised my grandfather I would keep it going and work to help others."

"First of all, you're pregnant, so focus on that for now. The time will come when you can get back to your work with the agency. I've got enough money, and the agency has enough money to keep going. Bert can run things while you're away. If you want, you can have another branch in Dallas. How's that?"

"There will be a lot of back and forth because of all my family living here."

"That'll be easy. I have my own jet. We have cars. You'll be able to get back and forth when you want to, or bring your folks to see us. Okay?"

"Okay. You're worth making a few little sacrifices for," she said.

He grinned. "Thank heavens for that."

"I still think this is the most beautiful ring." She admired it until he leaned close to kiss her, and she wrapped her arms around him to hug him tightly.

Later, still in each other's arms, he said, "Let's have this wedding soon."

"I agree. If we start planning tonight, we can get married this month."

"If you say we can have the wedding soon, then let's do it. The sooner the better, as far as I'm concerned."

"It's not late now. Let's get dressed and go tell my family. They'll love it."

"Sure. Your folks, my half brothers—I'll call them."

"Blake, I heard about you and William—that you donated baseballs, a bat and a glove—lots of equipment for him and for the kids. That was wonderful."

"I wanted to. I'd like to have him out to the ranch sometime. I suppose it's inevitable that we'll have all those kids out. I'll charter a bus or fly them there."

"We'll figure it out. That would be wonderful."

"This means I need to hire you and Eli and Lucinda and my contractor again. Now we'll need a nursery in the new wing, and we'll need a nursery in my Dallas home, too, unless you don't like that house."

"That is a gorgeous mansion. Of course I like it. And, yes, we'll need a nursery both places, but that's doable. Now let's shower, dress and go see my family. I can't wait to tell them. They'll be so happy for us. You'll see."

Hugging her tightly, he looked down at her. "You've given me faith in people, Sierra. I have never seen a married couple so filled with care and love for each other as your parents—I really didn't think that was possible. Because of you, I know there is good in people. I guess that rose-colored view is contagious—or is it just that I'm so in love that you've made me believe, and I see good everywhere now?"

She held him tightly. "I love you. Your life is going to change in lots of ways, but it will all be good."

"What's really good is kissing you," he said in a husky voice.

And he kissed away her response.

Epilogue

Sierra stood in the foyer with her arm linked through her older brother's. The church was packed with every seat filled, and an overflow crowd watched on big screens set up in other rooms while some just waited outside.

She looked at the row of bridesmaids. The last one was going down the aisle now. They were in pale yellow silk dresses and carried bouquets of spring flowers. Her oldest sister, Ginger, was her matron of honor, and there were eight attendants. The groomsmen were two of Blake's half brothers and his friends. Cade was the best man. Two five-year-old nieces, Viola and Tina, were flower girls. Sierra's gaze slipped past them and went to her tall, handsome rancher fiancé. In a black tux, Blake took her breath away.

She wanted to be finished with their vows and the

party and to be in his arms. She thought of all the joy Blake had brought into their family and the families of others through his donation to the agency, and she thought of how he had stopped holding on to the hurt he had experienced as a child.

On the groom's side of the church, she saw Blake's father sitting straight backed, facing his son. He was a solitary figure, and he looked as frail to her as he must have looked to Blake. She was surprised he was present.

Brad Benson squeezed her arm. "You look beautiful, Sierra. Dad told me to tell you that he just hopes you have what he and Mom do. He told me that when I married, too."

She smiled at her older brother and looked at her father, standing near the altar rail in his robe, waiting to say the vows that she and Blake would repeat.

She was filled with love for her dad, thinking what a contrast he was to the father Blake had.

"Blake's a good guy," Brad said, and she smiled.

The wedding planner shook her veil lightly. "Now, it's time," she said, and Sierra walked down the aisle with her brother to have her hand placed in Blake's.

Blake smiled at her as she stepped beside him, and they moved forward to face her father, who smiled at her before beginning the ceremony.

When they were man and wife, trumpets and organ music filled the church. Then they walked back up the aisle and into the foyer.

"Now we circle around to come back for pictures," she said, leading him through the church that was as familiar to her as her home.

The reception was at the country club. Blake had reserved the entire place. A band played in the ballroom, and there were tables of food in various rooms. People filled the club—friends and people Sierra had helped, relatives and employees, cowboys from Blake's ranch.

The party commenced, and Sierra only saw Blake across the room until it was time to cut the cake. Then they were again separated to talk to guests until the first dance.

Music became lively as the dance floor opened to the crowd, and arms waved in the air while people danced and sang.

Blake took Sierra to one side. "Think we'll be missed if we step into the library?"

She laughed. "Yes, we'll be missed. Let's go back and party for the next hour, and then maybe we'll disappear."

He glanced around. "There's no one out here right now." He kissed away her answer, and she kissed him in return.

"I can't believe we've been here alone this long. C'mon and join the fun," she said, taking his hand and returning to the dance floor to join the festivities.

Later she stood in a big circle with Blake's arm around her waist. Cade was there, and Gabe. She had finally met Nathan, but he and Lydia had left early to take baby Amelia home.

She was glad for Blake that his half brothers had made him part of their family, and she was thankful that their own baby would be welcomed by her big family.

Her sister Lenora came to get her. "It's time to toss your garter to the bachelors," she told Sierra.

"All right," Gabe said, laughing. "C'mon, Cade. That's us."

"Not me," Cade said, laughing with him and shaking his head. "No marriage in my future, bro. Sierra, throw it right to him, and we'll get my wild little brother married off."

She nodded and turned, feeling her white satin skirt swirl around her ankles.

When she tossed it, Gabe jumped into the air and grabbed it, grinning and waving it while he whooped with glee. She had to laugh. He had an exuberance that seemed to run in the family.

Friends turned to talk to her, and she forgot about Gabe. When she rejoined Blake, he slipped his arm around her waist as they stood in a circle talking to friends.

"I'm not the only one to make peace with my dad— there's my mom sitting by him."

Sierra had just met Veronica Callahan, Blake's mother, the previous week because she had finally arrived in Texas for the wedding. Now Sierra looked at the slender woman, whose white hair was turned under to frame her face. She was tall and attractive, with dark brown eyes that Blake had inherited. She sat at a table with Blake's father.

Nearby, Crystal Callahan, divorced from Dirkson and mother of Cade, Nathan and Gabe, was with a group of friends at another table.

"Let me see if I have this straight. Your dad's first wife isn't here, and they had no children."

"That's right."

"Your mom was his second wife, and she's sitting with him now. And she's very nice, Blake. I really like her."

"She likes you, and she is so excited to become a grandmother." He looked to where his mother sat with his father. "I don't think they've spoken since I was a little kid. Maybe he's made peace with her, too."

Sierra smiled. "I know your mother is very excited to be a grandmother. I've already received half a dozen presents for the baby. And back to wives—your half brothers' mother is Crystal, enjoying herself with friends and divorced from Dirkson."

"That's right. After all these wives, he's alone now. He had mistresses in that lineup, too. He just had no interest in his children."

"He made that choice," she said. "Blake, we're alone and the party is in full swing, and has been for hours now. Do you still have a waiting limo?"

"Do I ever, darlin'," he said, taking her hand. "Walk slowly, as if we're moving to find some friends, and we'll slip out and be on our way."

Smiling, she did as he said, and in minutes they sat in the limo as it pulled away and left the club, heading for the airport and Blake's waiting jet.

It was night when they entered the penthouse apartment Blake kept in New York. He turned to embrace Sierra, who had changed into a pale blue dress and matching heels. Blake was still in his tux, but he paused to shed his coat and tie while she unfastened the studs on his shirt. Before she finished, he wrapped his arms around her to kiss her, and she held him tightly, returning his kiss.

Joy filled her as she began her marriage to the rancher she loved with all her heart. His hand slid over her still-flat stomach. "Our baby, Sierra. This baby will have a world of love."

"Yes, this baby and our others, Blake. I love you with all my heart," she declared, gazing up at him with a faint smile, knowing life was good and they would have a marriage filled with love.

* * * * *

MILLS & BOON®

Why not subscribe?
Never miss a title and save money too!

Here is what's available to you if you join the
exclusive **Mills & Boon® Book Club** today:

* *Titles up to a month ahead of the shops*
* *Amazing discounts*
* *Free P&P*
* *Earn Bonus Book points that can be redeemed
  against other titles and gifts*
* *Choose from monthly or pre-paid plans*

Still want more?
Well, if you join today we'll even give you
50% OFF your first parcel!

So visit **www.millsandboon.co.uk/subscriptions**
or call **Customer Relations on 0844 844 1351***
to be a part of this exclusive Book Club!

**This call will cost you 7 pence per minute plus your
phone company's price per minute access charge.*